STOLEN LIVES

Also by the Author
Random Violence
The Fallen
Pale Horses
Bad Seeds

STOLEN LIVES

Jassy Mackenzie

SOHO CRIME

Published by
Soho Press, Inc.
853 Broadway
New York, NY 10003

Text design by forzalibro designs

Library of Congress Cataloging-in-Publication Data

Mackenzie, Jassy.
Stolen lives / Jassy Mackenzie.

ISBN 978-1-61695-067-5
eISBN 978-1-56947-910-0

1. Women private investigators—South Africa—Fiction.
2. Attempted murder—Fiction. 3. Kidnapping—Fiction. 4. Human trafficking—Fiction. 5. Johannesburg (South Africa)—Fiction.
6. London (England)—Fiction. I. Title.
PR9369.4.M335S76 2011
823'.92—dc22
2010044893

Printed in the United States of America

10 9 8 7 6 5 4 3 2

for Margaret Mackenzie

I

Detective Constable Edmonds saw the running man just a half-second before the unmarked car she was travelling in hit him.

A slightly built man, dark-skinned and dark-clad in a tight-fitting jersey and a beanie. He burst out of the shadows behind a flyover and sprinted straight across the A12, fists pumping, head bowed against the gusting rain, splashing through the puddles on the tarmac as if he were running for his life.

"Look out!" Edmonds shouted from the back seat, but Detective Sergeant Mackay, who was driving, had seen the man, too.

"Hang on, people."

A shriek of brakes, and then the car reached the puddle of water that had pooled on the tarmac and went into a skid. Edmonds' seatbelt yanked hard against her chest, squeezing the breath out of her in spite of the regulation Kevlar vest she was wearing under her jacket. She grabbed the seat in front of her, and a moment later her hand was squashed into the padded fabric by the larger, tougher palm of bulky Sergeant Richards, who was also bracing for the crash.

The car slewed sideways, and Mackay swore as he fought for control. Through the spattered windscreen Edmonds saw the running man look, too late, in their direction. He flung out a hand in defence, and Edmonds' heart leapt into her mouth when she heard a loud metallic thunk that seemed to shake the car.

The man stumbled heavily and went down, sprawling onto his side. But before Edmonds could even conceptualise the thought—is he hurt?—he got up again and set off at a shaky jog. He scrambled over the crash barrier on the opposite side of the road and disappeared from sight.

He didn't so much as glance behind him.

The tyres regained their purchase on the road and Mackay slowed to a stop.

"Jesus," Richards said. "What the hell was that all about?"

Nobody answered. For a moment the only noise was the ticking of the hazard lights, which Mackay had activated, and the flick of the wipers. Water splashed up as a car drove by in the fast lane, the motorist oblivious to what had just occurred.

Then Richards looked down and saw that his hand was covering Edmonds'.

"Oh. Sorry," he said, and removed it.

Mackay pulled over into the emergency lane, and two of the men climbed out and shone a flashlight into the darkness where the running man had vanished.

"He's nowhere in sight. Must have gone into that park over there." The detective who had been sharing the back seat with Edmonds and Richards climbed back in, and once again Edmonds found herself squashed, sardine-like, between the car door and the warm bulk of Richards' thigh.

"He's lucky you were wide awake." The detective sitting next to Mackay shunted the passenger seat forward for the second time that trip, in an attempt to give Edmonds a couple of inches more leg room.

"Lucky anybody is at this hour," Mackay said. "And that it's so quiet tonight." He let out a deep breath, then checked his mirrors and pulled onto the road again.

"But we hit him," Edmonds said. She could hear the unsteadiness in her own voice as she spoke, and she hoped the other detectives would put it down to reaction after their near-accident, rather than nervousness about what lay ahead. "Do you think he's all right?"

Mackay nodded. "He'll have a sore arm tomorrow, I should think. Nothing we can do about it now. I'll write it up when I make the report."

"Better hope you don't have a dent in the bonnet, or you'll be writing that up as well," Richards observed, and all the men laughed. Another clicking of the indicator, and they turned right off the A12, heading east towards Stratford.

In the three months since Edmonds had been promoted to the Human Trafficking team in Scotland Yard, she'd been surprised to discover that most of the operations they tackled did not take place in central London, but in the middle-class and respectable-looking suburbs. Like the one where they were headed now.

As they drove down Templemills Lane, Edmonds stared at the tall wire fences and enormous crash barriers that lined the road. The headlights flickered over the stiff mesh, ghostly silver in the dark, as high and solid as a prison fence. But the area protected by the fences and barriers was no prison. It was the construction site for the 2012 London Olympics.

"That's where they're building the athletes' village." Richards pointed across her, to the left. "More than twelve thousand people will be living there. Not all of them will go back home again, if our last Olympics was anything to go by. They'll stay in the UK and claim asylum. About a thousand, probably. Mostly from Iraq, Nigeria, Somalia, Zimbabwe."

Edmonds peered into the darkness at the endless wire fence and the solid concrete barriers flashing past, but she found she couldn't get the image of the man out of her head. Fists clenched, head bowed, seemingly oblivious to the fact he was running straight across a major arterial road.

Running towards something, or running away?

For a troubled moment, Edmonds wondered whether the near-accident with the man was a sign that the police operation tonight, her first-ever raid, was going to go wrong.

Then she shook her head and told herself not to be so super-stitious.

The crash barriers came to an end and, suddenly, they were in suburbia. Ranks of small, unremarkable-looking, semi-detached houses and flats, with shops and businesses lining the narrow high street.

"This is where you'll find the kind of places we're after," Richards had told her during her training. "Not in Soho and the West End. There, they work in pairs. One girl and one maid in one flat. That's legal. But what you'll find out here often isn't."

A police van was parked by the side of the road, waiting. Mackay flashed his lights at it as he passed, and it pulled out into the road behind them.

Peering through the rain, Edmonds made out a pub, a launderette, a fish and chip shop, and another business with a large sign written in lettering she couldn't understand—Turkish, perhaps. All dark and locked up, because it was already after midnight.

The unmarked car slowed as the establishment they were here to raid came into sight.

At street level, the place looked innocuous—a black-painted door with a small number six painted on it in white. Upstairs the windows were shaded by dark blinds and a sign hung, small and discreet, from a neat hook in the corner wall.

"Sauna? Yeah, right," Richards remarked drily.

The police van following them pulled to a stop behind their car.

"Right, everybody," Mackay said. "Let's get this operation going."

Heart pounding, Edmonds wrenched the door open and jumped out, slipping and almost falling on the wet, uneven pavement. Richards caught her arm.

"C'mon love. Round the back."

"Love"?

But there was no time to bristle at the word that Edmonds was sure, in any case, was unintentional. Time only to follow the plan which had been discussed in detail the previous day, to sprint round the back of the building with two of the uniformed officers and head for the fire exit.

She ran up the fire escape, the metal vibrating under her fleece-lined boots.

"Get in position." Richards was behind her, already out of breath.

Ahead, a solid-looking grey door.

As she reached it, Edmonds saw the handle move. Someone was opening it from the inside.

The door swung open and a middle-aged man hurried out. Tousled brown hair, furtive expression, busy buttoning his shirt over his paunch.

"'Scuse me, sir." Edmonds stepped forward.

The man glanced up, then stopped in his tracks when he saw the two uniformed officers behind the plainclothes detectives.

"I'm not . . ." he said. He whipped his head from side to side, as if wondering whether turning and running would be a better option, but there was nowhere to go.

"Please accompany the officers down to the police vehicles, sir," Edmonds said, aware that she sounded squeaky and not nearly as authoritative as she would have wished. "We need to ask you a few questions."

Footsteps clanged on the fire escape as the two officers escorted the unhappy customer downstairs.

Then a red-haired woman wearing a black jacket and a pair of dark, tight-fitting pants burst through the exit, almost knocking Edmonds off her feet. The policewoman grabbed at the railing for support.

The woman's skin was sickly pale, a stark contrast to her crimson hair. She looked older than Edmonds had expected; in her fifties, perhaps. Too old to be a sex-worker? Edmonds had no idea. She smelled of stale cigarettes and perfume, the scent musky and heavy.

The woman was past Edmonds before she could recover her footing, but Richards, standing a few steps further down, managed to grab her by the arm.

"Let me go!" She struggled, shouting at Richards in accented tones, but he had a firm hold on her.

"Nobody's going anywhere just yet, ma'am. Are you in charge here?"

"Me, no." The woman raised her chin and stared at him fiercely. "I am nobody, nothing. Forget you saw me."

"We can't do that, I'm afraid," Richards said, with heavy irony. "Who are you, then?"

Defiant silence. Then the woman snaked her head towards Richards, and for a bizarre moment Edmonds thought that she was going to kiss him. Before the big officer could stop her, she sank her teeth into the exposed strip of skin between the collar of his waterproof and his beanie.

Shouting in pain, Richards let go of her arm. He snatched at her head with both hands, grabbing her hair in an effort to pull her off him.

"Kick her!" Edmonds shouted, but in his panic, Richards seemed to have forgotten his basic self-defence training. Her stomach clenched. God, this was it. She'd have to take the woman down. Fumbling for the canister of pepper spray on her belt, she leapt forward, ready to tackle her, feeling the fire escape rattle as one of the officers below came running up again to assist.

Before Edmonds could act, the woman twisted away from Richards' grasp, leaving long strands of hair dangling from his hands. Edmonds had a brief glimpse of her mouth, bloodstained lips curled back in a snarl, and her gut contracted again because she looked just like a vampire.

To her astonishment, the woman then hooked a leg over the handrail and jumped. Edmonds saw her red hair fly out behind her as she landed on the tarmac below on all fours, like a cat.

"Grab her," Edmonds shouted, and the fire escape vibrated yet again as the officer on his way up did a hasty about-turn and made a hurried descent.

Edmonds thumbed her radio on. "Escaping suspect," she yelled. "Back entrance. Red-headed female. You copy?"

She glanced down again, just in time to see the woman dart into the shadows and disappear from sight. She was limping heavily, favouring her right ankle, which must have twisted when she landed.

The radio crackled in reply. "We've got the two main streets cordoned off. She won't get far. Over."

Edmonds turned back to Richards. He was swearing, breathing hard, his fingers pressed to the wound on his neck. He took his hand away and stared down at the sticky smear of blood.

"Bitch!" he hissed through clenched teeth. "Bloody bitch. Can't believe she did that. God knows what she's given me."

A strong gust of wind wailed eerily through the gaps in the fire escape's supports. Blinking rain out of her eyes, Edmonds saw the woman emerge from the shadows, then bend and fumble under her trouser leg before she set off half-running, half-limping, towards the young constable standing by the parked police cars.

Edmonds grabbed her radio again. Through the worsening downpour, she thought she had seen the gleam of a knife in her hand.

"Watch out! She's armed!" she shouted, directing her voice into the radio and also towards the uniformed officer manning the cordon.

The officer didn't hear her warning. He moved confidently forward to intercept the fleeing woman, obviously thinking, as Edmonds had done at first, that she was one of the trafficked victims trying to escape. There was a brief scuffle, and then he cried out and stumbled backwards, clutching at his stomach. In the bright beam of the police car's headlights, Edmonds saw blood seeping through the young man's fingers.

Kevlar offered little protection against a sharp-bladed knife.

Firearms were not commonly found in brothels, as there was always the risk that they could fall into the wrong hands. Because of this, the police didn't carry guns during raids.

Right now, Edmonds wished she had a gun.

"Officer down!" she screamed into the radio, staring at the scene in horror. "Call an ambulance. We've got a man injured on the street."

Another pair of high-beam headlights blazed in the darkness, and Edmonds saw a sleek black car speeding down the street towards them. It skidded to a stop a few metres away from the police blockade. For a moment the lights from one of the police cars shone directly through the windscreen, allowing Edmonds to glimpse the driver, a sunken-cheeked black man. Then the passenger door flew open, the red-headed woman dived inside, and water hissed from under the tyres as the car spun round in a tight U-turn and disappeared down the Leytonstone Road.

Two other officers sprinted over to the fallen man.

"Shit!" Richards had wadded a tissue onto the wound in his neck and was also staring at the departing vehicle. "That was an Aston Martin. Looked like Salimovic's car."

"The brothel owner?" Edmonds' eyes widened. She'd heard Mackay on the radio earlier, communicating with the team that had been on the way to his house to arrest him.

Now it seemed that despite their careful planning and preparation, he had managed to escape.

"Shit," Richards said again, inspecting the wet and bloody tissue. "How do these bastards always know?"

"Well, it wasn't Salimovic at the wheel," Edmonds said. "I saw the driver. He was black."

The radio crackled again and Richards jerked his thumb towards the door. "Don't worry about what's happening down there. They'll sort it out. We're going in now. Room-to-room search. Keep your pepper spray handy in case there's trouble inside."

Edmonds tripped over the ledge in the doorway and almost sprawled headlong into the corridor. Great going, girl, she thought. Look good in front of your superiors, why don't you?

She moved forward cautiously, glancing from side to side. It was gloomy in here, lit only by a couple of low-wattage bulbs. The walls were dirty and the floor was scuffed, the lino cracked and uneven. She caught another whiff of the unpleasantly musky perfume which she now realised hadn't come from the escaping red-head, but from the interior of the brothel itself. Underlying that was the stench of old dirt and another pungent odour that Edmonds suddenly, shockingly, realised was the smell of sex.

Pop music was coming from somewhere, piped through invisible speakers, but as she noticed it the sound was turned off. Now she could hear the voices of the officers at the front of the building.

"You three take the top floor."

"Bag that price list, will you?"

"Christ, it stinks in here."

"Oi! Where do you think you're going, sir? Hey! Someone grab him." Then there was the sound of running footsteps, followed by a brief scuffle.

She came to a closed door on her right. Aware of Richards behind her, she pushed it open. The room was gloomy; a purple lantern illuminated a single bed in the corner with a figure huddled on a stained mattress.

"Somebody here," she called, hearing the quiver in her own voice as she approached the bed.

A black girl lay there, eyes wide and terrified. She was on her side, her slender arms wrapped tightly around her legs, and Edmonds saw with a jolt that she was naked. She glanced around the room for something to cover her with, but there was nothing suitable in the small space. Nothing at all.

"Are you all right, miss?" Edmonds leaned forward. Now she could see the puffy swelling on the girl's left cheek, where the dark skin was mottled even darker with bruising. She could also see the massive, crusted scabs on her lips.

The girl flinched under Edmonds' concerned gaze.

The police officer breathed in deeply, suppressing her anger. Who had done this? The owner? A client? That middle-aged bastard who'd tried to wriggle out of the back entrance?

"Who hurt you?"

No reply. She whispered something in an almost inaudible voice, but it wasn't in a language that Edmonds could understand.

"I don't know if she speaks any English," Edmonds said aloud.

She reached out and gently took the black girl's hand in her own cold, damp one.

"Are you all right?" she asked again.

The girl looked up at Edmonds in silence, her eyes full of tears.

2

They came for him at night.

Eleven p.m. on a summer evening and Terence was in bed, propped up on his black continental pillow, fiddling around with something on his laptop. She was watching *Idols* on the big-screen TV, lying naked on the bedcovers, her hair spread over the pillow, listening to some teenager butchering a Mango Groove song.

Then, a noise. Loud, hard, frightening, cutting right through the hum of the laptop's fan and the screech of the South African *Idols* contestant's high notes.

He snapped his laptop shut and sat bolt upright. She raised her head from the pillow and stared at the window, as if she could somehow see all the way through it and down to the dark garden below.

"What was that?" she asked.

"Don't know." He pushed back the covers and climbed out of bed. "Turn the TV down, will you?"

He pushed back the curtain and peered out of the window. She felt around for the remote, nearly knocking the bedside lamp over. Where on earth was it? She fumbled in the folds of the duvet, checked under the pillow. Her heart was pounding, her hands trembling. What had made that noise? It was impossible that anything could be banging outside like that. But it hadn't sounded like a banging noise in any case. It had sounded like . . .

. . . like somebody knocking hard on the front door.

Which was even more impossible, because they were the only people on the property. It was well secured, as all the homes in this wealthy Jo'burg neighbourhood were, surrounded by a high wall and a five-thousand-volt electric fence.

She glanced across the bed. There it was, of course. On his table. It had gravitated to the man's side, as remotes invariably do. She stretched across, grabbed it and stabbed the mute button with nail-breaking force.

The teen's quavering voice cut off mid-wail.

"Can't see a thing," Terence muttered, turning away from the window.

Then they heard the noise again. It sounded louder in the silence.

Bam, bam, bam.

"Shit," he said. He hurried to the cupboard, flung it open, rummaged among the clothes.

"What is it?" she asked.

"How the hell should I know?" He pulled on a black T-shirt and grabbed his jeans. Searching through the cupboard once more, he took out a small silver gun. He did something to it that made a metallic, ratcheting noise.

She sat up and stared at him, wide-eyed, clutching the duvet and worrying it between her fingers. He turned around and regarded her coldly, as if she were a complete stranger, as if they hadn't been making love earlier that evening and sharing a jacuzzi an hour ago.

"Put on some clothes," he snapped.

Suddenly her own nakedness wasn't sexy or appealing. It made her feel vulnerable, afraid.

She leaned down to retrieve the outfit she'd worn earlier, now discarded on the floor. Short black cocktail dress, lacy panties, gold sandals. Hands shaking, it took her three tries to fasten her push-up bra. By the time she'd got the dress over her head, Terence was on his way downstairs.

She heard his footsteps on the tiles. Then nothing. She waited, perched on the edge of the bed, straining her ears. Was that the front door opening? She didn't know. It was too far away for her to be sure.

She waited for what felt like an eternity, expecting to hear a shout, a gunshot, something.

She heard only silence and the soft trilling of a cricket outside.

"Terence, are you okay?" she called.

More silence.

"Terence?" She tried again, louder this time.

She waited a few more fearful, stomach-clenching minutes. What should she do? Eventually she crept down the stairs, slowly, cautiously. Who would be waiting there? She didn't know. She needed a weapon, but what could she use?

Stopping at the foot of the staircase, she lifted an ornamental wooden spear from its resting place next to the painted Masai shield on the wall. It wouldn't be effective against a gun, but at least it was something. Its polished shaft felt comforting in her hand. She held it in front of her and cautiously made her way down the hallway.

The lounge was quiet. The hall was empty. There was no sign of Terence, no sound of anyone.

Ahead of her she saw the front door, gaping wide open. Beyond that—she froze, grasping the spear more tightly, feeling her heart hammer a panicked tattoo in her throat—the electric gate stood wide open, too. Wide open to the dark road outside.

The house was unguarded, vulnerable, its defences breached.

Terence was gone.

3

October 26

Jade pounded along the path that ran parallel to the main road and then wound its way through a grove of pine trees. Her feet skidded on loose sand, crunched over the dry needles. Shade at last. The air was cooler in the dappled cover of the trees. She slowed to a jog and concentrated on her breathing. Two steps breathing in, two breathing out. In, out, in, out. Her lungs burned. Her legs ached.

She hated running.

Every weekend, without fail, her police-commissioner father had got out of bed even earlier than his usual break-of-dawn start. He would pull on his battered running shoes and strap his service pistol around his waist. If Jade was up by that hour, which she occasionally was, he'd greet her with a grim nod. He'd always say the same words to her, in the same resigned tone.

"Can't let the bad guys outrun me."

Then her father would head out of the house, returning an hour later, redder, sweatier, and with an expression on his face even grimmer than before.

Jade suspected it was similar to the one she wore now.

She wore Nike trainers, which thanks to her twice-weekly runs were rapidly becoming as battered as her father's had been, but she drew the line at carrying a gun. She knew from experience that a loaded weapon might feel light at the start of a run, but it would have grown as heavy as a brick by the end.

Her father was dead, but his life lessons stuck with Jade.

Don't let the bad guys outrun you.

Jade lifted her gaze from the path in front of her and checked the road ahead. Slowing again, she glanced back. Nobody there.

The pine grove was behind her now. The path led down an uneven slope, the dry soil fissured and eroded, pale yellow-green weeds clinging to the sides, and then rejoined the sandy road.

Not far to go till home.

She increased her speed, forcing her tired legs into a sprint. She ran past the house on the corner, a gunmetal-grey monstrosity that looked like it must surely be owned by a retired naval commander. The outside wall had been painted white, which was an unfortunate choice for a home bordering a dusty dirt road. Jo'burg's winter had been long and dry, and although it was late October now, and hot, not a drop of rain had fallen. The wall was covered with brownish-yellow stains, just like the teeth of a sixty-a-day smoker.

Past the next house, an inoffensive bungalow with an electric-wire fence. Inside, a gardener stood aiming a hosepipe at a withered flowerbed. Jade waved. He waved back. The owners' Jack Russell raced up and down the fence line, yapping loudly.

Almost home. Past the next property. It was easy to run faster here, past the main house and the concrete staircase that led to the tiny flat above the garage. Jade didn't want to look at it. She didn't want to see the smart red Mini parked outside the garage. It belonged to the new tenant, a woman who was obviously prepared to pay more for her wheels than for her accommodation.

David had lived in those upstairs lodgings until a couple of weeks ago.

Superintendent David Patel, to give him his full title. Superintendent David Patel, who'd recently packed up his modest belongings and moved away. Lock, stock and barrel. His wife had been promoted, he'd told Jade. She had been transferred to the Home Affairs head office in Pretoria, and so he was moving back to his house in Turffontein, where she and their son Kevin had been living.

Jade had no idea whether that meant David was considering getting back together with Naisha. They were separated, not divorced. Easy to move back in with your married partner. Especially when it seemed her relationship with David was now history.

When he'd kissed her goodbye—a formal peck on the cheek—she'd looked for a sign of regret in his icy-blue eyes, but seen none.

His brown-skinned hand had clasped her fair-skinned one for a too-short moment.

"See you soon, Jadey," he'd said. Then he'd straightened up to his dizzying six-foot-five inches and sauntered over to his car.

Jade clenched her hands more tightly. She wouldn't think of the nights she'd spent with him up in that tiny room. How many nights had it been in all the time they'd spent as neighbours?

Not enough, Jade thought. Never enough.

"Get a bicycle."

Those had been the last words he'd called out to her as he sped down the road and passed her on the start of a run. He'd leaned out of the window looking amused, his unmarked vehicle so over-loaded with clothes, bedding, books and boxes that she'd meanly hoped he would be pulled over by the Metro Police and fined.

Get a bloody bicycle. What kind of goodbye was that? Damn him.

She hadn't spoken to him since then. She had to admit, though, that the advice he'd given her was well worth taking. Riding a bicycle would be a lot more fun than this.

Jade quickened her pace, elbows pistoning. If she could make it past his house in twenty strides, he'd come back.

Fourteen, fifteen, sixteen. She hurled herself forward, aiming for the boundary line. It was too far off. She wasn't going to make it.

Ahead of her, an engine roared.

Her head snapped up. She slowed her pace, and moved away from the centre of the road, ducking into the shade. She couldn't run here; the sand was too thick. She dropped back to a walk, propelling herself along on now-wobbly legs.

A shiny silver sports car fishtailed down the road and skidded to a stop outside her gate, dirt flying. The blare of a horn shattered the stillness of the morning.

Gasping for breath, Jade pulled her T-shirt away from her body to draw in cool air. Her hair had worked loose from its ponytail and hung around her face in wet rats' tails. She pushed it back and approached the car cautiously. She wasn't expecting company. Still less, company driving what she now saw was a new-looking Corvette convertible with a vanity plate that read PJ1.

The single occupant of the car was a blonde woman. Her face was turned away, looking back in the direction she'd come from, where the dust of her hurried approach still floated in the air. Jade could see the outline of her head in the wing mirror. If she checked the mirror, the driver would see Jade.

But she didn't. She turned to look straight ahead again, staring directly at Jade's rented cottage. Then she hooted a second time.

Jade walked up to the car and rapped on the window.

When she heard the sound, the woman screamed.

The sound was high and shrill and penetrated the tinted glass. The woman cringed away from Jade, cowering in her seat, arms flung up in defence.

Her face was ghostly pale, her features twisted with terror.

4

The woman peered through her raised hands at Jade. Looking more closely, she took in her faded baseball cap and sweaty pony-tail, her white T-shirt and her old running shorts. Then she lowered her arms. She glanced over her shoulder, reached out an unsteady hand, and buzzed the window down.

"I'm looking for Jade de Jong," she said, in a high, tense voice.

Jade stared at her, surprised. Although this woman obviously knew about her, Jade had no idea who she could be. She'd never seen her, or her car, before. Jade guessed she wasn't from the area, because people who drove regularly on the rough country roads in her neighbourhood tended to buy big, high-riding suvs or trucks, not low-slung sportscars.

Sandton, she decided. Everything about this woman screamed Sandton, from her big, gold-framed sunglasses and the silver Patek Philippe watch on her left wrist to the oversized diamond rings that sparkled on her red-manicured fingers. A wealthy woman from Sandton, asking for her.

"I'm Jade de Jong," she said.

The window buzzed down all the way.

"You're Jade?" The woman moved her elbow onto the door-frame and regarded her more closely. "I phoned you just now, but you didn't answer. I need your help urgently. Please."

Jade's legs were starting to stiffen up, and she was conscious of the sweat dripping off her hair and onto the back of her neck. She took the gate buzzer out of her pocket and pressed the button.

"Shall we talk in the house?" she said.

The woman clearly thought this was a good idea. The Corvette's engine roared again and gravel sprayed out from under the tyres as she accelerated through the gate without waiting for Jade. The car skidded to an abrupt stop in the shade of a syringa tree next to

Jade's vehicle, a small entry-level runabout which she'd hired from a company called Rent-a-Runner. Every month Jade took her car back to them and switched it for a different model.

Right then she was driving a Ford. Or perhaps it was a Mazda.

At any rate, parked beside Jade's hired car, the Corvette looked like a crouching silver dragon next to a little white mouse.

The woman climbed out, slammed the door, and hurried across to the cottage. Her high-heeled sandals were the same colour as her car. With the extra height they gave her, she was slightly taller than Jade.

Catching her up, Jade unlocked the security gate and the front door, and they walked inside.

The interior was gloomy after the glare of the morning sun, and the temperature dropped ten degrees instantly. That was thanks to the high, thatched roof. Although it made the place unbearably cold in winter, it kept it pleasantly cool in summer.

Jade shut the front door behind them and glanced at her cell-phone, which she'd left on the kitchen counter. A blue light was flashing, indicating she had missed calls.

"Take a seat." She gestured to one of the two sofas in the small living room. Pink floral upholstery, stacked high with a multitude of lacy scatter cushions in varying shades of pastel. When she first moved in, Jade had planned to stash these annoying items some-where out of sight, but decided against it when she realised that they would take up most of the available storage space.

For a moment she was slightly embarrassed by the décor. She was tempted to explain to the woman that it wasn't her choice; that she'd rented it furnished.

Jade didn't, though. She just watched while she moved three cushions aside to clear an area large enough to sit in, and then took a seat opposite her, shoving the rest onto the tiled floor and reaching for her notebook on the coffee table.

"I'm sorry," the woman said. "I haven't even . . . I came here in such a hurry, I haven't told you who I am. My name's Pamela Jordaan."

Pamela spoke with an accent so refined it made Jade wonder whether it was the product of elocution lessons.

"How did you know where to find me, Pamela?"

"Oh, I asked Dave. I called him earlier this morning and he gave me your details."

"Dave?" Jade frowned, confused.

"Dave Patel. You know, the police superintendent."

Dave?

"David recommended me?" Saying his name out loud made Jade's stomach clench uncomfortably. She wondered how on earth this woman knew him, and what their history was. David had never mentioned Pamela to Jade, that was for sure.

"Yes."

"What do you need?"

Pamela took a deep, shuddery breath. "I need a bodyguard. He said you would be able to help."

Jade paused before answering, surprised by Pamela's request. She'd protected women in the past, a number of them, but she had never once been hired by one directly. The job had always been assigned to her by a wealthy husband or boyfriend who needed close protection for his woman, but didn't want another man moving in on his territory.

In every single instance that Jade could remember, women who hired bodyguards for themselves wanted males, not females. Big, strong, muscular men to keep them safe.

"I can help you," she said. "Could you give me a few more details, Pamela? Is there a specific reason why you need a guard?"

"My husband disappeared last night," Pamela said in a shaky voice.

"Disappeared? From where?"

"From our home in Sandown, in Sandton."

So her guess had been right, Jade thought.

Pamela cleared her throat, swallowed, and spoke again, gabbling her words as if she had rehearsed them. "His phone is switched off. I can't contact him and I have no idea where he is. He was supposed to be at work this morning and he isn't there. I've already reported him missing. I don't want to start panicking unnecessarily, but until I know where he is and what's happened to him, I want some added protection for myself and my daughter. Just somebody around to keep us safe."

"Your daughter?"

"Tamsin's grown up." A small smile softened Pamela's taut

expression. Jade had noticed no such warmth when she'd mentioned her husband.

"She doesn't live at home anymore," Pamela continued. "She doesn't even know Terence—my husband—is missing yet. But she works for him, and if something's happened to him then I'm worried for her." She twisted her manicured fingers together, then stopped and adjusted one of her rings. Jade wondered whether the big diamond had been digging into her hand. "I've never had anything like this go wrong before, but we are involved in an industry where these things have been . . . well . . . known to happen."

"What industry is that?" Jade asked.

"One that has a rather unsavoury reputation, I'm afraid. Adult entertainment." In response to Jade's questioning glance, she continued. "Terence owns a chain of strip clubs. You might have heard of them. They're called Heads & Tails. They're upmarket, totally legitimate and above board. He offers his patrons good, clean fun."

"I've heard of them." Jade gave a small nod, struggling to keep her expression carefully noncommittal. Good, clean fun at Heads & Tails? But of course. Bring along the whole family for a jolly evening's entertainment. Even Granny would approve.

"The problem isn't Terence's business. The problem is the industry itself. It attracts more than its share of ne'er-do-wells; people looking to make quick money or who are simply obsessed by sleaze," Pamela said.

Jade nodded again. She couldn't remember the last time anybody had actually used the term "ne'er-do-well."

"Tamsin's not a dancer, of course," Pamela added hurriedly. "She runs the admin office at the Midrand branch. But I'm still worried for her."

"I can see why you would be." Jade nodded for a third and final time.

Given the nature of their business, she could now understand why Pamela might feel more comfortable hiring a female bodyguard to look after herself and her daughter.

"I operate on my own," Jade told her. "So if you're looking for full-time, round-the-clock protection for yourself and Tamsin, I can't help. You'll need to contact one of the big firms and get a team of guards."

"No, no, I don't think I'll need that. Just somebody to be with us when we're out and about, and to check on security wherever we stay."

"Will that be in Jo'burg, or are you planning on travelling?"

"In Jo'burg, I should imagine."

"And have you or your daughter had any other problems with security recently? Any reason for you to feel in personal danger?"

Pamela gazed out of the window for a few moments, then shook her head. "I don't think there's been anything," she said.

Jade nodded. This sounded like a low- to medium-risk job. She'd worked a few of those in the past, one-on-one with an employer who could not afford, or did not think it was necessary, to hire a team. Sometimes Jade had been stood down during her employer's working hours, but more commonly she had guarded the client during the day and gone home at night, leaving her employer's safety in the hands of the local police or home security company until the next morning.

In a job like this, it was common for the bodyguard to be asked to do other, unrelated tasks. Jade knew one close protection officer who had survived a two-year stint in Iraq, but had quit after a week when the spoilt Beverly Hills heiress who had hired him on his return assigned him "gardening" duties—walking the dog, scooping poo, mowing the lawn.

Although she'd spent innumerable hours waiting outside fitting rooms in clothing boutiques, Jade had never been asked to mow the lawn, but she had walked quite a few dogs in her time.

"I usually agree on a set period of time with the client in advance," she said. "Given the circumstances, though, I think it would be better if we take it day by day, and wait to see whether there's any news on your husband."

"Thank you."

In spite of her reassurances that there had been no problems with her own security, Pamela still looked tense—she was perched on the edge of the squishy sofa as if poised for flight. Her body language puzzled Jade. In her experience, disappearing spouses were usually a cause for anxiety rather than fear.

As if making a concerted effort to relax, Pamela let out a loud sigh, rifled through her white Gucci handbag and produced an orange emery board. She stared distractedly at the brightly painted nails on her left hand, then started filing the nail on her index finger.

There was silence, apart from the erratic scrape of the emery board. Then Pamela turned her head towards the door and asked, "What's that? I can hear something."

Jade listened too. She heard a low, drumming noise. It was the sound of a car approaching fast, its tyres hammering over the deeply rutted road. She got up, hurried over to the kitchen window and looked out. The car shot past the cottage without slowing. She thought she recognised her landlady's white Isuzu, but the clouds of dust made it difficult to tell.

"Just a local resident," she said. "Nothing to worry about."

"Oh." Pamela didn't stop watching the door.

"You'd like me to start right away, I take it?" Jade told Pamela her rate for full-time close protection and the blonde woman nodded in a distracted way, as if money was so completely irrelevant she didn't want to be bothered by it.

"I'd like us to go past my house first, so that I can check that everything's secure there," Pamela said. "Then we must go straight to my daughter's flat and pick her up. I've already left her a message to say I'll be coming."

She brushed distractedly at an invisible speck of dust on the leg of her cream-coloured trousers. They were worn with a belt with a logo on the buckle that Jade didn't recognise, but which she was sure she would have been impressed by if she had.

Jade tugged her now-clammy running shirt away from her skin.

"Give me a minute to change, and we can go."

She emerged from the bathroom five minutes later, showered and wearing black jeans and a dark jacket that concealed the gun on her belt.

Pamela was still busy with her manicure, but when she saw Jade, she put the nail file back in her designer tote and stood up. Then she opened her purse and handed Jade a thick wad of banknotes.

"This is your fee for the next three days."

Surprised that Pamela was carrying so much cash with her, Jade took the money. She couldn't remember the last time she'd been paid this way. She decided not to count it in front of her new client. The wad of hundreds felt thick enough to her. In fact, the bundle of notes barely fitted into her small leather wallet, making it chunky and uncomfortable when she stuffed it into her back pocket.

By the time Jade had locked up the cottage, Pamela was already in her car and revving the engine, her hard, crimson nails tapping out a rhythm on the steering wheel.

5

Jade had done her official close protection training in London. Her course lecturer had been a Scottish woman, who as far as Jade had known didn't seem to have a first name. They'd simply called her Stewart.

Stewart was built like a tank, as broad and solid as she was tall, with a voice to match her physique, and a thick Aberdeen accent. She had striking green eyes, a jutting chin, and a rough grasp that felt a lot like a donkey bite. One from a very large, foul-tempered donkey.

Would Jade have felt safe with Stewart guarding her? Absolutely. She'd have felt safe from armed assailants, a rebel invasion, even a meteor strike. She would certainly have felt a lot safer than she did with Stewart as her teacher; the muscle-bound instructor had inspired equal amounts of terror and respect.

Jade had been the only woman in the class, but she knew the lads felt the same way, because none of them had laughed or joked about their indomitable teacher.

There were guidelines to be followed when protecting a client, Stewart had explained. First, you will assess the level of threat and risk to the principal. Then you will plan and prepare in order to minimise it as much as possible.

She'd taken them through every page of the rule book, step by thorough step. She'd explained the different levels of security that existed in response to the various levels of threat, and she'd explained the difference between providing overt and unobtrusive security.

Then she'd told them that the rule book was as good as useless in certain circumstances; that bodyguarding was often about making the best of a bad situation and relying on your own instinct and gut feeling to know when things were about to go bad. And, when they did go bad, that was when a bodyguard would truly earn their fee.

"If it came tae the crunch, wud ye be prepared tae take a bullet fo' yer principal?" She'd stabbed her finger into the chest of the largest and most macho lad in the class, an American who'd told Jade in hushed tones the day before that he really wished his teacher could come with subtitles, because he couldn't understand half of what she said. The man had stumbled backwards, away from Stewart's prodding finger, with an expression on his face that Jade could only describe as panic.

"Well? Wud ye or no?"

Jade opened the Corvette's passenger door and got in. The car smelled new, of expensive leather and finely tuned engine. If wealth had a smell, Jade was sure it would be something like this.

It was common practice for bodyguards to do the driving, but since Pamela had hired her as a precaution and did not seem to be in any direct personal danger, Jade did not insist on taking the wheel herself.

Assess the threat . . .

Pamela's husband had disappeared yesterday evening. Where could he have gone? She could think of a few obvious possibilities. He could be with another woman. He could have been a victim of an opportunistic robber or hijacker. He could have driven off a stretch of lonely road and be lying in the wreckage of his car, unconscious or dead, but still undiscovered. There was no reason to panic yet—at least not as far as Pamela's own safety was concerned.

Or so Jade thought.

The Corvette was brutally powerful. It was built for speed, and Pamela drove it that way. When she reached the main road she pressed the sports mode button and put her foot down. Its big engine responded instantly with a throaty roar. The car shot forward, leaving the other drivers in their heavier four-wheel drives and luxury sedans gasping in its wake.

Jade tried to fasten her seatbelt discreetly, but the damn thing kept locking whenever Pamela accelerated, and Jade ended up having a tug-of-war with it. *Lady, I can't protect you from a* collision, she thought, gritting her teeth as Pamela shot past a taxi pulling out onto the main road, missing its front bumper by the width of an acrylic fingernail.

She'd been a nervous passenger with David at the wheel, too, but he just laughed when she complained and called her a control freak.

Perhaps she was. Perhaps that was why he'd moved back to Turffontein.

Forcing thoughts of David out of her mind, Jade focused on the task at hand, checking the wing mirrors carefully, watching as Pamela zig-zagged in and out of the slower-moving streams of traffic on William Nicol Drive. Cars behind them, cars beside them, cars, for a short time at least, in front.

Pamela turned left into Sandton Drive and then left again. They passed a sign for Sandown with an advertisement for gourmet catering services below it.

This narrow, two-lane road was also busy. Above the noisy traffic, Jade picked up the drone of a motorbike engine approaching fast behind them.

Pamela glanced into the rear-view mirror when she heard the bike, and gripped the wheel harder.

"Jade, I think——"

Jade never found out what Pamela thought, because at that exact moment the whiplash crack of a gunshot split the air.

She felt the bullet's deadly breath as it sped past her. A small, round hole appeared in the driver's window, surrounded by a milky web of cracks, and then Jade found herself staring at another neat little hole on the left-hand side of the windscreen.

The motorbike, Jade realised in horror.

Its rider had shot at their car. Shot at a woman whom she had considered to be a low-risk client, on a public street, in broad daylight.

Pamela's handbag tipped sideways and the contents scattered over the carpet as she swerved violently and started screaming. "Dear God! Help! I'm going to be killed!"

There are three stages to every attack. Stewart had counted them off on her thick, stubby fingers time and time again. Surprise, control, and escape.

Always act during the surprise stage, she'd growled. Because when they've got control of your client, it will be too late.

The roar of the bike, louder again, pulling alongside them. It was a red Ducati, and she could see the black leathers and dark-visored helmet of its rider. Tall and strong-legged. Definitely a man. A man gripping a black Beretta in his left hand.

"Keep calm," Jade yelled. "And keep still. I'm going to try and get a shot at him."

She wrestled her Glock out of the holster and leaned forward, trying to get a clear line of sight, but in the confined space of the car's compact interior, there simply wasn't enough room to manoeuvre.

Pamela was driving, and Pamela was also panicking. She ducked down, right into Jade's line of fire, screaming and shoving at Jade's gun hand as if she were the criminal. Then she flattened the accelerator and the car surged forward on a weaving, erratic path. Jade felt her stomach lag behind the motion in a queasy twist of terror.

An oncoming Land Rover flashed its lights at them, swerving violently as the Corvette veered over the white line. The blare of its horn faded into the distance behind them.

Jade looked over her shoulder. The bike had dropped back, but she saw to her dismay that it was catching up with them again. The only reason the rider wasn't shooting now, she guessed, was that he wasn't close enough to the rear window of Pamela's convertible to get a clear enough line of sight.

But she could see him.

Jade raised her gun before realising the shot was impossible. With Pamela's poor driving, she couldn't be sure of hitting him, and there was a minibus taxi right behind him. A large, vulnerable target crammed with innocent passengers.

She couldn't do it.

The motorbike pulled alongside them once again. It was close now, so close that Jade could almost feel the throb of its engine.

"Listen to me!" Jade shouted, wishing she was in the driver's seat. It was too late for that, and she'd made a critical error there. She should have insisted, even though the threat level had seemed low. "Drive into him, Pamela. Use your car as a weapon. Try and knock him off his bike."

"Help!" Pamela cried again, ignoring Jade's advice completely. As Jade made a grab for the steering wheel, Pamela floored the accelerator and the Corvette surged forward once more.

Another gunshot, followed by a whistling noise that told Jade this bullet had gone wide and shattered the side window.

A large white van clattered past in the opposite direction, forcing the motorbike driver to drop back.

"Watch the road!" A grinding scream as the Corvette's bumper made contact with the raised kerb. Hysterical, Pamela snatched at the wheel. Tyres screeched as she overcorrected the steering, then braked hard to avoid rear-ending a slow-moving car ahead of them. A stately old Mercedes, the driver's white head barely visible above the seat, oblivious to the commotion behind him.

With a sick sense of doom, Jade realised they were pretty much trapped. The elderly driver was blocking the road in front of them, and there was a solid stream of traffic coming from the other direction.

How close was their pursuer?

She looked back again.

The biker was directly behind them, aiming more carefully this time as he prepared to take another shot.

Behind him, the taxi. Approaching fast, showing no signs of slowing down. What in God's name was the driver thinking?

In an instant, Jade realised he must have seen what was happening, and he was coming to their rescue. As she watched, the accelerating taxi clipped the back wheel of the motorbike.

The bike skidded violently, leaving black slashes of rubber on the tarmac, its engine screaming as the rider fought to regain control. Going more slowly now, the taxi nudged the motorbike a second time. Again it skittered sideways, wobbling dangerously, and this time Jade really did think it was going to hit the ground.

Somehow the rider managed to right his machine and swung away, heading for a side street, but as he did he opened fire on the Corvette. Two ear-splitting shots in swift succession. One bullet smashed through the centre of the windscreen, and Pamela screamed, making a sound of pure terror.

"Pamela, it's okay, he's . . ."

But Jade's words were too late. Pamela twisted the wheel

violently and, before Jade had time to react, the car had mounted the kerb with a bang and a smash. They careered along the uneven pavement, ploughing through grass and bouncing over driveways.

Trapped in an out-of-control car; this was Jade's worst nightmare.

"Slow down!" she yelled. "He's gone!" She braced herself sideways, clutching her seat with one hand and pushing against the dashboard with the other, preparing for the inevitable crash.

The wing mirror hit a lamppost and snapped off instantly. Then, with a bang as loud as a gunshot, the Corvette cannoned into the metal struts of another sign.

The impact was hard and searing. As the passenger airbag exploded onto Jade's forehead and her seatbelt cut into her shoulder, Pamela, hurled forward without the protection of a belt, landed half on top of the deploying driver's airbag. Her head connected with the windscreen with a terrible smacking sound.

The car spun through 360 degrees, rocking violently, before finally coming to a standstill just beyond the mangled sign.

Steam hissed from the engine.

Pamela was immobile, panting, white-faced and wide-eyed. Conscious, though, in spite of the knock her head had taken.

"Get out!" Jade fumbled to undo her seatbelt. "Now."

The passenger door had buckled and she didn't rate the chances of getting it open, so she leant over and half-pushed Pamela out of the car through the driver's door. She was quivering all over, a delayed reaction to their predicament. Not a good state for accurate shooting if the gunman returned.

"My bag." Pamela turned back to the car.

Jade grabbed the Gucci handbag and scooped the contents back inside it. Or those she could see, anyway.

Not surprisingly, the traffic had slowed to form a fascinated queue of rubberneckers goggling at the unusual sight of a one-car accident on a suburban verge.

The gunman could return at any moment. She was sure she could hear the distant blurt of his engine. If he did, they would have nowhere to go. They were sitting targets, as would be any well-meaning people who stopped to help. Already, Jade could see two concerned-looking motorists had pulled over onto the opposite verge.

Looking ahead, she saw the taxi that had been following them had stopped to let out a passenger.

"Quick!" Waving at the taxi driver, she set off at a run.

She jumped over the buckled sign—glancing down, Jade saw they had just entered the suburb of Birdhaven—and down onto the paved pedestrian walkway. Pamela flailed behind her, battling to keep up in her unsuitable footwear. She stumbled as her high heel twisted sideways on the bricks, and almost fell. Jade grabbed her hand and yanked her along without slowing down, and it occurred to her that from now on she should insist that clients with errant husbands wear sensible shoes at all times.

"Here." They reached the taxi. "Get in."

"Inside this?" Pamela stopped in her tracks, staring at the battered white minibus.

"Yes. Hurry." Jade pushed her through the open door with more force than she'd intended.

The tinted windows made the taxi's interior look gloomy. It was hot and airless, and reeked of diesel and tightly packed humanity. As they scrambled in, fourteen chattering people fell silent and fourteen pairs of eyes watched them. A portly black man moved out of his seat in the first row and squeezed in next to the woman in a domestic worker's outfit behind him so that they could sit together. His chivalry was lost on Pamela, who promptly collapsed onto the cracked leather seat and closed her eyes.

The taxi lurched forward. Still nobody spoke. Jade realised she was still holding her Glock. She holstered it and tugged her wallet from her pocket. Then she sat down next to Pamela.

Was it her imagination, or was there a collective sigh of relief?

She had no idea how much a taxi-ride cost, or even where they were going, but she handed the driver a twenty-rand note and was passed a couple of silver coins in return.

"Thank you for helping us back there," she said.

The driver shrugged, as if trying to knock gun-wielding maniacs off their motorbikes was all in a day's work for him.

Slowly, muted conversation resumed.

Jade turned to look through the rear window, but it was

painted over with an advertisement for Lucky Star sardines and was impossible to see through. The taxi had two wing mirrors, both loosely attached and one badly cracked. They wobbled disconcertingly as the driver wove between the lanes of traffic, but all she could see through the unsteady glass were cars and other taxis. No motorbikes.

Pamela was breathing hard, her eyes brimming with tears.

"Jade, what . . . ? Why . . . ?" She massaged the crown of her head gingerly, and Jade noticed one of her immaculately enamelled nails had been torn off, leaving a pink, jagged line.

"Don't talk now," she said. "Later."

The taxi driver was busy peeling a banana with his knee propped against the wheel. While he ate the fruit, he conducted an animated conversation with the man in the passenger seat. Lots of unbroken eye contact, reminding Jade of the way David liked to drive.

When he had finished, the taxi driver flung the banana skin out of the window and, still steering with his knee, began to peel an orange.

The vehicle felt wallowy on the road, its uneven progress a testimony to ancient shocks, balding tyres, brakes worn down to the rim.

Jade remembered a newspaper article she'd read recently about Toyota Quantum panel vans that had undergone cheap, illegal conversions into death-trap minibus taxis. The seats were welded to the paper-thin body of the vehicle instead of to the chassis, and there was no rollover bar. This meant that in the event of an accident, the passengers could easily be crushed; their legs snapped like twigs as the seats broke loose.

Suddenly Jade realised that the loud, unpleasant-sounding rattle she'd noticed ever since climbing inside the taxi was coming directly from the row of seats upon which she sat.

Taking a deep breath, she tried to view the situation in a more positive light. Bad as the driver was, and unroadworthy as his taxi appeared to be, at least nobody on board was trying to kill them. So, for the time being, they were safer.

It was all a matter of perspective.

6

The taxi driver joined the highway at the Grayston Drive on-ramp and veered off it again—there was no other word to describe the manoeuvre—at the Marlboro Drive exit. Traffic was backed up at the light, but that didn't deter him. He swerved into the emergency lane and accelerated past the rows of stationary cars. Just ahead of them, another taxi pulled out and did exactly the same, forcing their driver to slam on the brakes. The vehicle slewed sideways, tyres squealing.

Pamela's eyes were shut tight, her lips moving. Jade wondered if she was praying.

A couple of blocks further on, one of the passengers shouted out a request to stop. Responding instantly, the taxi driver headed straight across the double-lane road and juddered to a halt.

"Let's get out here," Jade said. She'd had enough.

They were in Marlboro Gardens, a relatively new industrial suburb. She guessed it had been planned to provide easily accessible jobs for the residents of Alexandra township. On the opposite side of the main road, Jade could see what looked like the outskirts of the township itself. Narrow, crisscrossed roads, small houses, a forest of electrical poles. No match for the large mansions in nearby Sandton, but far better than the tumbledown shacks that had made up the original township residences.

Marlboro Gardens was dusty, with the feel of a place still under construction. Tall signs had been planted alongside the main road, advertising companies manufacturing plastic piping, engine parts, skirting boards, and pieces of equipment so obscure that Jade couldn't even guess at their intended use.

One of the signboards was for a coffee shop in a retail centre down the road. They walked there slowly, Pamela shuffling along because the strap of one of her silver sandals was broken.

The shop was empty, apart from two men in golf shirts seated at a table near the entrance, both peering at a laptop. A ceiling fan whirred at high speed, fluttering the edges of the Italian flags that were draped over every available surface. A male voice—Pavarotti, perhaps?—was singing "Nessun Dorma" in the background. Jade gently steered Pamela over to a corner table where they would have a clear view of the shop's two windows as well as its big glass door.

Looking at Pamela more closely, Jade saw she was so pale she looked as if she was going to faint. Her smart top was torn in two places and had a bloodstain on the right side. The blood came from a graze on her wrist. Jade was sure Pamela hadn't even noticed it. Her trousers were scuffed and grimy, and her hair had sprung wildly in all directions. She didn't sit down, but looked around the room until she saw the sign for the toilets.

"I must go to the Ladies," she said.

"No problem."

She checked the toilet before she allowed Pamela inside. It was small and empty, and smelled strongly of disinfectant.

Jade went back to her seat and let out a long, slow breath as she tried to make sense of what had happened to them. Who was the motorbike rider, and why was he after Pamela?

Had he been waiting near her house, and got lucky when he'd seen her car? Or had he been tailing her some other way?

While she waited for her client to reappear, she called David.

"Jadey," he answered loud and cheerfully. She couldn't help but feel a leap of hope when she heard him say her name. "Did Mad Pammie get in touch? She phoned me just now and I recommended you."

Mad Pammie?

"Yes, she did. And now . . ."

"Good. She's rich, so you can charge her double. And I've got some interesting news about the Hawks."

What on earth did South Africa's new crime-fighting squad have to do with Pamela, Jade wondered.

David took her surprised silence as an invitation to continue. "They might be absorbing our unit next year, in which case it will be the most senior in the police service when it comes to fighting organised crime. I've been whipping everyone into shape here. Hardball Patel, they're calling me. I've never met such—"

"David, please, stop talking about work and listen to me." Jade interrupted his monologue.

"Sorry." His voice was softer now. "What's up?"

Jade glanced around the shop and lowered her own voice.

"I think Pamela has a hit out on her. Her husband disappeared yesterday, and about half an hour ago somebody on a motorbike made a pretty serious attempt at killing her. Fired four shots at her car while we were driving back to her house. It was pure luck that she wasn't injured or killed. She crashed the car, a silver Corvette, which is now on top of the Birdhaven suburb sign on the side of Fourteenth Street. Closest intersection Willow."

A long pause.

"Holy shit," David said.

"Exactly."

"Are you okay?"

"I'm all right. So is she."

"She have any idea why someone's after her?"

"I haven't asked her yet."

David sighed. "Bloody hell. I'm sorry, Jadey. I had no idea . . . Pammie didn't tell me what was up when she phoned. Just said she needed a bodyguard urgently. I asked her if a woman would be okay and she said yes, a woman would be better. I thought she was having the usual problems. Husband smacking her around, you know."

"Are those Pamela's usual problems?"

"No idea. All I know is she married some rich bastard, so when she said she needed help, I assumed it was something along those lines. Isn't it always?" He sighed heavily. "Pammie's a real drama queen. She's been known to stretch the truth. Exaggerate. Sometimes fabricate a situation when it doesn't exist."

"Not this time," Jade said.

"Nope. Not this time. What can I do to help?"

"You could send a detective to check out the crime scene, and call me when he's finished, so that I can organise to have the car towed. And do the police have any leads on her missing husband yet? That would be useful to know."

"What's his name?"

"Terence Jordaan."

"Terence Jordaan," David said. "You know, that sounds familiar. Don't ask me why."

"You think he has a record?"

"No, not necessarily. I just remember hearing it somewhere before. Still, it's a common enough name, I guess. Must be a lot of them around. You know what line of business he's in?"

"He runs a chain of upmarket strip clubs called Heads & Tails."

Jade heard a rat-a-tat-tat sound as David tapped the desk with his fingers. Then something that sounded suspiciously like a snort. "Heads & Tails?" he said disparagingly. "No wonder his name's familiar. Maybe he does have a record after all. Did Pammie say anything about previous involvement with the police?"

"Nothing. Wouldn't she have mentioned it when she called you?"

If David called her Mad Pammie and she called him Dave, a liberty even Jade would never dream of taking, it surely meant the two must be on very friendly terms. Thinking about that, Jade was surprised to feel a tiny stab of jealousy.

"Nope, she didn't say a thing about him." To Jade's disappointment, David didn't elaborate on Pamela's situation any further. "I'll check it out and follow up. See if Terence Jordaan's name comes up on our system."

"Thanks. I appreciate it. I know you're busy."

"Tell me about it. I'm bloody swamped. But I feel responsible for this. I feel like I've dropped you in it. I thought looking after Pamela would be an easy job. If I'd known some nutcase with a gun was going to try and take her out, I'd never have recommended you take it on."

Before Jade had a chance to respond, David put the phone down.

7

David's computer was hanging again, its screen a bright blue that wouldn't change no matter how hard he wiggled the mouse or slammed his fingers down on the Control-Alt-Delete keys. He reached over and unplugged the damn machine at the wall, then plugged it in again and rebooted. Crude but effective.

While he waited for it to power up, he stretched his neck from side to side, ran his fingers through his short hair and then rubbed his thumbs against his temples. This went some way towards relieving the nagging headache he'd had all morning.

Breathing deeply, he glanced at the screen again. The password request had popped up. As he typed in the code, he saw that a stray hair was trapped under his wedding ring. David noticed that it was pure white.

Bloody hell. Captain Thembi, his new right-hand man, had been joking the other day that their monthly benefit package should include a box of Clairol. Now, David realised it hadn't been that much of a joke after all.

His head began to pound again. He opened the top drawer of his desk and took out the bottle of Panado that he kept next to his personal jar of extra-strong coffee. Jade had teased him about cause and effect when she'd noticed those two items side by side in his drawer.

But he wasn't going to let himself think about Jade. Not now.

David shook the last two pills out of the bottle and washed them down with a gulp of cold coffee from the mug on his desk, grimacing at the taste.

He checked the time on his watch. Ten-thirty a.m. and it was already turning into a bitch of a day.

He typed Terence Jordaan's details into the system and

drummed his fingers on the desk as he waited for the organised crime database to perform the search.

After the fatal shooting of the corrupt police commissioner who had headed up his old investigation unit, the suspension which the commissioner had given David had been overturned. That had been more than a year ago now, but his superiors had recently advised him that since the serious and violent crimes unit was going to be "restructured," David should consider transferring to another department.

The move to the Organised Crime Division had required David to pack his possessions in a cardboard box and walk them up two flights of stairs and along a corridor. His new office was bigger than the old one, which meant he had to share it with Thembi and two other sergeants from his team. It faced the same direction, with a view of a fir tree and a couple of bushes amid the urban sprawl of Johannesburg. The trees looked smaller from this fourth-floor office, and his working environment was somewhat noisier, but apart from that nothing much had changed.

This morning, he was the only person at work. Thembi and his team were on their way to investigate a notorious Sandton brothel after receiving a tip-off that the owner might have brought in a new shipment of girls from Thailand.

Drug trafficking and arms dealing were the two biggest money-spinners for organised crime syndicates, but David had been surprised to learn that trafficking in people was the third most lucrative criminal activity in the world.

While countries like Britain and the USA were destinations for trafficked women, and countries like Mexico and Bulgaria the sources, South Africa was both. In addition, it was a transit country for trafficked workers being transported into or out of the African continent. Corrupt immigration officials and the country's large and porous borders made trafficking a depressingly easy crime to get away with.

All this meant—in theory—that the government had a growing responsibility to fight this exploitation of human life with all its available resources.

In practice, South Africa's existing laws were hopelessly inadequate when it came to this particular offence. Although the South

African Constitution expressly forbade slavery, there were no stand-alone laws that directly opposed all forms of human trafficking. Instead, three different acts were used to prosecute offenders, which meant that putting together a case against traffickers was a haphazard, piecemeal affair. "A right bloody pain in the arse," was how Captain Thembi had succinctly described the process.

The Immigration Act in particular was a stumbling block for police officers, because its focus was primarily on arresting and repatriating illegal foreign residents. Inevitably, the main targets of this act ended up being the trafficked victims themselves.

Because of this, it had not surprised David to learn that South Africa had remained on the Tier 2 watch list in the United States for four consecutive years due to what their Department of State had described as "an inability to exhibit efforts to meet the minimum standards for the elimination of trafficking."

David had told himself he would give himself a year in the department, and then request a transfer to a Jo'burg precinct. That was his dream. To run his own show; to be the commander of his own little ship. To stamp out inefficiency and corruption in his unit, and fight the crime that took place on his turf. To have responsibility for just one area—he didn't mind which one—and show that a determined station commander could make a real difference to the crime rate in his neighbourhood.

Finally, the computer screen finished refreshing.

David leaned forward, surprised by what he saw.

The Organised Crime Division had, in fact, opened a human trafficking case against Terence Jordaan a few years ago.

Reading through the details, David discovered that Jordaan had been arrested after a routine check-up on the Midrand premises of Heads & Tails. There, police had discovered four exotic dancers from the Slovak Republic working without visas, the thirty-day visitors' permits in their passports long since expired.

According to the dancers, they had been lured to South Africa by the promise of a five-year work permit and a high-paying job, neither of which had materialised.

Jordaan had managed to wriggle out of a jail sentence, and the four Slovakian women had been swiftly deported. David could find nothing in the report that stated what the dancers' living conditions had been, or whether they had been forced into prostitution.

A more recent series of updates by Captain Thembi stated that Jordaan appeared to have been running a clean operation since then. The investigation team had discovered no further irregularities during subsequent checkups.

Even so, his history meant that Terence Jordaan was still a "person of interest" for the division.

When David attempted to exit the most recent report update, the computer hung again, forcing him to restart it for the third time that day. He didn't go back into the records. He'd seen enough, and the four case files he'd taken from the filing cabinet that morning were all awaiting his urgent attention. Two were drug-smuggling cases, one was the investigation into the Sandton brothel that was currently under way, and the final file was an investigation into a brothel in Bez Valley that was also suspected of employing trafficked workers, code name "Project Priscilla."

Tomorrow night, he and his team would be conducting a raid on that establishment, and in the meantime David had a mountain of work to get through.

He would call Jade later. Perhaps he could just send her an email. That way, he would be able to avoid speaking to her altogether, avoid that heady mix of guilt and desire that caused his stomach to churn whenever he heard her voice.

As he opened the Project Priscilla file, David frowned and shook his head. Not because of the contents of the cardboard folder, but because of the irony of his situation.

When he'd recommended Jade to his old acquaintance Pamela, he'd never dreamed that the wealthy woman's missing husband would have a criminal record for human trafficking.

Despite all his efforts to move on, it seemed that Jade was back in his life once again.

■

Pamela had now been gone so long that Jade started to wonder if she was all right. Perhaps she'd passed out, or collapsed in a delayed reaction to the stress of the shooting or the bang on her head.

That thought got Jade on her feet and halfway across the café, but she stopped in her tracks as the door to the toilets swung open and Pamela emerged.

Her colour was better. She'd tidied her hair and washed her arm. The only evidence of the bloodstain was a damp patch on her blouse. She limped back to the table, shunting her broken sandal across the floor, and sat down.

Considering what she had just been through, she was looking remarkably calm. Jade wished Pamela had been able to control her fear as effectively when she'd been behind the wheel of her car.

She poured the blonde woman a glass of water from the bottle she'd ordered after speaking to David. When Pamela stretched across the table to take the glass, Jade noticed she had sustained another injury; a livid, blue-black bruise on the bicep of her right arm.

Had her arm caught the edge of the steering wheel during the crash? Jade was about to ask when she realised that this bruise, with its deep purple centre and yellowed edges, was already a few days old.

Pamela put the water down on the table and tugged her sleeve hurriedly over the bruise again. Something about the way she did it made Jade decide to keep quiet about what she had seen, although she couldn't help remembering the comment David had made just a few minutes ago about rich bastards who smacked their wives around.

"I can't believe this is happening," Pamela said. She raised the glass to her lips—freshly lipsticked, Jade noticed. She didn't sound scared now. If anything, she sounded slightly annoyed. "I cannot believe that somebody has just tried to kill me."

"Do you have any idea who that biker might have been?" Jade asked.

"Not a clue." She picked up her bag and drew out the nail file, inspected her broken nail, and started to smooth its edge with quick, brisk strokes.

"Are you or your husband involved in any court cases? Any business dealings that might have a bearing on this? Any problems with employees?"

Pamela turned her attention to her other hand. "No court cases. I don't work, and I fired our maid last week. Terence's business does have its problems from time to time; it's the nature of the industry." Pamela looked up from her mini-manicure. "He did mention he'd be heading out of town in the next day or so. And I know in the past he has gone away when he's in trouble. Gone underground. When there's something he's trying to avoid. Or someone." She shrugged, managing to make the gesture look elegant, and turned her attention back to her nails.

"He couldn't have decided to leave early?" Jade asked.

"No, dear. Our plane is still in its hangar at Lanseria Airport, and all the cars are at home," Pamela said, somewhat testily. Then, "He goes . . . usually, anyway, to a private country residence we own in Dullstroom. It's state-of-the-art. He had it specially designed, you know, and the levels of security there are unsurpassed."

"So did Terence really disappear from your home, then?"

Pamela frowned. "What?"

"If all your cars are where they should be?"

The only sound in the sudden silence was the heartfelt tones of the tenor singing in the background. Jade noticed Pamela was now sitting very still.

"I don't want to talk about it," she said finally.

"If I'm going to be able to do my job properly, I need to know."

Pamela shook her head. Jade detected a stubborn set to her jaw.

The big steel espresso machine on the bar counter made a loud grinding noise, followed by a steamy hiss, and the smell of fresh coffee wafted across the restaurant towards them.

Jade sighed inwardly. This was getting more complicated by the minute. Was Pamela trying to protect her husband? Or did she know more about his disappearance than she was prepared to let on?

Jade had no idea.

"I need you to turn your phone off," she said.

Now Pamela glanced up in surprise. "My phone? Why?"

"That man on the motorbike knew where you were. Maybe he just got lucky because he was in the area looking out for you, but it's also possible he was tracking you via your phone. So, until we've ruled out cellphone tracing, I don't want you to turn it on again."

"But I need to call my daughter to tell her we'll be late. She'll be worrying by now."

Jade nodded. "Tamsin's our first priority. Call her on my phone and tell her we're on our way."

Pamela took the phone. "I'll text her, then, if it's all right with you. Tammy won't answer a call if it's from a number she doesn't recognise."

While Pamela was keying in the message, Jade walked across to the counter, where the waitress was busy making the second of two large, frothy cappuccinos. She paid for their water and used the restaurant's phone to call a taxi. Then she borrowed a silver paper clip from the receptionist and used it to do a temporary repair job on Pamela's sandal. Bodyguarding 101: Ways to keep your client mobile.

The taxi was one of the Gauteng yellow cabs, bright and shiny, with an interior that smelled new, but not in the same moneyed way that Pamela's Corvette had.

After a short drive, they pulled up outside Tamsin's housing complex in Illovo. Pamela had called it a flat, but looking at the spacious buildings that she saw through the bars of the gate, Jade guessed that an upmarket, self-contained, high-security, three-bedroomed palace with a private garden and a koi pond was probably a more appropriate description.

There were only five numbers listed on the intercom. Pamela told the cab driver to press the button for number three.

The bell made a muffled trilling sound. Pamela buzzed the back window down, leaned out and listened for a response.

Silence.

"Ring again," Pamela ordered the driver.

He rang the bell again, and they sat and listened to more silence. It was uncomfortably warm in the car, and the light breeze that wafted in through the open windows wasn't helping in the least. All it was doing was forcing more hot air inside.

"I'm worried," Pamela said in a small, quiet voice. "She didn't respond to my text message either, and I specifically asked her to."

"Do you have a gate buzzer for her house?"

Pamela shook her head.

Jade climbed out of the cab and walked round to the intercom. She pressed all five buttons in quick succession and was rewarded with a little orchestra of trills.

A minute later, a man answered. A light-sounding voice, rushed and breathy.

"Hello?"

"Hi. I'm looking for Tamsin Jordaan," Jade said.

"Sweetie, she lives in number three. You pressed the wrong bell."

Then he hung up on her. Jade heard a clunk that sounded like an intercom receiver being placed back on its rest.

The glare from the bright white wall in front of her was blinding. When she blinked, she saw the white-painted bars of the gate had seared themselves onto her retinas, forming floating black ghosts that drifted across her vision.

She had no idea which number the man lived in, so she pressed each button again.

He responded, this time sounding irritated.

"Number three, I told you."

"Wait." Jade said rapidly, before he could disconnect again.

A pause. Then, "What do you want?"

"I need to come in. Tamsin's mother is here to collect her, and she's missing. She's not answering her phone. Her mother's worried something is wrong."

"Pamela's here?" The man sounded surprised.

"Waiting outside."

Jade heard the sound of the intercom clattering down again, and a moment later, the gate rolled smoothly open.

She told the driver to park on a strip of grass in the shade of a nearby tree. Ahead of her, she saw five double garage doors arranged in a horseshoe shape.

"Which is Tamsin's house?" she asked Pamela.

"That one there. Shall I come with you?" Pamela pointed at the middle set of doors. Jade heard a tremble in her voice, a sign of the same fear that she'd noticed when the blonde woman had arrived at her house earlier that day.

"Better not," Jade said. She didn't want to elaborate any further on the reasons why, but looking at Pamela's face, she saw she didn't have to.

The house had a private garden which was fenced off by dark green palisades. Looking through the bars, she saw mowed grass and lush flower-beds blazing with colour.

And a koi pond. Perhaps she was psychic. Jade concentrated hard, but no other revelations were forthcoming. Glimmers of white and gold appeared briefly in the water as the fish lazily circled their little world.

"There you are." The light voice again, from behind her. Its owner was a young, slender man wearing trendily ripped jeans and a Calvin Klein shirt, with hair gelled into a series of ferocious-looking black spikes.

He glanced at the pond, then back at her.

"Do you like koi?" he asked.

It seemed an odd introduction.

"I've never tried them," Jade said.

"Sorry?" He frowned, looking confused.

Jade held out her hand. "Jade de Jong. I'm working for Pamela."

He clasped it in a gentle grip. "Raymond Arends. I'm Tamsin's neighbour, and her hairdresser. I also do Pamela's hair."

"Have you seen Tamsin recently? Do you know where she might be?"

The diamanté earring in Raymond's right ear twinkled as he nodded. "I don't know exactly where she is, but I'm assuming she's with her aunt right now."

"Her aunt?"

"Yes. She was with Tamsin when I popped round to borrow some Candarel earlier this morning. So I'm sure Tammy's fine."

"Oh." Jade said. "Thank you."

Raymond pulled a tiny silver phone out of his pocket and glanced down at the display. "Look at the time!" he exclaimed. "I don't want to be rude, but I must fly. I just popped back home to change my shirt because I splashed tint all over the one I was wearing, can you believe it?" He laughed merrily, then rummaged in his pocket again and drew a business card from his wallet. "Take this, sweetie. I'd love to do your hair. Come down to the salon any time. I work in the Thrupps Centre. Oh, and if you drive right up to that gate you'll activate the sensor and it'll open to let you out again."

He turned, trotted back towards the double garage to the right of Tamsin's house, and pulled out in an electric blue Peugeot. As he passed the yellow cab, he hooted and waved.

Jade hurried back to the cab, which was still too hot, in spite of the fact that it had been parked in the shade with the air conditioning running. The meter was still running, too.

"Does Raymond know where Tamsin is?" Pamela asked anxiously.

"He said she's with her aunt," Jade said. "Do you think she'll be safe there, or should we go and pick her up?"

Pamela stared at her with a blank expression for what seemed like a very long time.

"Tamsin doesn't have an aunt," she said slowly. "I'm an only child, and Terence's sister died way back when he was in the army."

Then she opened the back door of the cab, leaned out and vomited onto the lush, irrigated grass.

8

Cash Is King was located on the corner of Church Street and Central Road in Halfway House. Ten years ago, Halfway House had been a quiet village, so named because it was located halfway between Jo'burg and Pretoria. Today, thanks to the rapid development that had taken place in the surrounding area, it had become a mini CBD that, in turn, was becoming part of the megalopolis as Jo'burg spread north and Pretoria south. The two cities were gobbling up the empty veld between them at an ever-increasing rate, spitting out uniform housing estates, cramped office parks and busy road networks.

The traffic lights at the litter-strewn intersection were out of order. This had caused problems all morning and now, in the lunchtime rush-hour, it was creating chaos. Battered-looking taxis pushed their way in and out of the slow-moving queues of traffic, dodging pedestrians, tooting their horns, stopping wherever and whenever to cram yet another passenger into already overloaded vehicles.

Perched on a bar stool that was rapidly approaching the end of its natural lifespan, Garry Meertens glanced out of the dirty window on his left as the intermittent honking changed into one long, angry blare. Some arsehole had managed to piss everyone off at once. He squinted through the brownish glass, his view sectioned off into small squares by the thick metal mesh that covered every inch of his shopfront. He would have put his money on the offender being a taxi driver, but instead he watched the white Merc that had crossed the intersection out of turn swing off the road and park on the pavement behind his battered Ford Bantam.

That hour's sideshow over, he turned his attention back to the shop's interior. A couple of raggedly dressed customers were browsing the dusty shelves in the area where the second-hand hi-fis and music systems were displayed. One of them, a stocky coloured man, was a frequent visitor but had yet to buy anything. Garry was starting to suspect he was planning some kind of trouble. Moffat, his assistant, was busy nearby, ostensibly cleaning the display but in fact keeping a close eye on the two browsers.

Then the doorbell buzzed, and Garry's stool squeaked as he twisted round to check out the new arrival.

In contrast to the rest of the windows, Garry kept the glass around the entrance door sparkling clean so that he could check out every customer before letting them in. He'd looked down the barrel of a gun three times in his career, in spite of having the surrounding area pretty much sewn up in terms of security, and that had been three times too many as far as he was concerned.

A lone black man waited at the door. He held a walking stick in his right hand in a way that made Garry think he'd used the tip of it to ring the buzzer bell. He was slim, very dark-skinned, respectably dressed in a button-down shirt, jacket and dark trousers. His head was completely bald, and it gleamed in the bright afternoon sun. Apart from the cane, the man appeared to be empty-handed. Not a seller, then, unless he'd brought along small goods like jewellery, which they didn't deal in, because neither Garry nor his business partner was an expert in stone identification, and it was too easy to get ripped off.

A buyer, then. Garry's finger hovered over the button behind his desk for a fraction before he pressed. With a buzz and a clanging sound, the door sprang open.

The man walked slowly through the aisles. Past the other two customers, who were still staring longingly at the hi-fis that Garry had known from the moment they entered they could not afford. Past the ranks of mountain bikes and racing bikes that Moffat was now dusting. Garry saw the assistant's gaze follow the older man as he headed towards the furniture section, and then return to the coloured guy.

Garry shifted his weight on the stool and it squeaked again.

"Damn thing," he muttered.

He stepped off it and fumbled underneath, his fingers exploring the area where the seat was attached to the four steel legs. The problem was here, he was sure. A screw that needed tightening; a nut or a bolt that was misbehaving. He couldn't feel anything wrong, though. He squatted down, tipped the stool sideways and peered underneath. Couldn't see anything wrong, either. He'd have to take it home tonight and dismantle it, see if he could put it back together in a way that would make him feel he wasn't sitting on top of a badly tuned musical instrument every time he moved.

"Baas!" Moffat's voice was loud and insistent. At the same time, he heard a harsh, barking cough from the other side of the counter.

Garry heaved himself upright, catching the stool with his knee and sending it clattering to the floor. He'd expected to see the big coloured man there, but he was wrong.

The dark-suited gentleman was standing by the counter, leaning over it and examining the contents.

Rattled that the man had got so close without him noticing, Garry drew himself up to his full height of six foot three, and faced the smartly dressed man.

"Help you?" he asked.

Close up, the man was older than he thought. In his fifties or sixties, Garry guessed. His dark skin was dull, with a greyish tinge, and deep lines carved their way from his surprisingly aquiline nose to his full lips. The joints of his fingers, gripping the head of the walking stick, looked swollen and sore.

"Yes, please." The man spoke softly, dropping his gaze to the display under the glass counter.

That was where the knives were kept. A selection of about twenty, ranging from short to long, from smooth to cruelly serrated, all with their blades uncovered. Unusually for stock in a pawnshop, Garry's knives were always brand-new. In the entire history of Cash Is King, nobody had brought one in to sell second-hand. He got them straight from the manufacturers—ends-of-ranges, old stock, surplus items.

Garry didn't feel good about the knives, but he didn't feel bad either. They were just something he sold, like the secret stash of hard-core porn movies that he showed to only a few selected customers.

In the display there were a few fire department rescue knives, with their dark steel fold-away blades flipped outwards, and a couple of AK-47 fixed-bayonet knives. These were displayed out of their leather pouches, with broad, smooth six-inch blades and a button to hook them up to the rifle, should anyone who bought one possess such a weapon and wish to attach a knife to it.

But it wasn't those that the man was staring at.

He was looking at the four traditional Scottish sgian dubhs that Garry had noticed while shopping in Edinburgh a few years ago after travelling there for a friend's wedding. He'd bought six, kept two for his own collection, and put the other four in the shop. And at a hefty price, which was why they hadn't attracted much interest. Up until now, that is.

The short knives had plain black handles—he'd learned that the words "sgian dubh" actually meant "black knife"—and short, wickedly sharp spear-point blades forged from Damascus steel. When he first saw them, they had lain next to their simple sheaths, the same way that they were displayed now.

It had taken Garry a few tries to get the pronunciation right when he asked what the knives were called. The closest he'd been able to get was "ski-and-do."

"In the old days they were secret weapons," the buxom Scottish shop assistant had explained to him in her delightful accent, hooking her thick, copper-coloured hair behind her ears. "They're small, see, so they could be carried hidden. That way, if you had one, you'd have the element of surprise in a fight."

"The aily-ment of surprise, hey?" Garry had grinned at her, mimicking her accent, and she'd giggled and blushed. He'd bought the knives, asked her out that night, and taken her along to the wedding with him the following day. What had her name been? Morgan? Morag? Something like that. They'd lost touch soon after his return to South Africa, but looking at the knives always reminded him of that Scottish salesgirl.

"May I see one of those, please?" The black man was pointing to the sgian dubhs. Garry noticed that his fingertip did not quite touch the glass. Respect. Older guys had it. It made a welcome change from the youngsters, usually rough types who flattened their entire palms over the counter and peered inside, bending so close that their breath steamed up the glass, leaving greasy smudges and sweaty finger-marks behind them.

"Ja, sure." He unlocked the display cabinet, reached inside, and placed one of the knives on the counter. He stepped back, just in case the man was going to try anything funny with it, but he wasn't overly concerned. After all, they weren't throwing knives, and his gun was within easy reach.

But the man simply took it and, holding it in his palm, ran the back of one of his swollen knuckles gently down the blade. Then, as if reaching a decision, he nodded once and closed his fingers around the handle.

"I'll take them."

"Them? You mean . . . ?"

"All four, please."

"They're a thousand rand each, my friend," Garry said, in the particular accent he always used when dealing with black customers. "You sure you got the money for that? Cash only, hey."

The man reached into his jacket pocket and produced a bulky white envelope. He opened it, and offered it to Garry in the same way that a friend might have offered him a piece of biltong from an open packet. Inside the envelope, Garry could see a thick wad of two-hundred-rand notes.

"Please, take your money."

Surprised, Garry took the envelope. The man wasn't a local—he could tell that from his accent—but he sounded well educated. He could surely count twenty notes off a stack without help.

Perhaps those swollen knuckles would make the job too painful; although Garry's old man had worse arthritis than that, and he could still shuffle and deal a pack of cards like a croupier.

Garry counted out the notes, examining them carefully, holding each one under the uv light on his desk to check its authenticity. They looked genuine enough as far as he could tell. Genuine enough, at any rate, to be spent by him again.

When dealing with customers like these, Garry's standard policy was to short-change. Hell, why not? Especially seeing there was way more than four grand in the envelope that the man had so unsuspectingly handed over. Garry guesstimated that it contained over six thousand rand. He had nothing to lose and everything to gain. Just let his fingernail hook a bunch of notes all at once, and add a little onto his own personal Christmas bonus.

Money that he would not have to declare to the taxman, or to his business partner, who was away today doing a stocktake at their other shop in Jo'burg city.

He glanced up furtively, but his customer wasn't watching. He had his head turned away, and was looking around the shop.

Garry's right index fingernail snagged the extra notes easily, but then he hesitated.

He had a pretty strong sense of self-preservation—a must for any guy running a successful pawnshop in this area—and his instincts were starting to scream at him that, perhaps, doing this wasn't a good idea.

Perhaps, in fact, it was a very bad idea.

It was all too easy. Was this some kind of test?

Garry lifted his finger and the little bunch of notes riffled back into the stack. He carried on counting out the notes, and when he had reached the exact amount, he handed the envelope back to his customer.

Then Garry put the other three knives and their sheaths into a white plastic bag and pushed it across the counter, noticing that the man didn't add the fourth knife to it. While Garry had been packing the other three up, he must have done something with it. Garry had no idea what. All he knew was that the knife was no longer visible.

"Anything else?" he asked.

The man paused for a moment. Then he beckoned Garry closer.

The action was suspicious, particularly given the mysterious disappearance of that knife. Garry didn't want to feel that blade pressing against his throat, didn't want to have to comply with a hissed request to give that cash right back again, thank you.

Garry leaned partway across the counter, keeping his gaze fixed on the older man's hands.

"I heard you can organise South African passports," he whispered. Close up, his breath smelled sour.

Garry had just closed his hand around the grip of the Colt .45 he kept under the counter as a precautionary measure. The words caused him to recoil. He dropped the weapon back on the shelf. What the hell? Was this guy a cop?

"What's all this about?" He raised his voice, glowering down at the man.

Unperturbed, the black man beckoned him in again, speaking softly.

"I am asking you only because one of your customers told me you do it."

Garry blinked rapidly.

The man was right. He had organised docs for various people, including a couple of regular customers, a number of times in the past. For a while it had been a thriving sideline. But it had become too dangerous. He'd almost walked into a police trap last Christmas, and after that he'd decided it wasn't worth the risk. In any case, his connection in Home Affairs had recently retired.

"I don't do that anymore," he muttered.

"I can pay. Whatever it will take."

Garry considered his options for a moment.

A while back, he'd heard that a woman had set up shop somewhere in Pretoria, specialising in the procurement of South African documents. One of his old customers had told him about her. In fact, Garry had even taken her details down, but after the Christmas situation, had never used them.

Perhaps he should take the money the black man seemed so willing to invest and contact her now.

Or perhaps not.

An elegant solution to his dilemma suddenly occurred to Garry.

"If you want to pay, you can buy a phone number from me. Hand over the rest of the money in that envelope, and I'll give it to you."

The man twisted away from Garry and coughed again, his shoulders hunched. The noise was rough and rasping and sounded like it hurt.

Then, turning back, he shook the last sheaf of notes from the envelope onto the glass counter.

Garry scribbled the lady's details down on a sheet torn from his spiral notebook.

"Thank you," the man said, as he pocketed the paper. Then, once again, he leaned closer.

"You have done me a favour. So I will do one for you, too."

"What?" Garry snapped. He had been hoping the old gogo would go away now.

"You need to watch out," the man whispered. "One of your customers is armed."

"What the hell?"

Then Garry's head snapped up as he realised that the coloured man had moved closer to the other end of the counter and was fumbling for something under his faded shirt.

"Moffat!" he yelled.

His assistant dropped the duster he was holding. He glanced over at Garry and then, reading the situation instantly, dashed towards the coloured man.

"Hands up! Drop it!" Garry shouted.

Jesus Christ, the bastard had the gun out already, and now he was pushing Moffat aside, sprinting forward, and aiming it at him. He realised in an adrenaline-fuelled instant that it looked like an old police-issue z88 and leaped sideways, but caught his foot on the fallen stool.

He crashed onto the tiled floor, whacking his head hard against the back wall. The z88 fired with a deafening bang, and the bullet smacked into the wall above him.

Breathing hard, Garry crawled to the edge of the counter, his vision temporarily dulled, his mouth filled with a bitterness he would later realise was the acid tang of fear.

He reached up and scrabbled around for his own gun, but his fingers couldn't find it anywhere on the shelf.

"Baas!" Moffat's panicked voice distracted him. His assistant had grabbed the coloured guy from behind, pulling his gun arm out to the side, but the man was struggling hard. He twisted and turned his wrist, somehow managing to angle the z88's barrel round towards Garry.

Garry scrambled to his feet and hurled himself round the counter, but he was too slow; he had reacted too late. He was still a few feet away when his assailant, with hate in his eyes, pulled back on the trigger.

Silence, apart from a dull-sounding click.

The gun was empty or, more likely, it had misfired.

Garry cannoned into the duo before the man had time to try his luck again. The force of his tackle slammed Moffat back against a shelf. Steel cooking pots clanged to the floor as Garry grabbed the gunman's wrist, kneed him in the groin, smacked the edge of his other hand across his throat, and then wrestled the weapon away from him as the man sank to the ground, choking in pain, babbling what sounded, incredibly, like an apology.

"Grab the tow rope over there, Moffat. Get his hands behind him and tie him to that wall bracket. Right, you bastard. Stand up and shut up."

Garry hauled the man up with shaking arms. This was their closest call yet, by far. He'd been thinking for months that he should install a metal detector at the door, but he'd never quite got round to doing it. Well, he didn't need another wake-up call like this one. He'd phone the salesman this afternoon.

Only when the offender was firmly secured to the wall bracket and Garry had gone back to the till to call the police did he realise that the man in the dark suit was nowhere to be seen.

Perplexed, he checked the door leading to the storeroom, but it was locked. There was no other way out of the shop except through the main entrance, but how on earth had he managed to get through the locked security door?

Could the man have leaned over the counter and pressed the door buzzer with the tip of his walking stick? He must have done. He must have buzzed the door open himself and calmly left the shop during the commotion.

Garry was baffled. He'd looked the coloured man over carefully when he'd walked in. Moffat had checked him out, too. Neither of them had spotted the fact that a firearm was concealed under his shabby clothing. But that man—he'd walked past him just once on his way through the shop and picked up that he was carrying.

How could anyone have such sharp instincts?

On reflex, he checked the till's contents. All the money was still there.

It was only then, with a sudden giant clench of his heart, that he realised his gun was missing.

Garry stared blankly at the empty spot on the shelf under the counter where he'd placed his weapon.

It had been there, stashed safely out of sight, and now it was gone.

The man in the suit had stolen it.

9

"My life is falling apart. It's all just falling apart."

Hunched over in the taxi, arms hugging her legs, Pamela looked pale and drained and suddenly a lot older than Jade had first suspected.

The driver was twisted round in his seat, staring at her with a troubled expression. Jade didn't know whether he was concerned by the unusual behaviour of his passengers, or simply worried that Pamela might throw up again, this time inside his vehicle.

She asked him to take them to The Seasons.

The Seasons was a small, exclusive hotel in Morningside. It wasn't well signposted or advertised, and the only reason Jade knew about it was that she'd met a client there a few months back.

The Texan woman had been visiting South Africa for a breast augmentation, face-lift and tummy-tuck. While she was recovering, she'd wanted to trace an ex-employee who had apparently conned her out of a sizeable sum of money.

She'd given Jade the information from her bed in the dimly-lit room, speaking with some difficulty because her face was swathed in bandages. What little skin had been visible was mottled by bruising and swollen to disfiguring proportions.

Jade had returned to the hotel a few days later, after managing to trace the absconding staff member. By then her client's bandages were off and the swelling had subsided. When Jade arrived at her room, she found her eating smoked-salmon sandwiches under an umbrella on the balcony, looking out over the well-kept gardens.

Jade didn't know how the client had used the information. It had been a fifty-fifty chance, she guessed, whether she would have got the police involved or paid a couple of goons to beat him up.

If she had to call it, Jade would have guessed the wealthy Texan would have gone for the hired thugs. She'd had that look in her eye.

Through that assignment, Jade had learned that the reason that The Seasons had such a low profile was because of its clientele, who demanded the highest levels of privacy. The place was used almost exclusively by rich women, travelling from Europe and the States to have various types of cosmetic surgery done at the nearby Morningside or Sandton clinics, following it up with a recuperative week at its sister hotel, a luxury safari lodge in Mpumalanga.

Security at The Seasons was indeed extremely tight. It was as safe and private as a hotel could get.

They had a room available, and Jade booked them in under her own name.

The taxi driver dropped them off in a secluded spot near the covered walkway that led to the hotel's reception. Pamela was walking as slowly and hesitantly as a woman who had just had radical plastic surgery might have done. She had her hands clasped so tightly her knuckles had gone blue-white, and she was muttering the word "No" to herself over and over again.

When they were safely inside the large, comfortably furnished room, Jade sat her down on the bed and spoke to her in a gentle voice.

"Pamela, I'm going to try and find out where Tamsin is. I'm also going to make sure that everything is all right at your house, and bring you a change of clothes."

She nodded.

"Do you have your house keys with you?"

"In my bag," Pamela whispered.

Feeling rather self-conscious about looking through another woman's handbag, Jade searched the Gucci tote until she found a set of keys attached to a gate buzzer.

"Don't open the door to anybody while I'm gone," she warned. "Put the latch on when I leave, and keep it fastened until I come back. Don't even let room service in. And please, don't turn your phone on. If you want to check your voicemail, dial into it using the hotel phone."

Pamela nodded almost imperceptibly.

Jade left her sitting on the bed, hugging herself tightly, staring at the carpet and shaking her head. She informed the receptionist and the uniformed security guard who stood at the entrance to the bedrooms that the lady in the de Jong suite was not, on any account, to be disturbed.

After the strained silence in Pamela's hotel room, the buzz of hair-dryers in Salon Rose Anglaise in the Thrupps Centre was deafening.

Through a thick mist of hairspray, Jade could see Raymond putting the finishing touches to an elegant, blue-black hairdo. When the air cleared, Jade saw its owner smiling at her reflection in the large, gold-framed mirror, obviously pleased with the result.

When Raymond saw Jade, he scurried over. The sticky-sweet smell of hairspray clung to him.

"Sweetie! Here so soon? Are we going to do something with that hair now?"

The yellow taxi was still waiting outside, and Jade had no time to waste on chitchat.

"Tamsin doesn't have an aunt," she said.

"She doesn't . . ." Raymond stared at her, wide-eyed. Then real-isation dawned. He clapped his hands over his mouth. "Dear Lord in heaven. Something's happened to her, hasn't it?"

"Did you actually see Tamsin there this morning?" Jade asked. "What happened when you went round to borrow the sweeteners?"

"I—bye, luvvie!" Pasting on a wide smile, he waved at his beam-ing client, who had paid the receptionist and was about to leave. "Have a wonderful holiday." He turned back to Jade. "She's off to Paris," he whispered. "Flying first-class, too. Her ex-husband is a founder member of Medscheme. You must have heard of them?" Then, in a louder voice, "Anyway, this morning . . . well, I knocked on the door and after a fair while it was opened by this lady I'd never seen before. So I said hi and asked if Tamsin was there, because I'd run out of Candarel. The lady said she was her aunt, and Tamsin was in the shower. She told me to wait, and she went away and came back with the Candarel. She brought it to me on a plate, like a waitress. I thought that was a bit odd."

Fingerprints, Jade guessed.

"Anyway, she said I could keep it, that Tamsin had another one. So I went back home and drank my coffee and rushed off to work. Her car was still there when I left."

"Whose car?"

"Well, the aunt's, I guess. Or whoever she really was. It was parked outside Tamsin's garage. A big white Mercedes."

"Did you notice the number plate?" Jade asked.

Raymond shook his head, looking crestfallen. "No, no, I didn't, I'm so sorry. If I'd known there was anything wrong, I would have taken it down, of course. There was something about it . . . Oh dear, I do wish I had a photographic memory." Then his eyes brightened and he snapped his fingers. "It was a Cape Town plate. I remember thinking she must be from Cape Town, although she had an odd accent. Definitely not South African."

Jade nodded. The Cape Town plates were interesting, but they probably meant nothing at all. A few of her rented cars had had Cape Town plates, and so did many of the vehicles available from Jo'burg-based car hire companies.

"What did she look like?"

Raymond thought for a minute, propping his chin on two fingers.

"She was a good-looking woman. Reminded me of Pamela, now I come to think of it. Similar height, slim, blue eyes, good jaw, strong hands. Wearing a lovely black trouser suit. Oh, but she had terrible hair." He rolled his eyes as he said "terrible" and used his hands to illustrate. "It was badly cut in a longish bob and very badly dyed. Such an ugly shade of brown, flat-looking, no tonal depth. The lengths were oversaturated and darker than the roots. It was a home job, I could see immediately, the cut and the colour. We have to fix that kind of hair in the salon every day."

"How old was she?"

"Pamela's age. Fiftyish. But carrying it well."

Jade stared at Raymond in disbelief. "Pamela's fifty?"

"Sweetie, Pamela is actually fifty-one." Raymond winked at her. "Botox. She's been having injections for years. And the odd bit of surgery. Trust me on that. The hairdresser knows all the naughty little secrets."

And makes sure they don't stay secret for too long, Jade guessed. A pity there was no Hippocratic Oath for hair-care professionals.

"Is there any way I can get into Tamsin's house?" she asked. "I saw a gate in the fence between your property and hers."

"Well . . ." Raymond regarded her with what Jade considered to be perfectly justified suspicion. This was Jo'burg, after all, and she was a virtual stranger.

"I've got a key for it, because I feed her koi when she goes away. It won't get you into her house, though. Only the garden." He picked up the suede bag that lay on the shelf next to his scissors, took out a bunch of keys, but didn't hand them over straight away. "You'll have to go through my house to get to it."

Jade nodded in a manner she hoped looked reassuring. "I'll lock everything up again."

"Will you bring the keys straight back?"

"Yes. I won't be long."

Raymond sighed. "Here they are. But please be careful. My house . . ."

"I'll be careful."

Jade turned to go and then turned back again to give the hairdresser a business card from her wallet.

"Please call me if you remember anything else. And if Tamsin isn't home by tonight . . . you might want to start feeding her fish again."

10

It was a short walk from Raymond's tidy kitchen to the gate in the garden fence. Jade unlocked it, then locked it carefully again behind her. Somewhere nearby she could hear the hum of a lawn-mower, but it wasn't coming from this garden.

There was a splash from the koi pond as she passed it on her way to Tamsin's front door, and she saw a brilliant flash of orange in the water.

To her surprise, the front door was unlocked. It opened smoothly and she stepped inside.

Tamsin's place was as messy as Raymond's had been organised. Every available surface was littered with objects. The small hall-table alone was home to several bunches of keys, a large framed photograph, a fly swat, three bottles of perfume, a romantic novel, a crumb-covered side plate, a cigarette lighter, two unopened packets of Silk Cut, and a bank bag half-filled with marijuana.

The photograph looked like it had been taken at a party or a nightclub. Nightclub, Jade guessed, looking more closely at the poster in the background which advertised the occasion as The Bacardi Breezer Birthday Bash. In it was a young brunette that Jade guessed was Tamsin, wearing a pink lacy blouse, with her arm around an unsmiling man in a black leather jacket.

Tamsin was pouting sulkily at the camera. The man had thick dark eyebrows, a low hairline, and the first word that came to mind when Jade looked at him was "unsavoury."

If this was her boyfriend, Jade guessed she'd inherited her mother's attraction to sleazeballs.

She moved carefully through the house, past an expensive-looking wall unit piled high with magazines and CDs mixed by DJs she'd never heard of, picking her way over discarded clothing, shoes and underwear. The dressing table in Tamsin's bedroom was cluttered with perfume bottles, and her double bed looked like a breeding-ground for fluffy toys.

Tamsin lived alone, that was clear. There was barely enough space for one person under the mound of stuffed animals, never mind two.

The entire house smelled of stale cigarette smoke.

The woman was maybe twelve years younger than her, but standing and staring in bemusement at the chaos that surrounded her, Jade felt uncomfortably like her disapproving grandmother.

It was difficult to be sure with all the clutter, but she couldn't see any obvious signs of a struggle.

No sign of Tamsin, either, although Jade noticed that the tiled floor of the shower was still wet, and so was the pink towel crumpled on a chair in the bedroom. So she—or somebody—had been here recently.

Jade couldn't find a cellphone or a handbag anywhere.

There was a laptop on the desk in the second bedroom, but when she booted it up, she found it was password-protected, so she turned her attention to the stack of papers next to it.

"Heads & Tails Interview Form," the printed pages read.

Jade scanned the form. So this was part of Tamsin's admin job at the strip club. The questionnaire began with a section for the applicant's height, weight, build and colouring. Then it moved on to other details. Previous employment, place of birth, current residential address, identity number or passport number, and contact numbers of closest relatives.

Terence Jordaan certainly did a thorough job of checking up on his staff, that was for sure. Everything seemed to be done by the book.

She took her cellphone out of her pocket and dialled Tamsin's number. She waited till it started ringing and then walked from room to room, listening for a ring tone, or the muted buzz of a vibrating phone.

Nothing.

After eight rings, it went through to voicemail. Jade didn't leave a message, but she remembered Pamela saying that she had when she'd phoned her daughter earlier in the day.

Pamela had sounded confident that Tamsin would be waiting at home, ready to go. So, if the woman who had pretended to be Tamsin's aunt had listened to the phone message, she would have known that the girl's disappearance would be discovered very soon.

Jade sensed a small movement behind her and spun round.

Nobody there. Just the bedroom door that she'd pushed wide open, slowly swinging back to the half-closed position in which she'd found it.

Breathing deeply, she opened the door that led to the garage. A bubble-gum-pink Mazda MX-5 sporting a vanity plate was parked there. Custom-painted, she supposed.

Jade stood in the hot, airless confines of the garage, feeling sweat start to dampen the back of her legs and trickle down her cleavage. She tried Tamsin's phone again, but it wasn't in the car either.

Only when she walked back inside the house did she notice the piece of paper lying on the tiles just inside the front door. A mauve notelet which must have been pushed under the door earlier, but been moved out of her sight when she'd opened it.

The paper had a logo at the top. "Lerato's Manicures." Below it, handwriting in a script so bubbly that Jade was surprised it wasn't popping off the page.

"Hey doll, the gardener let me in! Did u forget it was Tuesday?! Lol!! Tried phoning u but no luck! See u next wk, hope u okay, luv Ler!"

Jade put the piece of paper back down on the floor, shaking her head because this cheery little message confirmed her worst fears.

She had been hoping that, by some lucky chance, Tamsin had not been home when the "aunt" had come looking for her. That she'd been staying at a friend's house, and had perhaps mislaid her phone.

But would Tamsin have missed what seemed to be a long-standing weekly appointment with her mobile manicurist? Jade didn't think so. She knew what Sandton girls were like about their nails.

She'd have to report her missing now, and hope that her phone was with her and that the police could triangulate its signal before the young woman suffered any harm.

Assuming, of course, that no harm had already been done.

II

Half an hour later, having returned Raymond's house keys to him, Jade arrived back at her cottage. She paid the driver using the money that Pamela had given her, noticing that the taxi fee didn't even make a dent in the thick wad of notes.

The road seemed quiet, but the uneasiness that Jade had felt in Tamsin's house persisted.

Jade had thought this would be a straightforward job. Look after the rich lady until her husband turns up, dead or alive. She'd never imagined that it would involve a gun-toting biker trying to murder Pamela.

And why do it that way? A shooting like that would never be a guaranteed way of killing somebody, especially not in those circumstances. Why hadn't the gunman waited until Pamela arrived home, or, at the very least, was stopped at a traffic light? Then he could have pulled up beside her—easy to do on a motor-bike—aimed and fired before roaring away.

Perhaps he had intended to scare Pamela, rather than kill her. Oddly enough, though, Pamela had seemed more scared before the shooting than she was afterwards.

Jade frowned. She was starting to wonder whether Pamela had known that something was going to happen that morning. She had just locked the front door behind her when she heard an odd noise from outside—a soft, persistent rustling.

She froze, holding the keys tightly, listening.

It was a small sound, but it hadn't sounded like the wind, and in any case there wasn't even the slightest breeze.

There it was again. It was coming from round the side of the house.

Jade unlocked the door again, walked quietly along the paved garden path and rounded the corner.

The noise seemed to be coming from one of the flowerbeds. Last year it had filled up with colourful blooms after spring arrived. This year, thanks to what David called her "gardening disability," only the toughest, spikiest shrubs and bushes had survived. Even their new spring leaves were wilting in the fierce, dry heat, but the foliage was still dense enough for somebody to hide in.

There it was again. A tiny rustle.

A shoot quivered.

Jade squinted, but all she could see was an endless mass of green and brown. She stepped forward. At which point the leaves gave a decisive shake and the Jack Russell from the house down the road scrambled out, scratched the grass with its hind legs, and trotted over, wagging its stumpy tail.

"Hello, little boy." Jade could hear the relief in her own voice. She squatted down and stroked its short, smooth coat.

"How did you get in here, I wonder?" She gently grasped the dog's collar and read the name on the brass disc. "Bonnie? With that name, I guess you're not a boy."

Jade stood and buzzed the gate open.

"Home, Bonnie," she said, in a commanding tone.

Bonnie ignored her. In fact, she sat down on the paving and wagged her tail even faster.

Jade sighed. "Okay, come with me. Let's take you back."

She picked up the dog and walked determinedly out of the gate, checking the quiet dirt road in both directions before she walked the short distance to the bungalow down the road. She rang the bell outside the gate, but there was no answer. There were no cars in the driveway, and the gardener had obviously gone home.

"So how did you manage to get out, then?" Jade wondered.

Looking round, she spotted a furrow under the electric fence where the dog had obviously dug her way out. But each time she pushed the little dog back inside, she just turned around and wriggled straight back out again. After the seventh attempt, Jade gave up.

She returned to the cottage with Bonnie gambolling alongside as if on an invisible leash. The dog trotted straight into the kitchen and turned to stare at Jade, her small sides heaving.

"Are you thirsty? It's hot enough, isn't it?"

Jade filled a china cereal bowl with water and placed it on the floor next to the fridge. Bonnie bent her head and lapped at it eagerly.

"I'm sure you've got a perfectly good bowl of water at home," Jade said.

The dog didn't respond. After she'd had enough, she headed off into the lounge and began to explore the cottage's cool interior.

"All right," Jade called after her. "You can stay here until I go. If you help with security."

She hadn't had anything to eat all day, and now she was starving and desperate for a cup of coffee. She'd grab a quick bite here, then drive to Pamela's house and pack up some clothes and toiletries for her.

She put the kettle on and opened the fridge. There were two tomatoes and a cucumber in the vegetable drawer. On the top shelf was half a block of cheese wrapped in tinfoil and an unopened box of tofu that she'd bought during an especially health-focused shopping spree. She'd successfully managed to ignore it since then, and she managed to do so again now.

Did she have pita bread in the freezer? Yes, she did. An easy decision, then.

She popped one into the toaster, and sliced the cheese and vegetables into bite-sized pieces. Bonnie reappeared when she heard the rustle of foil and sat at her feet, her tail wagging at top speed.

Jade looked down at her sternly.

"No. I am not feeding you," she said in a firm voice. "This is not your home."

She took the pita bread out of the toaster, chose a Nando's chilli sauce bottle from the selection in the cupboard and spread a thick layer of the fiery orange liquid over it. Then she added the cheese and vegetables and, just for luck, finished off with another dollop of the sauce.

She sat down at the kitchen table and, holding her makeshift sandwich in both hands and tilting it to avoid drips, took a huge bite.

As she put the pita back down on the plate and picked up her coffee, Bonnie started to bark. The small dog hurtled towards the security door and shot through the bars and out towards the gate, punctuating her progress with a volley of high-pitched yaps.

Jade stood up so fast she nearly knocked the table over, and hurried to the window. Who had arrived?

She stared at the beige Toyota Corolla outside her gate. The driver hooted impatiently. Bonnie's barking grew louder, and she darted from one end of the gate to the other.

It was David.

"What do you want now, you bastard?" Jade mumbled through her half-chewed mouthful of food, feeling her heart give a little leap and then accelerate, a physical reaction that she couldn't control, despite her efforts. "Why should I even let you in, Mr. Get-a-bicycle?"

She ran to the bathroom, swallowing the last of her mouthful of sandwich as she went. Despite herself, she had to have a quick look in the mirror. Did she have food stuck in her teeth? No. Sauce on her face? Yes, there was a bright orange smear on her chin. She wiped it off, ran her fingers through her hair, cast a glance at the perfume bottle on the glass shelf, but resisted the urge to apply some.

Then, hearing another long hoot, she returned to the kitchen and buzzed the gate open.

12

As Jade unlocked the security door she heard more barking, and David swearing.

"What the . . . Get off me, dammit. Ouch! Bloody hell. Off!"

She flung the door open and hurried outside. As she rounded the corner, she almost collided with David. He had a big, brown cardboard box in his arms and was dancing frantically from foot to foot as Bonnie dashed back and forth behind him, barking furiously.

"Jadey, your dog's trying to bite me."

Jade spread her hands. "She's not my dog."

"What's it doing here then? Off!"

"She lives down the road. She won't go home. I don't know what her problem is with you. She's been very friendly with me." Jade picked Bonnie up and held her while David hurried into the cottage. Then she shut the dog outside. The barking took on a forlorn note until Bonnie changed tactics and began to whine and scratch at the wooden door.

"Oh, that dog from number twelve." David placed the box on the kitchen table, almost upsetting Jade's plate of food. "I remember it used to bark at me every time I walked past the house. It's racist, I tell you."

"Not necessarily." In response to David's enquiring glance, Jade continued. "She"—she emphasised the pronoun just a little— "might just be a bit sexist."

David nodded in agreement, his expression grim. "Still bad news for me."

He rested his elbows on the box, which Jade saw was sealed with brown packing tape and had a musty, old-cardboard smell which was rapidly permeating the kitchen.

What was inside it, anyway? For a moment Jade wondered

whether David was returning all the stuff that she'd left at his place over the months. But there hadn't been that much of it. A toothbrush, a couple of t-shirts, a book or two. She was sure it could easily have fitted into a carrier bag.

"So, anyway," he said. "I was passing by, so I thought I'd bring you this."

"Passing by?" Jade asked, raising her eyebrows. She knew perfectly well that David worked in Johannesburg city, that his home was now in Turffontein, and that his wife lived in Pretoria. To her knowledge, there were no suspected drug-traffickers or money-launderers living in her neighbourhood. That meant David had no reason to come this way, unless it was to see her.

Not that he'd admit it. Not now, after what had happened between them a couple of months ago, when she had managed to stamp so hard on their fledgling relationship that she'd effectively squashed it to death.

■

They'd been lying together on their stomachs on his extra-long double bed, his fingers stroking her hair, freshly made cups of coffee steaming on the table as they scanned the pages of that morning's Sunday newspaper.

"Look at this, Jadey," David had said. "Rapper walks free after causing two deaths."

"Let me see." She'd pulled the paper closer and read the story.

A well-known South African rapper with a string of traffic offences to his name had lost control of his Hummer while driving home from a nightclub. Two pedestrians on their way to an early church service had died after he ploughed into them, and three others sustained grievous injuries.

According to the report, the wealthy star had pleaded not guilty, and his lawyer had got him off on a technicality. No fine, no jail time, no compensation for the families of the victims whose lives he had destroyed. Just a meaningless five-year suspended sentence.

Witnesses at the scene of the accident had confirmed that the man reeked of alcohol and appeared to be drunk. However, the police had been unable to breathalyse him because, for reasons that were unclear, the emergency services workers had already put him onto a drip. Jade had wondered whether the paramedics had been trying to protect the man because of his star status, or whether the rapper had paid one of them to get him out of trouble.

The star hadn't shown a trace of remorse for his crime. At the bottom of the article was a poorly worded, printed apology that had been issued by his agent because he was out of the country, performing at a concert in Kenya.

Disgusted, she'd passed the paper back to David.

"If one of those people who'd died or been injured was my relative, I'd kill him," she'd said.

She'd sensed the change in his mood instantly. He'd taken a slow, deep breath and then eased himself away from her, leaving a small, chilly gap between them in the winter-cold room.

"Would you?" he'd responded, in a deceptively casual tone.

"In a heartbeat. He's an arsehole. He hasn't learned from his mistakes. He doesn't care what he's done. He's only going to carry on and do worse."

"And you think killing him will help?"

"Well, he wouldn't be able to do it again."

"That's not funny."

"Tell that to the people whose lives he's wrecked."

"He was found guilty of culpable homicide. A revenge killing would incur a murder charge. So all you'd be doing is committing another, far more serious crime."

"Well, David, what else can you do when the guy's obviously untouchable? He's got the money, he's got the fame, he can take his pick of the best lawyers in town. I'm sorry, but I think that's wrong." She'd propped an elbow on the unopened business section and turned to him so that she could look him in the eye. At that stage, she'd still thought that David sympathised with her beliefs, and that his counter-argument was him simply playing devil's advocate. She'd honestly believed that they would talk it through.

"You mean every word you've said, don't you?" His voice was soft.

"Yes."

David had stared back at her, his eyes like pale-grey laser beams. Too late, she realised she had walked straight into his trap.

"How would you do it, Jade? Go on, share it with me. Tell me exactly how you would murder that man in cold blood. A drive-by shooting, perhaps? Is that how you'd try to get away with it?"

"No!" Her denial had been instinctive.

"How, then? I thought drive-bys were your speciality."

After those particular words, Jade had had to look away.

"I don't . . ."

"Oh, yes, you do." David pushed the duvet aside, stood up, and grabbed his clothes, which were slung over the arm of a chair. "Anyway, I don't think there's any point in discussing this further. I'm going to work."

Jade had been about to remind David that it was a Sunday, and they'd made plans to drive out to Hartebeespoort Dam that afternoon, but looking at his face, she'd realised those plans were history.

And so, it had transpired, was their relationship.

They hadn't spoken to each other again that morning. Jade had left soon afterwards, and walked the short distance back down the road to her cottage. Walked fast, head down, stomping her feet on the stony ground as if she could stamp out the sting of his words.

I thought drive-bys were your speciality.

She'd kicked at a stone and watched it skitter to the side of the road. And she'd shaken her head hard, trying not to think about how she had felt the first time she had killed. The night she had shot the man who'd murdered her father.

How she had leaned out of the car's passenger window, her hand steady as she'd aimed the Glock at her target's head, sighting carefully as the corrupt police officer strode down the dark street, back to his lodgings.

Why it had been so easy for her to pull the trigger? Jade hadn't hesitated. She hadn't felt a moment's regret at what she had been about to do, although soon afterwards she had been sickened by guilt and remorse.

"Damn it, David. He's a criminal," she'd said aloud, as she walked into her lonely little cottage.

But so was she. David hadn't been there to reply, but she knew that was what he would have said, and what he still believed.

So was she.

■

Now, watching him leaning on the big cardboard box, Jade wondered if David was also thinking about what had happened on that Sunday morning.

She moved the plate of food off the table and put it on the kitchen counter. Then she picked up her mug. Pointless actions, but at least it gave her something to do.

"Coffee?" she asked, but David shook his head.

"The detectives have finished with Pamela's car, so you can get it towed now," he said. "Are you okay after what happened this morning?"

"I'm fine, thanks."

"And Pamela?"

"She's safe, but worried. Her daughter's disappeared now."

His eyebrows shot upwards. "First hubby, now the daughter?"

"Yes."

"Think it's hereditary?"

"Very funny."

"You've reported her missing, I assume?"

"Yes."

"I don't know if this has any bearing on the situation, but I found out this morning Terence Jordaan has a criminal record," David said.

"He does?" Jade felt her heart quicken. "For what?"

"Human trafficking. A few years back, he was bust for employing illegal Slovakian workers at his club. He seems to have behaved himself since then, but who knows? He might have just changed his modus operandi to avoid getting caught again."

David rubbed his forehead. His hair was longer than its usual scalp-hugging crop, and Jade was surprised to see fine silver streaks in the rough-looking fringe.

"I'll ask Pamela about that when I see her," she said. "I suspect she knows more about Terence's disappearance than she's telling."

"Mad Pammie." David nodded. "Always been one for secrets and lies."

"How do you know her, anyway?" Jade asked, eager to learn more about David's connection with her client.

He mumbled something in reply, turning his head away as he spoke.

"Sorry, what was that?"

David muttered, "My father's girlfriend cleaned her house."

"And then what? Did she find Pamela living in a cupboard?" Jade started laughing, but stopped when she saw she was the only one enjoying the joke. She replayed David's words in her mind again and, too late, realised what he'd been trying to say.

"Oh. Oh . . . I see. Your father's girlfriend cleaned *Pamela*'s house?"

David nodded. "Apartheid days, Jadey. Cleaning was the best job she could get. She worked for Pamela's family. When I spent time in Durban with my dad, I'd often go there for the day with her. Pammie was older than me, and she was as bossy as anything. A real prima donna. 'Don't touch this.' 'Don't go into that room.' 'Have you washed your hands?' She made my life an absolute misery when I was small."

Small? Jade had difficulty with the concept that David had ever been small.

"Was her family rich?" Jade asked.

"Not particularly," David replied. "But Pammie always had an eye for the money. It might be cruel to call her a gold-digger, but she liked the good things in life. She hooked up and broke up with a series of boyfriends with increasingly fancy cars. She always did the hooking—'scuse the pun—and always did the breaking up, too. She left home and started working when she was about twenty. By then, her hair was already a different colour. Pumpkin, I think."

"I'm sure it wasn't called Pumpkin on the box," Jade said. "Not appealing enough."

David snorted. "Trust me, nor was Pamela's hair."

"What work did she do?"

"Oh," David said, "I thought she would have told you that. Or perhaps not, come to think of it. She was a stripper."

"A stripper?" Jade echoed. Her own eyebrows shot skyward as she tried to imagine the refined, blonde-haired woman with her legs wrapped around a metal pole, tossing her G-string to a baying crowd of men. "*Pamela?*"

"Started out that way. Ended up doing a lot more than that."
David sounded serious. "I was way too young to know all the
facts at the time, but when she stopped dancing, she went into
business with one of her ex-boyfriends. Got involved in organising parties for men, private bashes where the women provided
the entertainment. The girls were expected to be ... well ...
extremely 'accommodating.'"

Jade shook her head. "I can't believe it."

"Eventually the parties got a bit too wild. There were a couple
of accusations of rape. Pammie closed up shop and went overseas.
I heard from somebody that she'd got married and completely
reinvented herself, but I didn't see her again until she recognised
me the other day in Lonehill's Woolworths. Talk about a blast
from the past. By the time she'd finished grilling me on my life
history since we last met, I was wishing I'd decided to shop at Pick
'n' Pay."

Jade smiled.

"Anyway ..." David said. He didn't complete the sentence.
Perhaps he felt he'd said enough about Pamela. Or said enough to
Jade. This was the longest conversation they'd had for a while. The
longest they'd had since the one that had caused all the trouble.

Jade took a mouthful of her coffee, noticing that it tasted
suddenly bitter, in spite of the two heaped spoons of sugar she'd
added.

"What's in that box?" she asked, changing the subject.

"Oh, the box." David glanced at it as if he'd never seen it before.
"I found it yesterday, in my house in Turffontein, when I was looking for Kevin's cricket bat. It's been in the back of the cupboard in
the spare room for so long, I'd forgotten all about it. I should've
given it to you when you came back to South Africa." He patted its
top. "After your dad died, I sorted out his house, you know."

"Oh." Jade felt her face grow hot.

After she'd murdered her father's killer, Jade had fled the country and hadn't returned for ten years. Sorting out her dad's house
before she left? She hadn't even thought about doing that. All she
knew was that it had been sold in her absence and, in accordance
with her father's will, the modest proceeds deposited into her
bank account.

"There wasn't a lot of personal stuff worth keeping," David continued. "But what there was I put in here. I thought if you ever came back, you'd like to have it. If not—well, I didn't want to throw it away. There's things in here that I know have sentimental value."

He didn't say to whom. A small smile creased the corners of his mouth. It lit up his dark-skinned face, warmed his icy eyes. "I read one of your school reports from when you were six. It said you didn't play well with others." His smile widened.

"Yes, well, I was only six, I suppose." Now Jade's face felt as if it was on fire. Her school reports. What else had he read? What other embarrassing documents were in that stupid box? She took another gulp of coffee to cover her confusion, hoping David hadn't noticed her blush.

"Don't worry," he said, as if reading her mind. "I only looked at a few."

Jade put the cup down again, adopting a business-like tone. "I'm sorry you had to deal with packing up my dad's stuff. That was a job I should have done."

David shrugged. "You had other things on your agenda." His long, elegant fingers tapped the top of the box in a brief, rhythmic tattoo.

Another uncomfortable silence ensued.

People never change. That was one of David's favourite sayings, and for good reason, because as a police detective he'd seen it proved over and over again.

He knew what Jade had done to her father's killer, and why, because she'd told him. But perhaps he had been trying to convince himself since then that she was different; that she had changed.

For a while, after that Sunday-morning conversation, Jade had considered apologising. She'd toyed with the idea of telling David that she had been the one playing devil's advocate for the sake of a good argument, and that she hadn't realised what effect her words would have on him.

It wouldn't have been the truth, though, and David probably wouldn't have believed it anyway. And even if he had, was she prepared to live a lie for the sake of being with him?

The answer had been no.

And now here they stood, on a scorching, bone-dry summer afternoon, staring at each other over a musty-smelling cardboard box, the air around them thick with the debris of unresolved issues.

"Well, thanks for bringing it. And thanks for looking up Terence Jordaan. Are you sure you won't have a coffee?" Jade said.

He shook his head. "I'd better be going."

"Right."

Jade picked the keys up off the kitchen counter and unlocked the door, but David didn't move. He just stood there, leaning on the box, picking at the packaging tape with his fingertips, glancing over at the kettle as if he regretted saying no to Jade's offer.

Then he looked at his watch, heaved a deep sigh, and followed her outside like someone walking through glue. He didn't kiss her goodbye, didn't touch her at all. She stood in the shade of the wilting syringas and held the Jack Russell in her arms while David climbed into his car.

She could feel Bonnie's body quivering with anticipation. She was straining against Jade's grasp, and uttering tiny growls. Clearly, all she wanted to do was to bolt across the driveway and launch herself at the tall police detective. Jade couldn't blame the little dog. She wanted to do the same, but for different reasons.

13

"Detective work is ninety-nine per cent perspiration, one per cent inspiration. Just like genius, only more difficult."

Edmonds couldn't remember who'd told her that, shortly after she'd been promoted to Detective Constable, but she'd soon discovered it was only too true.

She was sitting in the front row of chairs in the small meeting room next to Richards, who smelled strongly of Brut. Perhaps she had plebeian taste, but Edmonds didn't find the fragrance unpleasant. She rather liked it; it reminded her of the first lad she'd kissed, back in the little village of Corfe Castle in rural Dorset where she'd grown up.

"Right, people." Mackay called the meeting to attention, jolting Edmonds out of her reverie. "Operation Platypus. Let's see where we are. What's the update on Number Six? Edmonds, will you give us your latest?"

Richards gave her a nudge and Edmonds scrambled to her feet, aware of the small sea of faces observing her. She suddenly felt flustered and disorganised despite her morning of careful preparation.

Operation Platypus—the police computer system that assigned the names to their cases was currently working its way through an alphabetical list of mammals—had been handed over to her, and she was now in charge of the investigation. She hadn't expected to be assigned her own case so soon, but as DS Mackay, the team leader, had explained, they were critically short-staffed and it was the best way for her to learn.

"I trust you," he'd said, words which had sent a nervous thrill down Edmonds' spine.

Now, standing in the meeting room, she almost dropped the folder with her notes inside, but Richards grabbed it before the pages could slide out. He handed it back to her and Edmonds nodded her thanks, her face hot.

"We've interviewed the victims, sir. All except one." Her voice was squeaky, like a little mouse. Nothing she could do about that. "They were recruited from South Africa. The only people they had contact with were the customers, each other, Salimovic, and his cousin Rodic, who we arrested during the raid. He—er—helped to—um—break them in. Unfortunately, none of the victims is willing to cooperate with us any further. They've chosen not to become witnesses, and they aren't offering any other information on how they were recruited in their home country."

"What about the victim you haven't interviewed yet?" Mackay asked.

"Hospitalised. She was badly injured and had to have three operations. Her grandfather's here from Senegal, and he's been with her almost constantly. She's recovering well, so I'll be going to the hospital straight after this meeting to try and have a chat."

Mackay scratched his chin. "And Rodic?"

"He's not talking either."

"Not talking?" Mackay asked, sounding surprised. "I thought he was going to do a deal with us."

"He's not saying a word, sir."

"Any updates on Salimovic's whereabouts?"

The team had discovered that the brothel owner, in a display of what was either dumb luck or an uncanny sixth sense, had taken a taxi to Heathrow and boarded a Croatia Airlines flight a few hours before the raid. By the time Edmonds had climbed the fire escape of Number Six, Salimovic had already landed at Butmir airport. His passport number was now flagged and, according to the Bosnian immigration authorities, he hadn't attempted to leave the country since then, but Edmonds knew only too well that people like him would have access to false passports and forged identity documents, allowing them to cross borders with ease.

The Bosnian police were investigating his whereabouts. As a matter of priority, too, if the number of increasingly desperate phone calls she'd had from her foreign counterpart was anything to go by.

"Nothing further on him yet. We've searched his house in South Woodford, but it had been broken into, so some evidence might have gone missing. We have had better success with identifying the red-haired woman, though."

Glancing down, she saw Richards touch a protective hand to the small dressing taped to the side of his neck.

Edmonds cleared her throat and continued, her heart pounding so hard she felt as if she were halfway up Everest. "We checked the footage of street cameras in the surrounding area, and we spotted her climbing out of a cab an hour before the raid. The cab driver said he picked her up from a hotel in Chelsea, and they had a photocopy of her passport. According to that, her name is Mathilde Dupont. The hotel staff told us she had a black partner, but we haven't been able to get any ID on him yet. The hotel forgot to ask for his passport, unfortunately."

Edmonds paused for breath.

Mackay nodded approvingly. "And where is Ms Dupont now?"

"When we searched the room, it was obvious they'd packed up and left in a hurry." Edmonds remembered the hours she'd spent in the palatial sixth-floor suite, in the hot confines of her protective overall, dusting for prints with the forensics team and crawling around on the pale, thick-pile carpet, collecting trace evidence. She'd earned herself a good case of backache as well as a friendly warning from Richards that her time was valuable and she should have let forensics do that job on their own.

"The night porter at the hotel told me he called a taxi to take them to the airport, but at this stage I don't know where they flew—if they flew at all. I've done almost two days' worth of investigation at the airport already, and I'm going back again later this afternoon, when I'm finished at the hospital."

Mackay nodded again, thoughtfully. "Try checking Dupont's passport number with South African immigration," he said.

Edmonds frowned. "South Africa?"

"Well, the victims came from there, didn't they? It's possible Mathilde Dupont or her anonymous black accomplice might have connections in that country. Now, we don't yet know exactly what these two were doing at Number Six that night, do we?"

"No, sir. Rodic denies knowing them at all—but then, he's denying everything."

"Hmm. At this stage I'm inclined to think they might be business associates. So, if we can trace Dupont or her partner, they could lead us to Salimovic."

"Yes, of course. I'll do the checks this afternoon, sir. Or I'll put one of my team onto it," she added hastily, remembering Richards' words.

"Thanks, Edmonds. Now, is that all for Platypus? Right. Richards, can you give me the report-back on Operation Raccoon?"

Relieved her grilling was over, Edmonds sat down. Her face was still warm, and to her dismay her underarms felt wet with sweat. Ninety-nine per cent perspiration was absolutely correct. Nobody had told her police work would involve a scarier equivalent of public speaking, but at least now she understood why Richards doused himself in aftershave before these meetings.

14

Back in the kitchen, the musty smell hit Jade immediately. The box was impossible to miss. It sat on the table like an accusation, dominating the room, daring her to ignore it for any longer.

By now, Jade's coffee was lukewarm and her half-eaten pita bread cold. She stuck them both in the microwave for sixty seconds. When she took them out, they were both steaming hot and the coffee smelled of chilli. Fusion food, de Jong-style.

She took a searing gulp of coffee and turned back to the wretched box. Steeling herself, she ripped the packing tape off the top, pulled open the cardboard flaps and stared down at what was left of her father's life.

The neatly stacked contents stared back up at her. All the papers were arranged in see-through document wallets as if they were sections of case files. She didn't know if that was her dad's doing or David's. Both, perhaps.

Jade risked another swallow of coffee, then set to work.

The topmost file contained her school reports. Thanks, David. She didn't read through them. She had no memory of what the teachers had said about her when she was younger, and she didn't want to be reminded now. She would just have to take David's word that she hadn't mixed well with other children. It sounded likely enough.

Her father's personal documents took up two large sleeves. She found his ID book, his passport. Commissioner de Jong stared up at her from the photo page, his face stern, his hair as grey as she remembered it, a navy-blue tie knotted around his neck. There were tax returns, insurance documents, her dad's birth certificate. He'd been born in Howick, Natal. She found a copy of her parents' marriage certificate. Elise Delacourt and Andre de Jong. So now Jade knew her mother's maiden name. There was Jade's birth certificate. She'd been born in Richard's Bay, where her father had been posted at the time. And her mother's death certificate just a few short months later, also in Richard's Bay. Cause of death, kidney failure. That would have been as a result of the cerebral malaria that her father explained had killed her, Jade supposed.

Her death had been quick, her dad had told her. Quick didn't mean easy, though. He'd never talked about it. In fact, he had spoken so little about her mother it was as if she had never been an important part of his life. But Jade knew she had, because he'd always kept one photo by his bedside, a tiny print of them on their wedding day. It was so small that all she'd been able to make out was that her mother was smiling and wearing white flowers in her hair.

Opening the next plastic sleeve, Jade was astonished to see that there were more.

She stared down at the pile of photos before examining each one carefully. Some large, some small. A few in black-and-white, the majority in colour. Some were of the wedding. Here were her parents together, sitting at an outdoor restaurant. Cars in the background, their boxy shapes and square-looking headlights evidence of an earlier decade, and beyond that a couple of distant palm trees. Had this one been taken on honeymoon? It was a close-up of her mother, strands of brown hair blowing across her face, her eyes narrowed against the sun.

Green eyes, Jade saw. Just like hers.

The portrait was a shock, because it could have been of Jade herself. Elise Delacourt, or de Jong, had the same slim build, the same pronounced cheekbones, the same determined angle to her jaw. Even her mother's hair was the same shade and length as her own.

At the bottom, Jade found one of Elise with a tiny, crimson-faced baby in her arms. Her heart skipped a beat as she saw the tender smile on her mother's face, the expression of utter love in her eyes. On her left hand, curled protectively around Jade's white-swaddled form, she saw the engagement ring her dad had told her about. Silver, with a clear green stone—the stone that she'd had been named after.

Jade slipped the photos back in their sleeve. What would their relationship have been like, she wondered, if her mother hadn't died soon after she had been born? Would she have grown up any different if she'd had a mother?

Perhaps they would have been best friends, with the type of giggly, let's-share-make-up-tips closeness that she'd seen a couple of her friends enjoy. Or would Elise have been more distant, more authoritarian? She didn't think so.

In that photo of her holding Jade, she looked so gentle.

Jade wondered what Elise Delacourt had thought about living the hard, uncertain life of a police officer's spouse.

At the bottom of the box, Jade found a hand-painted coffee mug she'd decorated for her father as a school crafts project, and a couple of ancient, hardcover Nancy Drew stories. The books' dust-jackets had long since disintegrated.

She smiled as she remembered the obsession she'd developed as a young girl with the fictional detective Nancy Drew. Her father had bought her the entire series of books—a few new; most of them from second-hand shops, dog-eared and smelling of mildew. He'd bought her other books, too—books written for younger readers "explaining" how to be a detective. How to hide behind a tree without your shadow giving you away, how to search for evidence in a criminal's hiding place, how to spot a character behaving suspiciously.

Her father had taught her some basic judo throws and defence moves, and they'd even shared a secret language, a coded method of communication to be used in an emergency, or a combat situation.

"Marseille" meant "dodge," "Toulouse" meant "drop," and "Lyon" meant "duck."

Jade had spent hours practising the moves, and had been fascinated by the unfamiliar words, which at first she hadn't known were the names of cities in France.

"Why did you decide on French words, Dad?" she'd asked, when she had found out. "You don't speak French, do you?"

He'd smiled, but his voice had sounded sad.

"I didn't choose them, Jadey," he'd said. "They were taught to me, too."

When she was much older, Jade realised that this secret language must have been something that her mother and father had shared.

Keeping the sleeve of photos aside, Jade carefully repacked the box. She glanced at the clock on the wall and saw she'd spent far too long looking at the pictures. She needed to get going. She'd better try to take Bonnie home again. Surely, if she took a spade with her, it would be possible to push the dog through the hole under the fence and block it up again behind her.

Then she'd drive to Pamela's house, check that everything was in order, pick out some clothes and toiletries for her, and get back to The Seasons.

The microwave hadn't done the pita bread any good at all. It had cooled to the approximate hardness of a brick, so she tipped it into the bin. The orange Nando's sauce was still pooled on the plate. It would be a pity to waste that. Jade wiped a finger through the sticky mess and licked it off, enjoying the distraction of the hard, hot burn.

Elise Delacourt had married the cop she'd loved. At the moment, Jade couldn't even get David to spend five minutes in her company, and seeing they couldn't even sort their issues out in English, she guessed sharing a secret language was definitely out of the question.

15

The shrill, piping sound of the pennywhistle being played on the staircase outside Lindiwe Mtwetwa's second-floor office in central Pretoria could mean only one thing.

She had more business coming her way.

Another customer. Would they never stop? It seemed there was no limit to demand. When she'd first set up shop she'd sometimes gone weeks without a sale. Now, people were in and out, in and out, their numbers rising steadily. Glancing at her with shifty eyes as they handed over their wads of crumpled, grimy banknotes. Treading dirt into the pale beige carpet that she'd had installed last winter, and which was her pride and joy.

She often complained her office was busier than the Bree Street taxi rank, even though, to be truthful, the most she'd ever seen was five people in one day.

Lindiwe rocked forward in her reclining office chair and wearily lifted her braids off her shoulders.

She'd had the coarse artificial hair in all winter. She'd been meaning to get it removed, get her hair relaxed and cut in a short, chic style for mid-summer, but the sudden heat had taken her by surprise. Now, in the early afternoon, the sun was blazing through the window behind her.

Her office was cooler than the two down the corridor, principally because its windows were unbroken and shaded by cream-coloured blinds that blocked out the view of the building across the road, with its crumbling balconies and colourful rows of washing.

The electric fan propped on the desk in front of her, and aimed squarely at her face, also played a role. It hummed valiantly, doing its best to make the temperature bearable, but on summer afternoons, even with the blinds closed, her neck and back usually ended up dripping with sweat.

Lindiwe watched the security gate, listening for the sound of the penny-whistle, but she didn't hear the tune again.

That meant she could expect only one arrival.

During apartheid, the clear, happy tones of this instrument had become one of the most famous sounds in the townships. It was traditionally played by young men on street corners to alert residents drinking and gambling in the illegal shebeens to approaching police, allowing them to make a safe and speedy getaway.

Apartheid was over now, but Lindiwe used the same system for her business. The instrument was played by Veli, her youngest nephew, who positioned himself in the building's stairwell and kept a lookout for her. She needed no electric doorbells or cameras, which was just as well, because in Pretoria's dilapidated inner city, power cuts occurred on an almost daily basis.

If there had been two men, Veli would have played the tune twice. For three or more, he would play it a third time. A simple system to forewarn her of the numbers coming up the stairs in case a returning visitor knocked at the door while his companions hid out of sight.

She never admitted groups, not even two people together. The inner city was a dangerous place, especially for someone who regularly accepted large amounts of cash. The Muslim clothes hawker, whose warehouse was downstairs from her and who also ran a cash business, had been robbed more than once.

To make matters worse, Lindiwe had come to realise that most of the customers she dealt with were nothing but common criminals. Scumbags. People she wouldn't ever risk turning her back on.

Because of this, she had a rule. Only one person in her office at a time. And if Veli thought the arrivals looked dangerous, she had told him he must run down to the Muslim trader's shop and call the security guard who now worked there full-time.

He'd taken that precaution a few times, although there had never been any incidents—probably because she was the last resort for the people who knocked on her door. They might be scumbags, but they were desperate ones. They had nowhere else to go.

Lindiwe tugged her blouse straight, glanced over the pitted surface of the wooden desk in front of her, and brushed away the crumbs from her lunchtime sandwich. The contents of the desk were entirely innocuous. Just an old calculator and a couple of invoices for the transport business that was a front for her real setup. For this there were no documents or stamp pads on view. No official forms or receipt books. No incriminating evidence at all.

That was all concealed in a locked filing cabinet in the small room that led off the office.

Lindiwe heard footsteps, and a moment later she saw her new client appear on the other side of the security door.

The man was of average height and slightly built, wearing a formal-looking jacket and black trousers, holding a leather briefcase in his left hand. Too dark-skinned to be a South African, she thought, as she assessed him with a swift, experienced glance. Nigerian, probably. Well-dressed; his clothes looked expensive. Clean shoes, too, so no need to worry about her carpet this time.

The little till in Lindiwe's head went "ka-ching!" as she took another look at those shoes.

"Good afternoon," the man said in a hoarse voice. "Are you open for business?"

He looked, and sounded, older than her average customer. And more polite, too. Quite the elderly gentleman.

Most importantly, he was not a policeman. Policemen didn't dress like that, not even plainclothes ones, which meant the biggest danger was out of the way.

The electricity was working, so she didn't have to get up to unlock the door. She simply reached for the button under the right-hand side of her desk and buzzed him in.

"Sit down." She indicated the single chair on the opposite side of the desk.

Close up, she saw the man was very thin. His cheeks were sunken and the whites of his eyes were yellowish and unhealthy-looking. He sat, placed his briefcase on his lap, and simply waited, lacing his swollen-looking fingers together as he looked round the small office.

"So. What do you need?" she asked.

Now the man stared directly at her.

"Tikukwazisei," he said, in his hoarse-sounding voice.

Lindiwe blinked, trying not to look shocked. The man had given her this formal greeting in fluent Shona, her native language. Certainly it had been spoken within these four walls before, but she had always been the initiator in such circumstances.

How did he know she was from Zimbabwe?

"Kw–kwaziwai." She stammered out the formal reply, suddenly terrified that her gut instinct had been wrong and this man was in fact a policeman. "How did you . . . ?"

He didn't answer. After a brief pause, he carried on in perfect English, as if he'd never used Shona at all.

"I understand you can help me with certain documents."

Lindiwe clasped her hands together tightly. Calm down, she told herself. He had recognised her accent, that was all. Her English was good, but even after five years in South Africa, she didn't sound like a local.

She'd had a few Zimbabwean customers who had sat in that chair and cried, and called her sister, and begged her to get their ID books at a reduced price. No matter their circumstances, her answer had always been no. So perhaps, despite his wealthy appearance, this man was hoping to do the same.

Well, he could keep on hoping. Lindiwe carried on in English.

"I can get you the South African identity book and the passport. One hundred per cent genuine, and officially registered with Home Affairs." She jerked her head in the general direction of Home Affairs' head office in Waltloo, east of the inner city. "I take cash only, and no discounts."

Then she folded her arms across her substantial bosom and waited for the man's next question. She was sure she knew what it was going to be, because they all asked the same questions. First, how much? Then, how genuine?

There were a couple of other suppliers that offered low-quality fake documents, so badly done that even a child could tell the difference. You'd never get out of the country with one of those passports. You wouldn't even get past a police roadblock with the ID book.

Thanks to Lindiwe's connections, she was able to supply authentic documents of many kinds. The document holder would have their name listed on the computers and their fingerprints put onto the system. They would become a South African citizen with a valid, legal identity number. Lindiwe had recently started offering a very popular service—for an additional fee, a code eight driver's licence could be printed on the correct page of the identity document for those individuals who didn't want to go to the trouble of actually passing a test.

Nobody else could offer what she did. The only other supplier Lindiwe knew of, a pawnshop owner, had stopped doing business last year after she'd reported him to the police.

The man cleared his throat. "What is the cost?"

Lindiwe glanced down at his smart leather briefcase. She loved window shopping in the expensive malls—Menlyn Park, Sandton Square—and she recognised luxury goods when she saw them.

Ka-ching, ka-ching.

She decided to double her price, just as she had done a fortnight ago for the drug dealer who needed a new identity in a hurry, and some time before that for three of the bodyguards employed by Zimbabwean president Robert Mugabe. They had wanted South African passports and identities as a fallback plan in case their boss ended up losing the presidency in the country's upcoming elections.

Thanks to the money that Lindiwe had charged them, she'd been able to buy the two beautiful diamond rings which she now sported on the middle and pinkie fingers of her right hand. She'd got them from a fence at a bargain price—considering the size and glittering clarity of the stones—and both were a perfect fit.

Lindiwe had chosen not to burden herself by worrying about how these pieces had been separated from their original owners. Such things were surely beyond her control.

What she did know was that the seller had shown her a lovely diamond pendant; their perfect partner.

In all likelihood, that piece of jewellery would still be available at the weekend.

"Four thousand rand per document," she said.

The man's mouth twitched.

Lindiwe waited for the next question, but it didn't come.

Instead, the man asked, "How long will four passports take?"

"Three days." Lindiwe was proud of the fast turnaround time. Normal South African citizens waited months, sometimes years, to get their ID books or passports. Choked to death by uncaring employees, or by those who refused to perform their jobs unless bribed to do so by the public who were supposedly their customers, the system had become so slow and inefficient as to be useless.

With documents so hard to obtain, officials so corrupt, and procedures so tangled in red tape, it was not surprising that Lindiwe had been able to profit from the many South Africans who were prepared to pay a high premium to get what they needed in a matter of days. And, as she had swiftly discovered, foreigners needing new identities were prepared to pay even more.

Lindiwe had obtained documents for men and women from every country in southern Africa, and a few others too.

"I need them sooner than that."

She frowned. This man wasn't following her script. "Quicker than three days? That is not going to be easy."

"If you can organise them by the end of today, I will pay you double."

Lindiwe shook her head in a show of reluctance, although her mind was racing at the possibility. Four thousand rand times eight? For that price, she was sure her colleagues in Home Affairs would be willing to come up with a solution. It would be far riskier, but they had pulled it off successfully once before.

"It depends on how you plan to use the passports," she said after a suitable pause. "If you're going to use them immediately, and only to leave the country, then I can do it."

Last time, she had done the favour for an Indian man who had needed to get out of South Africa as fast as possible, and under an assumed name. Instead of issuing a valid identity number and registering the man on the system as they usually did, the syndicate had simply substituted his photograph for that of a genuine applicant of a similar age and race whose passport was being processed that day. Her contact working in Computer Records had deliberately changed one letter of the passport-holder's name and forty-eight hours later, when the Indian was safely out of the country, had erased the "faulty" record from the system and re-issued the passport, this time with the correct photo. And fortunately for Lindiwe, nobody had been any the wiser.

The question now was whether four "mistakes" could be made and corrected without attracting unwanted attention. It would be much riskier. And she remembered one of her friends in Home Affairs had mentioned that security measures were going to be tightened up soon.

Lindiwe hoped it could be done.

"The passports will be used immediately," the man said. "And their holders will not be returning. That I can guarantee."

"Did you bring photographs?"

The man opened his briefcase and took out a big plastic folder. He shook two large manila envelopes out of it and onto her desk. Then he closed the briefcase and put it down on the carpet. Lindiwe noticed something glinting on his belt, but before she could think about it any further, her attention was caught by the topmost envelope, which was bulging with the distinctive shape of banknotes.

"For you." The man nodded towards her. "Your money."

It was crammed with hundred-rand notes, new and crisp, clipped together in groups of ten. It took her only a minute to count them, her long, pink-tipped fingernails separating the notes with the ease of long practice.

Thirty-two thousand rand exactly.

How lucky for him.

"Do I get a receipt?"

"If you like." Lindiwe opened the dog-eared duplicate receipt book lying on her desk, picked up a ballpoint, and scribbled out an entry that stated a cash purchase had been made from Mopani Transport Services. She ripped off the top copy and held it out to him.

He didn't take the receipt immediately. Instead, he doubled over, one hand pressed to his gut, the other gripping the chair tightly. He grimaced and half-closed his eyes.

Lindiwe watched nervously. The man didn't look at all well, and she found herself hoping he wouldn't collapse on her carpet.

He didn't. Just straightened up, breathing hard, and looked at her with an unsettling gaze as if nothing had happened.

"By the end of today?" he asked.

"Six p.m."

"Are you sure?"

"Yes."

"I can not afford a delay."

He spoke the words softly, but something about the way he said them made Lindiwe catch her breath.

Was this old, sick man threatening her?

"There won't be any problems," she snapped, making a mental note to tell Veli to run down and call the guard as soon as he saw this customer come back. Nobody was allowed to give her attitude in this office.

"Good. I will see you then."

Lindiwe buzzed the door open for him and watched while it swung shut again. As soon as he had gone, she walked through to her back office, unlocked the little safe, and stashed the money inside.

Then she picked up her cellphone and dialled the number for Eunice, her contact in Home Affairs, to tell her she had an urgent job coming through.

16

Pamela's house was situated in a cul-de-sac called Autumn Road, in a quiet part of suburban Sandown. The entrance was in the form of an elaborate wrought-iron gate which stood in the deep shade of an enormous oak tree. The gate—motorised, of course—and the face-brick perimeter wall were topped with electric fencing which looked unbroken and undamaged.

No rogue bikers had followed Jade here.

When she depressed the buzzer on the bunch of keys she had taken from Pamela's bag, the gate swung open smoothly, rustling a couple of the low-hanging branches as it moved. After a final glance in her rear-view mirror, she drove inside.

She went past a small wooden hut that looked like a guard-house, past a verdant expanse of lawn studded with trees. Near the house she could see a large swimming pool that sparkled in the sun. The grass was emerald green, the flowerbeds bursting with blooms.

She parked near the back wall of what looked like an outdoor entertainment area opposite the swimming pool, so her car would be invisible from the road. Then she walked around to the over-sized front door, listening to bees humming in the impressive display of French lavender under the windows. The door looked like it had been stolen from a giant's castle, and the key to the lock had equal character. It was long and heavy, and it rattled in the lock, making her feel like a medieval jailer.

Jade had expected clinical coolness and the smell of furniture polish or potpourri, but instead she wrinkled her nose at the whiff of blocked drains coming from the closed door on her right, which obviously led to a guest bathroom.

The smell was very un-Pamela. Perhaps she shouldn't have fired her housemaid so hastily.

As Jade locked the door behind her, the distant ringing of a telephone broke the silence.

She didn't think anyone was home, but she guessed she'd soon find out if the phone was answered.

She walked swiftly through the hallway in the direction of the sound.

The house was the ultimate in open-plan living. Pamela and Terence had gone big on the front door, and gone without any of the others. It made her job easier. She walked through an expansive lounge-cum-dining-room whose furniture was so ultra-modern that it looked more like a contemporary art gallery than somewhere to relax after a busy day. The kitchen could have been the control deck for the *Starship Enterprise*.

The phone was ringing in a little alcove off the lounge, where a chair, desk and bookshelf formed a miniature study.

Pamela's study, she guessed. An in-tray held a pile of letters from various charities, all addressed to Mrs. Jordaan. The ringing was coming from a smart but rather outdated-looking fax-answerphone.

It rang eight times before it gave a high-pitched beep.

The blinking light indicated there were new messages.

Jade pressed Play, and listened.

The first one was from someone with a deep voice and a rough South African accent.

"Pamela. Naude here. Call me, will you? As soon as you can."

The second message was from the same man. He spoke faster this time. Stressed or in a hurry, she guessed.

"Naude again. Call me urgently."

The third and final message was short and to the point—the sound of a replaced receiver.

She turned away from the study and headed towards the staircase. At the bottom she noticed an ornamental Masai shield with a wooden spear displayed on its right. Two empty brackets marked the spot where a second spear should have crossed its partner.

She carried on up to the landing and checked the other bedrooms and bathrooms before entering the master bedroom. Here, the large television flickered soundlessly. The bedcovers were rumpled and faint scents still clung to the fabric. A musky male cologne, a hint of flowery perfume.

Jade moved to the dressing-room and opened a cupboard at random. She was confronted with an ostentatious display of silk shirts, shiny suits, snakeskin belts and fashionably faded jeans.

So this was Terence's wardrobe. She wondered if he had ever worn the pair of form-fitting DKNY leather pants hanging right at the back.

Surely not.

On one of the shelves Jade saw an empty alligator-skin conceal-ment holster, but she couldn't find a gun anywhere.

She opened the double cupboard opposite. It was stuffed with colourful designer outfits.

Jade chose a few of the most casual clothes on offer, which wasn't an easy task. Pamela didn't possess any sensible shoes, so Jade picked out a pair of wedge-heeled sandals from the ranks of footwear that jostled for space on the bottom rails. What else? Underwear? Cosmetics?

She pulled open one of the wooden drawers in the cupboard. A tangle of bras and panties spilled out. Although the lingerie was high quality and expensive-looking, there were no garments that Jade would have described as sexy. The panties were full-cut, the bras designed to conceal rather than reveal, and all were in neutral colours. Whites, blacks, beiges.

Jade couldn't help thinking again about Pamela's early career as an exotic dancer and an organiser of private parties for men.

David was right. She certainly had reinvented herself since then.

Another drawer contained socks and stockings and, on top of them, a framed photograph. Jade took it out and held it up. It was a wedding portrait. Pamela and Terence, head-and-shoulders, smiling at the camera. Very much the happy couple.

Terence was brown-haired, fit-looking and tanned, with an aggressively jutting jaw. To her surprise, he was somewhat shorter than Pamela, who Jade supposed would have been wearing ridicu-lously high heels.

Jade had no idea why the wedding photo was face-down in the sock drawer.

She closed the cupboard door and turned away.

Terence hadn't been snatched from the house; Jade was certain of that. Nothing looked out of place, there were no signs of a struggle, nothing appeared to be missing apart from one of the two spears on the landing and the gun that should have been in the holster.

How had he disappeared, then? Had he rushed out of the house with his unholstered gun in one hand and the Masai spear in the other?

Jade smiled at the fanciful notion. People like Terence didn't walk out of their homes—they drove. So, if none of the cars were missing, someone must have picked him up. A "trusted" business associate, perhaps.

But wouldn't Pamela have heard him leaving?

Jade discovered a matching set of leather luggage in yet another cupboard. Four bags in sizes ranging from weekend-in-Cape-Town to fortnight-in-New-York. She packed Pamela's clothes into the former and added a selection of toiletries and cosmetics from the bathroom, which was fragrant with the scent of roses.

Then she made her way downstairs with the suitcase. Through the lounge, with its cloying smell of furniture polish. Past the shiny kitchen, which smelled of nothing at all, and back the way she had come.

With the front door closed, the stink in the hallway was far stronger. It hit her like a slap in the face. She breathed out hard, grimacing at the odour, which was suddenly, horribly familiar.

Surely it couldn't be . . . ?

Her spine contracted with shivery unease.

Jade walked up to the white-painted guest-bathroom door she'd noticed on the way in. She grabbed the handle and pulled it open.

Freed from the confines of the hot little room, the smell rushed out to meet her, bigger and nastier than she'd expected, closely followed by a swarm of excited bluebottles.

Jade staggered back, stifling a cry. She dropped the suitcase, which thudded down onto the tiled floor, and swatted frantically at the cloud of flies.

Propped up in the corner below the half-open toilet window, a woman stared at Jade with sightless blue eyes. Blood was matted in her blonde hair, and a thick trail of dried blood led from one of the two deep wounds on her temple to the corner of her gaping mouth.

The dead woman looked much younger than Pamela. She was wearing a short black dress and one high-heeled gold sandal. The other sandal was lying on the tiles near the door. On her lap, broken in half, lay the ornamental spear that was missing from the display on the landing.

17

The dead woman wasn't Tamsin. That was Jade's first, illogically relieved thought. She wasn't the same person that she'd seen in the framed photo earlier that day in the messy, cluttered house.

Who was she, then, and how had she ended up here?

The woman had been dead for at least twelve hours; the smell attested to that. A long streak of dried blood on the floor indicated that her body had been moved into its current position, but if she'd still been bleeding, Jade knew this must have been done either before or shortly after her death.

Perhaps the woman had received the first blow to the head elsewhere, and had then been dragged into this little room, where a second, fatal injury had been inflicted.

No doubt the pathologists would be able to paint a clearer picture of what had happened. One thing was clear to Jade, though. In spite of Pamela's insistence that her husband had disappeared from their house, she herself could not have spent last night at home.

Shaking her head violently as a fly buzzed around her face, Jade kicked the bathroom door shut. She'd checked the entire house and she knew it was empty, but that fact didn't stop her primeval feeling of dread that the woman's killer might still be nearby.

This was a job for the police. Rummaging in her pocket, Jade pulled out her cellphone. She was going to call the Flying Squad, and while she waited for them to arrive, she was going to search the rest of the property. The garden, the garages, the staff quarters.

She didn't want any other nasty surprises.

She was halfway through dialling when she heard a sound, faint but recognisable, through the thick walls and tall door.

The accelerating roar of a powerful motorbike.

Jade stood stock-still, grasping the phone.

She stared at the front door as if her gaze could somehow penetrate the thick wood and extend out to the paved driveway beyond.

Somebody else had arrived.

The engine cut out close to the front door. That meant whoever had just opened the gate to Pamela's house and ridden so confidently up the driveway might not have seen Jade's car parked in its secluded spot round the corner.

Not yet, anyway.

She heard footsteps approaching.

Did this person have a key to the front door? Probably, since the automatic gate had opened without any trouble.

Remembering her earlier thoughts about rogue bikers, Jade backed away from the door. Until she knew who this was, it would be better to stay out of sight. But where could she hide?

Moving as silently as possible, she carried Pamela's suitcase back into the minimalist lounge and crouched down behind the only object large enough to provide decent cover, a white leather three-seater in the corner. Not very effective, because the couch was raised rather than flush with the floor, which meant that her feet would be visible through the gap underneath.

She unclipped her gun as she heard a key in the lock.

Whoever it was who came in didn't go far. The footsteps stopped close to the door to the guest bathroom.

She gripped the butt of her gun tightly, forcing herself to breathe slowly, trying to calm the adrenaline-fuelled pounding of her heart.

The noise of a handle turning. Then a startled shout.

It was a male voice. Jade could picture him reeling backwards from the doorway, swiping frantically at the cloud of flies, just as she had done.

The door slammed and there was a muffled gagging sound. Jade knew how the man was feeling. She had felt nauseated, too, when she had seen where the smell was coming from.

The man didn't leave after seeing what was in the bathroom, as Jade had hoped he might, nor did he call the police.

Instead, he walked straight into the lounge and headed purposefully across the tiled floor towards the study. She could hear his breathing, which was rough and fast. Now he was passing by the window. She could see his shadow move across the wall behind her and then disappear as he entered Pamela's study.

There was a familiar click and then the same automated voice that she'd heard earlier on the fax machine.

"No . . . new . . . messages."

"What the hell?" she heard him mutter.

Jade's legs were starting to tremble but she didn't dare to shift her weight. The man had expected to find messages. Having found none, he would know that someone else had already checked the machine.

Her breath sounded as fast and hoarse in her own ears as the mystery man's. She willed herself to breathe more silently.

If he was listening for messages, that surely meant he must have left at least one. There had only been two voice messages when she had pressed the "Play" button earlier, and they had both been left by the same person.

Was the intruder the mysterious Naude?

There was another beep and the automated voice began again.

"Play . . . old . . . messages."

"Pamela. Naude here —"

"Message . . . deleted."

"Naude again —"

"Message . . . deleted."

The man also deleted the third message that Jade had listened to, the silent pause followed by the click. Then he started walking back towards the hallway. Once again his shadow passed over her, but this time it stayed put, a dark, fuzzy shape against the white-painted wall.

And then it started moving downwards.

Perhaps the man had seen, or sensed, something. Either way, he was doing what Jade had prayed he wouldn't. He was about to look underneath the couch, and if she didn't act immediately, she was going to lose what little advantage she still had.

Jade grabbed the back of the sofa and leaped to her feet, aiming the Glock at the chest of the tall, black-clad man who stood just a few paces away.

He started to lunge towards her, but when he saw the gun he stopped.

He wasn't holding a weapon, but he did have a holstered Beretta on his belt.

His eyes narrowed and he raised his hands slowly above his head.

Hands that Jade now noticed were covered by tight latex gloves. They were thick-fingered, large and strong-looking, in proportion to his solid physique. He was big, but carrying a few extra kilos. Dark hair, a heavy jaw and a thick moustache salted with grey.

All this she assessed in a split-second.

Her eyes moved back to his hands. If his right arm moved towards the holster, she was going to shoot.

"Who are you?" he said.

His voice was deep and grainy, and he sounded surprisingly calm. The same voice as the one on the answering machine? Definitely.

"You're Naude," she said.

His gaze darted left and right before fixing, sharp-eyed, on her again.

"You're not a policewoman."

"No, I'm not." Jade moved around the couch and took another step towards him. Naude took a step back.

She should have shot him there and then.

She should have put a bullet through his foot, immobilising him, and then called the police.

She should have, but she didn't. Something made her decide against it—perhaps the memory of that fateful argument she'd had with David about shooting and revenge. It was a spur-of-the-moment decision, and she soon realised it was a bad one, because she couldn't hold Naude at gunpoint forever.

She was going to have to force him upstairs and lock him inside one of the bedrooms. There she could keep him penned long enough for the cops to arrive.

"Go—" She was going to say, go upstairs.

Too late, Jade realised Naude had noticed her hesitation. Clearly believing that she wasn't going to shoot, he did something she hadn't even anticipated.

He turned and ran. He sprinted through the lounge, round the corner and out of her sight, his footsteps slamming on the tiles.

She was already in pursuit, furious with herself for not having blocked his exit route in time. She skidded round the corner, her hand tight around her gun. He would have had time to draw his own weapon by now, and for all she knew she could be running straight into his line of fire.

As she reached the hallway, the big wooden front door swung closed. It slammed shut with a bang that seemed to shake the house, and the key rattled in the lock.

As she snatched Pamela's keys out of her pocket, she heard the bike start up again.

Jade jammed the key in the lock, twisted it frantically and pulled the front door open.

Naude was already speeding down the driveway towards the opening gate, riding on a red Ducati that looked identical to the one that had pursued Pamela's car earlier that day. He twisted round, and this time Jade saw he was holding the Beretta.

They fired at exactly the same moment.

Naude swerved as he shot, and that must have allowed him to avoid the bullet she'd aimed at his centre mass, because he didn't go down.

His bullet thumped into the wooden door, so close to her body that when she checked, with trembling hands, she discovered two holes in the black fabric of her jacket, barely an inch from her waist.

Entry and exit. In and out, like the tracks left by a giant needle.

With a roar of his engine, Naude disappeared from sight.

18

Jade ran down the long driveway to the gate where Naude had recently made his escape. The sun was shining directly through the open door of the guardhouse, and the small building smelled unpleasantly of creosote.

She opened the main gate and jogged all the way to the inter-section in case Naude had ditched the bike and was coming back on foot, but he seemed to have disappeared.

Heading back to the house, the only pedestrian in sight on this hot, quiet afternoon, Jade thought about what Naude had said. About his entry into Pamela's home and the messages he'd deleted.

She thought about the bullet that had passed so close to her that it had made a neat hole in her jacket before ploughing into the solid wood of the front door.

The slug was embedded in there now. The hole in the wood had looked small from the outside, but Jade guessed it would be bigger inside, a cavity punched into the wood as the bullet flattened and deformed. She could poke the first joint of her finger through the holes in her jacket, which she'd now taken off and tied around her waist. Jade was uncomfortably warm, but even so, she shivered when she thought about that bullet.

That wasn't what was bothering her the most, though.

This was a wealthy area, and in Jo'burg the very rich were often specifically targeted by burglars. It was worth the risk, because well-off homeowners had so much more to steal.

She noticed that every single house that she passed had elabo-rate security precautions in place in addition to the usual electric fences and automatic gates. Some had cameras mounted on top of the walls, others had security guards sat in the driveway under giant umbrellas, looking bored and hot, but nonetheless present and doing their job. Some homes had packs of dogs that roused themselves from their shady resting places and barked at Jade as she passed by.

Big dogs for intimidation and attack; little dogs because they were more alert and faster to sound the alarm.

Every single one of the houses that Jade passed had a steel-blue-and-grey notice board attached to their wall or gate. "This Property Protected By Peacetime Security," the phone number and website address of the security firm printed underneath.

Peacetime Security had Autumn Road sewn up in terms of business. Except for just one home. Pamela's mansion had no reassuring notice board outside. It had no cameras, no infra-red beams, no armed guards and no dogs. Just an empty wooden guardhouse.

If having good security meant being better protected than your neighbours, then this house was a soft target.

That didn't make any sense to Jade at all.

On impulse she took out her phone and called Peacetime Security. The control room operator was unable to answer her questions. She asked to speak to the sales director, but was told he was out of the office. Then she asked for the owner of the company. He wasn't available either.

Out and about, working hard to spread the peace, she supposed.

Jade left an urgent message asking that one of them return her call. Then she walked back through Pamela's emerald-green garden, peering under bushes, looking around trees and checking under her own car.

She tugged her shirt away from her body to cool the hot sweat that had sprung up on her skin.

Two covered carports stood next to the garages. One of them was occupied by a black BMW X5 with tinted windows. The other, which Jade supposed had housed Pamela's car, was now empty.

She guessed the garage doors would be automatically operated by one of the other buttons on Pamela's remote control. There were four buttons—red, blue, yellow, green. The red one was for the gate. Jade pressed all the others in turn, and watched as the three garage doors rolled smoothly upwards.

The backs of three brightly coloured sportscars sparkled in the sun. Red, yellow and blue, just like the buttons on the remote control. Ferrari, Maserati, Aston Martin. Their angled, aerodynamic bodies looked as if they were ready for a rubber-burning getaway, coiled in the "Get Set" position on their thick, black tyres.

Expensive toys for a wealthy boy. Cars that, individually, were each worth millions of rand. These powerful machines made Pamela's Corvette look like a simple and economical choice.

She moved between the cars almost on tiptoe, aware that she was holding her breath. She let it out slowly and breathed in again. She couldn't hear anything suspicious, or sense anybody watching her. The garage was empty apart from the three cars, as shiny and expensive as precious jewels.

When Jade moved closer to the back wall of the garage, she heard a tiny noise. Looking up at the small window above her head, she saw a bluebottle buzz against it briefly, as if stunned, before recovering and flying away.

Then she picked up another sound, which seemed to be coming from somewhere beyond the garage wall. A soft but unpleasant scraping noise that made her think of fingernails on a blackboard.

What on earth?

Jade walked out of the garage and cautiously made her way around the building to the entertainment area that she'd glimpsed earlier when she'd parked her car. The tiled patio had a lovely view over the pool. Behind the row of smart cane chairs, she saw a large braai built into the back wall. It was a sturdy structure, with an adjustable grill supported by four thick metal posts.

But below the metal posts . . .

Jade's world spun around her and she sank to her knees, clapping her hands over her mouth in horror.

"Jesus Christ," she breathed. Unable to take her eyes off the dreadful sight in front of her, she stared and stared, swallowing hard.

The body of a naked man was sprawled on the tiles below the braai. His wrists had been bound with wire to the two front posts. His torso was slumped forward, his head lowered, hanging from his outstretched arms. His hands were blackened and grossly swollen from the wire's tight bite.

His ankles were trussed together with more of the wire. That must have prevented him from struggling and fighting against whoever had worked on him.

And worked on him they had. Peering at him, unable to breathe, Jade saw that giant tracts of his skin had been burned away. The flesh was puckered and scarred by terrible, oozing wounds, coal-black around the outside and deep red in the centre, populated by buzzing clusters of flies.

His eyes were missing. His genitalia were a scorched, bloody ruin.

A mound of coals, now greyish-white, powdery and cool, lay in the braai. Like every other meat-eating South African, Jade knew that the heat generated by the smouldering charcoal would have been ferocious.

The tools that his tormentor, or tormentors, had used still lay on the grill. Tongs, skewers, a solid-looking poker, their tips thick with ashy residue.

Grasping a chair for support, Jade stood up again. She felt dizzy and had no idea whether her wobbly legs would hold her, but she managed to take another step forward. She choked on the sweet-ish, smoky smell she'd noticed when she'd first arrived.

It was not the aftermath of a braai, as she had thought, but rather the lingering odour of charred flesh.

Lifting his chin with a gentle hand, Jade saw that the man's lips were studded with enormous blisters. In places, the flesh had been half melted away. Looking at the grey dust and darker, bloody patterns of saliva that oozed from the man's ruined mouth, Jade realised that a red-hot coal had been forced between his lips, all but burning his tongue away, searing itself immovably into his flesh, and no doubt suffocating him with the fumes of his own broiling body.

A destructive, deadly gag.

Her next thought was that identifying him might be difficult because his face had been so badly disfigured. But then she realised the strong shape of his jaw was exactly the same as the one belonging to the groom in the wedding photo she'd so recently seen.

This was Terence, Pamela's missing husband.

Missing no longer. Right here at home, in fact.

Why, then, had Pamela reported his disappearance to the police?

Looking more closely at the deep burns on Terence's ribcage, Jade froze in horror as she realised the most terrible fact of all. His chest was moving, erratically and almost imperceptibly.

As Jade looked on, his feet twitched. A tiny, weak effort, but enough to scrape the rough end of the wire that bound his ankles against the tiles to make the unpleasant noise that Jade had heard minutes before.

Terence Jordaan had not suffocated; nor had he died of his injuries. Somehow, impossibly, he was still alive.

19

Edmonds hurried along the corridor of the Royal London Hospital in the Whitechapel Road. She was on her way to meet Amanita, the Senegalese victim rescued from Number Six, who had been recovering here for the past fortnight.

Amanita had allowed the detectives to access her medical records. Scanning the report earlier, Edmonds had seen that her list of injuries was horrifying. Smashed left cheekbone, broken jaw, concussion, three broken ribs and severe abdominal bruising. The doctors had suspected damage to her internal organs but, in this respect at least, she'd been lucky.

She also had oral gonorrhoea. One of the doctors had explained to Edmonds that they took a throat swab from every sex worker admitted to check for infection, as unprotected oral sex was the norm at brothels. The victims at Number Six had been lucky that the punters were obliged to wear condoms for all penetrative sex. Many trafficked women and girls ended up at establishments where the men could pay an extra tenner for unprotected sex.

The police had discovered that Amanita was reasonably fluent in English, and that only her severe facial injuries had prevented her from speaking to them on the evening of the raid. She was now sufficiently recovered to do the interview, and straight afterwards she would be flying back to Dakar with her grandfather.

Edmonds hoped her nervousness would not show. This girl represented their last and only chance. All the other victims had flatly refused to cooperate with the police or testify in court. They had been offered a thirty-day reflection period to think about it and to change their minds if they wanted to, but every one had turned the opportunity down and had asked to go back to South Africa. With them would go any chances of a successful prosecution.

Toting her bag of interview equipment, Edmonds walked into the four-bed ward.

An elderly black man in crumpled-looking clothing struggled to his feet from Amanita's bedside. The anguish in his eyes was almost palpable.

Edmonds could only imagine how he must have felt after hearing about the physical and emotional abuse that his granddaughter had suffered. In her limited experience she had discovered that the parents and guardians were usually more traumatised, and harder to deal with, than the victims themselves.

Perhaps it was because the victims had been through the worst of their ordeal by the time she interviewed them, whereas for their parents, the hell was only just beginning.

Up close, she revised her initial impressions of the white-haired man. His clothes might be crumpled-looking after the hours spent sitting by his granddaughter's bedside, but they did not look cheap. She took his hand, aware that her own was cold and slightly clammy, but to her relief, Bernard Soumare's didn't feel any different.

She greeted him with professional warmth, and offered a "Good afternoon" to Amanita.

"If it's all right with you, sir, I'd like you to step outside while I have a chat with Amanita."

He gave an almost imperceptible nod.

"Please, be gentle with her," he said in accented English. He bent down again, exchanged a few whispered words with the injured girl in a language that Edmonds supposed was their native Wolof, squeezed her hand, then grasped his walking stick and slowly left the ward.

A hospital ward was not the ideal place to conduct an interview like this. In Scotland Yard there was a special room set aside for such activities, because the team's number-one priority was to put the victims at ease. The more relaxed and comfortable they felt, the easier it was for them to talk. The Yard's interview room was decorated warmly, with comfortable couches and unchallenging watercolours of flowers and riverside scenes on the walls. The room was unobtrusively wired, and the big wall mirror opposite the carefully positioned couches concealed a one-way observation station.

Since she had joined the Human Trafficking unit, Edmonds had spent many hours with her feet tucked up on one of the couches, wearing jeans and a comfortable top, talking to victims sat on the other. She found it took a long time to persuade the women to relax, open up and start talking, and if a certain topic was too difficult to speak about on a specific day, then Edmonds would simply change the subject and start chatting about music, food, hair care, or their life back home.

"Pink and fluffy," Richards had told her when she joined the department. "That's how we need to come across. We have to convince the victims that the police can be liked and trusted, which is not an experience many of them have had in their home countries."

Judging from some the questions she'd been asked, Edmonds was convinced that many of them didn't believe she was a police officer at all.

She drew the curtains around the hospital bed before adjusting Amanita's pillows so that she could sit up comfortably.

One of the black girl's eyes was covered by a surgical dressing that extended down the left side of her face. The other returned her gaze, steady and unblinking.

Edmonds sat down on the chair next to the bed and arranged her recording equipment on the little table, moving a vase of flowers aside to accommodate the sleek black machine. In a hospital, this was another potential problem, because the sight of the recorder might make Amanita nervous about talking freely. It was far better for such equipment to be unobtrusive or, better still, completely out of sight.

She pressed the record button and the red light on the machine began to flash.

"Amanita, I'm Eleanor Edmonds from the Human Trafficking unit at Scotland Yard. I don't know if you remember me from the night you were rescued. How are you feeling now?"

Amanita gave a small nod and began to talk.

"I remember you. I still have pain, but they look after me well here."

"We're going to be preparing a case against Mr. Salimovic, the owner of the place where you were forced to work," Edmonds continued, her voice gentle. When we find him, she thought. "And

Mr. Rodic, who helped to run Number Six. We're going to need to build a strong case against these two men, not just because they were running an illegal brothel, but because they were abusing their workers. This way we can push for the maximum sentence, and send them to prison for a long time. Fifteen years, hopefully."

Edmonds took a deep breath. "We're going to ask you to try and identify both men, using pictures, of course." The old identity line-up had long since been replaced by a photo-based system.

"We will also need you to testify in court. If you agree to do this, we'll help and support you the whole way through the process and afterwards. We'll fly you back here when the time comes, and you'll stay in a safe house, under a witness protection plan." Edmonds was deliberately emphasising the safety precautions that would be put into place. She had seen the fear in the eyes of the other girls when they'd refused to assist the police any further. Frustrating as it was, she could only feel sympathy for them, because they must have been intimidated to such an extent that they were simply afraid to say anything.

Amanita cleared her throat and spoke softly, through lips still swollen and smeared with salve.

"Are any of the others helping you?"

Edmonds paused, thrown by this unexpected question. What to say? Was the Senegalese girl asking this because she didn't want to be the only one testifying? She hoped not, because all she could do was tell her the truth.

"No. All five have asked to go back to South Africa as soon as possible."

She stared at Amanita, and the girl's dark eye met hers again. Edmonds saw the strength in her gaze, and her next words confirmed it.

"I will help you," she said softly.

Leaning forward on the plastic chair, her elbow propped rather awkwardly against the bed's side rail, Edmonds felt a huge surge of relief. Prematurely, she knew, because the victim might still change her mind. But at least, for now, they had a witness.

"Thank you," she said. "Now, Amanita, please tell me how you were brought to England to work at Number Six."

"I was travelling in South Africa with my friend Fariah," the woman said. "On a long holiday, before I started my studies." She looked at Edmonds with concern in her eyes. "Have you found Fariah yet?"

Fariah was the missing victim; the one who had been beaten up and sold on.

"We're searching as hard as we can for her," Edmonds said reassuringly.

"We were looking for work, some way to earn extra money," Amanita continued. "We were short, because Fariah's bag got stolen with a lot of cash inside. We did not want to ask Fariah's mother for more, because she had just lost her job, and I did not want to bother my family back in Senegal. Then Fariah saw an advertisement for extravaganza dancers in a newspaper."

"Can you remember which one?" Edmonds asked.

Amanita thought for a moment. "I do not know," she said.

Edmonds nodded. That was understandable.

"We were told to come to the dance venue the next morning," Amanita continued. "It was in Johannesburg somewhere, but I cannot remember where. There, a woman interviewed us and took our photos." She paused and swallowed.

"Here." Edmonds picked up the glass of water on the little table and held it carefully to Amanita's lips. "What did the woman look like?" she asked.

"She was young. Not very tall, with blonde hair in a ponytail, and blue eyes. She smiled a lot. She told us her name was Mary."

Mary? Edmonds jotted the name down, disappointed. She'd hoped that Amanita might give a description of Mathilde Dupont.

"Go on," she encouraged.

"Mary told us there were no jobs for us here, as they were full, but that she was looking for workers for a club in England. She asked Fariah if we had passports. I did, but Fariah's passport had been inside the stolen bag. Mary said it did not matter, that she would help her get a new one in time. She told us to meet her at the airport in a week."

Edmonds held the water glass to the victim's lips again.

"When we got to Heathrow, a man met us who said his name was Sam. He had black hair and a cruel face."

Edmonds nodded. She already recognised the description—Salimovic.

"Sam asked for all our passports. He said he needed them to get us a working visa. I did not want to give him my passport, but I was frightened that if I said no, I would not get the job. We left the airport and drove for a long time until we came to a big house, on the corner of Camargue Road and another street. It had a white wall and a high wooden gate."

Edmonds was encouraged to hear that the house matched the description of Salimovic's rented home in South Woodford perfectly. As the police had suspected from the trace evidence discovered inside the large detached mansion, the victims had indeed been taken there first.

"Then what happened?"

"Fariah and I were put in a room together. The rooms were smart, and I thought it was a nice place. But then I saw that I did not have my suitcase with me, or my handbag. And when I tried to open the bedroom door, it was locked."

Now Amanita looked down while she spoke, fixing her gaze on the shiny linoleum floor.

"I banged on the door and asked for someone to open it. Then Sam came. He unlocked the door, looking angry." Her voice dropped to a whisper. "He started shouting at us, saying that we owed him money for the flight and the passport, and that we must work for him for one year to pay it back. That we were using illegal passports, and if we tried to escape the police would find us and they would put us straight into prison.

"I said that was not true because my passport was my own, but he did not listen. He hit me hard on my face." Amanita raised a hand to her bandaged cheekbone and Edmonds nodded in sympathy. She'd suspected that the most recent injuries the girl had suffered had not been her first.

"Then he unzipped his trousers. He started to smile, talking to us in his own language, and although I could not understand what he was saying, I knew already the kind of work he was going to ask us to do. I knew he and Mary had lied to us."

She blinked rapidly. "I was wishing I could do something to get away, but I did not. I was too scared he would hurt me again.

Fariah was on the floor crying, and I think the man knew she would not fight him.

"So he raped her first," she said, in a small, husky voice.

Over the next half-hour, Amanita related more of her story. Edmonds listened intently, checking the recorder from time to time, struggling to maintain a level of professional distance and a sympathetic manner, to conceal the shock she felt.

Fariah had been taken to another room soon after that, and Amanita had been entirely alone. Her "breaking-in" had been brutal and methodical. If she complied, she was left alone; given food, even offered alcohol and over-the-counter drugs like painkillers or tranquillisers if she wanted them. If she resisted, she was beaten.

Either way, she was raped repeatedly by the cruel-faced Salimovic and her other tutor, who, from the description Amanita gave, Edmonds recognised as Rodic.

"Smile," Salimovic had told her. "For every client, you will smile."

When Amanita refused, he had grabbed the corners of her mouth with his thumbs and index fingers, and pulled them painfully upwards, then leered at her and pointed to his own expression.

"Smile," he had said again.

They moved her at night, she said, in the back of a car. She was not restrained, but she was blindfolded, and Sam sat next to her in the back seat as Rodic drove. Not a long ride, ten minutes perhaps; but she had no idea where they were taking her. No one in the car said anything during the journey. Still blindfolded, she was taken into a house, led up a flight of stairs and put in the tiny bedroom that, for the next few months, would be her home.

After the first client had raped her, Amanita cried. She told Edmonds she was punished for her tears with yet another beating. After that, she learned not to cry, but just to smile. To smile as man after man entered her little room and forced himself on her. Usually ten men a day; sometimes as many as twenty.

Food was brought to her room twice a day, but she felt constantly sick and had no interest in eating. When he saw the plates of congealing food on the rickety table next to the bed, Rodic had sat down beside her and put his pudgy arm around her. He told her in his broken English that if she did not eat, she would receive more beatings, and although he did not want that to happen, he would not be able to stop it. And, pointing to the toilet, he indicated that if she flushed the food away and pretended she had eaten, that would also not be wise. He poked her in her ribs, pinched her hipbones. Thin is not good. The clients will think you have Aids.

The universal terror.

So Amanita had choked down the meals, forced herself to swallow the overcooked meat and anaemic mixed veg, the hard bread rolls and the dry scrambled eggs. Every night, when "work" was finally over, the ancient, unsmiling receptionist—Rodic's mother, who was also under arrest and also refusing to cooperate—would bring her an alcoholic drink in a plastic cup.

Those, Amanita always flushed down the toilet. She was convinced that the drinks were spiked with drugs or sleeping pills.

"I drank only water," she said.

Edmonds took a deep breath. It was time to move on with the questioning now, to try and find the answer to a question that had been perplexing the team.

"Amanita," Edmonds said gently, "I have another question for you now."

"Yes?"

"We received the phone records for Number Six yesterday."

The landline records had proved to be disappointing. Apart from a few calls to Salimovic's home numbers in South Woodford and Sarajevo, most of the other numbers were for local fast-food outlets and pizza parlours.

Except for one.

"We saw that somebody phoned your grandfather's mobile number in Senegal a few days before the police raid. Do you know anything about that call?"

In the silence that followed, Edmonds realised how quiet the ward was. The only sound was the muted hum of the air conditioning doing its best to keep the room at the requisite comfortable temperature, despite the grim weather outside which heralded the fact that summer was well and truly over.

Then, in a whisper, the girl replied.

"I called that number. I phoned him."

Her eyes locked with Edmonds', and once again the police officer was surprised by the strength she saw there.

"How did you manage to get to a phone?"

"The man I was with, he was very drunk. He fell asleep. They did not lock our doors when the customers were there, so I went out. I saw there was nobody in the office, so I quickly made the call."

"What did he say when you spoke to him?" This was the question that had been puzzling Edmonds the most. If the girl had managed to get a message through to him that she was in trouble, why hadn't he called the police immediately? The raid had been pure coincidence; as a result of an anonymous but well-informed tip-off.

"I did not speak to him."

"You didn't speak to him? But the call went through." And it lasted for five minutes, Edmonds thought. Long enough, surely, for Amanita to have described her predicament.

Amanita turned her head to the right, looking away from Edmonds. Her fingers touched the white dressing on her cheek.

"He was at a jazz club in Dakar with his friends. I could not speak loudly because I was scared somebody would hear, and he could not hear properly because it was a noisy place. Because of that he did not know it was me at first. Then he said he would go outside and find somewhere quieter to talk. He did not know that it was urgent. I heard him telling his friends to wait and then walking through the club. Lots of voices and loud music. Then he was outside, I think, because the noise stopped. He said, "How's my girl?" Then Sam came back into the office and I dropped the phone."

"Then what happened?"

"He hit me many times. Then he pushed me down onto the floor and kicked me. I was screaming, but he would not stop. I thought I was going to die." She raised her hand to her cheek again and Edmonds saw that she was trembling.

"Did your grandfather phone back?"

"He tried to. But Sam saw a number from another country on the display, so he just carried on hitting me. Then he said that they were going to sell me and Fariah to another place, a place where the men do not use the condoms and all the girls soon die. A man came to look at me the next morning, but he said I was too hurt. He did not want to take me until my face was better. He told Sam that he would come back in a week. But you came first."

Amanita closed her unbandaged eye and leant back into her pillow.

"I am tired now. I am sorry."

Edmonds nodded. The injured girl had endured enough grilling, and she had given her all the information that the police would need for now.

"Thank you for cooperating, Amanita. You've been so helpful." She switched off the tape recorder. "Is there anything else you want? Anything I can get you while I'm here?"

"No, thank you. Is my grandfather still here?"

"I'll go and fetch him right away."

A nurse entered the room and nodded a quick hello. She was a short, smiling lady with blonde hair pulled back in a ponytail.

With a jolt, Edmonds saw that the name on the nurse's badge was Mary.

She turned back to the hospital bed.

"Amanita, are you sure . . . ?"

But the Senegalese victim's eyes were tightly closed and she did not respond to the policewoman's voice.

"I won't be long," Mary said. She checked the chart at the foot of the bed, jotted something down in a notebook, and left after opening the curtains again.

As Edmonds packed her equipment away, trying to keep as quiet as possible, she thought about the sequence of events that Amanita had described. The whispered phone call, the distracted man in the noisy jazz club, the unanswered return call.

From those few seconds of conversation, Mr. Soumare could surely have had no idea that anything was wrong.

No wonder he had sounded so shocked when Edmonds had contacted him after the raid and broken the news.

Edmonds walked out of the ward and headed down towards the lifts to the ground floor. Oh yes, it all made sense. It was an entirely plausible story. In addition, the human trafficking team members had been trained to accept that everything the victims told them was a possible truth.

Why, then, did she have the disconcerting suspicion that Amanita had been lying?

20

David knew he had to leave work early. Not because he'd finished his daily tasks—a detective's work was never done—but because he'd promised his wife that he'd pick up Kevin from his afternoon football practice and take him back to her rented townhouse in Pretoria.

"Don't be late," Naisha had insisted, with a tone in her voice that would have impressed a sergeant-major. "He's still a new boy. I don't want him waiting around after the game is over. It finishes at four, and he must come home straight away."

He knew exactly what she meant. They'd lived together for nine years, and been married for most of them. Naisha understood what police work involved. Late nights, cancelled holidays, broken promises. It was one of the reasons why they weren't living together now, although technically they were still married.

Despite his best efforts, he had to take two urgent calls as he was about to leave, and he was a quarter of an hour behind schedule by the time he'd sprinted downstairs to the underground parking garage and scrambled into his detective's unmarked vehicle.

The M1 highway from Johannesburg to Pretoria was already clogged with traffic. In another half-hour it would be at a standstill. Now, by weaving through the lines of cars, ducking into the emergency lane, grabbing opportunities wherever he could find them, David managed to keep moving at a reasonable speed.

Even so, it was ten past four when he took the final corner at thirty kilometres over the limit and roared up to the imposing entrance gates of Devon Downs College, hoping like hell the game was running late.

He parked in a hurry, under the watchful gaze of the security guard, his modest little unmarked car looking like a poor relation in the row of new, luxury vehicles.

Enrolling Kevin for this expensive school had forced David to make some unwanted changes to his own life. He didn't regret any of them, not even for a moment. The alternative—not seeing his son for months at a time—would have been so much worse.

He could still remember the panic he'd felt when Naisha had requested a special meeting with him a couple of months ago. Never mind that David was in and out of the Turffontein house regularly, picking up Kevin, dropping off Kevin, visiting Kevin. This was a matter that didn't concern her son, Naisha explained. She needed to speak to him alone, so they met up at the Mugg and Bean in the Eastgate shopping centre, a convenient halfway point.

"I have something to tell you," she said.

David was certain that Naisha was going to say she'd met somebody else, that she no longer wanted to give their marriage a second chance. The guilty twinge of premature relief he'd felt didn't last long. It was cut short by the words that followed.

"I've been offered an overseas job—Secretary of Immigration and Civic Affairs at the South African Consulate General in Mumbai."

"Mumbai?" David stared at her blankly. "You mean Mumbai, India?"

"That's the one."

David gaped, absorbing the implications of her words. Naisha had worked for Home Affairs for years, but the last time they'd spoken, she'd mentioned that the branch where she worked was closing and that she was about to be transferred to the head office in Pretoria, where she would take up a management position.

"That's . . . that's great. Well done. What happened with the Pretoria job?"

"That's still on offer," she said slowly. "I haven't made a decision one way or the other. I've been thinking it over. I'll be much better off financially if I take up the offer to go to Mumbai. Renting a place to live in Pretoria will cost a fortune, and I haven't been able to find any good schools in that area for Kevin."

Only then did the awful realisation hit David. "Hang on a minute. What about Kevin? If you're working overseas, where's he going to go?"

Naisha didn't answer immediately. She stirred some honey into her rooibos tea.

"Kevin will come with me, of course. There's a very good infrastructure in place over there for the children of embassy workers. Apparently they attend a great school for free in—"

"Naisha, no! Wait. Listen." David's words were so loud that a couple of neighbouring diners turned and stared. He saw his wife frown and carried on speaking more quietly, although his heart was pounding just as fast.

"Please. Don't take him away." He shook his head in frustration. "I don't want to stop you from advancing your career, but if you take this job, I won't see my own son for years at a stretch."

"That's not true. Embassy workers and their children get two flights home every year, fully subsidised."

"Dammit, you know what I mean. At the moment I see Kevin at least twice a week. I need that contact with him and he needs it too. He needs a father figure." Another thought occurred to David. "And what about crime? Wasn't there a terrorist bombing in Mumbai a while ago? There was, I'm sure. I don't want my son living in a place where there's any terrorist activity."

"There's crime everywhere," Naisha reminded him gently. "You of all people should know that. The embassy is very secure, and so is the staff accommodation. Besides, Mumbai is an amazing city. Do you know it's where Bollywood is located?"

"No, I didn't know that, and I don't care." Furious, David looked away from Naisha's smiling face, crumpling the tablecloth in his fists so hard that when he let go he saw he had made jagged creases in the starched white fabric.

"I knew this would upset you," Naisha said. "Don't think I haven't been agonising over it too. I only have to give them my decision in December, so we both have more time to think about this."

"Please stick to your original plan." David gripped the tablecloth again. "We'll find a school for Kevin. Didn't you tell me there was a good private school out in Irene somewhere?"

Naisha laughed, shaking her head. "Devon Downs College? Even with the salary increase I'll be getting, there's no way we can afford that school."

"Oh yes, we can." David contradicted her automatically, his mind racing as he searched for facts to back up his argument.

"How?"

The answer came to him in a flash. "I'll move back to Turffontein when you leave. We're paying the bond on the house in any case. Then the money I'm saving on my rental can go towards Kevin's school fees."

"Well, I don't know. I thought you didn't want to live in that area anymore. But if you're prepared to do that, then perhaps it could work." Naisha had given David a sidelong glance and for a moment he thought she was going to say something else. She didn't; she just sipped her tea and stared off into the distance the way she did when she was thinking hard.

To David's relief, Naisha decided on the Pretoria job a couple of weeks later and enrolled Kevin at Devon Downs. Even so, he still couldn't help feeling that there was a sword of Damocles hanging over his head. Naisha hadn't mentioned the Mumbai job since, but David knew he wouldn't be able to relax until December, when the offer closed.

He also wondered if she had been deliberately toying with him, in order to show him what could happen if he chose to walk away from the marriage.

David had spent many sleepless nights worrying about this, and every time he reached the same conclusion—he simply didn't know.

"Dad!"

His son's voice interrupted David's uneasy thoughts. The boy was pounding down the gravel drive towards him, his school bag bouncing on his back, his one-size-too-big soccer shorts flapping like white flags.

"Kevin!" He braced himself for impact as his son's head thudded into his stomach with the force of a small meteorite. "Did your game just finish?"

"No. It ended early, but Mum said you were coming to fetch me and that you'd be late, so she told me to wait in the library until quarter past four." Kevin beamed up at him proudly.

David shook his head. He'd been snookered.

"Let's get you home." He ruffled Kevin's dark, shiny hair, noticing it was shorter. He'd had a haircut since David had last seen him. The clean lines of the new style made his son's face appear different—a little stronger, a little more grown-up than his eight years.

For some reason, he found that small detail disproportionately upsetting. Kevin was his son, dammit. He should be the one who took him off to the barber's shop on a Saturday morning, the boy's fringe still rumpled from sleep. He should be the one who took Kevin to the local bookshop afterwards for an adventure story and a chocolate muffin from the café, his hair crisp and short, a few stray snippets clinging to the nape of his neck.

The small details of parenthood. The everyday episodes that marked the passage of time. Those were what tore at his heart when he realised he was missing out on them.

On the way out of the school grounds Kevin wound the window down and waved enthusiastically at another similarly clad boy walking towards the school gates with a domestic worker in a pink uniform. The boy waved back, but the domestic worker stopped and regarded their car with suspicion.

"Riaan!" Kevin shouted. "This is my dad!"

Now the black woman relaxed. She waved and smiled.

"That's Riaan, my new friend," he told David. "He lives in that house just round the corner, but Francina, she's their maid, she comes and fetches him and walks home with him every day to keep him safe. Mum says I can go and play there next Friday."

"That's nice, Kev. It's good you're making friends," David said in a falsely cheerful tone.

The boy chattered all the way to Naisha's new home, a rented apartment in a newly built townhouse complex in Faerie Glen. It should have been a twenty-minute drive, but a multiple-vehicle collision on Atterbury Road had blocked access in both directions and the rush-hour traffic was now being rerouted down a series of increasingly crowded and chaotic minor roads. David followed the signs, trying not to swear as they crawled down the unfamiliar streets, relying on his somewhat fallible sense of direction to bring them out again in the right place. It would be really helpful, he thought bitterly, if the South African police service would shell out for GPS navigation units in all their unmarked vehicles, instead of just a chosen few.

Despite his best efforts, he lost his way, but Kevin spotted a nature reserve he recognised and directed him from there. After more than an hour behind the wheel, he pulled up outside Naisha's townhouse complex. His heart sank when he saw her car was already parked outside. He'd been hoping he wouldn't have to see her.

She met him at the door, still in her work clothes with her dark hair pinned back, full of apologies. A kiss on the cheek for him, a warm hug for Kevin.

"Thank you, thank you. I've had an impossible day. I'm so glad you could fetch him. We had a late meeting this afternoon, and with the traffic, I would never have made it out to Irene before dark. Come in, sit down. Let me get you a drink."

He was about to decline, but Kevin's anxious face convinced him to change his mind.

"A beer would be nice." He lowered himself onto the couch in the sitting room and stretched out his long legs. He was stiff from the cramped confines of his car and his legs ached from working the pedals in the stop-start traffic. Kevin had disappeared into his bedroom. Listening to the muffled noises that emerged from the room, David guessed he was playing the Harry Potter computer game he'd given him for his birthday in June.

Naisha poured him a cold Windhoek lager in a tall glass and he downed half of it in one long gulp.

The flat was small but pleasant. Like the rest of the complex, it was fairly new. Everything was freshly painted, gleaming, and clean. There were ornaments on the sideboard, pictures on the mantel-piece. David glanced through the D-shaped archway into the open-plan kitchen where pots and pans hung from a rack on the wall. On the stove, a large saucepan of water was coming to the boil.

In the short time she'd been living there, Naisha had trans-formed the place into a home. It didn't feel like David's home, though, and he guessed it never would.

"What was the meeting about?" he asked Naisha as she bustled back through the lounge to the kitchen. She'd taken off her work jacket, changed into a casual top.

"I requested it," she said. There was an element of pride in her voice. She bent down to open the freezer, and after some consideration, pulled out one of the labelled Tupperware boxes and popped it in the microwave to defrost. "I'm implementing some drastic changes in the department this week, and I wanted to get my bosses' input, and their permission to go ahead with the next step."

"Changes?" he asked. "Your water's boiling, by the way."

"Oh. Thanks." She added some brown rice to the saucepan and turned the heat down. "We've got two big problems. Apathy's the first one—I've never seen such poor performance in a department—and corruption's the other. They're both serious and they're obviously related to each other, but the corruption needs to be addressed right now."

She took a tomato from the basket on the window sill and began slicing it, punctuating her words with decisive strokes of the knife. "In theory, it costs less than two hundred rand to get an official South African identity document or passport. In practice, corrupt officials are charging our uneducated citizens ten times that, or more, if they want their documents within a year."

David nodded. "I heard a news story a while ago about a man who committed suicide after waiting for more than eighteen months to get his ID book."

"Yes. The Home Affairs worker who was supposed to help him tore up his application form right in front of him and accused him of being a 'makwerekwere,' you know, a foreigner. It happens because the staff are too lazy or too corrupt to do the necessary work to process the forms. And as you can imagine, that's led to a whole syndicate of illegal document providers springing up."

Naisha reached for another tomato. "Now those documents are starting to cause trouble. Britain's Home Office informed us yesterday that as far as they're concerned most South African passports they see aren't worth the paper they're printed on."

"Ouch. That's a bloody insult."

"I know. They've just made it compulsory for South Africans to get a visa before they travel to the United Kingdom. Obviously, I can't do anything about that." She bent over the chopping board and started sawing at an onion with what seemed to David like unnecessary force. "But by God, I can turn the department around. I can show the world that our Home Affairs is not going to backslide any further. My aim is to get that visa requirement reversed in the next five years."

"They must have had problems, then, if they're insisting on visas now."

Naisha nodded, her expression serious. "Last week they arrested two suspected terrorists in Yorkshire. They were travelling on fake South African passports."

"How'd they spot the fakes?" David watched her pick out an avocado from the fruit bowl and prod it gently with her thumb before quartering and peeling it.

"Well, those passports were blanks, from a batch that was stolen out of a diplomatic bag last year. We managed to trace most of the reference numbers, but not all, so those two men just got lucky. British Home Office couriered the documents back to us yesterday and we had a look. They were good forgeries, but there were a couple of details that they'd got wrong." She glanced up at him, her eyes alight with enthusiasm, and with an expression David recognised well—the thrill of the chase.

"What were the details?"

"Firstly, the forgers had used the wrong version of font on the title page. If the immigration officials at Heathrow had been more on the ball they'd never have been allowed into the UK in the first place. We checked the names against our database, and of course they didn't match up to anything. Then, when we looked at the date of issue, we discovered it was actually Easter Sunday."

David finished the last of his beer. It was ironic, he thought, that their marriage had originally run into problems because Naisha had been disturbed by the police work he did. He recalled one conversation in particular from long ago, where he'd been telling her about a fingerprint he'd discovered that had cracked a case and led to the arrest of a serial killer operating in the Wemmer Pan area. Halfway through his story, Naisha had burst into tears. "Please," she'd sobbed, "I can't bear to hear anymore. This is all you do, all the time. You investigate these terrible acts, and you track down evil people."

"Well, yes," he'd replied, confused. "That's what I do."

"I don't want to hear about it!" She'd stormed out of the lounge and gone to comfort Kevin, who'd been two at the time, who had started to cry when he'd heard his mother's raised voice.

And now here she was, seeking to curb the criminal activities of people who were potentially just as evil as those he hunted every day.

"So what are you going to do about this?" he asked.

"I'm implementing new systems. The new blanks are under much tighter security, so I don't think an incident like that will happen again. But I'm more worried about the other type of fraud." She arranged the salad on a plate, and began squeezing lemon juice over the avocado. "I've had a look at the computer statistics for the last few months, and something's not adding up. I'm positive there's a syndicate working out of head office."

"What's your plan for them?" David rotated his glass slowly in his hand, watching the foamy residue trickle round its sides.

"This afternoon I put a freeze on all new passport and ID book applications received in the last ten days and disabled all the passwords that allow staff to change existing computer records or add new ones. Nothing will be approved or dispatched without being personally checked and authorised by myself or my assistants every step of the way. Not until I've completed my investigation into the irregularities I've found."

David's mouth was starting to water as a fragrant whiff of spices wafted across the room.

"Are you going to stay for supper?" Naisha asked. "It's your favourite. Chicken korma."

He struggled out of the chair, which seemed reluctant to release him from its comfortable embrace.

"Thanks, but I really must go. I've got a stack more work to do before I can call it a night."

To his surprise, she didn't argue.

"Next time, then." She walked through to the lounge, put a hand on his shoulder, and stood on tiptoes to kiss him goodbye. Her lips felt soft against his, and for a heart-rending moment he thought of Jade.

David stared down at his wife's upturned face. She'd had the affair; she'd insisted on the separation. But now he was the one who felt guilty, as if, through his actions since then, he had betrayed her.

Before he left, he stuck his head round Kevin's door. As he'd guessed, the boy's attention was focused on the computer screen, his hands poised over the keyboard, engrossed in his game. David heard tinny explosions from the speakers, and a sound that might have been a dragon's roar.

"I'm going now. Make sure you kill all the bad guys."

As he realised what he'd said, David winced at his unwise choice of words. He could see Jade looking at him with her right eyebrow raised in her favourite "Oh yeah?" expression, as if to say, "Look what you just told your son to do."

Kevin glanced up at him, frowning. Had he been doing anything else, David knew he would have been in for a few minutes of intensive grilling. Where are you going, Dad? Why do you have to go back to work? Are you coming here again afterwards? Why not? Questions that he always found difficult or impossible to answer. Today, though, David had timed his departure well. Another screech emanated from the speakers, and Kevin hurriedly returned his attention to the game, with a distracted, "Bye, Dad."

"Stay safe, hero."

Naisha was at the front door. She'd taken the key ring from the ceramic dish on the hall table and was opening the security gate for him.

"Well," David said, "see you soon."

Naisha was standing in his way, her fingers curled round the white-painted metal bars. He waited for her to move, but she didn't. Instead, she looked him in the eye and asked him a simple question.

"How's Jade?" Her voice sounded slightly strained.

He flinched, as if she'd slapped him. He couldn't help it. He blinked rapidly, trying to absorb the impact of this bombshell. Bloody hell. How did she know about Jade? He hadn't said a word about their relationship, hadn't wanted her to know; hadn't felt ready to discuss that issue until he'd sorted his head out.

On the other hand, Naisha wasn't stupid. If she had wanted to know if he was involved with anybody, there were a hundred ways she could have found out, and she'd clearly chosen one of them.

"I—er . . ." His voice tailed off as he felt sweat dampen his armpits.

Naisha spoke again, gently.

"I'm not a fool, David."

"Of course you're not, I know that."

"This arrangement we have." She swept her arm towards the inside of the house. "It can't carry on like this forever."

"No, it can't."

"You're going to have to make a choice." Her voice was gentle, but her eyes had the intensity of laser-beams. "And sooner, rather than later, I think."

Then Naisha stepped aside and allowed David to make his way down to his car, his stride automatic, his mind whirling in confusion.

21

David was dog-tired. He'd worked until after ten p.m. every night that week. Even so, going back to work was far better than going home to the empty house in Turffontein, to choose a packet of instant noodles from the three that were left in the cupboard, or buy yet another takeaway burger to be wolfed down in front of the television. And he knew he'd end up washing the taste away with one of the Black Label beers that were the sole inhabitants of his fridge right now.

He wasn't an alcoholic—two beers were just about his limit at the best of times—but if Naisha saw the contents of his fridge, he knew she'd freak out big-time and spend the next hour explaining to him, in no uncertain terms, why he was a sloppy male pig and a bad role model for Kevin.

Tonight, he'd work until nine, he decided, and then go home via the Engen garage shop. Buy a couple of pies for supper; that would make a change from burgers. And perhaps a box of cereal and a carton of milk for breakfast.

He removed a file from the cabinet and sat down at his tidy desk. Before he'd had time to do more than jot his first note in the margins of the first page, the phone rang.

Frowning because it had interrupted his train of thought, David grabbed the receiver. "Patel speaking," he snapped.

There was a pause and a tell-tale click. Then he heard a tinny male voice with a British accent.

"Good afternoon. This is Detective Inspector Richards from the Human Trafficking department in Scotland Yard. I wonder if you could put me through to Superintendent Van Zyl, please, if he's there." He pronounced "van" as if it were the car and "Zyl" as if it were the start of "xylophone."

"I'm sorry, but Van Zyl emigrated to New Zealand in July."

"Ah. Did he, now?" A short pause. "Come to think of it, I remember him saying something about that last time we spoke. Are you by any chance his replacement?"

"Yes, I am. Superintendent David Patel."

"Well, Superintendent, it's good to make your acquaintance."

"Likewise. How can I help?"

"I'm ringing because we've got a letter of request on the way to your department, so I thought I'd give you a quick heads-up on it."

This sounded interesting. David had dealt with those letters on a few occasions. They represented an official request for police assistance with an international investigation. The couple of times that he'd needed to send them off himself, he'd also discovered it was wiser to call ahead first.

"What's it about?"

"We've just identified a fugitive who's fled to South Africa, and we need your help in locating her."

"Right. Who is she?"

"Name's Ms Mathilde Dupont, a French national. She resisted arrest during a brothel raid in Leyton, and ended up injuring two of our officers rather seriously, so we've got a warrant out for her now."

"Right," David said again. More would-be cop killers, he thought. Just what we don't need.

"Anyway, your immigration officials have confirmed she landed at Cape Town International airport on the twenty-second of this month, although we're not sure yet what flight she came in on, because the information she filled in on her landing card was false. But the six victims we rescued from the brothel came from South Africa, so we can't yet say if Ms Dupont has a home base on your side of the world, or if she's involved in trafficking, and has come back to do more business."

"Send the information and I'll follow it up. You can email it if you like. That'll be quickest." He gave the British detective his email address.

"I'll do it in the next five minutes," Richards said. "I'll also send a passport photo of Dupont and a picture of her accomplice from a security camera in the hotel where they were staying. We don't have any positive identification for the accomplice yet. He may or may not have fled to South Africa with her. Either way, we're doing what we can to find them, and we'd appreciate your cooperation."

"You have it, of course." David glanced at his metal cabinet, which was already crammed to capacity with case files, and sighed inwardly.

"Our people will also need to be in touch with your Home Office about repatriating the five girls in the next few days. Is there a chance your Home Office might be open now?"

There was more chance of Cape Town putting up border posts and declaring independence from the rest of South Africa, David thought. "It would be better to try them in the morning," he said, diplomatically. Then, realising what the British officer had said, he frowned. "Five girls? Didn't you say there were six?"

"There were seven originally, from all accounts. We're still following up on that. Seems one of them was sold on somewhere else. Of the six, one is not a South African national. She's Senegalese."

David gave the officer his email address and rang off.

Two minutes later, with trademark British efficiency, the email arrived. David opened it and printed out the pages. Then he sat with his forehead propped against his palm, all thoughts of pies and burgers forgotten as he familiarised himself with his newest case.

22

Jade parked at an angle in a white-painted visitors' bay at The Seasons hotel, grabbed Pamela's suitcase from the boot and rushed inside, calling out a greeting to the receptionist as she hurried down the carpeted corridor. Ahead of her, a patient in a wheelchair was being taken back to her room by a nurse. Jade stepped round the wheelchair and then speeded up again as she saw Pamela's door ahead.

When Pamela opened it, Jade almost knocked her over in her haste to get inside.

"Sorry I've been so long. I . . ."

"Please tell me. Is there any news on Tamsin?" Pamela's eyes were swollen and bloodshot and worry lines carved deep paths between her eyebrows and across her forehead. In the four hours that Jade had been gone, she seemed to have aged ten years.

"Nothing yet," Jade said, closing the door behind her. "But there's a more serious—"

Pamela interrupted her again. "I've been checking my voice-mail using the hotel phone every ten minutes. I feel sick. I mean physically ill. And I've been praying." She smiled faintly. "I've been an atheist ever since I discovered what the word meant, but in the last few hours, all I've been doing is praying to whatever god might be listening that my daughter is safe."

Shoulders sagging, the blonde woman collapsed onto the bed.

Jade took a deep breath.

"Pamela, right now we have other major problems."

"What problems?" Pamela stared up at her through red-rimmed eyes.

"I went round to your house to get your things." She placed the suitcase on the chair as she spoke. "And while I was there, I found your—"

Yet again Jade was interrupted, this time by the ringing of the bedside phone. A moment later, there was a loud knock on the door.

Pamela leaned over and grabbed the phone.

"Hello?" she said, breathlessly. She listened, and then her entire body slumped.

"Yes," she said. "Yes, all right."

She turned to Jade with a stricken expression. "The receptionist said the police are here."

Captain Moloi was standing outside the door, his large shoes making sizeable impressions in the thick carpet.

He treated Jade to the same dour stare that she'd endured for the past two hours during her questioning. That had taken place in Pamela's garden while his investigation team searched the house. She'd also witnessed two paramedics gently loading Terence onto a stretcher. The younger medic had been as white as a ghost. He had looked the same way Jade felt when she thought about the not-quite-dead body of Pamela's husband and the scorched, oozing wounds where his eyes had been.

As he had done during the interview, Moloi gave nothing away now except the fact that he did not like Jade. Actively disliked her, in fact.

Pamela eyed the tall black officer apprehensively as he walked into the room.

"Mrs. Jordaan. First, I have just received some news on your missing daughter."

For a terrible moment, Jade thought he was going to say the words Pamela least wanted to hear. That Tamsin was dead. That they'd discovered her body and she'd been tortured as well, just like her father. She was so convinced by her own fears that it took her a moment to realise that wasn't what the officer was saying at all.

"She has been found."

Pamela's face flooded with relief.

"Tamsin's been found?" she repeated shakily. "Is she all right? Where is she? What happened to her?"

"A cleaner discovered her in a petrol station toilet on the N3 highway, just outside Heidelberg. She was unconscious and she has not yet regained consciousness. She's been taken to Heidelberg City Clinic." Seeing Pamela's horrified expression, he continued quickly. "She's unhurt, and she was fully clothed. The doctors suspect an overdose of a pharmaceutical drug, possibly GHB. Not fatal, but enough to send her into a deep coma." He eyed Pamela closely. "Your daughter has used such drugs before?"

"Well, only once or twice, I think—she does have psychological issues that sometimes require her to use . . ." Pamela blinked rapidly. Her voice sounded breathy and rushed. Jade knew she was lying. Lying like a rug, as the saying went, and watching Moloi's reaction she knew, for the first time that day, that he agreed with her.

"Once can be fatal, Mrs. Jordaan. Anyway, her cellphone is missing, but she had her ID and driver's licence on her, and also a gold chain around her neck with a small diamond pendant on it."

Pamela gave him a wobbly smile. "I gave her that for her eighteenth birthday."

"We'll be able to ask her more when she wakes up, but the evidence does suggest it was probably an experiment gone wrong," Moloi continued. "You should tell her to seek help for her problem. She was lucky this time, but the consequences could have been much worse."

"Yes, of course. Absolutely. I do agree with you. I'll have a serious talk with her. Perhaps I can get her some counselling, or send her to Tara for rehab. She went . . ." Pamela bit off the words, cutting short her own relieved babbling, but Jade was pretty sure she knew what she was going to say—she went there before.

"Now." Moloi squared his shoulders and adjusted the knot of his yellow tie. "Moving on to more serious matters, Mrs. Jordaan. We were called out to your house this afternoon by your hired guard." He nodded at Jade, managing to inject a disproportionate amount of disapproval into the small gesture. "We discovered the dead body of a young woman inside your house, and the semi-conscious body of your husband outside. Mr. Jordaan is very seriously injured and suffering from smoke inhalation after what appears to have been a prolonged session of torture. He's been taken to the burns unit at Netcare Milpark Hospital, where he is on life-support. I'm sorry to have to tell you that the prognosis is not good."

Pamela let out a small moan. The sound was loud in the quiet room. She clapped her hands to her mouth and stared at Moloi in total disbelief.

"Where was the dead woman?" she asked after a long pause, her hands now clutching at her face.

"In the downstairs bathroom," the detective replied, seemingly unperturbed by this odd question, and by the fact Pamela didn't appear more concerned about her husband's state of health.

"Who—who is she?"

"We're not entirely sure yet. However, one of my team has discovered that she matches the description of Celia le Roux, a dancer at the Midrand branch of your husband's business who went by the stage name of Crystal. The assistant manager of the Midrand branch is on his way to the Hillbrow mortuary now with one of our detectives, to see if he can identify the body." Then he leaned in closer, his face intent. Jade recognised the expression and although she wasn't sure exactly what Moloi was going to say next, she was certain that it was going to be more bad news for Pamela.

"The manager has also informed us that it was common knowledge at the club that Crystal was involved with your husband."

Oh no, Jade thought.

"Involved?" Pamela repeated in a high voice. "How do you mean?"

"They were having an affair, Mrs. Jordaan." Moloi sounded impatient now.

Pamela stood up and stumbled over to the window, where she stared out at the tranquil gardens.

"My God," she whispered, without looking round. "You can't be serious. An affair? I had no idea . . ."

"I am sorry to be the one to break it to you," Moloi responded with barely a trace of irony.

But she had known about it. Jade had seen it in her face. She could read it in her response to the detective's questions.

"I am going to have to ask you to accompany me to the police station, Mrs. Jordaan. We need to question you in connection with the torture and attempted murder of your husband."

"But I . . . this is crazy." Now Pamela turned back to the

detective. "I've just had an attempt made on my own life. I'm in danger. I need to be somewhere safe."

Moloi nodded sympathetically. "I am sure you will find Jo'burg Central Police Station safe enough," he said.

Pamela lifted her chin. "May I call my lawyer?"

Don't go there, Jade thought. Not with Moloi in charge.

Jade butted in before he had time to reply. "It's just a routine interview, Pamela," she explained. "In a case like this, the spouse is always under suspicion. The best thing you can do right now is to cooperate. I'll come and fetch you the minute you're finished."

Pamela's curls bobbed as she turned helplessly from Jade to Moloi and back again.

"All right," she said.

Moloi stood back to allow Pamela to leave, and then followed her closely down the passage. With the tall detective blocking the way, Jade couldn't even see the slender, golden-haired woman.

She felt like slumping down onto the hotel bed just like Pamela had done, and burying her face in the silk-covered pillow.

Instead, she left the room and pulled the door closed behind her.

Her client's husband had been brutally tortured, and his table-dancing mistress murdered. And Pamela herself was in the hands of the police and under suspicion for these terrible crimes.

Could anything else go wrong today?

As if providing an instant response to that question, her cell-phone started ringing. The number was unfamiliar, and so was the voice of the man on the other end of the line.

"Can I help you?" Jade snapped, aware that she sounded impatient, stressed and far from helpful.

"I'm returning your call, Ms de Jong. It's Mike Pienaar here, from Peacetime Security."

"Oh. Sorry. Thanks for calling back." Jade walked out of The Seasons, narrowing her eyes against the brassy late afternoon sun. Moloi was already driving out of the gate with Pamela in the passenger seat, staring straight ahead. Even through the tinted window glass, Jade could see the stubborn set of her jaw.

"What can I do for you?" Pienaar asked.

"I have a question. I'm doing a bodyguarding job for Mrs. Jordaan, 12 Autumn Road, Sandton. I noticed that her place seems to be the only house in the street that doesn't have any additional security measures, and I was wondering ..." How to phrase the question tactfully? Tact had never been Jade's strongest quality and she felt particularly low on it right then. "I was wondering if there was a reason for this. If you'd ever approached her with regard to security."

There was silence and then a disillusioned grunt.

"Well, I suppose it's no secret," he replied. "For years we supplied two armed guards in twelve-hour shifts, round the clock, to look after the Jordaans' property. As we still do for a number of other homes in that area."

"And then what?" Jade asked.

"Our contract was cancelled. Just a couple of days ago. No notice period—in fact, we're going to be charging a month's fees in lieu of that, but we were informed that the guards were no longer needed, so we removed our sign from the client's gate on Tuesday. I assumed the home-owners had made alternative arrangements with another security firm."

"Can you tell me who cancelled the contract?" Jade asked.

"Mrs. Jordaan cancelled it herself. She spoke to me personally. Said our services were no longer required and basically told us to pack up and leave immediately. To be frank with you, she was pretty rude."

"She didn't give an explanation?"

"Nothing. Not a word."

"I see," Jade said slowly. "That's all I needed to know. Thanks for getting back to me."

Staring down at her cellphone, she shook her head. Then she started her car, drove out of The Seasons and headed home.

23

Lunchtime had been hot, but the late afternoon was almost unbearable. The sun's rays blazed straight through the dirty windows behind Lindiwe's desk, blasting past the cheap blinds as if they weren't even there, turning the small room into a furnace. The pot plant on the cupboard near the door was wilting so fast that she fancied she would see it turn brown, wither and die in the next half-hour.

Lindiwe knew she should get up and water it, but she just didn't have the energy.

Worst of all, the fan had packed up. An hour ago, the motor had started to grind and the blades had slowed. A few minutes later, with a resigned thunk, it died completely. Without the fan's gallant protection, the air felt like treacle.

Her red blouse clung to her back and she felt sticky all over. She tried fanning herself with the invoice book, but soon discovered the effort of moving it was making her hotter instead of cooler. She dropped it back down on the desk and sat watching the hands of the clock tick over the endless minutes.

Although the office normally closed at six-thirty, she was going to leave at six, as soon as she had dealt with the dark-skinned man who'd said he would be coming back for his passports at that time. Then, if she hurried, and she was lucky with the taxis, she could get to the local Hyperama before it closed and try and buy a replacement fan.

She had warned Veli that he must run and fetch the security guard as soon as he saw the man arrive. She'd decided she wasn't even going to let him into the office. Better to give him the bad news about his documents with a solid gate between them, and with the guard standing by.

She'd never had to do this before. This was the first time ever that she had failed to get passports for a customer in time.

The minute hand moved up toward the top of its circuit, and then ever so slowly down again. Lindiwe watched it complete another full circle as if she'd been hypnotised.

She jolted out of her reverie when she realised that it was six o'clock exactly.

Thank God. He hadn't come, and now she could finally go home.

She put her cellphone into her bag, and pressed the button to open the security gate and let herself out.

But as she peeled her legs from the sweaty seat of her chair, a dark hand gripped the metal bars from outside and the gate swung open.

Lindiwe's legs went weak. She fell back onto the chair again and watched in silence as her unwelcome client moved swiftly over to the desk.

Where was Veli? How could he have let her down at such a crucial time? The young man seldom missed out on sounding the alert for a new customer, and he had always taken any potential trouble as seriously as she did, but now he'd allowed trouble to walk straight into her office. What the hell was he thinking?

She wasn't going to listen to her nephew's excuses. He was out of a job. Family or not, she wasn't even going to give him the ten rand for his taxi fare home.

"My documents, please," the man said softly.

Lindiwe shook her head.

"They are not ready. We couldn't get them done today."

He moved a step closer and she tensed and took a quick breath, getting ready to shout for help if he tried to lay a hand on her.

"Why not?" he asked. His tone was serious, but not threatening.

For a moment, under the man's unsettling gaze, Lindiwe found herself about to tell him what Eunice had told her earlier—that no documents could be done for at least a week because security had been drastically tightened. That the syndicate was scared and its members were keeping their heads down, praying that their transgressions would not be uncovered. That they were all living in fear of Mrs. Patel, the new manager.

Then Lindiwe lifted her chin, reminding herself that people

who came to visit her in this place were not customers. They were beggars, all of them, even this creepy man. They could go nowhere else if they wanted genuine documents.

"It is not your place to ask these questions," she snapped. "The reasons are not your concern. You can come and try again next week, and if we cannot get you the passports by then, I will refund you."

"You are wrong," the man said. "It is my place to ask these questions, and the reasons are indeed my concern." This time his tone was nasty and Lindiwe was gripped by the feeling that she was in a lift that was dropping too fast.

"Next week is too late," he continued. "I emphasised that this was urgent. You gave me your word that they would be ready by the end of the day."

"Well, I didn't know they couldn't be done. My contacts didn't tell me." Suddenly Lindiwe couldn't bear to be sitting here any longer, in this suffocating heat, trying to placate a frightening man who seemed to think she could do the impossible.

"I am going home now," she snapped. "Here is your money." She took the envelope from the drawer where she'd put it after Eunice had told her there was no point in bringing it through to Home Affairs, and slid it towards him. "It is all there, except for the ten per cent deposit, which is non-refundable. You must try somewhere else, or come back next week."

She slapped her hands, palms down, onto the desk, feeling her diamond rings knock against the wood. Glancing at the door, she opened her mouth to shout for Veli. He'd bloody well better come running, and take the man downstairs himself.

Before she could speak, the man dropped his hands to his sides. He didn't seem to move fast, but before she could react, she heard two loud thuds. A second later, she felt two bolts of pain, raw and red, more sudden and more agonising than anything she had ever experienced.

Then Lindiwe found herself staring down at the two slim knives which the man had stabbed through the backs of her hands, their razor-sharp points deeply buried in the desk's wooden top.

For a moment, she was paralysed by disbelief. This couldn't really be happening; not to her.

Yet the pain was growing worse with every second that passed, and she saw, to her horror, that the wood was already starting to turn dark and wet from the spreading pools of her blood.

Lindiwe gulped in air, opened her mouth wide, and screamed. Screamed as loud as she could. Screamed for Veli, screamed for her life.

But no sound came out. The shock had rendered her voiceless.

She stared past the man towards the door, praying that she would see her youngest nephew arriving with the uniformed guard behind him.

But the doorway was empty. Nobody was there.

Lindiwe managed to raise her head and met his eyes. Dark, pitiless, inscrutable. He reached out a hand and Lindiwe gasped as his knotted fingers stroked, then pinched, her cheek.

Was he smiling?

No. His face had tightened in the same way it had done on their first meeting, and he snatched his hand away.

Dark shapes loomed at the edges of her vision and spread inwards. Sweat started to pour down her body, and she was hit by an overwhelming wave of nausea. She slumped forward as the blackness suddenly grew huge, crowding out the room's four walls, but the movement caused one of her hands to push against the knife pinning it to the desk. The blinding pain that followed wrenched her back to full consciousness.

Abruptly, Lindiwe vomited down the front of her blouse. Retching and spitting, she stared up as her tormentor began to speak.

"Calling for help is useless," he said. "Your little friend with the tin whistle is . . . incapacitated. A precautionary move, and a prudent one, it seems, since you have not fulfilled your side of the bargain."

"I—I couldn't. Not my fault." Tears streamed from her eyes and she found she was shaking all over. She could hear her shoes drumming against the chair legs. She was struggling to keep her head upright, to keep her eyes off her hands. The blackness was still lurking at the corners of her vision, waiting to overwhelm her again, and the taste of bile was enough to make her gag.

"No. Not your fault, I agree." He was speaking to her as if they were having a friendly discussion, as if he hadn't just punched two knives through her living flesh. "But I still need your help. I need you to make things right."

He was smiling down at her now, a cruel, twisted grin.

"Yes," Lindiwe whispered, through lips that felt cold and numb. "Make it right."

"I need names."

"Names?" Her head was swimming.

"I need the names of the people you deal with. Your insiders, your contacts in Home Affairs." His smile hardened. "We are going to have to take this, as the saying goes, all the way to the top."

24

Back home, Jade found there wasn't a cupboard in the cottage large enough to house the bulky cardboard box. She transferred the contents into an old suitcase and put the box outside, where its presence wouldn't keep reminding her that, in terms of immediate family, she was now entirely alone.

She didn't know how long Moloi would spend with her client, but she guessed that he would take a while. The black detective was thorough, and Jade had a feeling that, despite her pleas for Pamela to cooperate, she would not be an easy interview.

Suddenly, Jade longed for David to be here, sitting at the kitchen table, so she could speak to him about the disturbing complexity of the job she'd taken on. No doubt David would respond with some typically irreverent comments, but he would also provide a valuable perspective on Pamela and her circumstances.

She reached for her cellphone, and before she could think too hard about what she was doing, she dialled David's number. He didn't answer immediately, and she hung up without leaving a message.

Successfully Resurrecting a Relationship by Jade de Jong. Definitely one of the shortest books ever written.

Jade wrapped a butternut in tinfoil and put it in the oven to roast. While it cooked, she did an hour of Pilates on the sitting-room floor and then had a quick shower. The exercise and the shower helped distract her from the unwelcome memory of the charred man's ribs moving ever so slowly in and out again as he lay slumped on the baking hot tiles.

By the time she went back into the kitchen, the butternut was smelling delicious. She took it out of the oven and put it on a large plate. She'd eat it with butter, salt and Tabasco. Difficult to think of a more perfectly rounded, nutritious meal.

She just wished she felt hungry enough to do it justice.

As she unwrapped the tinfoil, her phone started ringing. She snatched it up, hoping that this meant Pamela's interview was over. A glance at the screen showed that it was David, and her stomach did another of those annoying lurches.

"Hi. I called you earlier because——"

David interrupted her. "Open up, Jadey. I'm at your gate. Or rather, I will be in a sec. I'm halfway down your road now."

"You've come back?" Trying to keep the delight out of her voice, Jade retrieved her gate buzzer from the hook on the wall.

"Yup."

"Why didn't you hoot like you usually do?"

"Because I'm trying to be more civilised. If that bloody dog's there, tell it not to bite me, okay?"

"Bonnie is back home where she belongs." Jade couldn't suppress a smile as she squinted into the darkening gloom, making sure that there was nobody else waiting outside.

David's headlights swept towards her as he drove through the gate, dazzling her with their bright beams. He climbed out of the car carrying two brown paper bags, and hurried over to the cottage.

"I brought us supper. Proper food. Curry takeaways from Raj. I got you that fish one you like, extra hot."

"Thanks."

A peck on the cheek. She felt the prickle of his stubble.

Jade got David a plate and some cutlery and set a place for him at the kitchen table. She rewrapped the butternut in its tinfoil and put it on the counter to cool. Tomorrow night's dinner, perhaps.

"I got a phone call from a lady in Richards Bay this afternoon," David said. "I thought I'd better come and tell you about it."

Jade turned and stared at him.

"You drove all this way to tell me about a phone call?"

"Yup." David nodded, keeping his gaze fixed on the takeaway dishes he'd set out in front of him.

Jade was certain he wasn't telling the whole truth. Most likely he hadn't wanted to go back to his empty house with a lonely meal for one, to be bolted down in a few bites while leaning over the kitchen sink or slumped on the sofa staring at the television. She knew that was what David did when he was home alone.

"What about the phone call?"

"It was a bit odd." Now he looked up at her. "The lady who phoned . . . she's retired now, but she was a nurse at the hospital where you were born and where your mother died."

"Oh," Jade said. She realised she didn't even know the name of the hospital. No point in asking now.

"She was put through to me after being shunted around practically every department in Jo'burg Central Police Station. By that stage she was rather upset. She'd phoned looking for your father, and she'd just been told that he'd died more than ten years ago."

Jade poured herself a glass of wine and opened a beer for David. His favourites were Windhoek and Black Label, and even though he'd moved away, she hadn't been able to stop herself from keeping a six-pack of each in the fridge. She handed a Windhoek to him with an enquiring look.

"Thanks. So anyway, she said that someone was asking about your parents recently. Asking questions about your mother, at the hospital down in Richards Bay. Wanting to know where you were now."

Jade frowned, feeling a chill in her stomach that she recognised as the beginnings of unease. "Who was asking?"

David shrugged. "I've no idea, Jadey. I got the news third-hand, by pure coincidence. From the retired nurse who'd heard it from a matron at the hospital. I've no idea who was doing the asking. I thought you might know. Anybody contacted you out of the blue recently?"

"No."

"Well, keep your eyes and ears open," David advised.

"I will." Jade put the wine back in the fridge.

"Oh, and I've got a message for you from Moloi," he added. "He said he's arrested Pamela. He's keeping her in the holding cells overnight."

Jade spun round to face him, her disquiet at his earlier news forgotten. "What? Why the hell is Moloi doing that? And why couldn't he pick up the phone and tell me himself? He knows I'm guarding her."

David shrugged. "I saw him in the parking lot as I was leaving. I'm sure he would have phoned you otherwise. Seems Mad

Pammie wasn't too cooperative. In fact, from what I can gather, she threw a hissy fit when Moloi started questioning her. She tried to march out of the interview room and then she started demanding a lawyer. So he locked her up. Said she needed to cool off, and he also said something about her being a suspect now. What's the story there?"

Jade's annoyance at Moloi's behaviour suddenly seemed trivial compared to what she had seen at Pamela's house earlier. She sat down opposite David and told him exactly what had happened that afternoon.

"Jesus, Jade. Hubby tortured and mistress found dead, and on the premises too? And Pamela had cancelled the security guards? It's not looking good for her now."

Jade shook her head. "It isn't. She also fired her live-in domestic worker, which I'm now thinking was probably for the same reason. And there was no sign of forced entry when I arrived."

"So you reckon she paid this Naude to do it?"

"It's looking that way, isn't it? I mean, she denied knowing him, but he had keys to the house, and he'd left messages on the phone in her study."

"Then why would he have tried to shoot her the next day?"

Jade shrugged. "Maybe he was panicking. Trying to cover his tracks. Look at this."

She took her jacket off the back of the chair and showed David the bullet-holes.

"Bloody hell," he said. He put his beer down on the table and examined the damaged fabric, shaking his head. As Jade had done earlier, he poked at the two neat holes.

"That was a close call, all right." He looked up at her, but she couldn't read the expression in his eyes.

"He nearly got lucky, that's all." Jade didn't want to think about the corollary—that she had nearly got unlucky.

She took the jacket to her bedroom and tossed it on the bed. Perhaps she would take it to the dry-cleaners and get the holes repaired. More likely, though, she'd end up throwing it away. It was a cheap garment, and far from new.

When she returned, she saw David had recovered well from the shock of her near miss and was prying the lids off the takeaway containers. She noticed he had got himself chicken korma. An odd choice for meat-loving David, she thought.

He scooped a mountain of rice onto his plate and tipped the contents of his curry container over it.

"If Terence survives, they'll be able to question him. He must have seen the person who tortured him," David said.

"I don't think he'll make it, David. And even if he does, he has no tongue left, no eyes, and I doubt very much whether he will have any hands, because that wire was so tight that they were black and swollen from the wrists up. So questioning him is going to be a long process."

"He'd had a coal put right inside his mouth, you say?"

"Right inside."

"How the hell do you force anybody to open wide for that?"

Jade shook her head. "I don't know. And I don't want to think about it."

She stirred her curry, breathing in the aroma of chilli and coriander. David had generously left her a quarter of a container of rice, and she knew that if she wanted any of it, she'd better get to it fast before he finished his plate and started looking around for more. She felt sick whenever she remembered Terence, and she could easily have gone without eating at all. But David had brought it for her, so she tipped it out and spooned sauce over it.

David was nearly halfway through his overloaded plate, shovelling chicken pieces into his mouth as if attempting to break some kind of speed-eating record.

"Seems like two completely different modus operandi, though," he said through a large mouthful of food. "The two incidents, I mean."

"I agree. That's what's confusing me. Whoever tortured Terence knew what they were doing. But Pamela's attempted murder was a different setup. Amateurish. A drive-by shooting like that, in broad daylight, from a motorbike. It was hardly guaranteed to succeed. I mean, if I'd been . . ."

Jade put down her cutlery and sipped her wine, trying to cover her confusion. Idiot, she chastised herself. She was about to say— if she'd been going to do a job like that, she would have done it differently.

Not the most intelligent thing to say to David, given their current situation.

Thinking fast, she continued. "If I'd been quicker to grab the wheel, I could have knocked him off his bike. Even if he'd killed Pamela, there was no guarantee he'd have got away without being injured."

David nodded in agreement. Then he reached across the table and hooked a finger over the top of the rice tub. Tilting it towards him, he seemed surprised to find that it was empty.

"There's half a container of fish curry left, if you're still hungry. I can cook you some rice," Jade said.

David considered her offer. "Thanks, but no thanks. Extra hot is too damn fiery for me. I might be half Indian, but I can't eat a decent curry without regretting it for the next two days."

"So perhaps only your top half is Indian." Jade said, drawing an imaginary line across her own midriff with her hand, surprised to find herself smiling in amusement at the thought. "And the bottom half—"

"Isn't." David finished for her, looking slightly embarrassed.

"Well then, all I can offer you is some baked butternut."

"I'll pass on that too, thanks." He clapped a hand over his stomach.

"Middle-age spread's setting in. Got to start fighting it, Jadey." He grinned at her and his grey eyes sparkled with mischief. "You run, I diet. Looking at both of us, I'd say your regime is a hundred per cent more successful."

Taken aback by the unexpected compliment, Jade changed the subject.

"What are you doing after this?"

"After this?" David glanced at his watch and back up at her. His smile disappeared, replaced by a dubious frown. "Er . . . I'm, er . . ."

Too late, Jade realised he'd misinterpreted her question as an invitation. And now he was looking for a polite way to tell her that no, he didn't want to spend the night.

Before Jade could explain, David spoke, sounding relieved.

"I'll probably go back to work. I've got a stack of info coming through from detectives in London who need our help with a trafficking case." He pushed his chair back, stacked their empty plates, and carried them over to the sink.

"That's a shame," Jade continued. "Because I was going to ask if you wanted to go somewhere with me."

"What, now?" David spoke over the sound of splashing water.

"Yes."

"Where?"

"Heads & Tails."

"Terence Jordaan's strip club?" He turned to stare at her, sponge scourer in hand.

"Yes."

"Why d'you want to go there?"

Jade shrugged. "Curiosity. I'd like to get a feel for the place. To see what's going on there now, and whether the operation is still as squeaky clean as Captain Thembi said it was."

David slotted the plates into the drying rack and wiped his hands with the dish towel.

"It's been a while since that last report of Thembi's was made," he said almost to himself. "Might be a good idea to visit the place, since it is on our watch list."

Jade didn't reply, just waited for him to make a firm decision.

It didn't take too long.

"All right, then," David said, sounding decidedly more cheerful than he had done at the prospect of going back to work. "I'll come along with you."

"Give me a minute to dry my hair," Jade said, aware that it was hanging in damp, unstylish locks around her face.

"I'll wait in the car." David strode towards the kitchen door. Preoccupied with his thoughts, he hit his head on the lintel. It made a dull, thudding noise.

"Ouch," he said. "Shithouse!"

Rubbing his forehead, David walked outside and pulled the door closed behind him.

25

Eunice Nkosi's phone rang at half past eight that evening while she was helping her daughter with her maths homework. She picked up the cellphone, saw the number was withheld, and rejected the call. Probably some irritating telesales person on the night shift. And no, she didn't want to listen to some earnest soul from New Delhi gabbling about the benefits of an accident insurance plan she couldn't afford.

She turned back to the textbook, squinting down at the geometry figures, battling to assimilate the logic behind the rules so that she could help her child. Those two angles were equal—the curved line across them indicated that. So then, that angle opposite the first one . . .

The phone started to ring again.

Not a telesales caller, then—they didn't ring twice. Something urgent, perhaps? A relative, her mother?

Sighing, Eunice answered. "Yes?"

"Eunice Nkosi?"

She frowned. The male voice on the other end was unfamiliar.

"Speaking," she said, more cautiously now, worried about who the caller might be and aware that the distraction had sent the geometry solution right out of her mind, just as she had been about to grasp it.

"You have disappointed me," he said.

Eunice realised she was gaping in surprise. Disappointed how? Her first ludicrous thought was that this was something to do with her daughter's schoolwork.

"How do you mean?"

A chilly laugh. "I think you understand exactly what I mean."

She didn't have a clue—but then, suddenly, she did. A dreadful suspicion began to surface in her mind.

"Who are you? How did you get my number?" she stammered.

"Ask your Zimbabwean friend," he said. "She was very helpful when I asked her for information earlier this evening. In fact, I had difficulty making her stop talking."

"I . . . but . . ." Eunice suddenly felt deathly cold. There was no way that Lindiwe would have given out Eunice's cellphone number. Not unless she'd been forced to.

The man continued. "She told me that you could not get my passports today, but I cannot wait. I need you to organise the documents for me first thing tomorrow."

"But I can't! That's what I told Lindiwe this afternoon. Our new department manager—"

"You will find the necessary photographs in an envelope in your post box," the man continued, as if she hadn't even spoken.

Her spine contracted. "What do you mean? What post box?" For some reason, the image of her pigeon-hole at work came to her.

Troubled by the tone of her mother's voice, her daughter looked up at her anxiously.

"Mummy, what . . . ?"

Clamping a hand over the mouthpiece, with an angry frown at her daughter and a finger of the other hand on her lips in warning, praying that the caller hadn't heard her small voice, Eunice stood up. Stumbling and nearly falling over the chair in her haste, she turned and hurried out of the dining room.

"What do you mean?" she asked again. She could hear the tremor in her own voice.

"In the box on your gate. The blue one."

Oh, Lord, no.

It was fully dark, but the street lamp near her house offered some light. Peering out of the lounge window, she could see the shadowy outline of the post box attached to her gatepost. He knew what colour it was. That meant Lindiwe had told him where she lived.

Eunice squinted into the shadows, but couldn't see anyone at the gate, or any cars on the road outside. Even so, he had been here. She gripped the phone harder, with a sudden surge of anger. How dare Lindiwe give this man her home address.

"You'll find your payment there, too," the man said in the same dry, emotionless tone.

Then he hung up.

"Mummy?" the young girl said again, her voice anxious.

"Stay where you are, darling," Eunice said, trying her best to sound reassuring. She hurried back into the dining room and pulled the curtains tightly closed.

Taking a deep breath, she opened the front door and stepped onto the short path that led to the gate. A low gate, useless against intruders, which was why Eunice had installed industrial-grade burglar bars on all the windows, and a sliding security door on the front and back entrances.

A rustle in the flowerbed made her jump and she spun towards the sound, stifling a cry. It was only the neighbour's cat, who used the soft earth as a toilet and, Eunice was sure, was the reason why nothing grew well there.

For once, she didn't shoo the cat away. He stared at her, eyes bright in the dim light, looking oddly disappointed that tonight she wasn't playing her usual game with him.

A fat, brown manila envelope was protruding from the post box. She wrestled it out, hearing a small ripping noise as its side caught on the narrow, steel rim.

The envelope was heavy and strangely bulky. Holding it tightly, Eunice hurried back towards the house. She slid the Trellidor across the doorway, listening to the reassuring snick as the double lock sprang into place. Then she slammed the front door, realising her breathing sounded as if she'd just run round the block.

She couldn't open the envelope in front of her daughter—children notice, children talk—so she took it into the kitchen. Glancing into the dining room as she passed, she saw the little girl was focused on her textbook and chewing her pencil.

She slid a knife under the envelope flap and slit it open, then carefully removed the smaller, slimmer window envelope with the photos inside.

Eunice raised her head when she heard a soft noise coming from the direction of her bedroom. The damn cat must have sneaked inside while her back was turned. Well, he'd have to stay where he was for now, because she was too busy to chase him round the house and throw him out.

At the bottom of the manila envelope, she found a small, black plastic bag containing an oddly shaped object.

Was this the payment? There certainly wasn't any cash inside.

Eunice felt her heart speed up again as she took the bag out, because her first crazy thought was that it was drugs, that the man had paid her with a chunk of cocaine or a few baggies of dagga, that it was a setup and the drugs squad was now closing in on her house.

She slid her hand into the bag and touched the strange object. It felt cool and soft and oddly familiar.

Rethinking her approach, she upended the bag onto the kitchen counter.

Two severed fingers tumbled out and rolled onto the Formica, curled up like the legs of a dead house spider.

The skin was black, the nails neatly manicured. Protruding from one of the raw ends, Eunice could see a jagged piece of bone. With a lurch, she realised she recognised the enormous rings on each one. They were real diamonds, her friend had told her proudly. Valuable diamond rings.

Oh Jesus, he'd cut off Lindiwe's fingers.

Open-mouthed, panting hard, Eunice felt the scream building up inside her. A scream of pure horror, from somewhere deep inside her soul.

Somewhere along its journey, the sound morphed into a low, dreadful groan. Eunice turned away and leaned over the kitchen sink, gagging and spitting as the contents of her stomach rose up in her throat. Dear God, somehow she was going to have to pick up those fingers again and put them back in the bag, or risk her little one seeing them.

The thought of touching them made her retch again and she grasped the steel rim of the sink for support, gasping for air.

After a while, she turned on the tap and splashed her face with cold water. Now that her panic had subsided, although she was still terrified, she felt able to think more clearly.

Eunice wasn't stupid. She'd had a contingency plan in place for a long time now, to be put into action if the worst happened, even though she hadn't had any idea what the worst could be.

Now she knew.

Despite the potential consequences, Eunice wasn't going to cooperate. First, and most importantly, she was going to get in her car and drive herself and her daughter somewhere safe. Her ex-husband lived on the other side of Pretoria, in Moreleta Park, and they were still on good terms. Good enough terms, anyway, that she knew he would be prepared to take them in for the night.

Then she was going to call the police and blow the whistle on the syndicate. She'd lose her job, but if she gave the police the names of the other syndicate members, she hoped she'd avoid a lengthy prison sentence.

She was going to turn state witness. She was going to ask the police to protect her and her daughter, even if it meant spending the rest of her life under house arrest.

"Sweetie?" She called her daughter, surprised at how steady her voice sounded. "I need you to pack up your homework and put some clothes in a bag. And your toothbrush, and your jammies. We're going to see Daddy."

She wrapped a tea towel around her right hand. Then, half-closing her eyes and gritting her teeth, she managed to poke Lindiwe's severed fingers back into their little bag.

Eunice hurried down the short passage to her bedroom to pack an overnight bag for herself. She still felt sick, and she was shaking so badly she hoped she would be able to drive.

She would just have to manage. If she did, then in an hour they would be safe. And although her life was about to change for the worse, in a way it would be a relief not to have to keep on looking over her shoulder at work anymore.

Her bedroom was dark. As Eunice fumbled for the light switch, the shadows in the corner of the room seemed to shift. The next moment, a cold hand yanked her forward and another clamped itself roughly over her mouth. Her legs turned to jelly as she felt the prick of a sharp blade at her neck. As she tried to twist away from the pain, pinned by her invisible captor, she heard a fast, rough, snuffling noise that she suddenly realised she was making as she fought for air.

154 • JASSY MACKENZIE

"Have you forgotten you have a job to do, Eunice?" The man's voice hissed in her ear. His breath smelled rank, rotten. "One last job, before you run away."

Eunice froze, unable to reply, terrified to do so much as nod.

"Your little girl would not want you to let me down. I promise you that."

Then he coughed. His wiry body convulsed against hers and the action drove the blade deeper into her skin. Something warm and liquid landed on Eunice's sleeve and for a horror-filled moment she thought he'd sliced an artery open, sentencing her to a swift and bloody death.

Then, as he turned her roughly round and pushed her down the passage ahead of him, she saw another crimson gob on her shoulder. Had her captor coughed up the blood?

That thought stopped her in her tracks, but he shoved her forward again.

With the blade jabbing at her throat and his fingers crushing her lips against her teeth, Eunice stumbled towards the brightly lit dining room where she knew her child would be busy packing her homework away. All she could think, through her haze of panic, was that, if he allowed her to speak again, she was going to start begging.

Don't hurt my little girl. I will do whatever you want me to. And, dear God, please don't use your knife on me.

26

Jade hadn't been into Midrand for a while, so she was surprised to see a huge concrete flyover had sprung up, seemingly overnight, next to the main road. David told her it was part of the new Gautrain network.

Heads & Tails was in a small shopping centre just opposite the entrance to the Randjesfontein racehorse-training complex. Jade guessed that its location was only too convenient for the trainers and owners in the male-dominated world of racing.

A massive sign was lit up by pink and blue neon lights, the ampersand cleverly manipulated to look like the silhouette of a naked woman bending over. A security guard manned the gateway, and beyond it a large car park was already three-quarters full.

Three Mercedes Benz minibuses were parked next to the gate, all with tinted windows. Two of them were custom-painted in red and gold with the naked female logo on the side and the legend "Heads & Tails—Mobile Entertainment."

The third was plain white. Waiting for a paint job, perhaps? Or, more probably, used for those events where it would not be wise to arrive in a vehicle loudly advertising exotic dancers.

David parked, muttering something about people milking cash cows.

They made their way to the entrance, following a man who walked rather furtively inside after glancing behind him as if expecting people to be looking on in disapproval.

At the door a blank-faced receptionist dressed in bunny ears and a low-cut black jacket asked them for a surprisingly hefty cover charge.

"That'll keep the riff-raff out," David said.

Looking at the bouncer standing with his back to the wall, Jade guessed he'd do an even better job of keeping unwanted guests away. The man's shoulders were so massive and bull-like that she thought he must have to turn sideways to get through doorways. He was dressed in black from head to toe, with a shaven head, a bleached goatee and narrowed, aggressive eyes.

She insisted on paying for both of them. After all, she wasn't exactly short of cash, thanks to Pamela.

They walked through a metal detector and were patted down: David by a large, unsmiling man and Jade by an equally humourless woman. Then a blonde hostess dressed in six-inch stiletto-heeled boots, shiny tights and matching red hotpants and bikini top escorted them down the well-lit passage.

"Welcome to Heads & Tails," she said. Her tone was friendly and her smile welcoming, but her greeting was directed only at David. Her eyes flicked over Jade as if she didn't exist. From the thick sound of her accent, Jade thought she might recently have taken the bus from one of the small Afrikaans-speaking towns on the platteland. A pretty girl, rebelling against the confines of her sheltered rural life and leaving to seek her fortune here in the big, bad city of gold.

The main seating area was huge, with ranks of tables arranged in a giant semi-circle around a raised stage. The tables were occupied mostly by men, and a surprising proportion of them were on their own.

The lighting was subdued in a dull, reddish, slightly shabby way, and a Beyoncé song was playing at a volume just too loud to allow for comfortable conversation. The table the blonde hostess showed them to, flanked by two leather armchairs, was small but sturdy. Thick wooden legs, a firm top, not a hint of a wobble. Jade could see why, because next door to them a long-haired woman in black lacy underwear and impossibly high heels was preparing for a table dance. At least Jade supposed that was why a uniformed cleaning lady had removed all the bottles and glasses, and was spraying the table's surface with disinfectant.

In the meantime, the dancer sat on the customer's lap with her arms around his neck.

"Isn't there a no-touching rule in these places?" she asked David.

"Applies to the customers only, I guess," he said. "Not the dancers. They need to work the guys, get them excited, persuade them to shell out for the extras."

Jade watched the woman step onto the table and crouch open-legged, slowly easing her bra straps off her shoulder, rotating her hips from side to side in time to the music.

The man on the sofa was spellbound. He was so intent on the dancer that Jade was sure he wouldn't notice if the building started falling down.

"You're not supposed to watch another table's show," David shouted, pulling his chair closer to hers. "It's considered bad etiquette."

"How do you know?" Jade retorted. "I thought you'd never been to one of these places."

David grinned. "I told you I'd done raids back in Durban. Some of the customers used to get quite chatty while I was taking down their details."

A waitress in a similar black outfit and bunny ears handed them menus. Jade went for a sparkling water and David, after some deliberation, ordered a Coke.

Boy, did they know how to party.

"What else did the customers tell you?" Jade asked.

"They vehemently denied having sex with any of the ladies."

"Were they telling the truth? Or was it a case of protesting too much?"

"In some of the places I raided back then, it definitely wasn't the truth. But this strip club doesn't look like it's set up for sex on the side. I don't know how it used to be, but I guess Terence must have cleaned up his act after his arrest."

"How would you know the difference?"

"Look around you."

Jade surveyed the gigantic room. The dancer next door to them was completely naked now. She was sitting on the table with her legs splayed, an ankle on each of her customer's shoulders. He seemed to be enjoying the view. On the big stage three dancers in skimpy red and gold outfits were performing a sequence that, predictably enough, involved taking their clothes off. To her left was the entrance to a passage. According to the neon sign above it, this was the Tunnel of Pleasure.

Down the corridor she could see a number of booths with glass sides with clear and frosted stripes on them and plastic curtains in front. Another large, grim-looking bouncer stood near the booths. Jade watched a dancer leading a rather dazed-looking man by the hand past the bouncer and into one of the booths. Then the dancer closed the curtain and the pair disappeared from view.

"There." David pointed in the direction of her gaze. "That's what makes me think that sex isn't on the menu at a place like this."

"Why?"

"Because you can see what's going on. Not everything, of course, but you can see enough to know what's happening through those strips of clear glass on the sides. That means the girl can't offer any extras, and more importantly, the man can't take advantage. That happens a lot more often than the ladies offering sex, I've been told."

"Rape? Inside those booths?"

"Not inside those. But you get other places that have booths with solid walls. Some of them even have lockable doors. When I used to raid these joints, those were a clear warning sign. Inside those rooms anything could be going on, and probably was."

"What about the dancers meeting up with the men after hours? That must happen."

David nodded. "Yup. I think it happens from time to time. But it's strongly discouraged, of course. And these dancers earn good money, Jadey. They don't need to supplement their income and, trust me, they don't want to lose their jobs."

"Shagging the owner doesn't count, I suppose."

David's face lit up as he smiled. "That probably counts in their favour."

"Where do they come from?" Jade asked, glancing around the room again.

David shrugged. "The waitress sounded Eastern European, so I should check if she has a permit to work here. That girl at the door was definitely Afrikaans. And there's one black dancer there, on the stage."

"Sorry," Jade said. "I didn't mean it literally. I meant how do they find such particular types of woman to work here? They're all young, good-looking, with long hair and good bodies and big breasts. Like clones, Stepford wives. Or, in this case, Stepford strippers."

"The breasts aren't real."

"Did the customers tell you that, too?" Jade asked slyly.

David's grin widened and he shook his head.

"I guess it's the money," Jade said. "I see what you're saying. If I wasn't rigidly obeying strip-club etiquette, I'd tell you to look over there, at that table in the corner. Those are hundred-rand notes those guys are sticking into that woman's G-string."

"A lot of money moves around here. That's for sure."

Jade stabbed with the straw at the slice of lemon in her sparkling water, thinking of the sportscars gleaming in the garages at Pamela's Sandown home.

"Do you think money was the reason for torturing Terence?"

The song ended, and her words sounded oddly loud in the brief moment of quietness.

"I dunno," David said. "We'd have to answer the question your dad always told me to ask. Who benefits?"

Jade sighed. "Pamela benefits. That's the problem."

Scattered applause signalled that the dance on the stage was finished. The girls left through a curtained side exit, carrying their discarded outfits bunched up in their hands, their heads held high and their taut buttocks twitching as they walked.

A minute later, Jade spotted them again, exiting through a side door into a corridor that she now saw led to the Ladies' room. They'd already put their costumes on again. A reverse-Houdini act behind the curtain, she supposed.

"Where are you off to?" David asked as she pushed her chair back.

"I'm going to see if I can have a chat."

She walked towards the exit, aware that a number of men had turned to watch her go. In a place like this, she guessed any woman was fair game. Even if they were wearing tightly belted blue jeans and hadn't spent as long on their hair as they should have done.

She pushed open the squeaky door of the Ladies' room. The tang of soap and disinfectant filled the small space. There was no sign of the dancers. Only one cubicle was occupied, and as she watched, a waitress made a hurried exit.

Jade glanced at herself in the mirror as she followed the waitress out, noticing that she seemed to have aged alarmingly in the unforgiving glare of the fluorescent ceiling light.

The door squeaked again as it closed behind her.

Where had the dancers gone?

Turning away from the main hall, where she could hear the throbbing disco blare of yet another Beyoncé song starting up, she headed in the other direction. The door at the end of the corridor stood ajar. The smell of cigarette smoke wafted towards her, and she could hear low voices.

She walked outside, and the three dancers fell silent and turned as one to look at her, glowing cigarettes held in their French-manicured fingers.

They stood in a small yard under a bright outside light. The unglamorous backside of Heads & Tails. Uneven paving, a low brick wall doing a bad job of concealing a jumbled array of dust-bins, and a steel grating covering a foul-smelling drain.

Up close, and in this glaring light, illusions were also stripped away. She could see crow's feet around the nearest girl's eyes, fine lines around her mouth, a darker strip along the roots of her blonde hair. Her make-up was heavy, her tan a fake bronze.

"Hello, ladies," Jade said neutrally.

They stared back at her, their gazes suspicious and far from friendly.

"Hi," the blonde said. She drew deeply on her cigarette, pucker-ing her lips around the filter in a way that Jade guessed would have instantly doubled her tips, had any men been watching.

"I was hoping to have a chat with one of you. You see, my boyfriend and I came here to see what this place is all about." Her first words, and she was already telling lies. David, her boyfriend? If only.

The blonde said nothing in reply; just watched her.

"My younger sister is thinking of applying for a job here." Another lie. And the wrong thing to say, she knew that immedi-ately. The girls all stiffened and exchanged glances. The blonde flashed another look at her—a quick up-and-down assessment. Was Jade's younger sister going to prove to be a threat?

"Jobs here are not easy to get," the blonde snapped.

The brunette standing opposite her, a tall, willowy girl with multiple piercings in her ears, shook her head in agreement. "They're not looking for dancers at the moment. She can come in for an interview, but I'm telling you, the chances aren't good.

Especially this time of year. It's winter in Europe now, and there'll be a lot of girls from over there coming to work the summer season here. Does your sister have any experience?"

"No."

"Then definitely not," the blonde said emphatically. "Tammy only hires experienced girls." She adjusted a strap on her tiny outfit. The night was still warm enough for her to be comfortable standing outside wearing virtually nothing. God knows what they did in winter.

"Tammy?" Jade asked.

"Tammy Jordaan. The owner's daughter. She runs this branch. She makes all the decisions. You see, this place is the top of the range."

"Safe," the brunette nodded. "And upmarket."

"That too," the blonde said. She dropped her smouldering cigarette butt onto the tiles and crushed it with the tip of her stiletto-heeled shoe. "Clean. No rough types. No fights. And strict rules. You're not asked to do anything except dance. Most other places, the girls have to do a lot more than that."

"Where's the owner?" Jade asked.

The blonde shrugged. "In and out. He's busy opening a new branch in Fourways."

She didn't know what had happened to Terence, that was clear to Jade.

"I've heard stories about the bosses at these places dating the workers," Jade said. "Is that a problem here?"

The blonde exchanged another glance with her friends.

"Not really," she said.

"There's Crystal, though." The words were spoken by the black woman standing in the shadows, who until then had remained silent.

The brunette glared at her. "That's different," she said. "They're, like, an item, know. That's not the same as messing around."

"Anyway, back to work, I guess." The blonde gave her a tight smile, and made as if to move past her.

"Thanks for your help . . ." Jade gave her a questioning glance.

"Opal's my name."

A stage name, Jade assumed.

The brunette smoothed her hair back. "Amber," she said.

"I am Ebony," the black dancer offered.

Crystal, Opal, Amber and Ebony.

She'd always wondered what her own name would be useful for, and now, at last, she knew.

"Pleased to meet you all," she said. "I'm Jade."

27

"I think there's something wrong with me," David said, when she returned. He was sitting in solitary splendour, glancing from time to time in the direction of the Ladies' room.

"Why?"

"Nobody's come near me since you left. Nobody's even looked in my direction. The dancers are draping themselves over all the other customers like wet rags."

"What about the waitress?" Jade asked. "Did you ask her if she was legal?"

"She hasn't been back. Not even to find out if I want another drink." He indicated his empty glass. "I don't want a drink, I want to get the bloody bill. And I can't get the bloody bill if nobody will look at me."

"More strip-club etiquette, I should imagine." Jade drained her water. "If a man arrives with a woman, do not pay him any attention while she is absent from the table, or you will get your eyes gouged out when she returns." She waved a hand to summon the waitress.

Jade scrabbled in her wallet for cash while David produced his police ID and asked the young woman if she was working here legally.

"Oh, yes," she replied, smiling. "I have lived here for seven years now. I am a South African citizen. Nobody gets employed here unless they have a valid South African identity, or else a proper work permit. You are welcome to check with our admin office."

She waved a hand in the general direction of the exit door.

"Right, then." Pre-empting Jade's attempts to pay, David slid a twenty-rand note and a handful of silver into the leather folder that the waitress had brought. "Are we finished here?"

As they left, Jade saw the waitress quickly prepare the table for the small group of men waiting at the bar. The place was packed full now, loud and pumping. They walked back down the corridor, past the bouncer at the door, and headed for the car.

"Did you get any useful information?" David asked.

"There don't seem to be any dodgy extramural activities going on at all. The girls were very clear about that, and I believe them. Everything is above board, just like you thought."

Jade waited for David to unlock the passenger door for her. He'd explained earlier that this unmarked had a problem with the central locking and that the passenger door wouldn't open from the inside.

As he fumbled with the key in the lock, she heard the light tap of footsteps behind them and a voice called out, "Jade?"

Surprised, she turned to see Ebony, the black dancer, coming across the car park. She'd changed out of her skimpy red outfit into fleecy tracksuit bottoms and a white tank top. She had a gym bag slung over her shoulder and was dangling a bunch of car keys in her hand.

"I've had an idea about your sister."

"Your sis— oof." David's surprised interjection was cut short by Jade elbowing him in the stomach.

"Thanks for coming to find me," Jade said. Away from the other two dancers, Ebony seemed friendlier.

"Actually I'm on my way home," she explained. "I was on early shift today. I should have gone an hour ago, except I was covering an extra dance for Crystal."

Better get ready for more overtime then, Jade thought.

"What advice have you got for my sister?" she asked.

"Well, I've got two suggestions. The first is to do what I did. She could become a waitress and work her way up. It's just that most girls don't want to go that route because the money's not as good and the job's . . . different. A lot of the waitresses prefer not to do what we do." She smiled.

"And the other way?"

"There's a guy who used to work here as a bouncer a few years ago. He's got connections in the industry, I think, because I know Tammy has sent girls to him to look for work when they applied for jobs here and we were full. I can give you his number, if you like."

"That would be great," Jade said. She took her notebook out of her bag, flipped through it until she found a fresh page, and handed it over.

Ebony scrolled through her cellphone's directory. "I haven't spoken to him for a while, but this number should still work."

She wrote it down and handed it back to Jade.

"You know, a lot of people think that we're nothing but prostitutes. That's why they disapprove of what we do." She smiled again, a friendly smile. "I've told my family I'm a croupier at a private club. That way they can't try and visit me at work, and it explains my hours. It's ridiculous when you think about it. Here we are, earning good money, we're not doing any harm to anybody, nothing illegal. It's just a tease, just a bit of fun. We're acting out a fantasy, Tammy says. Like in Hollywood."

David made a grunting noise that could have been interpreted as agreement.

"I understand, I really do," Jade said.

"I think it's cool that you're trying to help your sister. That's why I want to try and help you. There's a huge demand for jobs at the moment, so maybe this will work better for her. And you just keep on supporting her, okay? You won't ever know how much it means to have family who understand."

She squeezed Jade's arm before turning and walking towards a smart black Alfa Spider parked nearby.

Jade didn't see Ebony get into her car. She was too busy staring down at the name and number the dancer had given her. Staring at it in complete confusion. She was so astounded by what she saw that she almost forgot to breathe.

On the slip of paper, in neat and legible handwriting, was a Vodacom cellphone number.

And below that, a single name.

Naude.

28

"It's the man who shot at Pamela," Jade said. "I'm sure of it."

They were driving back towards Kyalami. At David's speed, the twenty-minute drive would only take ten. Fuelled by the adrenaline that had surged through her when she'd seen Naude's name on the feint-lined notebook page, Jade was confident she would manage to get through the journey without grabbing hold of the dashboard, in spite of David's disconcerting habit of maintaining unbroken eye contact with her whenever either of them spoke.

"There are plenty of people called Naude," David said. The words were deliberately matter-of-fact, but his tone was not. He couldn't keep the excitement out of his voice.

Jade had wanted to storm straight back into the building, to question the receptionist and demand access to the office records and look up the man's details.

Impossible, of course. She didn't have any authority to act at all. It was Moloi's case, and all she could do was pass the phone number on to him and let him take it further.

David looked across at her and the unmarked began to stray over the white line in the centre of the road. Cats' eyes bumped under the right-hand tyres for a few seconds before the car drifted even further to the other side of the road. Jade tensed when she saw a pair of rapidly approaching headlights.

"Oncoming!" she yelled. She couldn't help it. Adrenaline only went so far. David corrected his course with a deft twist of the wheel, the approaching car shot past and Jade let out an audible sigh of relief.

"Naude might have instigated all of this," Jade added. "Perhaps he forced Pamela into cooperating with him."

"He might have done," David nodded thoughtfully as the

unmarked hurtled down the hill towards a green traffic light at what seemed like reckless speed.

Jade tried to force herself to relax. She told herself David had managed to get through more than twenty years of accident-free driving, so he could surely manage to survive just a little longer without ending up in a fatal collision.

Then the light turned amber and despite her best intentions, Jade found herself making a grab for the dashboard, even though the intersection was still a good distance away. David wasn't slowing down at all.

Was she going to warn him unnecessarily about a danger he must have noticed already?

Yes, she was.

"Light!" she called out, her hands moving up to grip the moulded plastic. David flattened his foot on the accelerator and hurtled through the intersection well after it had turned red.

"Chill, Jadey. There weren't any cars waiting," he said, slowing slightly to negotiate a bend before accelerating again. "This time of night, it's riskier to stop at a red light than it is to go through it." He grinned at her, his teeth white and even in his dark-skinned face.

"You're still thirty kilometres over the limit."

David shook his head. "Error of parallax."

"You're going to tell that to the Metro Police when they flag you down?"

"Nope. It's a scientifically proven fact. From where you're sitting on the left, the needle and the speedometer markings may look parallel with each other, but they aren't, so the needle appears further to the right than it really is."

Jade considered the logic for a moment.

"Not thirty kilometres further. No way."

"No," David agreed. "More like five or ten."

Jade punched him in the thigh.

The unmarked rattled and bounced as David headed down Jade's sandy road at a brisk pace. He flicked the headlights onto full beam, carefully scanning their surroundings as he skidded to a stop parallel to her gate. He waited while Jade buzzed it open with the remote control, and only then turned into the driveway itself and drove through. Then he braked again immediately and watched in the rear-view mirror until the gate was fully closed.

Exercising caution when arriving home after dark was standard practice in Jo'burg, but David was being even more watchful than usual. Jade guessed this was because of the phone call he'd told her about earlier. She wondered again who had been asking questions at the hospital in Richards Bay, trying to find out where she was now.

Had it been an old family friend? Or was it somebody who wanted to track Jade down, and had been asking questions about her mother as a smokescreen?

She didn't know, so she tried to push the thought out of her mind as David accelerated up the driveway.

As he parked close behind her car, she thought about the last time they'd come back home together so late. It had been at the beginning of winter, during an unseasonal and violent rainstorm. They'd stopped in just about the same spot they were in now. Then, while they waited for the worst of the downpour to abate, David had reached for her with his long, strong arm and pulled her towards him, a manoeuvre that had caused her seatbelt to lock and had made them both laugh. After undoing the belt he'd kissed her long and thoroughly, and she'd pressed herself against his solid chest, wound her arms around his shoulders, and kissed him back.

She couldn't remember how long they had spent in the cramped confines of the car, snogging like two love-struck teenagers. First, the only noise had been the drumming of the rain on the roof, but later she remembered the sound of David's breathing. The sounds he'd made, the words he had whispered to her. By the time the rain had stopped, the car's interior was so fogged up neither of them had noticed.

Jade had climbed out and breathed in the chilly, damp, night air. To her, it had tasted of freedom.

Thinking about that time now made her heart ache.

Damn it, she felt as if she were waging a desperate guerrilla war against a massive, well-equipped army. Although she had moved out, Naisha was still David's legally wedded wife and the mother of his child. She was a law-abiding career woman who would recoil from the crimes that Jade had committed.

There was every reason why David should go back to his wife, and none at all that she could think of why he should choose to be with her.

"Night, Jadey," David said. He grasped her shoulders and pulled her towards him and her thoughts suddenly went back to that rainy night. He was going to kiss her. Her heart sped up. Where might that lead?

Where indeed? To another snatched victory. Another single night to add to her modest store of memories. Another skirmish won on the sidelines while, on the main battlefield, the war raged on unchecked.

She took a deep breath, then reached up and removed David's hands from her shoulders. He stared at her, surprised. "That job I did last month," she said.

"Which one? That surveillance job for the IT company?"

"Yes, that one. Well, when I'd finished the work, Steve, the director, called and asked me out."

Silence. She couldn't even hear him breathing. Jade swallowed hard and continued. "I've been out with him twice. The second time was quite interesting. We met up at Emperor's Palace casino, had dinner, then took a walk through the place to see what was going on. There was a function on in one of the conference rooms—an awards ceremony for the South African Police Service. I saw you there with your wife. Of course, you're fully entitled to go with her anywhere you want, but you invited me to that ceremony back in June. Then you told me that it had been cancelled, and that you were going to be working late on that particular evening. Which means you lied to me."

She didn't dare look at him while she was speaking—she was too frightened of what she might see.

"I can't carry on living my life like this," she said, looking at his long-fingered hands which were now gripping the steering wheel. "It's not fair. Not fair to anyone—not to me, or you, or your wife." Jade couldn't bring herself to say her name out loud. "David, I know you have issues with who I am and what I've done, but you need to make up your mind, because as it stands, this situation is unworkable."

Now she looked directly at him and the pain she saw in his eyes made her want to cry.

"Jadey," he said in a soft voice, "maybe it's better that you go."

"Go?" Her voice was unexpectedly hoarse and she cleared her throat.

"Go out with Steve. Or whoever else. I think you're right. It'll be for the best. I can't ask you to put your life on hold indefinitely for a decision I don't know I'll be able to make."

"Okay. Well, 'night, then." Jade didn't trust herself to say anything more. She climbed out and slammed the door behind her. She didn't look back. She felt as if she'd just said a final good-bye to a part of her life she couldn't bear to lose.

Buzzing the gate open, she listened to the sound of David's car pull away and rattle off down the sand road.

Then she let herself into her empty cottage.

She'd tried to confront the army on the battlefield and her efforts had been met with a sweeping, instant defeat.

She should have stuck to the guerrilla tactics. One more night with David suddenly sounded like a sensible proposition. It sounded a thousand times better than what she was left with now.

"Well done, you idiot," she said aloud. Naturally, there was no reply.

Jade locked herself into her bedroom and climbed into her lonely bed.

29

Who was Mathilde Dupont's black accomplice?

That question had been preoccupying Edmonds ever since the raid. Hunting down a criminal was a challenge even when his identity was known to the police—Salimovic had been proving that with remarkable success so far.

So how to find this man, when all she had seen was a glimpse of his face through a tinted car window, and when the only description of him had been provided by an observant porter at the hotel where he had stayed?

"An oldish guy," the Australian porter had told her. "He was a bit shorter than me, so about five-eight, five-nine, I'd say. Very dark-skinned, and the couple of times I saw him he was wearing a suit. Oh, and totally bald."

In response to another series of questions from Edmonds, the young man had continued: "Nope. I didn't see any scars or anything like that. And he didn't speak to me. Just tipped me for carrying his bags."

The porter had looked down at his hands while he'd said that, and she had thought that perhaps he felt guilty about having profited from the proceeds of crime.

Following the movements of criminals in and out of the country was possible if their passports were flagged. If they weren't, it was a long and complicated procedure, especially if they did not require a visa to enter the UK.

Sometimes Edmonds wished that every human being could be micro-chipped. It might be a conspiracy theorist's worst nightmare, but it would make her job so much easier.

It had been Richards who'd suggested that the team take a look at the footage of the two CCTV cameras near the brothel. Luckily, they had caught Mathilde getting out of a taxi.

Edmonds was ashamed to admit that she wouldn't have thought of doing that. She preferred to get information from people—and she believed eyewitnesses were just as useful as security cameras. Slowly but surely, in interview after interview, she had pieced together what had happened after Mathilde and her black accomplice had fled from the brothel after the raid. They had returned to the hotel, where they had packed up and left before sunrise. They'd asked the Australian porter to book them a taxi to Terminal 1, Heathrow airport.

It had taken Edmonds hours of investigation in the terminal itself to establish what flights they had taken, and when she did she could have kicked herself.

Mathilde Dupont had not flown straight to South Africa, as she had assumed. As soon as the Croatia Airlines counter opened, she and her accomplice had paid cash for return tickets to Sarajevo—the same place where Salimovic had fled. They had never used the return. Instead, Dupont had gone on to Cape Town, and Edmonds guessed her accomplice must have done the same.

But now, at last, she could confirm her suspicions because she knew the black man's name. She was holding the photocopied page from the airline's passenger records in her hands.

Edmonds heard the sound of shoes on carpet and hurriedly lowered the A4 sheet which she'd been brandishing like a victory flag. She put it away in the folder with the rest of the growing paper trail.

When she looked up, Richards was leaning against the filing cabinet with a smile on his face. He had a waterproof jacket slung over his arm. From the drops of water she could see dripping off the dark fabric, Edmonds deduced that the weather outside, which had been miserable when she'd arrived early this morning, was getting worse.

"Hard at work?"

Edmonds nodded. "I'm finally getting some results on this case. I've just got an ID on Dupont's accomplice."

"That's good news." Richards' smile widened. He shook the jacket out and hung it on the coat hook.

"What's up with you?" Edmonds asked. "You're looking very pleased with yourself."

"So I should be. I got up early and went to gym. First time I've done that in a long while. Didn't even have time for a proper breakfast, because I went straight into a meeting for Operation Platypus." He glanced down and adjusted his navy-blue tie to cover a mark on his shirt that Edmonds thought looked suspiciously like an egg stain.

"I've got a lunch meeting with Crime Intelligence in just over an hour, which is a bit of a misnomer because those tight bastards never shell out for food. So, fancy grabbing a quick bite? Even canteen food is looking good now."

She was about to shake her head when Richards continued. "And I've got some good news for you, too. I'll tell you about it while we eat."

Edmonds put the other papers on her desk back into the folder slowly, one by one. She put the folder in the wonky desk drawer that she had discovered fell off its runners if it was opened too far. She pushed her chair back and stood up. And then, because she still hadn't been able to come up with a good reason why she shouldn't join Richards at the canteen, she followed him out of the office.

She was hungry. She hadn't eaten any breakfast either, not even an illicit egg. It wasn't the food she was trying to avoid now; it was the socialising. Why was talking to a victim for hours at a stretch so easy, but chatting to one of her own team over lunch so hard?

Edmonds wasn't ready to think about the answer to that. It was a subject she'd managed to avoid confronting for the past few years.

The Scotland Yard canteen was on the same floor as the human trafficking department, and just a short walk away. "Good news for your stomach, bad news for your heart," Richards had joked when he'd shown her around the building for the first time.

Now Edmonds walked with him along the blue-carpeted corridors and into the bustle of the canteen.

These days Edmonds was trying to eat more healthily—a desk job did nothing for the waistline. In fact, she was seriously toying with the idea of turning vegetarian, so it really didn't help that the first two dishes on display were always unapologetically meaty. Today it was Lancashire hotpot or beef stroganoff. Under the clean and well-lit counter, both looked far more appealing than the vague and uncertain prospect of a baked potato and sweetcorn further down the line.

Vegetarianism would have to wait for another day.

"Could I have the stroganoff, please?" she asked the serving lady. The minute she'd said it, the hotpot looked like a better choice. At least it had vegetables in it. "Or, actually . . ."

But the white-overalled woman had already ladled a large portion of the stroganoff onto the plate, and was turning to Richards, her next customer.

Discouraged, Edmonds pushed her tray along the metal rail. It caught on one of the corners and she managed to grab the plate just before it slid onto the tiled floor. Holding it down tightly with her now gravy-covered thumb, she took a bottle of sparkling water from the fridge, paid at the till with a crumpled five-pound note, and then followed Richards to the seating area.

"So," Richards said, pulling out a plastic chair and lowering his tray onto the table, "you want to hear my news?"

His plate was piled high with what looked like a double portion of the hotpot. He tucked his napkin into his collar and dug his fork into the food.

"I'd love to," she said, sitting down across from him.

"One of the Bosnian detectives phoned late last night."

"And?"

"She said they'd intercepted a call to Salimovic's home line. Apparently the call was made from a South African mobile phone."

"Now that is interesting."

"It is. And since the caller keyed in the access code and listened to the messages on the home line, there's a good chance it was Salimovic himself."

"So he's in South Africa, too?"

"Looks like it." Richards exhaled deeply and wiped his chin with the napkin. "I've emailed the info to Superintendent Patel to follow up."

He glanced down at the piece of carrot on his fork before popping it into his mouth.

Edmonds chewed thoughtfully on a piece of beef as she considered this new development. It seemed they were all sticking together. Salimovic, Dupont and her black accomplice. Where the brothel owner went, the others followed. First to Sarajevo, and then to South Africa.

Edmonds wondered whether this pattern would help the South African detectives to track them down. What were the chances of success? Surely they couldn't be high. She'd heard so many conflicting reports about that country. Beautiful but lawless, Mackay had told her recently. He'd said he'd been there on honeymoon years ago. Great wine, stunning food, fantastic weather, but the guests in the next-door chalet had been robbed at gunpoint the night before they left.

From what Edmonds had read, the levels of corruption in South Africa were as high as the crime, which was doubly bad news for law enforcement officials. If Salimovic paid off the right people, she supposed he could soon be back in business.

But Superintendent Patel had sounded competent when she'd spoken to him the day before, if somewhat stressed, and in her dealings with him so far, she'd found him to be extremely efficient. Perhaps he would be able to accomplish the seemingly impossible, and arrest them.

"So you've ID'd Dupont's partner?" Richards' voice interrupted her thoughts. "Who is he, then?"

"His name's Xavier Soumare. He's French, like Dupont. According to his passport, anyway."

"Xavier Soumare? That's quite a mouthful."

Edmonds nodded without speaking. She had a mouthful of her own to deal with, and the beef was proving rather tough.

"An alias, you think?"

Another nod. Edmonds' jaw was starting to ache.

Then Richards frowned. "Hang on a minute. Isn't Amanita's surname also Soumare?"

Edmonds finally swallowed the much-chewed piece of meat.

"Yes, it is," she said.

"Do you think Xavier chose that name on purpose?"

"He might have done." But then Edmonds corrected herself. "No, he couldn't have. That passport wasn't a new document. I remember the lady at the Croatia Airlines counter saying she'd noticed it was due to expire in December."

"Oh, well. Coincidence, then." Richards began mopping up his gravy with a piece of bread.

Suddenly, Edmonds wasn't so sure.

She remembered the uncomfortable suspicion she'd had in the hospital that Amanita had been lying to her. The black girl's description of her South African trafficker hadn't applied to any of the suspects on Edmonds' list, but had been an exact match for her ward nurse. Amanita had even used the same name—Mary.

Had Amanita been trying to cover up the fact that Xavier Soumare was a relation? Or worse still, had her grandfather asked her to lie in order to protect Xavier, because he had been instrumental in trafficking her?

Surely the elderly man would never have asked Amanita to do such a thing, and even if he had, his granddaughter would never have agreed to it.

Or would she?

Back at her desk, Edmonds took her case folder out of the drawer and dialled Mr. Soumare's home number. Amanita's flight would have landed in Dakar early that morning. She would be home by now, and Edmonds wanted to speak to her, just to reassure herself that she was wrong and that all was well with the Senegalese victim.

But the number simply rang.

She checked the folder again and found two more contact numbers. One was Mr. Soumare's personal cellphone, which he'd answered within two rings every time she'd phoned him on it, and the other one he had told her was an alternative home number.

She tried both the numbers three times, but got the same result. Mr. Soumare's mobile wasn't answered, and nor was the other house phone.

As she sat and listened to the hollow ringing of an unanswered phone in another country, Edmonds found herself biting her lower lip hard.

She was seriously worried that her hunch was correct, and that there was a connection between Amanita and Xavier Soumare.

But Amanita had flown back to Senegal, and it was too late for Edmonds to do anything about it now.

30

Pamela Jordaan was spitting mad. Literally. Standing in the corridor outside the holding cells at Jo'burg Central Police Station, she showered Jade and Moloi with a fine but fast-moving spray of saliva as she loudly voiced her opinion of the South African Police Service, of jails in general and her cell in particular, and about the rights of women who were treated as if they were common criminals just because somebody else had tortured their husbands.

"And what kind of bodyguard are you?" She turned on Jade, who stepped back in surprise. "You did nothing to stop me getting stuck in a cell for a *whole night* with a fat, snoring gogo who's never heard of the word 'deodorant,' and some toked-up crack whore who tried to molest me as soon as I was locked in. Is that what you call keeping me safe?"

"Mrs. Jordaan, I——" Moloi began.

"Don't you 'Mrs. Jordaan' me!" Jade found herself staring at Pamela's back as the blonde woman swung round and pointed a finger in the detective's face. "I promise you one thing right now. My lawyer is going to have a field day with this. An absolute field day. I'm calling him as soon I'm out of the building. I'm going to sue the backsides off both of you. Me, arrested. An innocent citizen. Is that how the system works these days?"

As she stalked past them towards the exit, she tripped over a crack in the tiles and would have fallen headlong, if Jade hadn't grabbed her.

"Pamela," she said, checking that the woman had regained her balance before she let her go, "I'm sorry about what happened, but if you'd cooperated with the detectives you wouldn't have spent a night inside."

Pamela spun on her heel to face them. She stood, posed dramatically in the doorway, and glared at Jade.

"You are fired," she said. "As of now. I'm going to call Executive Limo Services to take me to Heidelberg City Clinic. I'm not riding for one minute in that cramped little runaround of yours."

"Mrs. Jordaan, you will need to inform the police where you're—"

Yet again, Moloi was prevented from completing his sentence.

"Like I told you earlier, as soon as I've been to visit my daughter, I will be checking into the Sandton Holiday Inn. And I'd appreciate it if you would inform me when my own home is no longer a crime scene, so that I can call my new security company and have them make it safe for me to live in again."

"Have you thought about your own safety in the meantime?" Jade asked.

"The hotel will take care of that," Pamela said.

Chin high, she turned and marched outside. The retreating click of her heels was the only sound in the sudden silence.

Jade and Moloi exchanged glances. If Jade had imagined she was going to see any sympathy on Moloi's face, she was wrong.

"Is she still a suspect?" Jade asked.

"Ms de Jong, you are not involved in this case," Moloi said, stony-faced. "There is no reason for me to give you any further information on it, and I do not intend to."

"Well, she is my client."

"I am not deaf. And although English is my second language, I am still fluent enough in it to understand what the words 'You're fired' mean."

Jade sighed. "Temporary insanity," she muttered, stomping away, bitterly regretting the fact that she'd left a helpful message on Moloi's phone first thing that morning giving him Naude's cellphone number.

She passed Pamela pacing up and down outside the main entrance, phone pressed to her ear. The blonde woman didn't look up or acknowledge her in any way.

Jade climbed into her white car. The seats were in good condition; their padding firm, their design ergonomic. Stretching her legs as far forward as they would go, she could only just touch the front carpet with the tips of her toes.

"Cramped little runaround? I don't think so," she said aloud.

Jade took the Glenhove Road exit off the highway and drove past Rosebank, weaving her way through the one-way street system that had been put into place to accommodate construction work for the Gautrain, which seemed to be taking place everywhere at the moment. Traffic on the major highways was being halted for fifteen minutes every day so that blasting could take place. Great concrete supports were intruding into the familiar Jo'burg skyline in every area from Midrand to the airport.

Jo'burg, a city of endless change. When Jade was growing up in the humble suburb of Turffontein, the massive, flat-topped mine-dumps had been the only landmarks on the flat, dusty horizon. Most had since disappeared. New technology had made it possible for their residual gold to be extracted, and slowly but surely, ranks of bulldozers and earth-moving equipment had levelled the land.

Jade had liked the mine-dumps because she'd always associated them with home. But now, she guessed the Turffontein residents would have to learn to live without any landmarks at all.

She parked outside the Rose Anglaise hair salon and walked inside.

Raymond was busy attaching an ornate hairpiece to a dummy head on a metal stand. The mannequin stared expressionlessly at Jade when she walked in, but Raymond's face fell when he saw her.

"Oh no. It's you again," he said dolefully.

"Seems everyone feels that way today." Suddenly tired, Jade sat down on the plush orange chaise longue by the door.

"No, no, sweetie." Fluttering his hands in apology, Raymond hurried over. "I didn't mean it personally. It's just that . . . well, for me, this salon is a peaceful haven, you see. A place where everybody leaves their cares at the door and feeds on the positive energy that's created inside. I only try to speak about happy things in here and I'll tell you frankly, this whole business with Tamsin yesterday has just shattered everything I've been trying so hard to build. I still feel that there's a sadness in this room." He gesticulated at the cream-coloured walls which Jade noticed were lined with posters of pouting models sporting odd-looking hairstyles. "Is there any news on her?"

"She's been found," Jade said. "She's in hospital in Heidelberg. She passed out in a highway garage after what the police think was a drug overdose, but she's expected to be fine."

Raymond raised his head and placed his hand over his heart. "Alleluia," he said solemnly.

Jade decided that she wasn't going to add to the atmosphere of sadness in the room by mentioning that Pamela's husband was fighting for his life in hospital, or by explaining that in all likelihood, his blonde-haired client was a suspect. She was certain that Moloi had only released Pamela because he hadn't yet managed to obtain enough evidence for an arrest. But she wasn't here to talk about that.

"Have you got time to do my hair?" Jade asked.

"What, now, sweetie?" Raymond's eyebrows disappeared into his spiky fringe.

"Yes, now." She still had a thick wad of cash burning a hole in her pocket. Money she'd been paid, but thanks to her abrupt dismissal, hadn't earned. What better way to spend it than by giving some back to her ex-client's hairdresser?

Raymond flipped through the pages of his appointment book. "Actually, yes I have. And that's nothing short of a miracle, you know. From lunchtime today, I'm full, full, full for the next three months."

"I want a natural look, please," Jade said. "Nothing flashy. Something low-maintenance."

"Darling, I understand. Trust me, I knew the minute I saw you that you wouldn't like fuss or curls or too many highlights. We'll keep your colour exactly the same. Just give you some shine, and add a few lowlights, and cover up those roots. I can see you've got a bit of early grey coming through. Although in this salon, we like to call it 'executive blonde.'"

He took a colour chart out of a big folder and frowned down at the gleaming swatches of hair.

"I was actually expecting the police to come along and do an identikit with me," he said. "You know, the way they do it in the movies?"

"I expect they would have if Tamsin hadn't been found," Jade said.

"I've got an excellent memory for faces. I'm not so good with names, though," Raymond confessed. "That's why I call everyone 'sweetie' and 'darling.'"

It soon transpired that Raymond also had an excellent memory for gossip. As Jade tried to relax in the chair, her head swathed in tinfoil, he treated her to a choice selection.

"I feel so sorry for Pamela," he sighed. "She's such an unhappy lady, with that ghastly husband of hers running off every five minutes with another of those strippers from his clubs. I'm sure that's where he is now, you know. Off again with one of them."

Jade filed that away in the section of her brain labelled "Interesting Facts on Pamela." So she'd not only known about her husband's infidelity, but had shared that knowledge with her hairdresser.

"Sometimes he even entertains those girls in his own marital bed, can you believe it? Pamela travels quite regularly to visit her mother, who's in a retirement home down in Durban, and she often spends a night or two at the Sandton Holiday Inn when she needs some time alone. She told me she'd get home to find lipstick smears, perfume smells, even different-coloured hairs on her pillow. I don't know about you, but I think that's quite revolting."

"I do too," Jade agreed. "Why hasn't she divorced him?"

"Oh, she's too scared to leave the marriage, sweetie. Besides, Terence would never let her. Personally I think he can't bear the thought of not controlling her. You've never met him, have you? He's a horrible man."

"Too scared, you say? Why?"

"Well, when she wanted to separate from him a while ago, Terence started making threats. He said if she went through with it, he couldn't be responsible for her mother's safety. And soon afterwards, the old lady slipped when she was going down a shopping-centre escalator. She banged her head quite badly and ended up in ICU. It might have been coincidence, but . . ." Raymond shrugged expressively, "it probably wasn't."

"And Tamsin?" Jade asked. "What does she think of all this?"

Raymond shook his head and gave a heavy sigh. "Tammy is a troubled soul. A very troubled young lady. She has her own problems, but I'd be betraying her trust if I spoke to you about them."

With that, the hairdresser folded the last piece of tinfoil carefully into Jade's hair. He placed a selection of magazines in front of her with a flourish before wheeling his trolley over to the sink.

Jade didn't have time to glance at the magazines, because her phone started ringing. Taking it out of her bag, she saw that it was Moloi.

She lifted the phone to her ear, hearing the tinfoil rustle loudly.

"Moloi," she said. "What can I do for you?"

A surprised pause.

"Where's David?" Moloi asked.

"Well, he isn't here." Jade glanced around the small salon. She wished he was here, sitting on a chair next to her with his long legs stretched far beyond the footrest, paging through a magazine while he waited for Raymond to finish with her hair.

Reluctantly, she dismissed the unlikely vision of domestic bliss. In an environment like this, David would be pacing the room like a caged tiger. He got his hair cut at a little barber's shop in town. He'd told her once that it took ten minutes from start to finish, but that he tipped the barber extra when he could finish it in eight.

"Well, how come you have David's phone?" Moloi snapped.

"I don't have his phone," Jade replied, equally snappily.

"But why . . . okay, I must have made a mistake dialling. Sorry."

He disconnected abruptly. A minute later, her phone rang again. Again it was Moloi. She let it go through to voicemail.

Almost immediately she had another call. This one was from the United Kingdom. She recognised the +44 dialling code.

The caller was a young-sounding English woman with a pleasant but stressed voice. She asked for Superintendent Patel, and Jade took a message. It was Detective Constable Edmonds, from the human trafficking team at Scotland Yard. She wanted David to call her as soon as possible, please.

"Certainly," Jade said.

Jade kept her cellphone in her hand, waiting for the call that she was sure would come. In a few minutes, it did.

"Jade. I've diverted my calls to your phone." It was David, and when she heard his voice she felt suddenly sick with nerves.

"Why have you done that?" she retorted. "After what we discussed last night, I would have thought you'd be considerate enough to forward calls somewhere else if you've gone and lost your bloody cellphone."

"Look, I'm sorry," he said. "I don't have time to argue. I'll explain when I see you. I'll be at the cottage in half an hour. Jade, it's serious."

Something in David's voice was dissolving her righteous indignation. And he'd called her Jade, twice in a row, instead of Jadey. She couldn't remember the last time David had spoken to her without using his pet name for her.

"Half an hour?" Jade glanced into the mirror and saw Raymond frowning and waving his hands in warning. "David, I'm sorry. I can't get back that soon."

"Please."

The desperation she heard in that softly-spoken word was enough to convince her that she should.

"All right. I'll make a plan."

She put the phone away and glanced at Raymond in the mirror. "You're going to have to rinse me now, I'm afraid."

Raymond paled. "Sweetie, I can't possibly do that. The colour will be ruined. It won't have had time to develop properly and the copper lowlights will be bright orange."

"How much longer does it need?"

"Another thirty minutes, minimum."

Jade stood up and pulled off the cape. "I'll rinse it myself at home then. Now I must pay you, because I need to go."

Raymond rushed to the till, arms a-flutter. "This is not happening," he cried. "I've never, ever had a client walk out of my salon in the middle of a tint. Sweetie, it's seven hundred rand for the hair, but Lord knows what it's going to look like. This is my reputation on the line, you know."

He crammed a couple of bottles into a pink paper bag and handed them to her.

"Here's a professional shampoo and conditioner as a gift to you. You must use them when you rinse. Shampoo twice, condition once. And please don't leave through the front entrance, or somebody might see. Go out through the back door over there."

Jade put the money on the counter, grabbed the bag and ran. Tinfoil flapped deafeningly around her ears as she sprinted out of the back entrance. Above the rustling, she was aware of Raymond calling forlornly after her, "Shampoo twice, condition once. It's vitally important, sweetie, and for God's sake, please use the products I gave you!"

31

David hadn't slept since he'd left Jade's house the previous night.

He'd driven back home wrapped in a cloud of sorrowful self-righteousness. He'd made a sad decision, but it was the right one. He and Jade were always going to be an uneasy partnership at best, and an impossible one at worst. Far more sensible to bring this troubled relationship to an end.

In fact, thinking about it with even more brutal honesty—what a roll he'd been on at the time—David acknowledged that Jade was a real catch. Intelligent, fun, beautiful; a woman any man would be proud to call his girlfriend . . . or even his wife. Thinking about that particular concept made David feel ill, but he'd stubbornly pursued his train of thought.

Yes, you would need to have a certain amount of broadmindedness where guns and shooting were concerned if you dated Jade de Jong, but hell, this was Jo'burg. Every man and his dog carried weapons, and half of them, no doubt, illegally acquired.

The IT director—had she mentioned his name? Yes, Steve, a name David now realised he had always hated. At any rate, Steve sounded wealthy. David allowed himself to wonder whether Jade might settle down if she was married to a well-off businessman. She surely wouldn't need to take on the cases that saw her risking her own life and, occasionally, taking the lives of others?

With an effort, David silenced the small voice in his head that was muttering he was wrong, that if Jade was subsidised by a wealthy partner, then all she would do would be to take on pro bono cases that would only expose her to a darker side of society, and to more danger.

Back at home, he'd listened to the messages on his landline. There was only one, from Naisha. Could David please check his car, because they'd hunted everywhere for Kevin's maths workbook and it was nowhere to be found. Kevin thought it might have slipped out of his school bag while David was taking him home and, if so, could David take it to Devon Downs before ten tomorrow morning, which was when his boy's next maths lesson was scheduled.

Suppressing his irritation at the fact that Naisha thought his time was flexible enough to undertake another mammoth voyage to Pretoria and back during morning rush-hour traffic, David deleted the message.

He went back out to the car. Sure enough, under the seat, he discovered a slim, brown-covered notebook with pages of sums painstakingly written in Kevin's childish hand.

David let out a frustrated sigh. If Kevin hadn't been a new boy he would have been tempted to phone his wife and ask her if his son could do without his book for a couple of days. But he was, and David couldn't bear the thought of upsetting his still-fragile world. Nor did he want to upset Naisha, or do anything that might cause her to doubt the decision she'd made to accept the Pretoria job. She'd made a huge sacrifice by turning down the overseas posting, and only because he had begged her to. He'd just have to start work early, then drive to Devon Downs and hand the book in at the admin office.

David got into bed and as his head touched the pillow, the self-righteous cocoon enveloping him dissolved.

He'd been an absolute idiot.

What had he done?

He knew Jade wouldn't come back to him. Not after what he had said in the car last night. He'd lost her now, and lost her for good. And, furthermore, he had to acknowledge that in the process he'd been a complete arsehole to the two most important women in his life.

He'd enjoyed Jade's hospitality, her meals—and, talking of meals, why on earth did he end up having the table manners of a pig whenever he'd eaten with her? Was it some kind of rebellion against Naisha's constant nagging that he conduct himself properly while at the table? He didn't know.

He'd been eating at Naisha's place, too. Sleeping there on the odd occasion, and even sleeping with his wife again on one recent, regrettable night when he'd managed to convince himself that getting back together with her was the right thing to do.

What in God's name was wrong with him? He'd been shirking his responsibilities, refusing to make a commitment, or rather, shying away from making any decision at all, foolish or otherwise.

And he'd lied to Jade about the awards ceremony being cancelled. Why had he done that? He'd invited her along and he'd had every intention of taking her with him. But then they'd had that disturbing argument, where Jade had revealed the side of herself that David had hoped no longer existed.

Her words had filled him with fear.

Lying to a private investigator, David now realised, was an exercise in futility. It had surely been no coincidence that Jade and her consort had ended up going to Emperors Palace that night.

What an idiot he'd been.

David pounded his forehead against the pillow in frustration.

The night seemed endless, and when his alarm clock finally went off at four a.m., David was no closer to reaching a conclusion. All he knew was that he'd never felt so miserable in his life.

He stood under a steaming shower in the hope that the hot water would somehow relieve the leaden exhaustion that had penetrated his bones. When he was a young officer, he'd often spent the entire night dancing and drinking in Durban's dodgiest clubs and had always managed to get through the next day without a struggle. On really busy weekends, he'd even managed two party nights in a row.

Now, after five sleepless hours, it was all he could do to keep his eyes open, and he had a long day ahead. A meeting with the director of security at OR Tambo airport in the afternoon. A conference after that with the management at South African Airways, in connection with a drug trafficking case that had seen two of their flight attendants arrested at Heathrow Airport. Finally, he would be leading the night-time raid on the notorious brothel in Bez Valley.

He shaved, dressed in a white, collared shirt and beige tie, and checked the fridge to see if any breakfast fare had magically appeared inside.

Fourteen neatly stacked Black Label beers looked out at him.

Sighing in disgust, David slammed the door shut again.

Male pig.

When he got to work, David found that an urgent email from Scotland Yard had been sent late last night.

"A very good morning to you, Superintendent Patel," the mail from Sergeant Richards began. The British detective's writing style, like his voice, seemed to be permanently set on "cheery" mode. David glanced out of the window and saw that a faint ribbon of light was starting to show on the horizon.

"I think 'morning' might be an exaggeration at this stage," he muttered.

Scanning the text, David learned that the messages on Salimovic's home phone had been accessed from a South African mobile number, which Richards had included in the email.

David made a note to get a subpoena issued to the service provider immediately and have the caller identified and the line tapped.

Reading on, he discovered that the team had another urgent question for him. While reviewing evidence from a search carried out on Rodic's home, one of the detectives had noticed that his passport was missing. They suspected that this passport might have been taken by Salimovic, and perhaps even used to enter South Africa.

David grunted and made another note to check the passport number with Immigration. If Salimovic had used Rodic's passport to get into South Africa, David would be able to get it flagged as stolen.

The British detective had also attached digital photographs of the two men. Salimovic looked thuggish and brutal with his thin lips, narrow eyes, and stubble-short dark hair. Rodic was plumper, but otherwise not unlike his cousin in appearance.

David got hold of his contact at immigration at seven-thirty that morning, and the man called him back half an hour later to confirm that Rodic's passport had indeed been used to enter South Africa on the twentieth of October. He also told David he would flag the passport number immediately.

Pleased with the immigration official's fast turnaround time, David hit the Reply button on Richards' email, and relayed the good news to Scotland Yard. Now, if Salimovic tried to use that passport again, he would be arrested on sight. If David had his way, the next plane the man would be taking would be a British Airways flight back to the UK, securely handcuffed to his seat, and under police guard.

"Gotcha," David said, staring at the unsmiling faces of the two criminals on the computer screen with some satisfaction.

32

It was well after eight when David finally sprinted down to his car and set off for Pretoria, worried that his preoccupation with his morning's work might cause him to be late for his son yet again.

The main road leading to the Pretoria highway was clogged with traffic. He sat, frustrated, in his car, watching the hawkers threading their way through the queues backed up at the traffic lights, selling knock-off perfumes, dodgy-looking biltong and cheap sunglasses.

If they'd been selling coffee, David might have been interested.

Perhaps he should buy a pair of sunglasses, though. His trusty pair of Ray Bans had lost a lens the day before. Now, he had to squint against the bright morning sun without as much as a layer of tinted glass between it and him.

He was about to beckon the salesman over when his phone rang.

The caller was Moloi, and he sounded concerned.

"Superintendent, do you have a minute? I need your advice urgently."

"Fire away."

"I've just got to Heidelberg City Clinic, where Tamsin Jordaan was supposed to have regained consciousness this morning."

A stab in David's heart. Tamsin's name made him think of Pamela and then, immediately, of Jade.

Then Moloi's words hit home.

"Supposed to regain consciousness?" he asked, surprised. "What went wrong? Is she still in a coma? Is she dead?"

The motorist behind him hooted, but the noise wasn't directed at him. It was meant to attract the attention of the roadside news-paper seller, who rushed over with a copy of the morning's paper in his hand.

"She's not Tamsin Jordaan," Moloi said.

"What?" David's voice was so loud that a passing hawker stared curiously into the car.

"She's not Tamsin Jordaan. She is a woman of similar age and similar appearance called Raquel Maloney. She does not know Tamsin, has no obvious connection to her, and cannot explain how she ended up at a petrol station on the N3 highway when the last thing she remembers is having coffee alone at Hyde Park Centre."

"What the . . . ? Piss off, for God's sake!" David waved an impatient hand at a hawker who was brandishing an array of cellphone devices at him through the car window.

"Sorry, is this a bad time?" Moloi asked.

"No, no, carry on, I was shouting at somebody who's trying to sell me a bloody hands-free kit for my phone."

Usually, Moloi would have laughed at a scenario like that, but he was too rattled.

"I made a huge mistake, boss. I assumed we had the right girl."

"I thought you said she had ID on her."

"She did. She had Tamsin Jordaan's handbag with Tamsin Jordaan's ID inside. The photo looked similar enough that our officers didn't question it. Young slim girl, brown hair. Oh, and she was wearing a diamond pendant around her neck which Pamela Jordaan recognised when we described it to her."

"Does Mrs. Jordaan know what's happened?"

"I haven't been able to get hold of her yet, but she should be here any minute. She's coming to visit Tamsin. She still thinks she's safe and sound."

"She hasn't had any requests for ransom?"

"I'll check when I speak to her, but I'm sure if she had, she would have notified us."

"Look out for something like that." David felt his forehead crease into the familiar folds of a frown. So, Tamsin was still missing. Abducted, or possibly kidnapped. But why would somebody have grabbed her and then gone to all the trouble of substituting another girl in her place?

To buy time.

That was the most obvious answer. Whoever had done this had known that Tamsin would be reported missing and had arranged for a near-identical girl to be found so that the search would be called off. But called off before what?

"Look out for a ransom demand," David said again.

Kidnapping happened fairly frequently in South Africa, and occasionally a high-profile case would make media headlines. The most common form of kidnapping, though, was to snatch children or teenagers and demand a relatively small ransom. These cases happened far more often than statistics showed, because many parents chose to pay up without informing the police, hoping it would guarantee their child's safe return. In most cases it did.

Moloi thanked him and rang off.

David rubbed his temples, feeling the throbbing beginnings of another headache, and closed his sore eyes. The darkness offered him momentary relief from his fiery prison.

He opened his eyes again, and a movement at his window made him turn his head sharply.

Another hawker, this one offering sunglasses.

David buzzed his window down and hot air rushed into the car.

"How much?" he asked.

"Fifty rand." The shabbily dressed black man jabbered out the words, eager to close the sale instantly, before the lights changed and his potential customer was gone. "Only fifty rand for you, sir."

Before David could blink, the man had thrust a pair of mirrored shades into his hand. "These very good, these ones. Big, too. The right size for you."

"No, goddammit, I'm not walking around wearing those, I'll look like a gangster. Give me a plain pair. Just a pair of ordinary dark glasses. Yes, those ones, the ones with the steel rims."

David pulled out his wallet, glancing in his other wing mirror to check that nobody was approaching the passenger side wielding a brick or a spark plug. Smash and grabs were common at traffic lights, and hawkers provided a useful distraction, allowing the lurking robbers to strike.

He handed over a fifty to the salesman and put on the glasses. The relief from the sun was instant and they were a good fit. He leaned his finger on the window buzzer and got it back up as fast as he could, before the man selling the hands-free kits could come back.

Half an hour later he was outside Devon Downs. A couple of late arrivals were hurriedly dropping off their kids, not even bothering to park properly. David saw children trotting down the long, paved walkway towards the school buildings, bags bouncing on their backs. They broke into a run as a school bell sounded in the distance.

David tried to call Naisha to ask her where Kevin's classroom was so that he could surprise his son by giving him the book in person, but her number was engaged.

He headed for the admin office—a white, double-storey building that faced onto a courtyard with a fountain in its centre. Easier to leave the book there than trying to find Kevin among all those small, blue-uniformed children in a school whose grounds occupied roughly the same area as Lesotho.

But in the admin office, the secretary's attention was occupied by a distraught-sounding domestic worker who had rushed into the office as David had been climbing the outside stairs.

Wishing he could have been ten seconds ahead of her instead of ten seconds behind, David waited, glancing at the clock on the wall with increasing impatience, tuning out the uniformed woman's anxious explanation.

Until he heard the words "Kevin Patel."

He didn't recognise the domestic's face, but now he looked at her more carefully, her pink smock was familiar. He'd seen her the previous day, walking home with the boy that Kevin had said was his new friend Riaan.

A knot of dread formed in David's gut and began stretching out long, cold tentacles. He stepped up to the counter.

"What's this about my son?" Now he could hear the stress in his own voice, too.

"Mr. Patel? Oh, I'm so glad you're here. Perhaps you can explain." The school secretary's greying perm bobbed as she looked up at him. "Francina says she's just seen Kevin leaving the school grounds in an unfamiliar vehicle. We've checked, and he's not in class today. I've been trying to get hold of his mother, but she isn't answering her phone."

"I don't know anything about this," David said. "He should be at school today. I was just bringing his maths book in." He stared down at the brown-covered book, realising that his hands were cold and sweaty.

"We've never had anything like this happen before." The secretary was on the point of tears. "I'll be glad to help any way I can. Would you like us to send somebody round to Mrs. Patel's home, or her work? Perhaps she'll know where he went."

"No." David's mind was racing with plausible, happy-ending scenarios—Kevin had been sick, he hadn't gone to school, Francina had made a mistake—but his gut told him differently.

"I'll take a drive to the house right now, and see if he's there. I'll call you as soon I know what's going on."

The detective in him kicked belatedly into action. He turned to the domestic worker. "Francina, please could you give the secretary a full description of the car you saw, and the occupants. Anything you can remember will be helpful."

David sprinted out of the office and raced back down the walkway to the car park, now deserted apart from his vehicle. He started the engine and accelerated through the exit gates, his foot flat on the pedal and the tyres wailing in protest, driving as fast as he could, but still unable to outrun his fears.

33

David sped along the main road in the direction of Faerie Glen, sick with worry. Every few minutes he tried redialling Naisha's home, work and cell numbers, but no one picked up.

Why? Had something happened to her, too? Or was she in a meeting at work, phone on silent, unaware of the nightmare unfolding around her?

Ahead of him, a yellow Audi indicated to pull out into the fast lane.

If I get past the driver before he changes lanes, Kevin will be safe.

Mashing his foot down on the pedal, David shot towards the car. The driver hadn't noticed his last-minute acceleration, and began pulling out regardless.

David swerved into the emergency lane. The tyres squealed and he felt the car start to skid. The concrete barrier loomed on his right, so close his wing mirror was almost scraping it, but he felt no fear. Avoiding the crash seemed easy compared to facing what lay ahead.

Hands tight on the wheel, he managed to accelerate out of the skid and swing back into the fast lane ahead of the Audi.

The blare of its horn soon faded into the distance behind him.

Don't do it, David warned himself, breathing hard. Don't start indulging in superstitious behaviour. It can't change what's already happened. All it will do is get you killed.

Even so, he found himself attempting the same dangerous action a few minutes later.

Children disappeared all the time. Some were taken for muti medicine, most commonly young children in the townships. They were killed, cut open and carefully dissected. Each organ had a special significance. Even their flesh had value.

Children were also easy prey for kidnappers, and his blood ran cold as he recalled the conversation he'd just had with Moloi. Kevin was attending a wealthy school, although if a kidnapper did his homework he would quickly realise that Kevin was a bad choice, because his parents were among the poorest at Devon Downs.

Even so, if money was involved, David knew he would do anything to get a ransom together and bring Kevin safely home.

Anything.

Children were stolen for sex. He didn't even want to consider that possibility, but a good-looking young boy like Kevin would surely fetch a high price if he was sold to . . .

Don't think about it.

He's bunking school, he's at a friend's house. Please, please let it be something like that.

A few minutes later he parked outside Naisha's flat and sprinted to the front door. Her little house looked so peaceful, so normal. The white-painted security gate was shut and locked, and so was the door. He hammered with his fists on the varnished wood.

"Kevin!" he called. "Kev, are you there?" He listened carefully. Nothing, no response. "Naisha?"

His son wasn't there. The truth hit him with a punch, even though he'd known, deep down, that Kevin was missing, not sick, not skiving off school. And Naisha must be at work, where he would now have to go to break the dreadful news.

As David turned away, he noticed a familiar-looking red vehicle in the residents' parking area. He stopped and frowned at the little Nissan Micra. From here he could just make out the number plate.

No, he wasn't hallucinating. It was Naisha's car.

Bemused, David strode through the narrow ribbon of garden to the back of the house.

He'd warned Naisha repeatedly that it was pointless having a front entrance with a state-of-the-art security gate when her kitchen door had no protection at all. It was a standard wooden stable door with a flimsy, low-spec lock that any half-skilled criminal could pick in less time than it would take to phone the Flying Squad.

It was time to put its flimsiness to the test.

David peered through the kitchen window, which was bordered by cheerful yellow curtains. No point in breaking the door down and running straight into the muzzle of a gun.

But the kitchen was neat, tidy and empty. Next to the sink, a coffee cup and two cereal bowls were drying on the dish rack. Clearly Naisha and Kevin had had their breakfast. Then something had gone wrong.

He stared at the kitchen door, assessing it. It opened outwards, so not even the strongest and most dramatic rugby-tackle would force it inwards. Could he pull it open?

After a few minutes of futile wrestling, he realised the answer to that question was no. Rubbing his throbbing palms, David realised he'd have to go and buy a crowbar, call a locksmith, make another plan. Seething with frustration, he gave the stubborn door a hard, angry kick and turned away.

Then, to David's utter astonishment, he heard a key rattling in the lock. He spun round as the door flew open and gave an involuntary gasp when he saw Naisha standing there.

Her eyes were red-rimmed and puffy and black streaks of mascara had tracked their way down her cheeks. Her lips looked swollen, too. She was in her work clothes, but they were crumpled and creased, and she had make-up stains on the collar of her blouse.

"Naisha, what . . . ?" David felt the blood drain from his face—his first and immediate impression was that she'd been raped. He took a tentative step towards her.

"Go," she cried. "Just go away."

"I can't go."

"Call me tomorrow."

She tried to close the door but he grabbed the handle, yanked it back open and pushed his way inside.

"What . . . ?"

David yelled as his wife's nails raked savagely across his cheek. Before he had time to back away, her bunched fist connected with his jaw. His head snapped back and he tasted blood as he bit right through his own tongue.

Jesus, she's gone insane, he thought. What had happened?

Before Naisha had a chance to hit him again, David managed to grab her wrists. Her arms felt as strong and thin as steel cables as she struggled against him and he had to twist sideways when she aimed her knee at his groin. He heard a ripping noise as her efforts tore the seam of her skirt.

"What is it?" he shouted. "Naisha, stop this! Stop trying to hurt me and tell me what the hell is wrong."

She looked up at him wordlessly. Then the fight went out of her and she sagged in his arms.

"You've killed Kevin," she whispered.

"What?" David roared out the word in panic, as if the volume of his own voice could drown out what she had just said.

Naisha started to cry.

"They've got him. They've got my little boy. And they told me no police, or I will never see him alive again. No police and particularly not my husband. They said if I contact you, if I tell you anything at all, Kevin will die." Her breath was coming in harsh, rapid sobs, a sound that David had heard many times from victims and their families at murder scenes, shootings and violent robberies, but had never expected to hear inside these pale yellow walls.

"And now you've come here, and I'm sure they already know, and that means it's too late now, because they will have killed him."

David stared at her, open-mouthed.

"But you . . ." he began, in a voice that sounded strange and didn't seem to belong to him.

Then, in his pocket, his cellphone began to ring. Without even thinking about what he was doing, he pulled it out and answered.

"Mr. Patel." It was the school secretary. She sounded relieved; happy, even. "There's nothing to worry about. I spoke to your wife a few minutes ago and she said she kept Kevin home from school today because they've both come down with a bad cold. I do apologise for the scare earlier. Francina must have made a mistake."

"I see," David said, unable to contradict her. "Thanks for letting me know."

At that point, Naisha's knees gave way. Feeling strangely disembodied, David lowered her gently onto a chair. She slumped onto the table and buried her face in her arms. For a short while the only sound in the quiet space was her gasping cries.

34

David crouched down beside Naisha, stroking her shoulders and murmuring words of comfort that, even to him, sounded hollow.

Meanwhile, his mind was racing.

Kevin had been abducted. And he'd been targeted deliberately. Naisha had been ordered not to call the police, and specifically not to call David. So Kevin's captors had done their homework. They knew who he was and who she was.

By knocking on Naisha's door, had David already signed his own son's death warrant?

The thought made him feel physically ill. He clung to the hope that the kidnappers' words were only a threat, and that Kevin's captors, whoever they were, didn't have anybody watching Naisha's house. After all, his coming here was entirely due to a series of coincidences—the forgotten maths book, the traffic delays, the domestic worker noticing the unfamiliar car.

When Kevin was younger, one of Naisha's relatives had given him a hamster in a cage. The tan-coloured Brownie had proved to be a wayward animal. It bit both Kevin and him on numerous occasions and was prone to fits of frantic activity, where it would climb onto its wheel and run for hours, spewing wood shavings and fine yellow dust all over the desk in Kevin's bedroom.

Brownie hadn't lasted long. The hamster had escaped after giving Kevin's thumb a well-timed bite as he was taking it out to clean the cage. Despite its aggressive personality, David privately hoped that the small animal had gone on to live a happier life outdoors.

Right now his thoughts too were going round and round, in a frantic and repetitive sequence.

Who had taken Kevin? Why had he been snatched? Would his captors follow through on the threats they had made?

Dear God, let it not be so.

Naisha's wailing had calmed down to a rough, intermittent sobbing. David got to his feet and tore off a couple of sheets of kitchen paper. He handed them to her, then helped her up and led her outside into the small, walled back garden.

They sat down on a bench in the shade of the eastern wall and in a croaky, halting voice, Naisha told him her story.

She'd received the phone call on her way to work after she'd dropped Kevin at school. A private number which she nearly hadn't answered because she was wary of being caught on her cellphone while driving.

"Mrs. Patel?" A man's voice, soft and cold. "We have your son."

At first she hadn't understood. Then she hadn't believed him. He'd warned her not to phone the school, not to phone anyone, or it would mean instant death for the boy. He'd told her he was sending an MMS image from a SIM card that would be discarded as soon as he'd ended the call. A moment later, her phone had beeped. She'd stopped at a traffic light outside the Home Affairs building and peered down at the screen, and there it was—a picture of Kevin, in his school uniform, his eyes closed, with a copy of that morning's *Beeld* on his chest. She'd driven past a street vendor and noticed the headlines just a few minutes ago.

"Why are you doing this?" she'd asked her unknown caller. She'd been on the point of tears, but somehow managed to control herself. At first, she'd suspected that this had something to do with one of David's cases. It was a scenario she'd always feared; that she and Kevin would become victims as a result of one of his investigations.

The man's reply was short and sharp. She'd interfered with something she had no business in. She was to take the day off work but, before she left the building, she was to reactivate all the passwords that she had disabled yesterday in the security clampdown, so that "business" could go on as usual. If she did this, Kevin would be returned to her, safe and sound, at the end of the day.

"Don't go anywhere," the man had warned. "Stay home all day. You can expect another call on your landline later."

Someone had hooted behind her, signalling that the light had changed, but, gasping in shock, she'd stalled the car.

This wasn't about David. It was about her. It was about what *she* did.

She'd started to curb the activities of the criminal syndicate that she'd suspected was operating within the Home Affairs building. But already, it seemed, the syndicate was biting back.

No police, the man had warned. Tell nobody. Not even your husband. If you do, your child will die.

After the man had hung up, Naisha noticed two missed calls, one from David and the other from Devon Downs College. The school secretary had left a message to say that a domestic worker had seen Kevin leaving the school grounds in an unfamiliar car.

Panic had crushed Naisha like a lead weight. She'd sped through the underground parking garage, tyres squealing on the smooth floor. Then she had rushed up the stairs and into her office. Heads had turned as she'd run through the open-plan admin section.

Who was involved in this? Which of the people watching knew that she had just been coerced, in the most dreadful way, into letting them continue with their crimes?

How was she ever going to face any of them again?

Unable to fight her emotions anymore, she'd started to cry uncontrollably. People would notice; she must think of an excuse. She'd logged on, reactivated the passwords and then gone straight to her boss's office and lied. She'd just had news that her sister had been involved in a serious car crash, and was being rushed to hospital. Naisha had to leave the office immediately to be with her. She'd be back as soon as she could, but she would like to apply for a day's leave.

Of course, her boss had said, looking at her tear-streaked face with concern. Of course. Go straight away. What are you waiting for?

She'd reactivated the passwords, Naisha had told him, so that the issuing of passports and ID documents could continue in her absence.

"I appreciate that," her boss had said—and he was surely not one of the people involved in the syndicate, because if so, he would have prevented her from disabling the passwords in the first place. Knowing that he trusted her, that he believed her, had made her cry even harder. "Call me if you need anything at all," he'd said. "We'll carry on with the security clampdown when you're back."

She'd stumbled out of the building and, when she got home, called the school and told the secretary another, different lie.

She'd been pacing in her bedroom, weeping hysterically, when, to her horror, she'd heard David banging on the door.

Think, David urged himself. Think.

But looking at his wife's anguished face, he couldn't form any coherent thoughts except for the obvious one—that all this was his fault.

He had begged Naisha to turn down the overseas job. He had pleaded with her to take the position at Home Affairs' head office in Pretoria. He'd done it all because of Kevin, because he didn't want to be parted from his son.

Now, if Kevin ended up being hurt or killed, David would have only himself to blame.

He couldn't stay at Naisha's house any longer. He needed to leave, for Kevin's sake, and hope that nobody had seen him arrive. But he did need to stay in touch with Naisha.

David scrolled through the menu on his cellphone and diverted all his incoming calls to Jade. She would be able to handle the situation. In a crisis, there was nobody he trusted more.

Then he handed his phone to Naisha.

"I don't know if they're watching this place or monitoring your calls," he said, "but this phone's transmission is scrambled, so you should be okay if you use it outside. At least it'll give you a safe means of communication. I'll get a new one and sms you the number. When I do, go outside and call me immediately."

He wished he could stay with her, but it was too risky. At the time when she most needed his support, he was powerless to offer it. Guilt tore at his heart.

"I'll speak to you soon," he said. "Be strong. We'll get Kevin back. I promise you that. Whatever happens, we will get him back."

Checking nervously around him, he hurried back to his car and drove away.

35

Edmonds checked her watch for the third time that hour. Then she glanced out of the window, pushing aside the blue blinds and peering down through the rain-streaked glass to the building's entrance. She could usually spot the people who were arriving on business as they strode purposefully past the slow-moving groups of tourists, but on this rainy morning all she could see were a couple of umbrellas, bobbing black boats in the river of the street.

She flipped the blind back into place, her hand hovering over the telephone, ready to snatch it up as soon as the call she was expecting came through.

Edmonds had never thought they would get another potential witness for this case, but that was exactly what they had.

Last night, the Yorkshire police had raided a brothel in Brad-field. The test purchase officer who had investigated the place three weeks earlier had reported that there were seven women working there, none of whom ever seemed to leave the premises unless they were accompanied by the brothel owner. Without a doubt, they were trafficked workers. But when the raid had taken place, they found there were not seven women inside. There were eight.

The Yorkshire police had swiftly established the identity of the eighth woman, a relatively new arrival.

Her name was Fariah Sidibaye, and she was the victim who had been sold on from Number Six.

Edmonds had been woken in the early hours of the morning by a phone call from Mackay telling her the news. She'd been so hyped up after hearing it that she'd found it almost impossible to get back to sleep. Eventually she'd dozed off, and she had dreamed of the running man.

She'd seen the accident in perfect slow-motion, just as it had happened on the night of the raid, only more clearly. The swipe of the windscreen wiper flicking the rain away. The slow turning of the man's head, his sideways stumble, the heart-stopping bang as his hand had slammed against the car's swerving bonnet.

And then his body, rolling away across the tarmac.

In her dream, the man hadn't got up. She'd climbed out of the car and rushed over to him, skimming over the road the way one could only do in dreams, and she'd suddenly known that this was Salimovic, that they had him at last.

Then he had pulled back his hoodie and staring down in shock, Edmonds had realised it wasn't Salimovic after all. Under the black hood, she had seen the face of Xavier Soumare, staring at her with cold, dark eyes.

"Who are you?" she'd asked him. "Why is Amanita lying about you?"

Xavier hadn't answered. He'd just smiled, his lips stretched open all the way to his ears, exposing huge, jagged teeth in a shark's grinning mouth.

Edmonds had woken herself up shouting in fright.

Now, in the grim reality of a wet morning, her dream seemed silly. She wasn't going to tell anybody else about it. They'd think she was mad.

Edmonds heard footsteps outside, and Richards came in, followed by a waft of cigarette smoke. He shrugged off his jacket and Edmonds saw the front of his shirt was drenched.

"Not very nice out there," he said. "It's enough to make me want to give up the habit." He patted his pocket where Edmonds saw, beneath the sodden fabric, the outline of a cigarette packet. "Waiting for your interview?"

She nodded.

"I hope it goes well. I'll be watching from the observation room."

"I hope so too," Edmonds said. "I'm starting to feel as if this case will never be solved. Or maybe it's me. Perhaps I'm not cut out for this work. I don't know if I have the right instincts."

"No. Don't say that." Richards moved closer to her, and for a moment she actually thought he was going to take her hand in his. To her astonishment, she realised that she wouldn't have minded if he had.

204 • JASSY MACKENZIE

Stocky Richards with his smoking habit and his infectious laugh and his carrot-coloured cow's lick. Not the type of man she'd ever gone for.

But then, seeing she had been determinedly single for a long time now after a disastrous relationship, Edmonds had to acknowledge that perhaps she had never gone for the right type of man at all.

"You're a fantastic detective. Why do you think you got this promotion? Mackay wanted you right from the start. You know that test you had to write, with all those questions on what you'd do in various situations?" Seeing her nod, he continued. "Well, you got the highest marks out of all the applicants. In fact, I over-heard Mackay telling his boss that you got the highest marks that he's ever seen."

"Oh." Edmonds' face felt suddenly hot. Was she blushing, she wondered.

"So don't doubt yourself. You've just got a doozy of a case, that's all."

"I'd feel better if I could get hold of Amanita. I tried phoning her again this morning, on all three numbers, but no one answered this time, either."

"Perhaps there's a network problem in Dakar or something. You know what I think?"

Edmonds never found out what Richards thought, because the shrill ring of the telephone interrupted him.

It was Mackay, informing her that Fariah had arrived, and was waiting in the interview room.

Sending up a short prayer to whatever god was listening that this might finally represent a turning point in the case, Edmonds grabbed her jacket and headed for the lift.

Fariah looked exhausted. She was flopped on the couch facing the door with her feet tucked up underneath her, her arms crossed on the round, padded arm of the chair, and her head resting on them.

Edmonds noticed her hair first. Once long and beautiful braids that must have cost a fortune to attach, they were now loose and uneven, with knotted, clumpy roots that had tangled as they had grown out.

When Fariah heard the door open, she pushed herself upright, blinking. Her eyes were puffy, and there was a dull resignation in her expression that worried the police detective. Her denim-clad legs looked thin, and Edmonds saw that her wrists, jutting out of the sleeves of the brand-new fleecy tracksuit top she wore, were bony and fragile-looking.

"Hello there," Edmonds said, with a welcoming smile. "I'm Eleanor."

She wasn't used to using first names during working hours anymore. Nobody called her by her first name apart from the victims. Not even Richards, whose first name she'd found out by chance a few weeks ago. It was, rather oddly, Stavros. Perhaps he had a Greek mother?

"I'm Fariah," the black girl said, holding out her hand. Her handshake was gentle.

The girl yawned widely, covering her mouth with her other hand, and on the tips of her fingernails Edmonds could see the remnants of the pink nail polish she must have applied before she left South Africa and ended up in hell.

"I'm sorry," Fariah said. "I'm so tired. The nurse gave me a pill before we left. It was a tranquilliser, I think." Her voice was soft, and although she spoke with a noticeable accent, her English was good.

"That's okay," Edmonds said. "We've got lots of time. We don't have to talk about anything much today if you don't want to. We can just have a little chat, and then you can go back to the safe house and sleep." She sat down on the other couch and adopted the same position as Fariah. Legs curled up, arms on the armrest. Comfortable and non-confrontational.

On the wall opposite Fariah was a painting of a wooden wheel-barrow surrounded by colourful beds of flowers. Above this was what appeared to be a light, but which was actually a video camera.

Edmonds really didn't want to think about how much footage the Human Trafficking department had of her discussing movies, books, clothes and food. Hundreds of man-hours would be spent fast-forwarding over the bits where Edmonds was agreeing enthusiastically that yes, Lady Gaga was incredibly talented, and no, she didn't believe for one minute that she was a hermaphrodite.

"I don't mind talking," Fariah said. She picked at the polish on one of her nails, then stared at Edmonds.

Her gaze was flat and blank, like the light had been switched off behind her eyes.

"Where would you like to start?" Edmonds offered. "From the beginning, where you were first recruited? Or when you met Amanita?"

"The other girls haven't told you anything, have they?" Fariah asked, but Edmonds knew from the tone of her voice that it wasn't really a question at all.

Oh God, she thought with a sinking heart, not another one.

"They've helped us as much as they felt comfortable doing," she said. "It's important for you to remember, though, that your testimony will help us to send Salimovic and his accomplices to prison for a long time. The stronger the case we can put together, the longer their sentence will be."

Fariah gave a tired shrug.

"I will start by telling you why the other girls will not talk," she said.

"Thank you. That'll be helpful."

"When we arrived in England, we were taken to a house, somewhere in London, I think. There, we were put in separate bedrooms while the men took turns to rape us."

Edmonds nodded. So far, her story matched up with Amanita's.

"Then, some time later, I am not sure how long, they said we were ready to start work. But first Sam said that they were going to show us something. A motivation, that's what they called it. A motivation to obey the rules and not to run away. He brought us all into the lounge and he told us all to sit in front of the big movie screen."

Edmonds swallowed. She didn't like this. She had a bad feeling about what she was about to hear.

"Go on," she said. She leaned forward and took a sip of water from one of the glasses on the coffee table.

"The movie started playing," Fariah said in the same dry, flat voice. "I looked at the screen and I saw my mother."

"Your mother?" Edmonds couldn't keep the surprise out of her voice.

The young woman nodded. "My mother was in the film. First they showed her outside our house in Boksburg, getting out of the car. She was coming back from church, I think. Then they showed her again. It was dark this time. They had taken her somewhere, inside a building, and tied her up. They had put a piece of black cloth over her mouth. At first I was afraid they were also going to rape her. But then the person—the people—I could not see them, but they started burning her with hot coals.

"They were burning her and she was screaming so loud, and so was I. I saw the red coals touching her skin. Her arms, her stomach, her breasts."

Fariah wrapped her arms around her knees, huddled deeper into the corner of the couch, and squeezed her eyes shut.

"They burned her in so many places," she whispered. "They burned her, and they made us watch, and they told us that they knew where all our family and our friends lived, and if any of us tried to escape, or gave any trouble, or ever talked about what had happened here, then the same thing would happen to them."

Fariah was crying now in great gasping sobs. Edmonds was off the sofa before she could think about what she was doing. She took the girl in her arms and Fariah sobbed harder, burying her face in the policewoman's shoulder.

Edmonds rocked her back and forth, offering reassuring words, saying that no, it hadn't been her fault at all, that she had been brave and strong, that she had done the best she could do in those terrible circumstances.

"It was all my fault!" Fariah voice rose to a harsh shriek. "All my fault that she died!"

Died?

By the time the young woman could speak again, Edmonds' own vision was blurring with sympathetic tears which she tried to blink unobtrusively away.

"She died from her injuries?" Edmonds asked softly.

The girl shook her head. "When I phoned her last night to tell her that I was safe, her friend answered. She told me that my mother had been in a car accident. She had been going to hospital three times a week to get her burns treated. On the way back from the hospital one night, the taxi was in an accident and she was killed."

Edmonds reached for the box of tissues that was a permanent fixture on the coffee table, and handed a thick wad to Fariah.

Now she understood why the nurse had administered a tranquilliser. To have had to live with the awful guilt that she had inadvertently caused her own mother to be tortured, and then to learn that she had died on her way back from treatment, without knowing where her daughter was.

Edmonds had seen people pushed mentally over the edge after going through far less than this.

She could see how the shocking footage of Fariah's mother being tortured with smouldering coals would have intimidated all of the victims into remaining silent forever.

For the sake of their families.

Edmonds doubted whether the traffickers would have bothered to track down all the families and friends of the girls they had captured. That would surely have been an expensive waste of time, when all they needed to do was find one.

In the observation room, Richards reached for the telephone and dialled Patel's number to inform him about this latest development in the case.

As soon as he put the phone down, it rang again. Mackay was on the line and he sounded excited.

"You need to get to the airport straight away," he said. "You and Edmonds. I've booked you on a flight to Cyprus. We've had another breakthrough. I've found out where Xavier Soumare and Mathilde Dupont's home base is."

36

Deep frown lines carved furrows between David's elegant brows. His eyes were haunted and his shoulders were hunched over as if he was carrying the weight of the world on them.

"I can't believe this has happened," he said softly. "I just can't believe it."

He was slumped in a chair at Jade's kitchen table, staring down at his hands.

Jade was sitting opposite. She had her notepad in front of her; a pointless gesture, since she hadn't taken any notes. All she'd done was to listen as David had told her, in an unsteady voice, what had happened earlier that morning.

When she'd heard Kevin had been kidnapped, Jade had felt as if she'd been punched in the stomach.

"It's crazy, Jade—I mean, for years Naisha has been on at me about how dangerous my job is," David continued. "How, one day, one of the criminals that I'm after is going to target my family."

Jade nodded. She had also assumed, at first, that this was something to do with one of David's cases.

"And now it's happened, and it's bloody well happened because of her. Which still means it's my fault. If I lose him, it's all my fault."

David raised his head and looked over at her, desperation in his eyes.

"It's not your fault," Jade said gently. "It's no one's fault. Don't blame yourself."

"I—I haven't told you any of this, but a while ago Naisha dropped a bombshell on me. She said she'd been offered a job working at the South African embassy in Mumbai. I begged her not to take it up, because Kevin would end up spending most of his time overseas, and that would have meant that I'd hardly ever have seen my own son."

David stood up, pushing his chair back so hard that it fell over. Apologising, he righted it again and began to pace up and down the little kitchen.

"I persuaded her to apply for a promotion to Pretoria head office instead," he continued. "I told her it would be better for Kevin; that we could manage to get the money together to send him to private school, to Devon Downs. And Naisha agreed. She made that decision because I wanted it. And now look at this mess. Dammit, I should never have interfered. I should have let her go to Mumbai."

"You couldn't have known this was going to happen," Jade said.

David leaned over the table and slammed his fists down on the wooden surface. "Shit, shit, shit! Why didn't the guards at the gate notice that somebody arrived with no child, then drove out with one?"

Jade shrugged helplessly.

Stewart the bodyguard trainer had loved quoting statistics.

"D'you know that about ninety per cent of kidnapping attempts are successful?" she'd told the class. "Ninety per cent. And of those, about eighty per cent take place on weekday mornings. What does that tell you?"

Her words had been followed by a resounding silence. Jade could see her fellow students weighing up the consequences of admitting they didn't know against the potentially more serious consequences of giving the wrong answer.

Jade had cleared her throat. "It means your principal shouldn't leave the house at the same time every day, because it will make the kidnappers' job easier."

"Exactly!" Stewart had stabbed the air with her finger. "That's exactly right, lassie."

She'd gone on to explain that routine was the kidnapper's greatest friend. The work run and the school run provided the best opportunities for a target to be snatched. "Remember, the kidnappers are not interested in taking the guard along too," she had warned. "That means unless you stay super-alert at all times, you'll either be jobless or dead."

David surely knew these statistics as well as she did, but even so he could have done nothing to prevent his son from being snatched.

She pressed her fingers into her forehead as she tried to focus her thoughts.

Think like a criminal, her father had always advised her. So Jade tried to think in the same way that Kevin's kidnappers might have done, tried to apply logic and intuition to the facts as she knew them.

"This doesn't sound like something that's been organised by the syndicate working inside the building," she said eventually.

"Why?"

Because Jade's gut was telling her so. Opening her eyes, she struggled to articulate her feelings in words that David, and she, could understand.

"I don't think the syndicate would be powerful enough. It must surely be a small-scale operation. A few people who have good jobs at Home Affairs, earning an extra couple of grand a month putting through a few fake passports. If you're in that situation you're not going to have the means or the manpower to organise something like this, and you're certainly not going to have the motive to do it either. Not during a security clampdown, not if you want to keep your job as well as the chance to earn extra money on the side. A month from now people will be getting fired because of this. So, they must have been forced to do it, just like Naisha herself. Chances are there are a couple of frightened people working in those offices today."

David nodded slowly. He walked back to the table and sat down again.

"Jadey, you're right."

"So, Naisha's clampdown interrupted the plans of whoever is behind this. They need to get out of the country in a hurry."

"That makes sense."

"And the person—or people—can't travel on their own passports."

"Why not?" David asked. She knew that his rather obvious question was simply a prompt, an encouragement for her to continue with her train of thought.

"Because they must be known to the police. Wanted criminals can't travel under their own names."

David slammed his fist down on the table, but this time not in anger.

"Dammit, Jade, we need to follow up on this."

Then he looked at her more closely, as if he were really seeing her for the first time that day.

"'Scuse me for asking, but what's that on your head?"

"Oh, shit," Jade said, clapping a hand onto the crackly silver paper that she'd forgotten all about since arriving home. She jumped up, grabbed the packet Raymond had given her and bolted for the bathroom.

37

Jade wrestled her clothes back onto her still-damp body, and wrapped a towel around her dripping hair after obeying the hairdresser's instructions to shampoo twice and condition once. Never mind that she'd done it at a speed that she was sure had broken all records for that particular procedure.

She hurried back into the kitchen, the floor cool against her bare feet.

David was standing by the door, grim-faced, gripping his new cellphone and speaking in a tight, strained voice.

"Yes," he said. "Absolutely. I'll get onto it right now."

He snapped the phone shut, then leaned against the wall, pressing his forehead on the cream-coloured plaster.

"I don't know how I'm going to get through today," he said. "I've got a day from hell, starting now. Meetings at the office, meetings at or Tambo, the Bez Valley raid tonight. Right now, I can't imagine having a coherent, focused conversation with anyone. All I can think about is my son."

"Can't you reschedule the meetings?" Jade asked. "Spend the day following up on Kevin instead?"

David turned to her and she saw a flicker of hope in his eyes, but it was swiftly extinguished.

"No," he said. "Not now. I've already confirmed that I'm going to be at the OR Tambo meetings, and there's no way I can tell my team what's really going on. Not after the threats the kidnappers made."

Jade bit her lip. David's words made logical sense, but she knew that for him to battle his way through a long working day in these circumstances would be torture at best, and impossible at worst.

The kidnappers had said that Kevin would be returned unharmed at the end of the day. But that had been before David's unexpected arrival at his wife's house. If they had somebody watching the place, Jade knew Kevin might now be dead.

Didn't they say that outliving your children was the fate that every parent feared the most?

Jade had taken the framed photograph of her mother out of the box and put it up on the D-shaped arch that separated the kitchen and the sitting room. She glanced over at it automatically.

Elise Delacourt, née de Jong, hadn't outlived her daughter, but she hadn't lived to see her grow up, either.

Jade wondered if that was the second fate that every parent feared.

Thinking of her parents reminded Jade of something her father had once said when he'd investigated a kidnapping case involving a young girl from a wealthy family. The parents had been warned not to call the police, and they had only done so in desperation, after they had paid the ransom and the deadline for their daughter's return had passed.

"One of the worst things about this type of crime is the isolation the parents feel," her father had explained to her when he'd arrived back late that night. "Whatever happens now, at least their burden has been shared. They can get help from us, and comfort from their family and friends. It doesn't sound like much, Jade, but believe me, it's far better than dealing with something like that alone."

The young girl's body had been found the next day, dumped in a field, shot execution-style through the back of her head. Two weeks later, her father had arrested the suspect who would eventually plead guilty to the crime.

Now, her father's words echoed in Jade's head.

Share the burden. It's better than shouldering it alone.

"Please let me help you," she said to David.

He turned round to face her and she could see a glimmer of relief in his eyes. Then he shook his head.

"I don't think there's much you can do."

Jade shrugged. "There must be. And I'm willing to do whatever it takes to help him come home safe. What about trying to get a description of the people who grabbed him?"

"No. If anybody contacts the school again, the secretary might realise something is going on."

Jade thought it over and then had an idea.

"You told me that a domestic worker had seen the car. Perhaps I could get her details, saying that you wanted to thank her for her help, and then speak to her about what she saw. That's a plausible story, surely?"

David's eyes lit up again. Properly, this time.

"Jadey, I can do better than that," he said. "I know where she works. Kevin pointed out the house to me. It's just round the corner from Devon Downs. Pass me a pen and paper and I'll draw you a map. If you could drive there and get a description from her, I can compare it to our open case files, and we might just be able to get an ID on the people who snatched him."

"I'll go there straight away," she said.

But Jade didn't. Barely a minute after she had let David out of the gate, she heard the roar of a powerful engine and the drumming of tyres travelling at speed over the rutted road.

She peered out of the kitchen window, and saw the streamlined bonnet of a red Ferrari approaching. The car skidded to a stop outside Jade's gate, tyres digging deep gashes in the sandy soil.

The loud blast of a horn shattered the quiet of the afternoon.

Jade took a deep breath, closed her eyes and offered up a brief prayer for patience.

She buzzed open the gate and watched as the Ferrari shot through. It went too fast over the metal rim of the gateway, and she winced as she heard an unpleasant scraping noise from the under-carriage.

Pamela climbed out and slammed the door. She teetered over to the front door of the cottage, wobbling on yet another pair of strappy high-heeled shoes.

Her face was pale and her hands were trembling. She wasn't wearing her dark glasses, and her eyes were red-rimmed and vulnerable-looking.

"I'm hiring you again," she said in a hoarse voice.

Jade opened her mouth to say no, that she wasn't available, that she didn't give clients like Pamela a second chance, especially when they didn't offer an apology or an explanation. But the blonde woman didn't give her the opportunity.

"I've just had a call from Netcare Milpark hospital to tell me my husband has passed away from his injuries. And Tamsin is still missing. I went to see the girl that—whoever it was, that bloody fake aunt—substituted in her place, and it's not her. It's not her. I'm a widow now, and I have no family left in the world apart from Tammy." She took a deep breath and continued in a pleading tone.

"Oh, God, Jade, please. I'm sorry about what happened earlier. I'm going to go to prison, I know it. The way that black detective was looking at me and the questions he was asking, I'm going to end up behind bars, and I just want to be sure my daughter's safe before I do."

With a despairing yowl she launched herself at Jade, who staggered backwards as Pamela flung her arms around her and started sobbing, her face buried in Jade's shoulder.

Jade's cuttingly worded rejection dissolved on her tongue.

She patted Pamela's back rather awkwardly.

"It's okay," she found herself saying to the blonde woman. "We'll find her. I'll do my best to make sure that Tamsin comes home safe." She realised that her soothing words were a disturbing echo of what she had said to David just a quarter of an hour ago.

Guiding Pamela back into an upright position, Jade stared at the bright, copper-hued horizon.

Two missing children. One kidnapped; the other simply vanished.

Who had taken them, she wondered, and where were they now?

■

Xavier Soumare turned off the highway and, after a few more turns, headed down a narrow tarred road. The car bounced over the uneven surface, dry grass hissing and swishing along its side as he swerved to avoid a large pothole.

The distant hills swam, mirage-like, in the fierce heat.

He kept his gaze fixed in front of him, watching the road, looking out for the place they were going. Not once did he turn his head to check on the child sleeping on the back seat.

The establishment that he and Mathilde had contacted that very morning, after some careful research, was in a run-down cul-de-sac, which in turn was located in a shabby suburb not far from an informal settlement. Xavier had been surprised to learn

that an establishment like this existed in such a place—and particularly a setup that specialised in children—but he supposed that
everybody had needs.

And needs, as Xavier knew well, begged to be fulfilled.

At this hour the place was all but deserted, baking quietly in the
fierce afternoon heat. He was sure that as the afternoon cooled
down, the activity inside would warm up.

He parked inside the walled property after making a phone call
to announce himself. The front door was open to allow air inside,
but it was guarded by a heavy security gate.

Xavier scanned the area around him; he wanted nobody to see
what he was about to do.

He opened the back door of the car. The boy lay curled up on
the seat, his breathing deep and regular. He lifted him out. He was
light, but even so, Xavier found his arms trembling more than he
would have liked as he stood upright.

"Xavier."

Panting with the effort of holding the boy, Xavier turned
towards the sound of Mathilde's voice.

"Wait. Don't do it."

She spoke with some urgency.

Xavier frowned. They had settled on this plan yesterday. It was
foolproof, watertight in every way. She had handled the kidnapping professionally, immaculately, like the seasoned criminal she
had been and, he had thought, still was. But now, what was
happening? Had she lost her nerve?

"Why not?" he asked, trying to keep his voice steady, to stop it
from shaking with the effort of holding the boy.

Mathilde walked around the car. Her sunglasses prevented him
from seeing the expression in her eyes, but she was wearing the
small, fierce smile that he remembered from the past, when a job
was going well.

"Because it will be better if I do it," she said.

Xavier almost sagged with relief as she took the boy's weight in
her strong arms and set off, brisk and business-like, towards the
entrance. He got back into the car and turned the air conditioning
up high, drying the sweat that had sprung up on his forehead.

A moment later and Mathilde was inside.

Xavier could see her speaking to the dour-faced receptionist. There would be some negotiation, he guessed, before money changed hands. In a place like this, though, rates were never going to be top dollar.

A wave of exhaustion washed over him. It was so cool in the car, so peaceful. He blinked, slowly and heavily, and, to his alarm, found himself jerking awake with his head resting on the steering wheel, an inch away from activating the horn.

The painkillers. Until now, Xavier had never taken medication when he was on a job, and he was remembering exactly why. But this week, without his medication, he could hardly function.

He struggled out of the car. The heat felt like a furnace. He didn't want to go inside. It would be unwise to interrupt Mathilde during her discussions. Better to walk.

He made his way around the side of the building, where a row of young karee trees provided a thin layer of shade. He passed a few windows, noticing that all except one were shielded by thick navy-blue blinds.

Cupping his hands against the glass of the uncovered window, Xavier could just make out a small, shabby room with a black boy who looked a little younger than Kevin lying on an oversized bed. He wasn't sure, but he thought the boy's wrists were attached to the metal sides of the bed, effectively holding him prisoner.

Then the door opened and a tall, middle-aged man walked in. He turned and closed the door behind him. Xavier moved away, into the shade. He didn't want to see what was going to happen next, but he couldn't stop himself from looking back.

When the boy saw the man, he began to cry and struggle against his restraints.

The man stared down at the boy with an expression on his face that could almost have been sympathy. He took hold of the flimsy sheet that covered him and tugged it back. Then he moved to the window and closed the navy blinds. Perhaps he'd sensed Xavier's presence; perhaps he'd simply felt exposed.

The boy's cry still sounding in his ears, Xavier hurried back to the car. Mathilde was already sat in the passenger seat, tapping her feet and checking her watch.

Mathilde's business here was finished now. She'd done all that she had to, and now he wanted her to leave. He would handle the final part of the job on his own. Her flight out of South Africa was departing in four-and-a-half hours. They had just been to pick up her passport from Eunice at the Home Affairs office, and had then phoned a travel agent and booked an international ticket in her new name. It was time to take her to the airport and say goodbye.

Xavier went round to the driver's side. As he opened the door, a stab of pain made him double over and clutch his gut.

"All done?" he asked, when he could speak again.

She smiled again, that same hard, brisk smile.

"All done," she said.

38

David's day was inching past so slowly that time seemed to have stopped altogether. Now, back in the office after his final meeting of the day, he felt incapable of working, unable to do anything except watch the leisurely progress of the hands on the wall clock.

His thoughts were paralysed by the sickening knowledge that his son was in the hands of criminals.

David couldn't let himself acknowledge the terror the boy must be feeling. Had his captors hit him, abused him, threatened him with violence? He was gripped by the fear that the incident would leave Kevin with lasting scars—physical or mental; that even if the boy was returned to his mother at the end of the day, he would never be the same as the boy who had been snatched from the grounds of the expensive private school.

Stay safe, hero, he urged Kevin silently, narrowing his eyes in concentration as he tried to project his emotions to wherever his son might be. Do what they tell you, cooperate with them. Be strong, be brave, for God's sake, stay alive.

Guilt gripped him again, the emotion so powerful that David uttered a low groan of despair.

He had to accept the fact that, thanks to his own actions, Kevin might already be dead.

Naisha had texted him a couple of times, brief messages to say that there had been no further communication from the kidnappers. No phone calls at all, although she was waiting just a few steps away from the phone at all times.

Suffering through the endless day, just like him.

Now, with eyes half-closed and hands clenched, David did his best to project mental waves of compassion onto the kidnappers.

"He's only a boy," David muttered, feeling his fingers bruising his palms. "He's just a boy. Please don't harm him."

"Sorry, Sup?"

David opened his eyes to find Captain Thembi staring at him, in some concern, across the open-plan office.

With an effort he tried to relax his face and hands, but he feared the attempt would be as unsuccessful as it had been during his two earlier appointments at OR Tambo airport. He'd battled through the meetings somehow, but several times he'd been asked if anything was wrong.

"Just got a lot on my plate," he'd barked, and instantly realised that he had made a mistake in saying that, because it gave the impression he was not coping; that he was overwhelmed by his workload.

Not a great way to inspire confidence in the members of the public he was supposed to serve.

Now David tried another angle.

"I didn't hear you come in, Thembi. I wasn't speaking to you. I was thinking out loud."

Thembi nodded, but the captain's quizzical expression showed David that he was still puzzled. He sat down at his own desk and glanced over at his boss again before pulling a case file towards him and picking up the phone.

David's own phone rang, providing a welcome distraction. The caller was the security manager at Cell C, an acquaintance of David's who he'd contacted earlier that day about the cellphone number which had been used to access Salimovic's messages.

"Good afternoon, Superintendent."

"Afternoon," David replied. "Have you received the subpoena for the line tap yet?"

"Not yet, but I'm sure it'll be served tomorrow." The man sounded sympathetic. David knew that if he'd had a choice, he would have begun tapping the line immediately, but procedures had to be followed.

"I do have some information on the number for you in the meantime, though."

"Great. Fire away." He reached for his pen.

"It's a cellphone contract that's been running for three years now."

David's eyebrows rose. "Not a pay-as-you-go?"

"No. A contract. I don't know if this will help you, but it's in the name of a Miss Tamsin Jordaan."

"Tamsin Jordaan?" David repeated, so loudly that Thembi, who was now busy on a call, clapped his hand over his own phone's mouthpiece to muffle the sound.

"That's the one. I hope it helps, Superintendent. I'll let you know as soon as we get the tap up and running."

David thanked the man and rang off. For a moment this new discovery distracted his attention, allowing him a brief reprieve from the acid worry burning in his gut.

In all probability, Salimovic himself was using Tamsin's cell-phone.

"So there is a connection between the two disappearances," David muttered. "He's got Tamsin, for sure. Has he got Kevin as well?"

He let out another frustrated sigh and saw Thembi replace his receiver and look round again in concern. The black detective cleared his throat in a hesitant way that made David think he was about to ask him if anything was wrong, but before he could speak, they were interrupted by a knock at the door.

Looking up, David saw Jade standing in the doorway. Her face was strained, and her hair was escaping from the ponytail she'd scooped it into and hanging in shiny locks around her shoulders. The reddish-brown lowlights gleamed among the darker strands.

She nodded distractedly to Thembi, then turned to David.

"We need to talk," she said in a soft voice. She didn't say the words "in private" but she didn't need to. Thembi was already on his feet.

"Got to go and check some information in the archives," he said, heading for the door.

As he hurried out, he glanced at Jade and then at David, in a way that made David realise the captain had just reached a some-what erroneous conclusion about what was troubling his boss.

Problems on the domestic front.

Jade pulled up a chair and sat opposite David. Its vinyl seat was hard, and it squeaked when she sat down.

"Have you got any news on Kevin?" she asked, although she could see from David's face that he'd heard nothing. He shook his head and rubbed his forehead.

"Did you speak to Francina?" he asked.

"Yes, I did." Jade had spent fifteen minutes chatting to the domestic worker in the kitchen of the house where she worked. "I couldn't fool her with the "thank you" story, though. She's a sharp lady, and the family she works for have made her very aware of security threats in general and kidnapping in particular. She was in no doubt about what she saw. I made her promise to keep it a secret."

"What did she see?" From David's deliberately casual tone, Jade guessed he was trying to suppress his anxiety about the answer.

"She saw Kevin walking back from the school towards the parking lot with a woman that she didn't recognise, but who looked like a teacher. Or so she thought at the time. She had dark brown, jaw-length hair and a navy-blue skirt, and was carrying some books."

"So they intercepted him on the way into the school," David said.

Jade nodded. "You know that long paved walkway that leads up to the school buildings? I reckon the woman must have been waiting there, looking out for him. I'm sure she was ready with a plausible story. My best guess is that it was something to do with you. "Come with me, Kevin. We've just heard your father's been in an accident and we need to take you to the hospital straight away." I would have believed that if I'd been his age. It would explain why he followed her so willingly."

David nodded, feeling a cold fist squeeze his heart.

"The woman opened the back door of a white Mercedes, and after that, Francina says, everything happened very fast. The next moment the door slammed and the car pulled away. Francina wasn't sure, but she thought the driver was black. She didn't manage to get the car's number plate, but she did notice it had a Cape Town registration."

David blinked, narrowing his eyes in the way that he did when he was thinking hard.

"This sounds as if it could be the same woman who was at Tamsin's house," Jade said. "Raymond's description of the hair was similar, and I know the Cape Town number plate isn't conclusive, but he mentioned it as well. Do you think . . . ?"

David turned away and took a cardboard folder from his filing cabinet. He slid it across the desk.

"I do think it's the same person. Or rather, the same people.

Xavier Soumare and Mathilde Dupont. They're fugitives, wanted by Scotland Yard. Dupont resisted arrest during a brothel raid and Soumare helped her get away. They've been playing catch-up with a lowlife called Salimovic, the brothel owner and a human trafficker, who's also fled here. Here's the file. Their photographs are inside, and you'll find some interesting info on Salimovic as well. Seems he has a history of torturing people with hot coals, so there's a probable link between him and Terence Jordaan. It's all in there. Open up and have a look."

Jade took the folder from him, trying not to show the shock she felt at David's words.

The photo of Xavier Soumare was blurry and heavily pixellated. The man's features were in shadow, his eyes a vague smudge of hues in the darkness of his face. Jade shuddered as she examined his face, but it was more because of the evil he represented than because of what she could see on the printed page.

Mathilde Dupont's image was clearer. An attractive-looking middle-aged woman with strong features and a self-assured demeanour that reminded Jade of Pamela's moneyed confidence.

The rest of the file contained a fair-sized wad of printed and handwritten notes. The information was confidential, but Jade knew that David could, at his discretion, share it with a private investigator if that investigator was helping him with the case.

"Can I read through all of this?" she asked. "I'll be quick. I don't have much time, because I've got to get back to Pamela. She's waiting for me at the cottage."

David made a "go ahead" gesture. "You won't be wasting your time."

Propping her forehead on her hands and pulling the pages closer towards her, Jade began scanning the contents of the file.

When she had finished, she lifted her head and stared at David in shock.

Everything was connected.

Pamela's missing daughter, Terence's torture, Kevin's kidnapping, and the fugitives who had fled to South Africa and were now trying to evade the police.

The four different cases were one.

39

As Jade pulled up outside her gate, she heard shrill and familiar barking.

It was Bonnie, the little Jack Russell. It seemed the dog was becoming a national champion at fence-burrowing. Jade had found her in her garden again that morning. This time, she was happily roaming the empty plot on the opposite side of the road. Jade's mouth twitched as she opened the driver's door.

"Come here, girl," she said, trying not to sound amused.

Bonnie sat down in the sandy soil and started barking.

With a sigh, Jade climbed out of her car and went over to fetch her.

She picked her way through the dusty soil and coarse, scratchy grass, only to have Bonnie scamper deeper into the undergrowth.

"This is not a game," Jade called. "Come here, you silly dog. I don't have time for this. We are not going for walkies."

She ducked under the branches of a shrub, disturbing a roosting bird that flew out with an annoyed squawk and a clumsy flapping of wings.

What kind of bird? She had no idea.

She'd been able to tell the difference between a Beretta and a Glock when she was still in primary school, but her father's interests hadn't included an appreciation of the country's fauna and flora. Jade didn't have a clue what kind of shrub it was, either. All she knew was that it had dark green leaves with a waxy sheen . . . and that, in the pool of shade next to the shrub, where Bonnie was now sniffing around intently, the grass was oddly squashed and flattened.

Jade also noticed a distinctive pattern in the sandy soil nearby, which Bonnie thankfully had not disturbed.

A large footprint.

Nearby, another series of marks. Three small but clear indentations in the ground. They formed a neat triangle, with one of the dents pointing towards the window of Jade's cottage. Jade realised what they were in an instant. The ends of a tripod.

My God, somebody had been crouched in the shade, concealed by the overgrowth, staring at Jade's kitchen window and aiming . . . pointing . . . something at it.

Only two pieces of equipment would require a tripod in this situation. A camera or a gun.

From here, the window looked small and distant. Jade knew that with a telescopic sight it would appear so large and clear that the hidden viewer would have felt that they could reach out and touch it.

Jade had no idea how recently the watcher might have left. It could have been an hour or a week ago.

She automatically recalled David's words. Somebody had been asking about her. Asking questions, down in Richards Bay, at the hospital where she was born.

And now this.

Jade squinted at the window, but with the late afternoon sun reflecting off it she couldn't tell whether the glass had been shattered by a bullet or not.

Pamela, she thought.

She straightened up and ran back towards the house, skidding in the sandy soil, the dry grass whipping her shins. Bonnie hurtled after her. The dog's short legs pistoned as she dodged the bigger tufts of grass, sailing over the rocks and branches in her way.

Let Pamela be all right.

A camera, Jade prayed. It must surely have been a camera.

She and Bonnie arrived at the gate together, and Jade fumbled in her pocket for her remote control.

At the same time the security gate rattled, then swung wide open and Pamela stepped out. She looked worried and tired, but she was alive and unhurt.

Jade felt sick with relief.

"What's the matter?" Pamela called. "I saw you running. Is everything all right?"

"Everything's okay for now," Jade said. She picked up the Jack Russell and carried her to Pamela. "This is Bonnie. Please hold her while I bring my car inside. I've got some news on Tamsin that I need to tell you about."

Jade drew the curtains across the kitchen window while Pamela went indoors and sat down on the same sofa she'd occupied when she'd first come to ask Jade about bodyguarding services. She held the little dog in her lap and stroked her with her red-painted nails, staring anxiously at Jade as she did so. Jade hadn't labelled Pamela as a dog person. She'd thought the blonde woman was far too immaculately groomed to take kindly to animal hair and dusty paws.

But now Bonnie was revelling in the attention. Her little body was wiggling with pleasure and her stump of a tail was wagging madly.

There's no way of softening the blow, Jade thought, sitting down next to her. Better to get to the point straight away.

"Tamsin's fake aunt is wanted by the British police after escaping a brothel raid in London. The brothel, a human trafficker, has also fled to South Africa, and the police have just discovered that he's been using Tamsin's cellphone."

Pamela stopped stroking the dog, and sat very still. Bonnie looked up at her inquiringly and grunted before settling down on her lap again.

Jade hated having to break bad news. She just hoped that the shock of this revelation might force Pamela to open up and tell her the full truth.

Tamsin was in terrible danger now, and so was Kevin.

"Any information you can give me will be helpful. David told me that your husband was arrested for employing trafficked workers a few years ago. Do you know anything about that?"

Pamela remained silent and stared fixedly at the wall, her lips slightly parted.

Jade got the bizarre impression she might not even have heard the question.

She tried again. "Pamela . . . ?"

Still nothing. Jade reached forward and gently tugged her arm.

Snapped out of her reverie, Pamela turned to Jade, with the same distracted look on her face.

"This can't be happening," she said in a shrill voice. "It absolutely cannot be."

Bonnie jumped off Pamela's lap, perhaps sensing the woman's tension. Jade heard the click of the little dog's claws as she trotted into the kitchen.

"Pamela, what can't be happening?"

"Any of this. It's not possible. He was arrested. I read a report about it just the other day on *The Daily Telegraph* website. They said the brothel was raided and the manager, an Eastern European, was taken into custody."

Now it was Jade's turn to stare.

"How do you know who Salimovic is?"

Pamela gave an impatient shrug, ignoring Jade's question. "Salimovic's in prison. He must still be there. He couldn't have escaped, could he?"

"He was never arrested, Pamela. I've just read all the information on the case."

"He was." Her chin was high but she sounded unsure. "I know it for a fact."

"The brothel manager is Salimovic's cousin, Rodic," Jade explained in a gentle voice. "He is the one who was taken into custody after the raid."

Pamela was quiet for a moment. Then she leaned forward and covered her face with her hands. "Oh, God," she whispered. "Oh, dear God."

"Why is it so important to you that Salimovic was . . . ?" Jade fell silent as her own thoughts raced ahead. Suddenly she remembered the photo she'd seen in Tamsin's cluttered house, the unsmiling young woman arm in arm with the unsavoury older man.

Now she thought she understood.

"Tamsin knows Salimovic, doesn't she?" Jade said. "She's been—or maybe even still is—in a relationship with him."

Pamela nodded. Huddled in her chair, she suddenly looked very small.

"You're right," she said. "But that's not all. There's something else, Jade, something terrible, that I haven't told you."

She turned towards the D-shaped arch where Jade had placed the photo of her mother cradling the newborn in her arms, her eyes filled with all the love in the world.

Pamela stared at the portrait.

"That was me, once upon a time. I was so happy when Tammy was born. She was a loving, lovable, beautiful little girl. Oh, God, why did it all go so wrong?"

Then she burst into floods of tears.

40

Where had it all gone so wrong?

Salimovic turned away from the guesthouse window where he'd been looking out at the view of Jo'burg city. A crisscross of roads, now twinkling with the headlights of cars as it grew dark. The skyline against the setting sun—a postcard-perfect picture; not that he gave a shit about the way it looked.

The Hillbrow Tower with its spindly stem and dome-shaped head; the tall cylinder of Ponte. Other high-rise buildings, although he didn't have a clue what they were. Why should he? This wasn't his goddamn city. It was a place he came from time to time, to do business, and now it was a place where he'd been cornered, trapped, all his escape routes cut off one by one.

Salimovic pulled down the sash window with a bang. It didn't wake the sleeping girl sprawled on the bed, snoring gently, the sheet damp with sweat wherever it touched her. He'd known it wouldn't. Tammy slept like the dead after GHB and she slept like a corpse after sex, and right now that meant that she was out for the count. Doubly dead.

He sat down hard on the squeaky bed.

It had been sheer luck that he'd avoided the police raid. Total dumb luck. He'd been booked to fly home to Sarajevo the previous week, which meant he should have been back in London by the time the raid took place, but crap weather and traffic jams had meant he'd missed his first flight. As a result, he had already landed at Butmir airport when the detectives banged on the brothel door.

He could have been arrested at his penthouse apartment in Ciglane, Sarajevo. Thinking about that made him shiver, because it had been such a close call.

He'd switched on his mobile phone in the taxi on the way from the airport, and the first message had been from Tammy. Her voice had been high, breathless, worried.

"Sam, call me as soon as you can. It's urgent. I just found out the detectives are raiding Number Six."

A shock, like a block of ice against his back.

"This the building?" the cab driver had asked, slowing down outside Salimovic's apartment.

Christ, if Scotland Yard was involved, the local police could already be outside his front door, waiting for him.

Thinking fast, he'd told the cab driver to keep going. "I've just had a message that the meeting here has been cancelled. You can take me straight to my hotel."

He'd asked the driver to drop him outside the Hotel Michele. He'd walked inside and waited in reception for half an hour, edgy and paranoid, then got into another cab and driven to the Hotel Kovaci.

There, he'd called Katja, one of Rodic's many girlfriends in the UK. A short while later she'd called back and confirmed that Rodic was in jail.

Cold panic had descended on Salimovic. He needed to get out of Bosnia, and fast . . . but how? It was far too risky to travel under his own name now, and he hadn't brought his other passport; a fake South African one. He'd gone and left it in his goddamn house, so by now it was doubtless in the hands of the police.

He'd phoned Tammy back.

"How the hell did you know?" he'd asked.

"Long story," she'd replied. "I'll tell you later. Are you all right? What can I do to help?"

"You can buy me a ticket. Business class to Jo'burg. Use a false name and make sure it's fully transferable. I don't know what passport I'll be travelling on."

"I'll do that."

She'd sounded pleased, excited at the thought of seeing him again. He couldn't have cared less at that stage, but he'd played along because, right then, he needed her badly. He couldn't access the safe in his apartment in case the local detectives were watching, and when he'd travelled to another part of the city to try and draw money from an ATM, he'd discovered that his bank accounts had been frozen.

He'd had no idea how he was going to get out of the country safely, or how he was going to get hold of a travel document that wasn't his own. His connection in Bosnia had been arrested years ago, which was partly why he'd started the South African operation. He'd subsequently hooked up with another dealer who worked in Moscow, but this man was proving to be uncontactable.

In prison or in hiding? One of the two, he was sure.

Since then, Salimovic had been on the run, checking into different, and increasingly seedy hotels every night, paying cash from a stash that was starting to run terminally short. His frustration at the situation made him so goddamn angry that he could have murdered the plainclothes policewoman he saw stationed outside his apartment, standing and watching. Waiting for him. He could have walked right up to her and flung her out over the balcony, forced his way inside, grabbed the wads of cash that were tucked away in his safe.

He'd murdered a woman that way before, years ago, when his half-sister—his whore mother hadn't stayed with any man longer than a few months—had been living in the penthouse and working for him. Having a reliable female was necessary in his business, because women trusted other women more easily than they trusted men.

But she'd got drunk one night and an argument between them had escalated into a fight. She'd leaned back against the balcony, elbows resting on the rail and glass in hand, and started hurling insults at him.

Salimovic had not been able to restrain the eruption of fury that had taken him over to where she was standing in three long strides. Her smug expression had dissolved into horror when he bent forward, slid his arms under her knees, and heaved. The last he saw of her alive was the crotch of her pink knickers, neatly sandwiched in between her fish-white thighs, when she somersaulted backwards over the rail.

She'd screamed as she fell, and the sound had followed her tumbling body down, floor after floor, as she plummeted to the tarmac far below.

When the police arrived, he'd acted the part of a grieving brother. His sister was drunk, he had told the police. It had been a tragic accident.

He'd avoided arrest then, but Salimovic knew he couldn't risk getting rid of the plainclothes officer in the same way, because there might be other detectives nearby. Besides, there was no guarantee the cash would still be there, the local police being what they were.

In any case, that was how people got caught. By being careless. He wasn't careless, and he wasn't stupid. He'd had contracts out on him before—it was the nature of the game—and he had gained something of a reputation for being the invisible man, disappearing the instant he smelled a rat.

He'd relieved his tension by paying a visit to a trusted friend's brothel. A good friend who owed Salimovic a favour; so there was no charge and no questions asked. He'd spent an hour there and left the slut bruised and bleeding, inside and out.

Then, on the way back to his shitty hotel, he'd had another call from Katja, sounding nervous this time.

"Rodic called me from prison," she'd said. "He said I should tell you that his passport is still at my house, if you need to use it. And he said something else, too. He told me you need to be careful, because he thinks there is something else going on."

"What are you talking about?" Salimovic shouted.

Katja didn't know. Rodic had also been nervous, and hadn't been able to say much. She promised she would find out more when he called again. In the meantime, Salimovic told her to courier his cousin's passport to a friend's address.

It was a huge gamble, because the prison officials could have been monitoring the call Rodic had made, but it was his only hope. He'd got on the plane to South Africa the day after the passport had arrived. By then, his money was just about finished. He'd walked through Immigration, shitting himself with fear that the document had been flagged, but he'd been lucky. The police had been too slow.

He knew he couldn't use Rodic's passport again, but he hadn't thought he'd need to.

Until he'd found himself trapped in South Africa, too. His usual connection for passports was no longer doing business, and his emergency contact had temporarily closed shop due to a security clampdown at Home Affairs.

South Africa was a big country with a police force that, in his opinion, could be kindly described as "inefficient." It would have been easy for him to lie low for a while, but he knew that the police would soon be hunting for Tammy again, and he needed her to stay with him because she was his only source of money.

There was another reason Salimovic was in a hurry.

Tammy didn't yet know what he had done to her father.

He'd kept her drugged to the eyeballs, placid and drowsy, and so far he'd managed to stop her from turning on the television or radio and hearing about her dad on the news. He'd hidden the remote control of the set in their room just in case and, as an extra failsafe, broken the plug.

He wouldn't be able to relax until they were both out of the country and on their way to Brazil. There, he had a "friend" in São Paulo who was interested in buying her for his establishment, and for a very good price.

That money would allow him to start up his own operation again somewhere else.

Now all he had to do was to wait for Xavier Soumare to get their goddamn passports organised. He'd promised he could get it done fast, and although Salimovic wasn't convinced, he'd had no choice but to organise all the necessary photos as well as a small deposit. In case it was a trap, he'd made sure he wasn't around when Xavier and his woman partner had gone to Tamsin's place yesterday morning to collect everything.

The passports had already been delayed by an extra day for some reason—Salimovic wasn't sure exactly what. From the brief phone conversations they'd had, Salimovic got the impression that Xavier was totally paranoid, as suspicious and mistrusting as Salimovic himself, and in a way that reassured him.

Tammy stirred and murmured something sleepily. In an instant, Salimovic was by the bedside.

"How are you feeling, prejilepa?" he asked her. "Hungry? How about I go and get us takeaways and some wine?"

He smoothed her hair back from her sweat-damp brow. The

sheet had slipped and, looking down, he was surprised at the surge of lust he felt.

"Perhaps I go for the takeaways later," he said, smiling as he cupped one of her taut, silicone-enhanced breasts in his hand while his other prised her legs open.

He could sense she was sore, unwilling and tired, and she pushed back against his fingers.

"Not now," she mumbled.

Salimovic's smile widened. "Yes, now."

"Go'way. I'm still asleep."

In a swift, fluid movement he reached across to his bedside table and grasped the silver pistol that lay there.

He watched her eyes fly open as she felt the cold kiss of metal on her thighs. Slowly, he eased the weapon higher.

"You are not allowed to say no, prejilepa. It is one of our rules. In fact, now I think about it, it may be the only rule."

He was trembling with arousal now, his finger caressing the trigger as the muzzle of the gun moved over her soft, pink flesh. She flinched as she felt the pressure of the cold metal, but she did not say no.

Women like Tamsin learned the rules fast. It was why they were so useful to him.

With a swift motion, he buried the barrel of the gun deep inside her, hearing her gasp and her fearful whimper as he began to thrust it in and out.

Penetrating the daughter with the gun he had stolen from her father. There was a poetic justice in there somewhere.

As he thought about what Tamsin's bastard father had done, Salimovic's finger tightened on the trigger and for a white-hot moment, even he didn't know whether he would be able to stop himself from pulling it.

41

Traffic crossing over the highway at the Allandale Road bridge was heavy with the afternoon rush.

This time, Pamela was perched on the black leather passenger seat of the Ferrari. Jade had insisted on driving.

The traffic began to move, and she eased the vehicle carefully forward.

She hadn't broached the subject of Tamsin and Salimovic since they'd got into the car, mostly because Pamela had needed time to pull herself together. She'd stopped crying as they had driven past Kyalami racetrack, and blown her nose while they were waiting at the Vorna Valley traffic lights. Now, as the Ferrari inched across the highway bridge, Pamela had her bag open and was reapplying her make-up with the help of a compact mirror.

Jade judged that the time was right. "How did Tamsin and Salimovic get together?" she asked.

"It happened a few years ago," Pamela said. "Terence met him on a skiing trip in Slovenia, and soon after he came back, they brought the first lot of girls in. It didn't work out, as you know, and he got into a lot of trouble with the police, but the damage was done. Salimovic had been to South Africa and Tamsin took one look at him and—" Pamela made an expressive gesture with her hand.

"I see," Jade said evenly. She could imagine the attraction that the young, troubled woman must have felt for a man who was wealthy, foreign, and above all, bad.

"They kept it a secret at first," Pamela said. "When I found out Tammy was actually dating Sam, I hit the roof. I banned her from seeing him, of course, and Terence cut off all business dealings with him immediately."

"But it didn't work?"

Pamela shook her head sadly.

"It didn't work at all. All it did was to alienate her, and from me in particular. She moved out of home, into her own place. She was supposed to start at varsity—we had her enrolled for a BA at Wits—but she dropped out after a few weeks. She'd been helping out at Heads & Tails occasionally, and she was very good at doing the admin and the management, so she ended up easing herself into a permanent position there. Within a year she was just about running the Midrand branch, and doing a good job of it, which left Terence free to open other branches and expand."

And meant that Terence was no longer constantly looking over his daughter's shoulder, Jade thought.

They were over the bridge now. A couple more minutes and she'd finally be able to turn left into Old Pretoria Road. From there, Jade hoped, the journey would go more quickly.

"She never forgave me," Pamela said.

"How do you mean?"

"We'd been—well, not close. But we were friends. After Sam came into her life, Tamsin withdrew. We barely spoke. I think she regarded me as the enemy."

Jade made a sympathetic noise. "Well, your daughter was dating a brothel owner," she said. "I think any reasonable person would have done what you did."

Pamela shook her head.

"No. I overreacted. I know I did. At that stage I didn't know he was a brothel owner. All I knew was that he was bad news."

"If you were estranged from Tamsin, how did you know what she was doing? How did you know that she was still seeing Salimovic, and how did you know he owned Number Six?"

Pamela twirled a blonde lock around her finger, and the gesture made Jade realise what she was going to say an instant before she said it.

"Raymond," she said. "Our hairdresser. We were never at the salon at the same time. Tamsin made sure of that. But when she was there, she confided in him. She made Raymond promise that he wouldn't tell me anything, and he said nothing for a long time. Recently, though, he'd realised that things were getting out of control. He called me in and told me everything. From what Tammy had said—and the phone calls she'd taken when she was at the salon—he'd learned that she was still involved with Sam, and that Sam owned a brothel in London." Pamela removed a tissue from her handbag and dabbed her eyes again. "A brothel where illegal workers were employed."

The Ferrari's gleaming red bonnet inched round the corner. Open road at last. Jade put her foot down rather tentatively and was rewarded by a throaty growl from the engine and the sensation that a thousand horses were bursting out of their starting stalls.

Jade reined the horses in to a hand gallop. When the car was moving up the hill at a steadier pace, she focused once again on Pamela's words.

"What did you do then?" Jade asked. "Did you tell Terence?"

"Oh, God, absolutely no way. He would have killed her, and I mean that quite literally, Jade. No, I asked Raymond to try and find out where the brothel was. Eventually he managed to get the name, and the area. And then I did a silly thing. I know it was wrong, but Sam was changing her, I could see it, and Raymond agreed with me. She wasn't the sweet girl she used to be. She'd become . . . I don't know. Secretive. Hard. Evil. It was beginning to worry me badly, so I made an international call. I phoned Scotland Yard. I told the police what Sam was doing, and I asked them to go to Number Six and arrest him."

Jade took her eyes off the road for a moment to stare at her.

"You were the person who reported Number Six?" she asked incredulously.

"I was." Pamela nodded with some pride.

"I don't think doing that was silly, Pamela."

"No, it wasn't. It was what I did next that was stupid."

The gates of Heads & Tails stood open, and the guard stood to attention when he recognised the Ferrari. Jade drove through, the tyres scrunching over the tarmac, her skin prickling with uneasiness at Pamela's words.

The car park was half-full with the lunchtime crowd, and Jade noticed two black women walking slowly and dispiritedly towards the gate.

Perhaps they had arrived for a job interview, only to be turned away because Tammy was not available.

They would never know what a lucky escape they'd had.

"And what did you do next?" Jade asked Pamela.

"I thought . . . You see, I wanted to make things right with Tamsin. After Sam was arrested, I thought that it would be a good opportunity to rebuild our relationship. So I told her about the raid the minute I heard about it on Sky News. But I said that Terence had been the person who'd reported the brothel. I thought it was better to blame him, so that Tammy wouldn't start hating me all over again."

Jade stared at her, open-mouthed.

"Jesus, Pamela."

She realised now that Pamela's tip-off had signed her own husband's death warrant.

Death by torture, the orders, and probably the execution too, handed down by Salimovic himself. A fitting revenge for the man he believed had betrayed him.

Did Pamela realise what she had inadvertently done?

Jade guessed that, by now, she did.

She had just one question left for Pamela, and she was going to ask it as soon as they had finished their business at Heads & Tails. When they had another chance to speak in private, she was going to ask her about her involvement with Naude.

She parked near the club's door. Pamela climbed out, but instead of walking towards the entrance, she asked Jade for the car keys.

"There's a private parking bay round the back," she said. "If you don't mind, I'll take the car there. I don't want it to be in view of the road. I'll meet you inside."

Jade watched the Ferrari disappear round the corner, and then headed for the entrance door.

Just as she reached it, she heard the familiar blast of a powerful motorbike engine. Jade spun round, hoping that this time she was wrong, and that it was her own recent thoughts that had fooled her into believing this was Naude.

But to her dismay, she saw the now-familiar red Ducati speed in through the gate. The black-clad rider steered the bike into the shade of a tree. He kicked down the stand, dismounted, and hooked his helmet over the handlebar.

Then Naude saw her and froze.

42

Jade grabbed her Glock and yanked it out of the holster, her finger curling round the trigger as she aimed. Across the car park lot, she saw Naude mirroring her movements. Just as fast, just as practised. He raised his Beretta and pointed it in her direction.

Whatever happens, don't let him get to Pamela, Jade thought.

She sighted down the barrel of her Glock, her mind racing.

This wasn't the right time or place for a gun fight. Shots fired now would mean police, questioning, delays. Shots fired to kill would mean certain arrest, even if she could prove to the detectives that Naude was a dangerous criminal.

Of course, she wouldn't be able to prove anything if he killed her first.

What to do, then?

She dived for cover, landing spread-eagled behind the nearest vehicle, the solid white-painted people carrier.

Where was he?

She peered round the wheel arch, her heart banging in her throat, a new surge of adrenaline flooding her bloodstream.

Naude had taken cover too, behind a tree. She could see the sun glinting off his gun. She didn't know if he'd thought the situation through in the same way she had.

At any moment, he might try to shoot his way out.

"You might find, one day, the only thing left to do is talk your way out of a situation. If that's ever the case, Jade, make sure you choose your words carefully."

Her father's voice, as soft and dry as the breeze.

"Naude!" she shouted.

No response. Only the rustle of leaves.

Jade inched round the side of the white people carrier. If Naude wasn't answering, he might be adjusting his aim instead, using her voice to guide his gun.

But then he shouted back.

"Jade?"

He sounded . . . confused, was the best word she could think of. Had she been wrong about him?

Choose your words carefully.

"Put your gun down," she called.

A pause.

"Put yours down," Naude shouted back.

"No shooting, okay?"

"Why are you still holding onto that Glock, then?"

Jade tensed when Naude identified her gun. That level of awareness indicated professionalism.

"Here. Look." She held the Glock by its barrel and stretched her hand out, past the back bumper of the white van, where Naude could see it clearly.

Her hand was steady. She was glad about that, because the rest of her body felt as if it was vibrating.

"Now you," she called. "Your turn."

Slowly, a large, leather-clad arm appeared from behind the tree, holding the Beretta in the same position.

Jade stood up and pushed her gun back into the holster.

Across the car park she saw Naude doing likewise.

At that point, a white Audi shot across the parking lot and accelerated out through the exit gate. The blare of its horn was deafening.

A client making a break for freedom. He must have seen the whole thing. Had he alerted the people inside the club? Had anyone else seen?

They had. Jade saw a beefy, black-suited figure appear at the door. Shielding his eyes with his hand, the bouncer stared out into the parking lot.

"It's okay, bru,'" Naude called. "Everything's under control."

The bouncer looked at Naude, then at Jade. He shrugged, then turned round and walked back inside the club.

Whatever happened now, Jade knew she was on her own.

Naude strode across the parking lot towards her. He was

sweating profusely. His hair was sodden, and rivulets of sweat were running down his face. He wiped them away with his sleeve, leaving a wet, shiny streak on the leather.

Jade kept her eyes glued to his right hand. The minute it dropped towards his holster, she was going to act first, and to hell with the consequences.

Naude stopped when he was just a few paces away and folded his arms. The sun backlit his hair, giving him an incongruous-looking halo.

"You've been making a lot of trouble for me," he said.

"You've been making your own trouble," she responded, lifting her chin and looking him in the eye.

What had David said a while ago that she'd found so hurtful? Something to do with the fact that he'd stared into a lot of killers' eyes, and they all looked the same. They all had the same expression, he'd said—something hard; something cold.

Then David had stared directly at Jade. "You have it," he said.

"What?" she'd asked, rattled.

"That look. Killer's eyes." He'd smiled, but without mirth. "You have it in spades. I can see it whenever I look at you."

He'd left soon after that, and Jade had walked straight to the bathroom and spent a few minutes staring, concerned, into the mirror. Killer's eyes? What was David going on about? Try as she might, all she had seen was that her own eyes were wide, green, and worried-looking.

Looking closely at Naude, she didn't have a clue whether he had the eyes of a killer or not. She obviously didn't have David's instincts in that regard.

Naude gave a low chuckle. "Never had the chance to make trouble for myself."

"How do you mean?"

Before he could answer, the bouncer appeared at the door again and shouted out, "Bru', the security guard says he already called the cops. They're on their way."

"Right. Thanks," Naude called back. "I'm out of here," he said to Jade. "I'm having to avoid the police at the moment. Thanks to you."

He started walking back towards his bike.

"Wait," Jade called after him. "Just a minute. You were telling me why you never had the chance."

Naude lifted his helmet onto his head and swung his leg over the bike's seat. It started with a roar and he spun it round in a tight turn, sending grit flying.

Jade thought he was going to ride straight past her and out of the open gate, but when he reached her he brought the big motorbike to a stop.

"You want to know what's going on?" His voice was muffled by the helmet.

"Yes."

"I can't help you there. I don't have a clue what's going on myself. But I can tell you what I know. Not here, though." He patted the seat behind him. "Get on."

In a heartbeat, Jade weighed up the pros and cons.

Going with Naude might get her killed. But it would give Jade her only chance to find out his side of the story.

"You don't know if it's a hornets' nest until you poke it with a stick." Who had said that? Her father, probably. The logic behind the saying was simple enough—it basically defined police work. If you dig around enough in the right place, something will come buzzing out looking to sting you.

Jade hesitated for only a moment before making a firm decision. Then she climbed onto the leather seat behind Naude and grasped him around his waist.

The butt of his Beretta dug into her forearm. As she had expected, there was no way he could draw his own gun now. That single fact had convinced Jade it would be safe enough to go with him.

"Don't shoot me, okay?" said Naude. He sounded amused, as if he'd just had the same thought.

Then, before she had time to change her mind, the bike leaped forward. They were out of the gate and down the road by the time Jade heard the first sirens, faintly, behind them.

43

Jade's eyes were streaming, thanks to the hot, dusty air flying past her face. She'd tried twisting her head and looking back, but her hair, blown by the slipstream, had whipped around her face and ended up lashing her eyes as well.

Now her forehead was braced against the back of Naude's leather jacket and her eyes were tightly shut, apart from a few instances where she'd dared open them to stare down at the tarmac flashing past below her as the bike angled around a corner.

They rode for about fifteen minutes before Naude slowed, came to a halt, and switched off the engine.

They were in the shade of a tree, near the junction of two minor roads. She had no idea what area they were in, but judging from the angle of the sun on her face, she thought they'd been heading north.

Jade slid gratefully off the pillion. Naude kicked the bike's stand out and swung one leg over the saddle. He pulled off his helmet and hung it from the handlebar, just as he had done back at the club. Then he leaned against the bike, arms folded, staring at her.

Jade noticed his arms weren't crossed through each other. Instead, his right hand was cradling his left elbow and the palm of his left hand was face up in the crook of his right arm.

He saw what she was looking at.

"Your shot grazed me," he said, nodding down at his arm. "That day at Pamela's house. Your bullet caught me on the inside of my forearm. Bled like hell. Burns the crap out of me whenever I bend it."

"You swerved as I fired. I was aiming for your chest," Jade said.

Naude nodded. "I was aiming for yours, too. At first I was going to aim for the head. But in motion, at that distance, I thought it was better to shoot at centre mass."

"You got my jacket. Just a couple of centimetres to the right of my ribs."

"My front wheel caught on a loose brick," Naude said. "It threw my bike off balance. Funny, that probably saved both our lives. I've never shot at a living person before, only targets, but I wanted to put you down."

He reached into his jacket pocket with his right hand and pulled out a pack of cigarettes.

"You smoke?"

Jade shook her head.

Naude lit up and exhaled a grey cloud that quickly vanished into the dusty air.

"Good shooting, anyway. I'm glad I got a chance to tell you that." He inhaled again.

"I thought yours was a lucky shot," Jade said.

Naude shook his head and tapped his chest with his index finger. "Central Gauteng Practical Shooting Association open champion, handgun section, almost every year from 1992. The times I didn't win were when I didn't enter."

Jade remembered the man on the motorbike pursuing them down the road just after Pamela had appointed her as a bodyguard. Shots had been fired; glass was shattered. But nobody was harmed. Neither of them had been touched by a bullet.

A sharpshooter would certainly have hit his target from that distance, even mounted on a motorbike. It would have been the equivalent of point-blank range.

That left only one explanation.

"Pamela hired you."

Naude nodded. "Ja. She hired me."

"To torture and kill her husband?"

"Nope. She paid me to shoot him in the head with a silenced weapon and dump his body somewhere out of the way. Ditto his girlfriend. I told her I didn't have a silencer, so she told me to wrap a pillow around my gun. She said she'd watched people doing that in movies and it seemed to work just fine. I thought it was a bloody stupid idea, myself, but what could I do? Money talks, and it spoke loud enough to convince me."

Jade could well believe it had. She saw now that the Ducati he was riding was a 1098R, the most expensive model by far. For a moment she wondered how an ex-bouncer could manage to afford these luxury wheels, and what other work he had been doing since he left Heads & Tails.

The motorbike creaked as Naude shifted position. A car swished past on the quiet road.

"Why didn't you shoot them, then?" Jade asked.

Naude stared down at the glowing tip of his cigarette.

"Pammie and I have been friends a long time," he said. "Since we were youngsters. Good friends. Friends with benefits at one stage, know what I mean? We've been in business together. We've played together. No secrets between us."

Jade nodded.

"That's how I know she's been wanting a divorce. Terence opposed it, of course. No good reason, I don't think, just that it was something she wanted and he didn't. He was a piece of shit, by the way. I'm not saying what happened to him in the end was fair or right, but Jesus, he sure as hell had something coming to him." Naude dropped his cigarette butt on the stony verge and stamped it out with his boot. "Anyway, back to Pamela. Time went by, she pushed harder, he started threatening her. If she divorces him, she's in trouble. If she divorces him, he's going to start hurting people."

"Pamela's mother?" Jade asked.

Naude nodded. "So you heard about that? Could have been organised by Terence, could have been an accident. Who'll ever know?"

"So then she asked you to kill him?"

Naude shook his head. His grey-streaked fringe, clumped and flattened from the snug-fitting helmet, flopped from side to side. "Wasn't as simple as that. She waited. See, from time to time in his line of work, Terence gets threats made against him. It's happened before when he went up against a rival chain of clubs. They started fighting back, and things got really nasty. I was working for him at the time, and I saw how badly he was shitting himself. Talking about emigrating. In the end he just left Jo'burg for a while and went underground. Came back and sorted out the people who'd threatened him, and it was business as usual."

Another car drove past and Naude turned to watch it go.

"So Pammie decided to wait," he said.

"For another threat?"

Naude nodded.

"Wait till Terence was nervous again, wait until she thought there was more trouble coming his way. Then, if the police investigated, they'd stumble upon whatever had been scaring him. Because, as you know, the spouse is always the first suspect. So she reckoned, that way, she'd have an alibi."

Jade nodded.

"And I had another idea," Naude continued.

"Involving me?"

"Well, involving somebody like you. Anybody, really. I just said, go hire somebody to keep you safe, but for God's sake don't make it some trigger-happy man who'll try and shoot me when I do the job."

"So she hired me." Jade nodded slowly. Now she realised that Pamela's panic, and subsequent crash, hadn't been caused by Naude's pursuit. It had been caused by the fact that Jade was getting out her gun and preparing to return fire.

"But nothing went the way it should have done. It was a total screw-up, start to finish."

"Why?"

"Pammie made a plan to be away for a couple of nights. She knew Terence would have Crystal there. She gave me the keys to get in and I drove there just before midnight. Had no idea what I was going to do, or how I was going to do it. I was shitting myself too, right enough."

"And what happened?"

Naude shook his head. "The gate was wide open. Terence's car was in his carport, and some other car I hadn't seen before was parked at the top of the driveway. I went away. Thought maybe they had company. Came back a couple of hours later and the other car was gone, but the front door was still open even though there was nobody around. I went inside; checked the bedroom." He grimaced. "I didn't know the girl was already dead and Terence had been tortured, but I guessed something had gone badly wrong for them, so I locked up and got the hell out."

"Is that why you went ahead with the mock shooting the next day?"

"Yup." Naude grimaced. "When that taxi hit my bike from behind, I thought I was history. Wished I'd asked Pamela for danger money on top of my fee. Then I realised I'd left voice messages on her home answer phone instead of her cellphone. I rushed over there to delete the messages, and saw the girl's body in the bathroom. And then I saw you."

He shrugged. "That's all I can tell you."

"Do you know where Tamsin is?" Jade watched him closely.

"I know she's missing. It's not unusual for her. She goes away from time to time on business. Disappears for a few days, then she's back again as if nothing's happened."

"A dancer at the club told me you've done work for Tamsin."

Naude frowned and started to shake his head again. Then he stopped, seeming to realise what Jade was talking about.

"Oh, you mean placing girls in other jobs?"

"Yes."

"I don't do that anymore."

"Why?"

"Tammy hasn't referred anybody to me for a long time. It used to be a good system. If the girl worked out somewhere else, I'd kick a finder's fee back to her. Win-win."

"Do you know anything about a man called Salimovic?"

Naude went silent and Jade saw his jaw tighten.

"Don't know anyone who goes by that name." He glanced down at his helmet, then turned his head to watch another passing car.

Was he lying? Jade had no idea.

Then his cellphone beeped and he pulled it out of his pocket. He read what must have been a text message, and pocketed the phone again.

"Time to get going. You want me to drop you back at the club?"

Jade nodded. "Thanks."

He swung his leg over the bike, then hesitated and turned back to her. In an even voice, he said, "If there's anything I can do to help sort this out, let me know. Pammie's a good friend. I don't like seeing her in trouble."

Jade got back on the bike and tucked herself in behind him,

inhaling the sweet smell of warm leather and the sharp tang of fresh sweat.

Then he started his bike and pulled away so fast that Jade nearly fell off. She grabbed at his jacket and clung on for dear life.

Jade couldn't see any police cars when they got back to the club. She guessed Naude's bouncer friend must have told them the call-out was a false alarm. All the same, Naude stopped just long enough to allow her to dismount before roaring back out of the gate, and turning in the direction of the highway.

Jade rubbed her stinging eyes, blinking away what felt like a whole flock of small flying insects. Then she pulled her shirt straight and raked her fingers through her hair.

Thinking it over, she realised that Naude's account of what had happened over the last couple of days answered a lot of questions. Even though she still didn't trust the moustached man, she did believe his story.

Almost.

44

After a search, Jade found the private parking area that Pamela had mentioned; a garage just a few steps to the right of the back door where the dancers had stood smoking.

The only problem was that it was empty.

Pamela's red Ferrari was no longer there.

Outside Heads & Tails, twilight was deepening, and Jade noticed dark, angry storm clouds gathering on the horizon. Inside, the black-painted ceiling and neon overhead lights steeped the place in permanent night.

Nobody in Heads & Tails had seen Pamela Jordaan. Not the bunny-eared worker at the front desk, nor the grim-faced bouncer, nor the waitress hurrying to the kitchen with a tray stacked high with empty glasses and dirty ashtrays.

Jade could think of only one possible explanation. After parking her car, Pamela must have walked around the building and seen Jade leave on the back of Naude's motorbike.

She would have known then that the game was up.

Jade was pretty sure that Pamela had told the truth about her daughter while they were driving to the club. However, up till then, most of what she had said had been lies. In her efforts to organise her husband's murder, Pamela had lied to Jade, she had lied to Moloi, and she must have lied to countless other people. Lied with a straight face, looking them in the eye.

Jade wondered whether she would have left a money trail when she paid Naude. If she had, Moloi would easily be able to follow it. Hadn't David told her once that Moloi had an accounting degree, and a nose as keen as a bloodhound's when it came to sniffing out the truth?

Unless Jade could prove beyond doubt that somebody else had

murdered Terence Jordaan, Pamela would be facing a guilty verdict and a lengthy jail sentence. As would Naude.

Jade wondered why Naude hadn't seemed more worried about that. After all, he surely couldn't hope to evade the police forever—not unless he was planning on fleeing the country.

She called Pamela's cellphone number, but wasn't surprised to discover it was unavailable.

Putting her phone back into her pocket, Jade stood outside the club's entrance, momentarily indecisive. She had no transport now, but a lack of wheels was the least of her worries.

As the manager of the Midrand branch of Heads & Tails, and the person responsible for hiring staff, Tamsin was perfectly placed to procure an endless supply of victims for her lover to traffic both locally and abroad. She could easily have done so without her father knowing. When Jade had seen the interview forms in Tamsin's house, she'd assumed that the contact numbers of the applicants' closest relatives had been requested for the sake of thoroughness. Now she knew better. That information had allowed Salimovic to locate and torture the trafficked victims' loved ones.

Jade remembered the two black women wandering despondently away from the club. Young women with no close family ties, recently arrived in Jo'burg, would be desperate to find work in the city where highways were jammed with SUVs and luxury vehicles, and where the rich lived like Hollywood film stars in their high-walled palaces.

The city that lured its visitors in with the promise of endless riches, only to renege on the deal in the most brutal ways.

Jade turned round and walked back into the club.

■

If a client had strayed into the back offices of Heads & Tails, Jade was sure he would have retreated fast, confused and disappointed.

The club's darkly lit glamour stopped at the door to the admin office. Inside, Jade saw no semi-nude girls—not even any pictures of them. The only wall hanging in evidence was a calendar featuring luxury cars. It made sense when she thought about it. Motor mechanics traditionally had girlie calendars in their offices, so why shouldn't girlie-club owners go for cars?

The offices were small in size and decorous—modest, even—in

appearance. A middle-aged woman with permed hair and a sour face sat at one of the desks, hunched over her computer screen, working her way through what looked like a pile of invoices.

"This is where Tamsin sits." The bunny-eared receptionist who had brought her inside pushed open the door to another small room. It had taken some persuasive talking for Jade to gain access to the admin section. The bouncer hadn't wanted to let her through. He'd made her wait in reception for over an hour, and it was only when she threatened to call Pamela—an empty threat, given the fact that her phone was switched off—that he had given her grudging permission. She could see him even now, hovering at the main door. Watching her.

Jade walked into the office, out of range of the bouncer's steely glare. She had braced herself for the same clutter that she'd picked her way through in Tamsin's house. To her surprise, the place was tidy.

Extremely tidy, now that she took a closer look. A pink jersey was folded on the back of a chair, and a few pens and pencils were set squarely on the desk.

Jade stepped over to the desk and opened a drawer. It slid out easily on smooth runners. Then she tried the handle of the cupboard, and the door sprang open with a metallic clang. Both the cupboard and the drawer were empty.

She closed the door again carefully and checked the other drawers, but she already knew what she would find in them, which was nothing.

Apart from the furniture, the jersey and the most basic station-ery items, the office was empty.

No perfume, no cigarette packets, no hand cream, no chewing gum, no water bottles, no framed party photos. Not even any of the blank interview forms she'd seen in Tamsin's study. No completed ones, either.

She wondered if there had been anything else in the office an hour ago.

"Where's all Tamsin's stuff?" Jade asked.

Bunny Ears fidgeted with her bunny ears. "I—well, Tamsin usually brings her laptop when she comes to work."

"And the records for the staff who work here? Where are they kept?"

"Oh, Clara deals with those." The receptionist indicated the lady with the perm, who was now tidying her desk. "She does all the filing."

From the doorway of Tamsin's office, Jade saw two large metal cabinets behind Clara's desk. Three of the drawers were labelled "Staff."

Clara raised her head and stared at Jade through thick, horn-rimmed glasses. Her gaze had all the warmth and friendliness of a nest of vipers.

"Thank you," Jade said to Bunny Ears. "I've seen enough."

David answered on the second ring when she called him. He sounded as if he was driving.

"Where are you?" she asked.

"On my way back from a meeting," he replied. From the despair in his voice, Jade knew immediately that there had been no news of Kevin. She feared that he had given up hope; that he no longer believed his child would be coming home safely.

"Are you anywhere near Midrand?"

"I could be, in about twenty minutes."

"Could you possibly give me a lift home? I'm at Heads & Tails."

"Okay," he replied tonelessly. He disconnected without saying goodbye.

Jade stared down at her phone in concern.

Then she walked over to the gate and stood there, in the parking lot, watching as cars arrived and other cars—fewer of them—left. To pass the time, she thought about the logistics of what Tamsin had been doing.

Trafficked victims had to be sourced. That was easy enough. She remembered the staff advertisements she'd seen in the papers. Dancers Needed. Earn Big Bucks. Full Training Given. That was a lie, because the club hired only experienced dancers, many of them on contract from Europe. Only inexperienced applicants who fitted certain other criteria would be candidates for trafficking.

What had happened to those girls next, Jade wondered.

The victims who had ended up at Salimovic's brothel had been "broken in" by him personally, at his London home. But if Tamsin had also been supplying girls to other, more local establishments, they would have needed to be broken in beforehand.

Kept prisoner somewhere while they were raped. Held until Salimovic, or one of his accomplices, could locate and torture one of the women's family members in order to ensure their silence forever.

"She goes away from time to time on business. Disappears for a few days, then she's back again as if nothing's happened."

Staring at the white van with the tinted windows, Jade replayed Naude's words in her head. Her arms covered themselves in goosebumps as she suddenly realised what Tamsin must have been doing.

Without a doubt, she was the one who had hired the trafficked women. And Jade was willing to bet that she had also transported them from place to place. Driven them away to a secure location where their nightmare would begin, and a few days later, delivered them to their final destination.

Her thoughts were interrupted when tungsten headlights on full beam lit up the club's entrance gate and a bright orange Mazda with mirrored windows and an oversized rear spoiler swung in and roared towards her.

Jade recognised the car David was driving. It was one of the unmarked vehicles from the detectives' car pool, which she guessed he would be using as the undercover vehicle for the brothel raid later that evening. Although it was not exactly unobtrusive, a casual observer would never have suspected it was a police car. It looked more like a low-end drug dealer's runaround.

The first time she'd seen it, she had immediately christened it the Pimpmobile. David's expression of outraged embarrassment as he'd wound the window down had made her laugh so hard she'd ended up sitting on her driveway, tears streaming from her eyes.

Happier times.

Now she jogged over to an empty parking spot and waved David in. He hesitated, then swung the car hard left and parked. He unfolded himself from the car and walked towards her with exhausted, foot-dragging steps.

"What's going on now?" he asked.

"This van." Jade pointed towards the people-carrier with the darkly tinted windows. "I think this is how she's been transporting the victims."

David rubbed at his eyes using his knuckles, as if this was too much information for him to absorb.

"Who transports what?"

Jade gave him a brief rundown of what she believed Tamsin had been doing.

David listened, nodding occasionally. Then he lowered his head and pressed his fingers into his temples the way he did when he had a bad headache. Jade realised he was having to force himself to concentrate on the job at hand.

"Makes sense, doesn't it? Let's have a look inside it, then."

He walked over to the van and tried the door. It was locked.

Squaring his shoulders, summoning up what must have been a final reserve of energy, David set off towards Heads & Tails. Jade was at his shoulder as the bunny-eared receptionist let him in, a decision that she was sure the lady would soon regret.

"Welcome to Heads—"

"Police Superintendent Patel, Organised Crime Division." David interrupted her, shouting over the throbbing music as he showed her his detective's ID. "I have urgent questions about criminal activities relating to one of your vehicles."

Bunny Ears smiled nervously. "Which one would that be?" she asked.

Before David could respond, the bouncer stepped forward. It was Naude's friend, the same man who had been watching Jade when she was in the offices earlier. Mr. Expressionless.

He was about six feet tall, and so muscle-bound that she doubted whether it would be physically possible for him to clean his own teeth. Up close, he smelled odd. A sour, chemical odour. The smell of steroids leaking out of his pores, she decided.

"I'll handle this, Pearl," he said to Bunny Ears.

Pearl. Of course. Given the stage names in this place, perhaps the hefty bouncer would turn out to be called Granite.

"You want to come this way?" He indicated the door leading to the admin offices that Jade had seen earlier. "We can talk in there.

Less noise." He stretched his lips into a smile, exposing a row of white and entirely false-looking teeth.

After the hubbub in the club's reception, the silence of the offices was a welcome relief.

"Which vehicle are you interested in finding out about?" The bouncer's words sounded very loud in the quiet room.

Jade noticed with a start that the snake-eyed admin lady—what was her name? Clara?—was still tidying up, bent over one of the filing cabinets. As Jade watched, she moved back to her desk and glanced up with an expression that looked like she'd been chewing on a lemon rind.

"The plain white van," David said. He walked through the door that the bouncer indicated, into Tamsin's small office.

He sat down on Tamsin's chair, leaving Jade the one in front of the desk.

The bouncer pushed a third chair across the carpeted floor into the office.

"Your name is?" he asked again.

David sounded irritated at having to repeat himself. "Superintendent David Patel, from the Organised Crime Division."

The bouncer closed the door behind them and sat down.

"You need information on this van?"

"Yes. Firstly—"

"Do you have a warrant, sir?"

"A warrant is on its way," David said, with such assurance that only Jade knew it was a bluff.

Jade heard a muffled creak from outside the door. Clara, getting up to do another bout of tidying.

"Sorry," the bouncer said. "But I'll need to check the warrant as soon as it arrives. What else do you want to know?"

When she heard keys jangling, Jade realised she had guessed wrong. Clara wasn't doing anymore filing. Clara was finally going home. To dance widdershins round her cauldron or sacrifice a goat in her back garden, or whatever the hell she did for fun in her spare time.

"Firstly, who is the vehicle's designated driver? If there is more than one person, I'll need every name. Secondly, how long has it been owned by this company, and was it purchased new? Thirdly, where has it been . . ."

256 • JASSY MACKENZIE

Then Jade heard the faraway rattle of a big diesel engine starting up.

She was on her feet as fast as if an electric current had been run through her chair, before David could say another word and before she could offer any explanation for her actions.

The big bouncer was ready for her. He was quick on his feet, too, despite his size. He moved just as swiftly. Before Jade could get to the door, he was positioned in front of it, blocking her exit. Feet apart, knees slightly bent, arms at midriff-level in front of his body.

Braced for a fight.

On certain occasions, Stewart had explained to her trainees, a bodyguard would not be able to avoid getting involved in physical conflict. When that happened, she said, she was going to share the only rule for success.

"Martial arts?" the American student had asked, and Stewart had turned on him with a withering glare.

"Martial arts are bugger-all use to you in a street fight, laddie. I've seen black belt experts knocked out cold by street fighters because the experts couldn't decide which of their fancy moves they should begin with. The only rule is this. Act fast and act first. Practise one or two moves until you know them better than your own name. Use them instantly, and with all the force you have."

Jade was at a disadvantage in terms of height and weight, compared to most of her opponents, so she'd rehearsed a routine as swift as it was dirty.

By the time David shouted "What the hell?" Jade was already making her move.

A feint with the left hand to draw the bouncer's stronger right away by throwing a weak punch; a move that only tricked people because she was a woman. He grabbed her left hand hard, crushing it in his meaty fist, but that didn't matter, because before he could do any damage, Jade let rip with her double whammy. Her right knee hammered into his groin, and her right fingers straight into his eyes, as stiff as prongs.

The bouncer let out a strangled gasp and doubled over, clutching his groin, just as David half-leaped over the desk to help her, pens and pencils scattering.

"Jadey! What on earth's the problem?"

"Knock him out!" she shouted. She wrenched the door open so fast that it slammed into the bouncer's back. Pounding her way through the now-empty office towards the door at the back with the big green Fire Exit sign above it, she was relieved to find that Snake Eyes Clara had left it unlocked when she'd left.

When she'd left to drive away in the white van with the mirrored windows.

Jade sprinted across the car park. Clara had already reversed the van out of its parking place, but she seemed to be having difficulty engaging first gear, because when she saw Jade racing towards the driver's door, she put her foot down and it promptly stalled.

Jade flung herself at the driver's door and grabbed hold of the handle.

Locked, of course. Bloody central locking. And now Clara was turning the engine over again, glaring through the window at Jade. In a couple of seconds she'd be on the move.

Wrenching her Glock from its holster, Jade smacked the butt against the window glass with all her strength. Despite her efforts, the window didn't break. One of the drawbacks of owning a gun made largely of polymer, perhaps.

The engine roared into life and Jade heard the gearbox engage. She was sure that, this time, Snake Eyes would have worked out where to find first gear.

Jade angled the gun away from Clara's head and aimed at a place where she had a clear line of sight through the opposite back window. With her left hand she grabbed a tight hold of the vehicle's roof-rack.

As she fired, the van surged forward, so fast and suddenly that the rack ripped out of her hand and she went sprawling, face-first, onto the rough tarmac.

Jade thought it was over then, but, wonder of wonders, the abrupt leap forward had been caused by Snake Eyes stalling the car a second time, startled by the sound of the gun.

She scrambled to her feet. Her shoulder throbbed and her right cheek was stinging. Her elbow was grazed where she'd used it to break her fall, but her right hand was undamaged, and so was the gun it held.

The bullet-hole in the window that was now a web of cracks had given her the opportunity she needed. She punched the Glock's butt into the hole, and this time the glass gave way so easily that Jade's arm just kept on going. The side of the gun clubbed Clara on her right temple.

It was a hard and uncompromising blow. The woman reeled sideways, stunned. Her horn-rimmed glasses flew off her head.

Jade fumbled for the door handle through the rough-edged gap. She pulled it up, and she was in. Another whack on the head for Clara. Two points scored for the Glock. The admin assistant collapsed sideways, lolling onto the passenger seat.

Jade grabbed her ankles and yanked them towards the door. The woman was wearing brown court shoes. One of them fell off as Jade dragged her out of the vehicle. As she did so, Clara's skirt rode up and exposed her legs and her knickers, both of which were off-white and thick-looking. Jade slid an arm under her head to stop it from thumping down onto the tarmac. She didn't want to kill her. Dead bodies were far harder to question than admin assistants with a nasty headache.

"How much did Tamsin pay you?" Jade asked the prone woman rather breathlessly, as she moved her none too gently into the recovery position. "Were you and Granite-Face getting good money to keep quiet about what she was doing?"

Jade didn't expect an answer to her questions. Clara's snake eyes remained closed and she groaned softly.

"I hope it'll be worth the prison time," Jade said.

As she stood up, a glint of orange caught her eye.

David was scrambling out of the unmarked, which he'd parked sideways-on so that it blocked the exit gate of Heads & Tails.

"You're crazy," she shouted. "If this woman had got the van going, there's no way she would have stopped. She'd have smashed straight into your car and knocked it out of the way, with you inside."

David didn't react. He just stared at her, taking in her rumpled hair and bleeding elbow, her ripped jeans and grazed cheek. Taking in the people carrier's shattered driver's window and the bullet-hole in the glass opposite. Eventually, he replied.

"No," he said slowly, shaking his head. "I'm not the crazy one here, Jadey. You are."

45

David moved the unmarked away from the gate, and Jade heard him using the radio to call for backup. Job done, he locked the car and started striding purposefully towards her, his large shoes scrunching on the tarmac.

Jade wanted to hug him for the brave but foolish action of parking his car across the entrance. She wanted to tell him she loved him, that her heart was breaking for him and everything he was going through.

Instead, she pointed out that one of his shoelaces was coming undone.

While David bent down to sort it out, Jade took a look inside the van.

There, she saw what she had expected to see in Tamsin's office.

Although the interior smelled pleasantly of strawberries, there were crumpled tissues on the floor, a stack of dance CDs strewn over the passenger seat on top of a pink sports top, and a bottle of perfume, a lipstick, some gum, a granola bar, and a half-empty pack of Silk Cut all stuffed into the central console.

And, most tellingly of all, an instant Polaroid four-photo passport camera was lying on the carpet on the passenger side, half-in, half-out of its padded bag, on top of a large box of film.

Staring at the now-empty seats in the back, Jade shivered to think of who had sat in them, where they had been taken, how their hopes and dreams had been brutally shattered.

To her, those seats reeked of despair.

A GPS navigator was positioned on the dashboard. Aware that the police would need to fingerprint this device, Jade folded her jacket sleeve over her index finger and pressed the "On" button.

After a few false starts, she discovered a list of the most recently travelled destinations. The airport, the Michelangelo hotel. Two other addresses in Sandton, one in Bez Valley, one in central Pretoria and one in Dullstroom, Mpumalanga.

Dullstroom. That was the one Jade needed. Her cellphone had GPS, and she copied the coordinates into it. Then, frowning, she double-checked the routes that were shown on both.

"Why did Tamsin take those roads?" she said aloud.

At her feet, Clara was starting to utter a series of dazed-sounding grunts. David opened the unmarked's boot and tossed Jade a pair of handcuffs. She cuffed the woman's hands together behind her back and threw her shoes under the Mercedes van. Without them, she wouldn't get far.

By the time David's team arrived, together with a police car from the Midrand precinct and a forensic technician, the admin assistant was fully conscious and spluttering threats at Jade.

Jade stepped back and watched the action from the sidelines, feeling oddly left out, even though she had watched similar scenes many times when her father was alive. Over the next few hours, she knew that the officers would question the club's employees in detail and, when a warrant arrived, search the premises and gather evidence.

Police questioning and investigation. A lengthy, pedantic process. A series of tiny jigsaw pieces that, if you were thorough and lucky, would eventually be joined together to reveal the full picture. No way to speed it up; not with the team still awaiting the necessary search warrant.

But Jade didn't have any time to spare. She needed to get going as soon as possible.

David was inside the club with Captain Thembi, who was barking commands at his team. With the music now turned off, his voice sounded very loud.

Somebody had switched on all the overhead lights, and in the brightness Jade could see peeling paint on the walls and scuff marks on the floor. The nightclub staff were lined up on one side of the room. She recognised Opal and Amber, who were whispering together and looking scared, but was relieved to see that the helpful Ebony had obviously had the night off. A number of rather dumbstruck-looking clients were lined up on the other side. All were waiting to be questioned.

The bouncer, who now sported a swollen lump on the side of

his head courtesy of David's elbow, was sitting at the end of the line, his hands cuffed behind his back.

When Thembi had finished speaking, Jade tapped David on the shoulder.

"I'll see you later," she said.

"What . . . Where are you going? I thought you needed a lift."

"You're busy here, and I've got to get going. Now. I've called a taxi to take me home."

David stared at her, eyes narrowed. "I'm not too busy to drive you back to your place. Why the urgency, Jadey? What's up?"

"I'm going to get my car. Then I'm driving to Dullstroom."

"Tonight?"

"Yes."

"Why?"

"I studied the GPS in that van. It's been driven regularly to a few destinations. One of them is a place in Bez Valley, so they may have been doing business with the brothel you're raiding tonight. One of the other destinations is Dullstroom. That's a small town, it's out in the middle of nowhere, and I don't believe for a moment it's a hotbed of illegal sexual activity. But Terence owns a country lodge in that area, a top-security place which he's apparently used from time to time as a hideout. I think Tamsin has been taking the trafficked women there to get them broken in."

David didn't reply, and from his expression she knew he was thinking of Kevin.

Every step that led them closer to Tamsin and Salimovic might also lead them closer to his son.

Then he took the keys for the orange unmarked out of his pocket and jangled them in his hand.

"Come on, then," he said. "I'll take you home."

A strong wind had started to blow and as they pulled onto the highway, Jade could feel it buffeting the car.

The first summer storm was on the way.

"So Terence has a country lodge?"

"Well, it looks more like a small farm."

She glanced down at her phone to double-check the coordinates. To her consternation, David leaned over too and peered down at the screen.

"Should take you about three hours to do that distance, I'm guessing."

"You'd do it in two." She glanced up and immediately panicked. "David! Tanker!"

The noise from the growling engine noise of the slow-moving tanker ahead filled their car. A timely swerve, and David just managed to avoid ramming the unmarked into its tailgate. They whipped past its solid steel flank.

Jade's heart was leaping in her throat, and she prised her fingers away from the dashboard with some difficulty.

"The Mercedes van used a lot of back roads to get there," Jade said, when she was capable of calm speech again. "A real zig-zag of a route. It certainly wasn't a shortcut. I'm guessing Tamsin did it so that the women wouldn't have any idea where they were headed. Going along minor roads, sand roads, back routes, you'd never be able to tell anybody exactly where you had been taken."

"Fewer road signs, and less risk of running into a police road-block," David observed.

"That, too."

"You think this Naude chap knows what's going on?"

"David, I don't know. Perhaps he's in on the conspiracy, perhaps he isn't. If I'd got five rands for everyone who's told me the truth in this case, I still don't think I'd be able to buy a loaf of bread."

"Yup. That's people for you." David shifted his grip on the wheel. "Bastards when it comes to getting the facts."

"Naude told me Pamela paid him to shoot Terence and Crystal with a silenced weapon on a night when she wasn't home. He said he didn't know if he could do it."

"Why?"

"He said he's never aimed his gun at a living target before."

David glanced at her, frowning. "He didn't seem to have too many scruples when he tried to take you out."

"That's what's getting to me, too. I . . ." How to say it? Better to tell the truth, she decided. After all, somebody had to. "I know what the first time's like, David. I know you do as well. Tell me that you didn't hesitate before you fired at your first human target."

There was a telling silence.

"Yes. I did. I did hesitate," David said.

Jade didn't expect him to say anymore about it, but to her surprise, he did.

"It was back in Durban, when I was on a night patrol near the city centre. On foot. It was summer and humid as hell. I remember wishing I wasn't wearing my service pistol, because it was making a huge patch of sweat on my hip. Then we heard running, and round the corner came two guys wearing balaclavas. Just like that. It was surreal. We found out later they'd just robbed the Curry Palace down the road, and they were on their way to their getaway car. Talk about wrong place, wrong time."

Jade made an encouraging noise, wanting him to finish his story.

"I drew my pistol. I was very calm—it all happened so fast, I didn't have time to get scared. I should have fired then and there, because the leader had a gun in his hand. I shouted at them to stop. But the leader didn't stop; he just shot. He could have killed me, could have killed my partner. Neither of us was wearing Kevlar. I didn't act fast enough to prevent it. But he missed."

David swallowed hard.

"Then I shot him in the chest," he finished.

Jade didn't know what to say. She wanted to take David's hand and lace her fingers in his long brown ones, and squeeze it hard.

And she did.

Perhaps it was because of the near miss they'd just had with the tanker. Perhaps it was for some other reason. In any case, to her own amazement, she found herself reaching over and taking his left hand, which was curled around the gear stick, with her right. She slid her palm over the back of his hand, pushed her fingers in between his and clasped his hand tightly.

For a few moments, David squeezed her hand back. And, for those few moments, Jade wouldn't have minded if he'd crashed the car right there.

46

Edmonds had expected Cyprus to be warm. In fact, it was hot. She'd discarded her jacket as soon as she and Richards disembarked from the plane at Larnaca Airport in Southern Cyprus, and the long-sleeved top she was wearing underneath soon followed.

T-shirt weather in October. Who would have thought it?

They drove north in their hired car and crossed the Green Line at the Agios Dometios gate in Nicosia half an hour later. Here, they showed their passports at the checkpoint and were soon heading into Northern Cyprus.

The tiny village of Malatya was set high in the mountains. The Beshpa-mark, or the Five Fingers, according to Richards, who was happily bombarding Edmonds with local facts and figures. Sitting in the passenger seat, Edmonds was only half-listening to him as she took in the bleak, rugged scenery while the car wound its way up the narrow pass.

"Criminal bolthole." Edmonds tuned Richards back in again. "That's what this place is. A hideaway for every deadbeat that's ever stolen, smuggled, blackmailed, or laundered money. You know there's no extradition treaty between here and the UK? That's caused a lot of problems in the past, and I think it's why the authorities are pretty much cooperating with us now. They don't want their country to get anymore of a reputation as a place where the lowlifes can evade arrest."

Two detectives from the Turkish Cypriot police were waiting outside the villa, which was set back from the road, down a long driveway, behind ornate gates. They were leaning against the low wall that separated the white-painted buildings from the surrounding gardens.

The villa that was owned by Xavier Soumare and Mathilde Dupont.

This information had been gleaned by Mackay, who had been investigating the British Airways flight which the two suspected traffickers had taken from Cyprus. Although the pair had left no paper trail this time round, the airline recovered their address via a previous booking, when they had flown first-class to the Seychelles.

Mackay had told Edmonds that they had either made a stupid mistake in revealing their home address, or else been super-confident that they wouldn't be traced.

"The police raid on Number Six was an unlucky coincidence for them, that's for sure," he'd said. "If it hadn't been for us arriving at that time, they'd have got away free and clear."

The shorter of the two detectives, a sleepy-looking man with a large black moustache, stepped forward and shook their hands. He introduced himself as Barak. Edmonds was glad that he spoke good, if strongly accented, English. Earlier, in the southern part of the country, Richards had earned her undying gratitude by communicating with the car hire company in fluent Greek.

"You can go inside," Barak said to her. "We have searched the place and taken fingerprints. The information has been sent to our offices. We are waiting . . ." At first Edmonds thought the detective had paused to search for an English word, but then she noticed the well-dressed woman approaching on foot. A neighbour, perhaps.

When the woman started speaking, Edmonds was surprised to hear a distinctly British accent. An expat, then; one of the five thousand or so who lived in this part of the world. And, if Richards was to be believed, hopefully one of the few who were not criminals in hiding.

"Good afternoon, officer. I'm Maggie Rawlins from across the road. I got a message you wanted to speak to me. What's the problem? Is Mr. Soumare all right?"

The house wasn't a crime scene, so if the Cypriot detectives were prepared to allow her inside, Edmonds definitely wanted to take a look around. Moving away from her Turkish colleague into the cool, high-ceilinged hallway, Edmonds could hear Maggie Rawlins' outraged responses to the questions she was being asked.

"Impossible! Absolutely impossible. Xavier and his partner Mathilde are lovely people. I've known them for years. They'd never do anything like human trafficking."

Edmonds stepped further into the house, through the archway that led to the living room. The floor was tiled, the room felt surprisingly cool. Apart from the silvery smudges of fingerprint dust that Edmonds noticed on several surfaces, the tasteful interior was pristine.

Taking in the plush leather furniture, paintings on the wall that she didn't recognise, but which looked like expensive originals, a cabinet with a collection of porcelain, Edmonds felt the same choking rage rise up inside her that she'd experienced the day she had searched Mathilde's room in the five-star hotel.

How dare they? How *dare* they enrich themselves in this way, by abducting young women, subjecting them to the worst and vilest invasions of their being, changing them in such a way that even if they escaped their prison one day, they could never escape its legacy?

Human traffickers were thieves, but what they stole could never be given back or compensated for, because it was the very souls of the people they trafficked that they took.

"Officer, you *don't* understand." Maggie Rawlins' high-pitched voice was still clearly audible. "These people have done an enormous amount for charity. They are certainly not criminals. Ask their staff—they have a cleaner who comes in every morning and a gardener twice a week. And Mr. Soumare couldn't possibly commit a crime now, in any case, not with his health the way it is. He's been going to the BOC Oncology Clinic in Nicosia three times a week for aggressive radiotherapy and chemotherapy. He has cancer, you see."

A triumphant silence, as if the woman was sure this fact would change everything.

Hearing this, Edmonds clenched her jaw so hard that it hurt.

"Good," she uttered fiercely.

She stomped across the room, out of earshot of Maggie Rawlins' irritating voice. In a smaller adjoining room that opened onto a verandah, two comfortable-looking armchairs were positioned on either side of a glass coffee table. In contrast to the other furniture, these chairs looked as if they had been regularly used.

So this was where Xavier and Mathilde had sat. In the evenings, perhaps. Looking out at the sunset, sipping on cool drinks, paging through one of the books that she saw on the coffee table. And all without a twinge of conscience, she supposed.

A Lladro china figurine also stood on the table, next to a slim white cordless telephone slotted into its charger.

The idea came to Edmonds in a flash.

She picked the phone up in her left hand and turned it on, while digging in her jeans pocket for her own mobile.

She had the phone number for Amanita's grandfather in its memory.

He hadn't been answering any calls from the United Kingdom—but would he answer a call that came from here?

The keys of the cordless phone gave shrill beeps as she punched the number in. The noise seemed very loud to her, and she found herself glancing nervously over her shoulder. She wasn't sure if she was allowed to do this, and she knew she should check with Richards first, but she had no idea where he was now. He hadn't followed her into the house; that was all she knew.

Edmonds finished dialling the number and waited, standing alone in the quiet room, aware that her legs felt as tense as if she was waiting for a starting pistol to go off.

After a short pause she heard the ringing sound that had become all too familiar to her. It rang three times, four times, and she was beginning to think that it would go through to voicemail yet again.

Then, with a click that seemed to stop her heart, the call was answered and she heard Mr. Soumare's voice.

He said just one word.

"Xavier?"

That was enough. Edmonds snatched the phone away from her ear as if it had bitten her. Then she punched the disconnect button and quickly replaced the mobile on its rest. Her haste made her clumsy; on her first try it fell off and clattered onto the coffee table.

She couldn't believe that her suspicions had been so easily confirmed. Without a doubt, Amanita's grandfather knew Xavier Soumare, and from the sound of it had been expecting him to call.

Edmonds jumped as she heard footsteps on the tiles outside, and a moment later Richards walked onto the verandah.

"There you are. Come and have a look at this," he said.

Edmonds followed him outside and across the lawn to a covered patio where Barak was waiting. Nearby, a swimming pool of near-Olympian proportions sparkled in the sun.

Her mind was racing. She wanted to tell Richards about the call she had just made, but she didn't want to do it while she was within earshot of the Cypriot detectives, in case her actions ended up getting them both into trouble.

She decided it would be more sensible to tell him later.

"Down there." Richards pointed to a stone archway. "In the wine cellar."

Following the men down a steep flight of stairs, Edmonds saw the sturdy steel security gate at the bottom had been cut open—by the police, she supposed—and was standing ajar. She stepped into a gloomy room that didn't just feel cool, it felt cold. Wooden shelves lined the walls, with curved indentations on which hundreds of bottles rested.

Edmonds stared at the opposite wall, where two large wine barrels had been moved, stained rings on the floor indicating that they had been resting there for years.

The Cypriot police had done their work well. Behind the barrels, in a small recess, was a sturdy-looking safe door.

"This is what Barak just showed me," Richards explained. "They've got a professional safe-cracker already on the way, coming to open up. Another hour or two and we'll know what's inside. Apparently the house is clean. The detectives found no criminal evidence anywhere upstairs. So whatever secrets Xavier and Mathilde have been hiding, it's my bet we're going to find them in here."

47

On the highway to Dullstroom, Jade felt as if she was driving straight into a vast wall of cloud. Occasionally, lightning flickered eerily across the bulky piles of cumulus, or forked, hard and bright, to the ground. The trees swayed theatrically in the high wind, throwing leaves and small branches against the windscreen. When particularly strong gusts blew, the unmarked shuddered as if a hand were pushing it gently but insistently sideways.

The weather was as disturbed as Jade's own thoughts as she considered what motives Salimovic, Tamsin, Naude, and the mysterious Xavier and Mathilde might have for their actions. They seemed to her like pieces placed randomly on a chessboard—but who was on which side? And why?

Jade was beginning to worry that they were missing at least one crucial piece of information. She wished she could call for police backup, but police backup could mean certain death for Kevin.

Better to arrive quietly.

She reached the town just before eleven p.m. and drove slowly along the main road. Dullstroom was situated in the highlands of Mpumalanga, and she remembered it well because her father had taken occasional fishing trips there in the past. It was typical highland country—forested slopes, rolling hills, and countless dams. These, her father had optimistically informed her, were filled with trout, although Jade couldn't ever remember him having caught so much as one.

She was surprised to see that the town itself had tripled in size since she'd last been there. From the direction signs she passed, fly-fishing was still the main attraction, but now ranks of new-looking shops, restaurants and other businesses lined the main road, clamouring for customers' attention.

She was now just a few kilometres away from her destination.

There was the turnoff that would lead her to the country house. She left the main road, and after a couple more turns was soon driving through dark and empty countryside, down the long and rutted road that led directly to the smallholding.

A flash of sheet lightning illuminated the scene ahead. A winding sandtrack flanked by tall, dry grass; two or three animals grazing near a bushy copse. Jade had no idea what they were. Buck of some kind, with long, straight horns that looked almost silvery in the lightning.

They regarded the car with quiet curiosity.

"Headlights off," Jade muttered, wishing for a moment that David was in the car with her. "Better not to let them know I'm coming."

A twist of the knob, and her little car was careering into the pitch-black night at a speed that suddenly seemed far too fast.

She fumbled a gear change and the car veered off the track, hit a bump with a metallic scrape, and for one dizzying moment became completely airborne.

Jade clamped her lips together and braced her feet against the carpet. Her heart was pounding hard as the car slammed down again, bounced violently, and then she was back on course, braking hard and slowing to a crawl.

Another flash of lightning revealed a tall, solid gate ahead. It was set in a high palisade fence crested with vicious-looking coils of razor wire.

She stopped outside it and frowned into the darkness. She could just make out the lights of the farmhouse in the distance.

She had expected to find tight, Jo'burg-style security near the house, but the height of this perimeter fence meant that getting in was going to be more difficult than she'd thought.

Another pair of lights far to the left caught her eye, and she twisted round in her seat.

They seemed to be moving. An optical illusion? Or . . .

There it was again. The distant twinkle of approaching headlights, the beams bobbing and bouncing, intermittently swallowed by the undulating terrain.

Damn. Somebody was coming this way.

Jade reversed the car, then swerved off the sandy path and into the veld. Coarse grass scraped the undercarriage and she flinched as she hit a rock with a deafening bang.

She needed to find cover fast, but how could she tell where cover was? At least the strong wind would blow away the dust that had billowed out from under the tyres, so whoever was approaching would have no idea that another car had recently driven this way.

But all it would take would be one lightning-flash for her to stand out, as bright and visible as a beacon.

A hideous scraping sound told Jade that her poor little car would be due for a visit to the painters when she took it back to Rent-a-Runner, and quite possibly the panelbeaters too.

She'd driven right into the thorny embrace of a thick-looking bush.

The car rocked and bounced as she reversed and drove cautiously round the bush. She could see nothing now, and could only hope she'd done a good enough job of hiding herself.

Peering through the whipping leaves, Jade saw a dim glow. Then a moment later she was dazzled by a set of headlights on high beam. She blinked and instinctively ducked down in her seat.

Then the shadows swung away and she guessed it would be safe to look up again.

A big, dark vehicle was heading towards the gate, which Jade saw was starting to roll open.

This could be her only chance to get inside.

She swung her door open, and a gust of wind nearly ripped it off the car. It roared across the veld and whistled through the tree branches. Flying dust stung her eyes and made them water, but she could see the ruddy glow of brake lights disappearing as the car drove through the entrance and the gate started to close.

Jade set off at a run over the uneven ground. She bashed her shin against a rock, and felt her ankle turn as her foot slipped into a hole. She went sprawling and landed, face-down, in a shallow ditch.

As she scrabbled to her feet, she realised she'd reached the dirt track and that the ditch was actually a drainage channel. A smoother surface. Easier to run.

She didn't think it was possible to go any faster, but she managed to increase her speed.

The gap was barely a metre wide. If she didn't get there in the next few seconds . . .

Jade flung herself at the gate. Her shoulder crashed against its steel frame, slowing it down just enough to let her slip through the narrow gap before it closed. She spun round and grabbed the bars, gasping for breath, trying to jolt it out of its rhythm and force it to stay open, but the powerful motor didn't skip a beat.

She'd got in, but now she was trapped.

She fumbled with the metal box that housed the gate motor, but wasn't surprised to discover it was locked with a large and solid padlock.

Frustrated, Jade turned away from the gate.

As she crept cautiously up the long driveway, she thought back to when David had dropped her at the cottage. He'd wound down the driver's window and called out to her, but the gathering wind had blown his words away.

Now, Jade realised he had said, "Be careful."

48

Salimovic hurried down the carpeted corridor and into the master bedroom.

The storm had caused the power to dip, a problem that happened regularly in this area and was known as a 'brown-out.' As a result, the whole house was steeped in semi-darkness.

He'd just got back from the petrol station where he'd driven his hire car to buy diesel for the generator, in case the brown-out turned into a black-out. To avoid any incriminating documentation, the car had been hired by Tamsin using the credit card and driver's licence of Raquel Maloney, the decoy they'd snatched from Hyde Park shopping centre and later dumped at the petrol station on the N3 highway.

Now, in the bedroom, Tamsin lay naked on the bed. He'd stuffed a nylon stocking into her mouth as a gag, and tied another round her head to secure it. The nylon was biting into her cheeks. Her hands were bound behind her with cord, and livid bruises mottled the flesh of her thighs and upper arms. Salimovic hadn't marked her face—after all, she had to get through immigration without any questions asked—but he hadn't needed to.

He'd smacked her around before, from time to time, but never as badly as this. She looked up at him, and for the first time he saw real fear in her eyes. She was utterly submissive. All the fight had been beaten out of her.

He hadn't wanted to do this, but he'd needed the PIN codes for her bank cards, so he could continue to draw on her account after he'd sold her on. In an uncharacteristic show of stubbornness, Tammy had refused to give them to him.

She'd told him eventually, but it had taken time. Time he didn't have. And now other things were going wrong, too. He had assumed that by now Pamela Jordaan would have arrived. He had a nice little setup waiting for her, and was looking forward to getting the details on her bank accounts as well.

But the blonde bitch's cellphone was turned off, so she obviously hadn't read the SMS he'd sent from Tamsin's phone.

"My princess," he whispered, easing onto the bed beside Tamsin and running a fingertip over her face. "My sweet little princess."

She flinched from his touch, breathing hard. Near her mouth, he saw the stocking was running with saliva, and he wiped it away. He felt her relax slightly at this gentle gesture.

"I'm so sorry, my darling," he said. "But why did you make me do that to you? You know how angry I get when you say you don't trust me. We're a team now. I don't know why you can't understand that. Now, let me undo you."

As he picked at the tight knots he'd made in the stocking, he heard Tamsin's phone give a familiar beep.

He'd plugged the phone into the charger in the lounge. Abandoning his efforts, Salimovic ran through to the semi-dark room. He hoped this was Pamela, messaging to say she was on her way.

As he picked up the phone, the lights flickered and dimmed again.

He had two voice messages, but neither one was from Pamela.

The first message was from Rodic's whore, Katja. Her voice sounded slurred, and he would have bet a million euro that she was stoned.

"Rodic called again. He said the police told him someone was driving in your Aston Martin."

Salimovic couldn't believe his ears. His Aston? How the hell? Clamping the phone to his ear, straining to hear her mumbled words, he listened to the rest of the message.

"The police said they saw the car outside Number Six on the night of the raid. A woman attacked a cop and then escaped in it. They found it later, in a field."

Salimovic's puzzled frown remained, but he felt he could relax. At least the car had been found. It had cost him a fortune, and was one of his most treasured possessions.

"It was burned out," Katja continued.

"Shit!" Salimovic shouted. He punched the sofa cushion in a fury.

Christ, what was going on? Some bitch escaped Number Six in his car? Who, and how? Surely not one of the sluts who worked there. They were weak, harmless. After breaking them in, he'd seen the terror in their eyes.

"Oh, and something else important. Rodic said the police were . . . Oops. Battery dead!" Her laugh cut off abruptly as the message ended.

Definitely stoned.

Cursing, Salimovic called her back, but he only got her voice-mail. "Call me the minute you get this," he snapped, resisting the self-destructive urge to fling the phone down on the tiled floor. He hoped to hell she'd plugged it in to recharge before she passed out.

The second message he listened to carefully, twice, before nodding with satisfaction. His frown disappeared and was replaced by a thin, humourless smile.

Salimovic flicked the switch that turned on the outside lights and pressed the button to open the gate.

"Prejilepa," he called cheerfully. "I'm sorry, but you're going to have to wait just a little longer before I untie you. We have company arriving soon."

Pocketing the phone, he strode back towards the master bedroom to fetch his stolen gun.

49

It had taken Jade what felt like hours to cover the short distance between the gate and the house step by careful step, keeping her eyes peeled for sensors and security beams. As she drew closer she saw that a number of the rooms were dimly lit.

Hugging the white plastered wall, she edged her way along the side of the house. It was cold now; it was always cold in Dullstroom at night, and with the wind blowing face-on, she found herself having to clench her jaw to stop her teeth from chattering.

A flash of lightning lit up the car she'd seen arriving earlier, which was now parked on the paving near the front door. She was sure the gate buzzer would still be inside it. But to reach the car, she would have to get past a pair of French doors.

Jade crouched down. She'd have to leopard-crawl past them in case she activated a sensor or an alarm. But as she edged forward, an outside light went on by the front door and another light flickered into life down by the gate, which Jade saw was rolling open again.

That could mean only one thing—somebody else was about to arrive.

As quietly as she could, she tried the rattly and rather loose handle of the French door. It was unlocked, and no alarms sounded when she eased it open, but despite her efforts at stealth, the door itself made a loud scraping sound. She froze, forcing herself to count slowly to five.

Since nobody shouted or pulled the curtains back, she guessed she had been lucky, and that the room was empty. She slipped inside, closing the door behind her, then flattened herself against the wall, her heart pounding hard.

That was when she realised the room wasn't empty after all.

Hunched up on the bed, arms tied behind her, was a naked woman.

It was Tamsin, but not as Jade had expected to find her. She was bruised and beaten, trussed and gagged. A victim now, just like all the women she had helped to traffic.

In Jade's opinion, the young woman deserved everything that had happened to her, and more. Under other circumstances she would have walked away, ignoring her plight without a twinge of conscience, but she couldn't do that now.

Tamsin was a key witness in David's case, so Jade had to get her to safety. More importantly, she would know who else was in the house, and Jade needed that information urgently.

She stepped over to her side and began wrestling with the cruelly tight gag. But the knots in the stocking resisted all Jade's attempts to undo them, and although she had a gun with her, she had no knife.

"Tamsin," she whispered. The woman blinked when she heard her name.

"Is there a little Indian boy being held anywhere in this house?"

Tamsin shook her head.

So Kevin was somewhere else. Swallowing her disappointment, Jade turned her attention to Tamsin's wrists.

"Who did this to you?" Fumbling behind the woman's back, Jade gritted her teeth as she tried to work the knots open. "Was it Salimovic?"

No response.

"How many people are in the house now, besides you?"

Tamsin wiggled an index finger.

"One? Are you sure?"

The brown-haired woman nodded.

That levelled the odds.

"When I've untied you, I suggest you get dressed fast." Jade pointed to the pile of clothes on the floor beside the bed. "Then go out through that door and try to get out of the gate. My car's behind a bush about fifty metres to the left. Hide behind it."

At that moment, Jade heard a male voice from inside the house. He shouted something she couldn't hear and then, "We have company arriving soon."

Then she heard footsteps approaching the wooden bedroom door.

Salimovic.

Looking up, Jade saw there was no key in the door's lock. No chance to buy anymore time for Tamsin.

Adrenaline surged through her as she scrambled to her feet, tugging her Glock from the holster. Turning away from Tamsin, she faced the door, feet shoulder-width apart, aiming the weapon chest-high. No time for negotiation; not with other people arriving soon. She was going to take him down, shoot to kill as soon as he entered the room. With the element of surprise, she would have the advantage, even if he was holding a gun too.

The handle turned.

Breathe out. Aim. Wait.

When the door began to open her finger tightened on the trigger.

And then Jade's knees were kicked out from under her by a pair of bare feet.

She had just time to think—*Tamsin did this?*—before she fell forward hard, twisting to protect her gun as she sprawled onto the floor. The dark-haired man who had entered the room reacted, leopard-fast, to the situation and wrenched the weapon roughly out of her hand.

Another kick; this time from him. A heavy boot smashed into her jaw. Jade's vision went as her head snapped back, slamming into the corner of the bed, and her teeth bit deep into her tongue.

It had been Tamsin, Jade realised in despair. She had seen Jade aiming her gun at the door, and had done what she could to save Salimovic from being shot. Jade had made a fatal mistake in turning her back on the young woman. She should have guessed that, despite the abuse she had suffered, she would still be loyal to her tormentor.

She tasted blood in her mouth as she was dragged to her feet, shoved out of the room and hauled down a dimly-lit corridor. She struggled, tried to boot him in the shins, but she wasn't quick enough. Salimovic wrenched her left arm up behind her back so hard that the pain was sickening and, for a moment, she thought he had dislocated her shoulder. Then he grabbed hold of her hair and smacked her head against the wall. Once more, Jade saw a dizzying array of stars before her world became a grey blur.

She was dimly aware that he had manhandled her into a large room and was heading straight towards a heavy-looking wooden table. He didn't slow down, but shoved her straight into it. Pinned against the table, she heard him grunt as he tugged something tough and narrow tight around her wrists. Then she was pushed to the floor and the rope was fastened to something behind her.

She was a prisoner now. She was at his mercy, just the same way that Tamsin had been.

Jade's head was pounding, and her hands were beginning to throb.

As her dizziness subsided, she saw she was in a large flagstoned room, a dining room fit for a king. Enormous glass windows, free of burglar bars, were framed by heavy velvet curtains.

Mounted high on the walls, a row of animal heads stared back at her, their glass eyes cold, their fur dull and greasy-looking, the way Jade supposed all fur must look after its wearer had been shot, stuffed and hung on a wall.

The kudu she recognised, and the zebra of course, but the others Jade was less certain about. Was that a blesbok, perhaps, the one with the magnificent spiral horns?

No, this wasn't a dining room, she realised. This was a trophy room. A place for the hunter to show off his kills.

Jade also realised her back was starting to feel uncomfortably hot.

A sharp crackle and a shower of sparks from behind her confirmed her worst fears. She'd been tied to the metal support of a large Jetmaster fireplace.

Then Salimovic was standing in front of her again, breathing hard. A boot in the ribs from his foot sent her slipping sideways, the bonds cutting into her wrists, the rough floor grazing her knuckles.

"Who the hell are *you*, bitch?"

He stared down at her in contempt.

She said nothing, and her silence earned her a jab in the gut from her own Glock.

"And what are you doing here?"

Jade did not reply.

"Are you a policewoman?"

Still she said nothing.

"Jesus, I don't have time for this," Salimovic muttered. "You'll talk now, and you'll talk fast."

He reached up and lifted a pair of steel tongs off a hook on the wall, leaned over her and rummaged in the grate. Then he stepped back.

Salimovic had picked up a burning coal.

It had been in the fire for long enough for its outside to have formed a grey, ashy mantle, so thin it looked almost translucent, and for it to have developed a fiery inner core. When he waved it in her face, its heat seared her skin and the air around it shimmered. Jade could almost feel the oxygen being sucked into it.

"You have the count of five to tell me what you're doing here," Salimovic said. "Or this goes into your eye."

How do you force a red-hot coal into a person's mouth?

Suddenly, Jade knew the answer.

You push it in when he screams.

"One," Salimovic said.

The bonds around her wrists were viciously tight. Her fingers were throbbing and they felt as if they were starting to swell.

"Two."

Jade kept watching the coal. It was a hand's length from her face; so close her eyes felt dry and irritated and her skin was prickling with fiery pinpoints.

He was close enough for her to reach him with a kick. But she couldn't risk it, because the coal was closer.

"Three."

Jade took a deep, fast breath.

"You were expecting Pamela, weren't you?" she said.

Salimovic pulled back the tongs and stared at her in astonishment.

"You had this all set up. The fire, the coals, the rope. Not for Tamsin. You've already beaten whatever you need out of her. This is for Pamela."

The trafficker's rapid blinking told Jade that her guess was right.

"Were you hoping to get your hands on her money? To force her to give you her Internet banking details before you flee the country?"

Salimovic took a step back, out of her range, and lowered the tongs.

"You think I'm the only person who's worked this out?" Jade lied. "Pamela's been arrested. Naude, too. They're both in custody and the police are on their way. They will be here any minute."

She'd said the wrong thing. She knew that immediately. Salimovic's thin lips twisted into a smile and Jade realised with a sinking heart that the trafficker had realised she was bluffing.

"I don't think so," he said. "I think you're trying to fool me."

He raised the tongs again.

"Four."

There was nothing to do now but try to and fight him off. Numbly, Jade wondered whether Terence had struggled, too.

But Salimovic never reached five. His count was interrupted by a loud knocking on the front door.

Cursing, the trafficker dropped the tongs. They clanged onto the tiles and the coal skittered to the floor in a shower of sparks and came to a stop next to her knee. Jade wriggled away from it.

Then Salimovic turned and strode out of the room.

"Xavier?" she heard him call.

50

In her small apartment in Hackney, Katja blinked as she came to. She was lying half-on and half-off the low couch. Her pillow, a knit-covered cushion which smelled strongly of smoke, had left a rough, indented pattern on the side of her face. It was wet with drool, and she moved her head away from its sticky surface in sleepy disgust.

She needed a big glass of water, with three aspirins dissolved in it.

She needed to turn the lights off.

She needed . . . Oh, God.

Katja sat upright, jolted to full wakefulness as she remembered what had happened before she went to sleep.

She'd shared a couple of joints with the girls after they'd been at the pub, and then Rodic had phoned while she was on the bus home. She'd been too paranoid to relay the information he'd told her to Salimovic immediately, but she'd called as soon as she was inside her flat.

Then her phone had died and she'd passed out.

What had she told Rodic's dangerous friend?

She rubbed fiercely at her eyes, which were itchy and dry. Shit. She'd never even managed to take off her make-up. Leaving it on was supposed to age the skin.

She'd told Salimovic about his car. But she hadn't told him the most important fact of all, the one that Rodic had begged her to write down.

Blinking, Katja picked up her handbag from the floor and rummaged inside it.

There. She had written it. In red lip-liner on a white panty-pad. Classy. She stared down at the smudged letters and gave a short laugh, which made her head hurt even more.

Two words. He'd spelled them out for her.

Xavier Soumare.

The police had been asking Rodic who he was, over and over again. Apparently he'd driven Salimovic's car away from Number Six with some woman, and the police were convinced that the two of them were working with Salimovic.

Rodic had told Katja it was important that Salimovic should know the name.

Katja stood up, yanked her phone out of the charger and stabbed the redial button. She'd hoped that the call would go straight to voicemail like it did the last time she'd called, but to her surprise it started to ring.

■

Jade managed to flip onto her stomach and pull herself up onto her knees. Her arms were already aching from the painful position Salimovic had forced her into.

She needed to get her hands in front of her so that she could try to untie herself. Shifting as close to the fireplace as she could get, she managed to slip her wrists under her backside and wriggle her legs through one by one.

Now she was crouched on the floor with her wrists crushed together by the thin length of washing line, which was so tight that her fingers were beginning to swell.

Kneeling in front of the fire as if she were worshipping it.

After a short struggle, Jade realised that no matter how hard she yanked, sawed and twisted, the thin rope was unbreakable.

All she was doing was cutting into her own skin.

She leaned forward, easing the pressure on her wrists, breathing deeply as she considered her options.

She had just one left.

A line like this was impossible to break by hand. You could cut through it if you had a knife, which she did not.

Or you could burn through it.

Jade stretched out her leg and hooked her shoe over the hot coal that Salimovic had dropped. With gentle tapping movements, she manoeuvred it towards her until it was in front of her hands.

It had cooled a little since it came out of the fire. Its crimson heart was paler, but at least it was still glowing. Bending closer to it, she could feel its heat.

She knew that burning the line would mean burning her own skin as well.

She had to do it.

Gritting her teeth, Jade lowered her wrists onto the smoking coal. As she did, she thought of Terence Jordaan.

The hiss of the coal when it touched her skin was echoed by her own muffled hiss of agony. The reek of her own scorched flesh made her want to vomit and the pain was hideous.

She snatched her arms away. Now they were shaking almost uncontrollably. Her eyes were wet, and she was panting for breath.

Despite her efforts, the rope still wouldn't break.

The heat had allowed it to stretch just a little, giving a modicum of slack in the loop, but not enough to get her hands through.

In the distance, she heard the noise of a phone ringing.

"One more try and it'll be done," she whispered.

She lowered her hands, but stopped as soon as she felt the coal's fierce heat.

Go on, she thought. Don't be a sissy about the pain.

But she couldn't make her trembling arms obey.

Then she jumped as, from somewhere close by, a gunshot split the air.

Do it now.

Jade squeezed her eyes shut and forced her wrists onto the coal again. This time the rope broke, so suddenly that her hands slammed down on the floor.

She was free.

51

Salimovic's instinct for survival kept him alive. It stopped him from opening the front door to Xavier immediately, even though he was certain that this was a done deal.

Instead, he called out, "Let me see the goods first."

After a pause, three small, navy-blue passports were pushed under the heavy door.

Salimovic tucked the Glock into his belt, opened them and flipped through the pages. All three looked fine, with the correct photos in place, and he had to admit it was nothing short of a miracle that Xavier had managed to obtain them.

Xavier had apparently told Tamsin that he wanted to do more business with Salimovic, that there were other passports he could provide. Greek and Spanish. Both those would be extremely useful.

It was time to open up, then, to meet Xavier and start the negotiations.

As he went to slide back the bolt on the door, his cellphone started ringing.

The caller was Katja.

"Yes?" he snapped, clamping the phone between his shoulder and ear as he wrestled with the large bolt which was stiff and rusty and needed a strong, two-handed grip to open.

Her voice sounded toneless, the way it did when she was coming down from a monster high. He struggled to make out what she was saying above the metallic crunch of the bolt sliding back and the howling of the wind outside, which was rattling the door on its hinges as if Xavier were fighting to be let in.

"Speak louder, for God's sake."

The phone slipped away from Salimovic's ear as he twisted the Yale lock with one hand, and the key with the other.

"Who? I can't make it out. The man who stole my car and helped a woman get away in it? Yes, I heard that part. Say his name again."

This time, as the door swung open, her words were as clear as day.

"He is called Xavier Soumare," Katja shouted.

Salimovic reacted instantly. He dropped to his knees and the phone spun across the floor as the barrel of a Colt .45 appeared in the gap, followed by a black, swollen-knuckled hand. The gun went off, but the shot was too high. It exploded above him as he rammed his shoulder against the door, trapping Xavier's wrist with a sickening crunch. The bastard didn't drop the gun—his fingers were just about welded to its grip, but Salimovic managed to force his hand up and away, digging his nails into the man's dark skin. Christ, his arm was as skinny as a crow's leg, with dry, tough hooks on the end.

Then a shove from outside forced the door open again. Its edge connected with his head, nearly toppling him over, and for a moment he thought he'd lost the battle. But he wasn't ready to give up. He flung himself back against it one more time, with all his weight behind it, and just before it finally slammed closed, Xavier pulled his arm back.

Salimovic was on his feet in an instant. He wrestled the bolt across, then sprinted down the corridor to where he could get a shot at the man from one of the darkened and empty guest bedrooms.

He snatched the door open, ran across to the window, crouched down and sighted over the sill.

Sighted at nothing.

Xavier Soumare had disappeared.

Had he driven away, or was he still on the premises? Salimovic didn't know. From this window he could only just see the rear bumper of his own car. If another vehicle was parked in front of it, it would be invisible from this vantage point.

"Bastard!" Salimovic hissed. "Jebi ga!" He was trembling in reaction, or perhaps it was simple rage. If it hadn't been for Katja's phone call, right now he'd be lying dead in the hallway with a bullet in his brain.

Xavier must have been planning all along on doing this. Slowly gaining his trust, meeting up with Tamsin, even going to all the trouble of supplying him with the passports. But why?

Salimovic didn't have a clue. It wouldn't be the first time, though, that a deal had gone sour like that for no apparent reason.

He remembered that Tamsin, and now Katja too, had told him Xavier was working with a woman. That meant he must be with the whore who had sneaked through the open French door in the main bedroom and pointed the Glock at him earlier.

Who was now tied up in the trophy room, a helpless prisoner, awaiting his revenge.

With a jolt, Salimovic realised that the French door in the bedroom was still unlocked. Xavier could have got in that way, just as the other bitch had done. He could be inside the house by now. He could be right behind him.

He spun away from the window, his eyes straining into the semi-darkness, cursing the wind for its wailing when what would help him most right now was quiet.

Moving as silently as possible, he made his way back to the master bedroom.

He smelled the blood as soon as he entered the room; a coppery whiff, subtle but unmistakable. He froze in his tracks when he located its source.

He was too late. Xavier Soumare had already got to Tammy.

She lay face-up on the bed, still gagged, still bound. The right side of her face was soaked with blood. It had spilled onto the pillow and pooled in her hair.

The dark hilt of a knife was sticking out of her right eye-socket while her left eye stared ahead sightlessly.

Staring more closely at the gruesome sight, Salimovic noticed that her head was twisted sideways at an awkward-looking angle.

After stabbing her, Xavier must have broken her neck in a silent, deadly and expert manoeuvre.

"Shit," Salimovic whispered.

Now he couldn't take her with him and sell her, as he had been planning. Worse, he couldn't use her to get to her rich-bitch mother, which meant he was going to end up seriously short of cash again.

Soumare had stolen his property, his prejilepa, his little darling.

Salimovic knew what he had to do, but he was going to have to act fast. The French door was standing wide open, so he guessed Soumare must have fled outside after murdering Tamsin. He'd start the hunt for him later; but right now he was intent on revenge.

He locked the door, so that the black man couldn't get back inside. Then he reached out and took hold of the knife's hilt. He'd seen worse in his time, but all the same he had to grit his teeth before he wrenched it out of her eye-socket. It came free with a wet, sucking noise and he wiped some of the bloody residue onto the sheet, noticing his hands were unsteady.

"An eye for an eye," Salimovic whispered, pleased with the irony of the expression.

Silent as a shadow, he began to make his way back towards the trophy room.

■

Jade climbed to her feet. She'd expected Salimovic to be back by now, but after she had heard the gunshot there had been silence, followed by the far-away slamming of a heavy door.

Thanks to Salimovic's brutal treatment, her left arm was virtually crippled and both her hands were swollen and weak. She flexed her fingers, hoping the movement would help the circulation get going again.

The only potential weapon she could see was the pair of long metal tongs that Salimovic had used to pick up the coal. Using her stronger right hand, she eventually managed to pick them up. The tongs weren't much of a defence, but they might allow her to break the padlock on the gate motor if she needed to get away.

And, right now, she did need to get away. She was outnumbered two to one, and she had no gun. There was no time for anymore heroics.

The trophy room had an archway at each end. Which one to choose?

Salimovic had taken the one on the right. To be safe, Jade took the other one.

It led into a big kitchen, with a scullery door which proved to be locked. Another passage led to two bedrooms. Empty of all furniture, with no keys in the locks. From there, a short corridor led into a lounge. Double doors opened into a hallway, and beyond that Jade could see the big front door.

Stepping as quietly as she could, Jade crept into the hallway.

Cold air flooded in under the door. She grabbed hold of the bolt and tried to push it open, but it was old and stubborn, and her hands were still so weak that the metal proved impossible for her to shift.

As Jade turned away, something on the ground caught her eye. Bending closer, she saw three new-looking South African passports.

These must be the fakes that the syndicate at Home Affairs had been forced to supply. For these, David's wife had been threatened and his son had been abducted.

Now, here they were, lying discarded on the floor.

Jade hesitated only a moment before picking the passports up. With difficulty, because bending her wrists was agony, she slipped them into her jeans pocket.

Then she tensed as, right beside her, a cellphone began to ring.

The phone was under the hall table, where somebody must have dropped it.

It must surely belong to Salimovic. And any moment now, Jade was sure he'd be coming to find it.

She had no choice but to go back to the trophy room, where she'd been tied up.

As she entered the room, the coals shifted in the grate and the sound made her jump.

She knew she couldn't have much time before he came back.

Think, she urged herself.

She could hide. But where?

Behind one of the heavy velvet curtains that framed the main window, perhaps.

But as she moved towards the window, Salimovic walked into the dining hall. He was aiming her gun at her and when he saw she was free, he grinned widely.

"Still all alone?" he said, a comment which she didn't immediately understand. "You got out of those ties by yourself? Your precious Xavier didn't manage to rescue you?"

He spat out the last words, and with a sick feeling, Jade realised that Salimovic and Xavier were not, in fact, on the same side. Worse still, he now clearly believed she was the black man's female accomplice.

"Hands up," he said. "Drop those tongs. And if you try and run, I'll shoot you in the back."

Jade released the tongs and they clattered to the floor. Then she raised her hands slowly above her head. Or tried to. Salimovic's grin widened as he saw the red-raw skin on her wrists.

"So you burnt your way free. Did you enjoy it? Want to do it again?"

He took a step closer, and Jade saw his gaze focus on her bulging pocket.

"Take them out."

"What do you mean?"

"The passports. You've got them there. You're hiding them in your jeans pocket. Throw them to me. Now."

No point in resisting. Wincing, Jade managed to tug out the three documents. She tossed them towards Salimovic's feet. They landed in a little riff, like cards dealt in a casino. He picked them up and put them in his own pocket.

"Your friend tried to screw me using these," he said. "So I screwed him back. I never paid him. But you know what? I think you can be the payment."

Jade said nothing.

"Where is he now?" he asked her. "Tell me where Xavier is, and I'll let you go free."

"He's not my friend," Jade said. "I don't know why he tried to rip you off. And I don't know where he is."

The fingers on Salimovic's left hand twitched and Jade saw a knife appear in them. On its blade was a streak of blood that still looked fresh.

"Oh, I think you do know," he said, and took another step towards her.

Xavier Soumare stood very still, his emaciated body pressed back against the window, staring through the tiny nick he'd made in the velvet curtain with his fourth and last knife.

It was an awkward shooting angle, because he couldn't let the muzzle of the gun disturb the fall of the curtain. In addition, he was consumed by the need to cough, so badly he could feel blood bubbling in his lungs. Working slowly, with every movement a monumental effort, he managed to get his right hand into a workable position.

Through the tiny gap, he could see the woman's back. She was just a few feet in front of him. He couldn't see Salimovic at all—the woman was blocking his narrow view—but he could hear him speaking.

Xavier aimed for the exact centre of Jade's black jacket.

He let his breath out slowly, his hands steadying as his finger tightened on the trigger.

52

David been on raids before; many of them. Most of them in his younger days, back in Durban, before he was promoted to detective.

Most of them had been routine raids on illegal casinos, night-clubs, adult entertainment venues. And yes, the occasional raid on a brothel. He remembered one of the sex workers, a well-built coloured woman, pretty until she'd opened her mouth. Boy, she'd let rip, sending a volley of curses his way in a high-pitched screech.

"Fokken big policeman, I've got a right to earn an honest wage. Why don't you fokkoff and go hassle daaie charras that are busy giving cheap BJs next door? Jou ma se poes!" she'd yelled, and David had been glad that his sketchy knowledge of Afrikaans hadn't allowed him to translate her last words with any accuracy.

He'd got the idea, though.

He'd seen a lot in his raiding days. He'd thought he had seen it all.

Now, David realised that he hadn't. He hadn't had any idea how bad it could get.

They pulled up outside the Bez Valley brothel in the orange Mazda, the Pimpmobile as Jade called it, because nobody could possibly suspect it was a police vehicle. It was followed at a distance by two unmarked backup cars which would cordon off the entrance as soon as the Mazda was safely inside.

Once a modest residential suburb characterised by small, quaint houses, Bez Valley had been engulfed by the urban rot spreading southwards from Jo'burg's city centre. The streets were empty of everything except crumpled plastic packets and smashed bottles; the low walls in front of the houses chipped and eroded. Every bit of glass that wasn't already broken was protected by wire mesh and thick with dust.

For the brothel's customers, off-street parking was mandatory. Thembi rang the bell and the guard shone a torch into the Mazda before allowing it inside.

David was glad he was sitting in the back. He was so distracted, so concerned about his son, that even with the help of the GPS he knew he would have lost his way. A BMW with similarly mirrored windows left the premises, driving fast, as the Pimpmobile parked in the otherwise empty lot.

This property had replaced its low wall with a high, barred fence and an electric gate. Not just to keep criminals out, but to keep prisoners in.

Where was Kevin now, David wondered, as he eased the back door open and climbed out into the hot, breezy night. He'd checked in with Naisha on an hourly basis throughout the afternoon. The last time he spoke to her she had been crying, and there was still no news.

Where the hell was his boy?

Unlike their British counterparts, the South African police were fully armed when they conducted raids. David's service pistol was securely holstered on his hip, and he was wearing a Kevlar vest.

"The main entrance is this way," Thembi whispered. "And there's a second door just down there, if you follow that path." He'd been into the brothel the previous week, under the guise of a client who would prove too nervous to avail himself of the facilities, and had given David a full report on the building's layout and the numbers of the staff who worked there. Without a doubt, Thembi had confirmed that this establishment was using trafficked workers who, from the looks of things, were permanently imprisoned in their rooms.

When he'd checked the GPS coordinates on the white van from Heads & Tails after driving back from Jade's house, David had seen that the van had indeed travelled to this address.

He couldn't wait to begin questioning the owners.

"Go round to the back," David directed the third officer in a low voice. On the way to the main entrance he walked past a dirty window with thick blinds. He followed Thembi to the front door.

The rusting security gate that protected the premises was standing wide open.

"Police," Thembi announced, stepping inside. "Now, if everyone could please . . ."

He stopped just inside the door, and behind him David stood in silence as he took in the cramped and stinking room.

The reception area, where the Nigerian manager should be, was deserted. His threadbare chair was knocked over; a cash box lay open and discarded on the floor.

Moving inside, David saw that the owner's office in the adjoining room was also unoccupied, although the radio in the corner was still playing softly, the DJ's cheerful voice incongruous in this rathole.

All evidence of a hurried escape. Thembi shook his head in dismay. "They obviously had a tip-off. Somebody warned them we were coming."

"The car that left when we arrived," David said. "Get one of our backup vehicles onto it. That could have been them, making a last-minute run for it. They must have had a lookout on the street who phoned in when he saw the backup waiting. Jesus Christ, the slippery bastards." With an effort, he controlled himself, fighting the surge of anger that threatened to overwhelm him.

A failed raid. No arrests made, no suspects detained.

But at least they could help the trafficked victims.

"Let's get the workers out of here." David gestured towards the dimly lit passage.

He made a detour into the owner's office as he passed. Surely there must be some evidence here? With so hurried a departure, perhaps something of value had been left behind.

David was out of luck. Apart from one full magazine of nine-millimetre bullets at the back of the desk drawer and two empty syringes on the floor, there was nothing. He smashed his fists onto the desk in frustration.

David had already turned back towards the door when a shout from Thembi made him break into a run.

"Sup! Come here, quick!"

David pounded down the passage, over weathered floorboards that creaked loudly under his weight.

Thembi was in the first bedroom, a gloomy, cramped prison. The naked bulb in the ceiling had blown, and dark blinds covered the room's small window.

His captain was crouched over the bed in the corner.

"There's no pulse here!"

David felt his own heart quicken with fear.

"He's got no pulse at all," Thembi repeated.

He?

Pulling the torch from his belt, David switched it on and aimed the beam at the figure on the stained foam mattress, curled into a semi-foetal position, one arm outstretched.

A slight, brown-skinned figure.

Kevin?

David felt his world tilt. The torch-beam wavered, arcing up onto the filthy basin near the bed before he forced it back down again and stared numbly at the sight before him.

A young Indian man, naked and emaciated, his eyes staring sightlessly ahead. Peering down, David realised, with sick relief, that the youth was too tall and his hair too long for him to be his son.

He trained the beam on his face. It wasn't Kevin, but it could so easily have been.

Would he end up suffering the same fate?

In the crease of the dead youth's left arm, a forest of needle tracks bore witness to the methods that his captors had used to subdue him.

David lifted the arm gently. To his horror, it was still warm.

"They obviously gave him an overdose," he said in a voice that sounded hoarse and tense and strange. "Forcibly injected him with something—heroin, probably—to get him dependant, to keep him subdued, and then used it to kill him."

Thembi glanced up and David saw his own dismay reflected in his captain's eyes.

"The others," he said. "What about the others?"

Together, they rushed from the room.

An hour later, the failed raid was over.

Paramedics had pronounced four of the trafficked victims— two men, two women—dead on the scene. The fifth, a woman, had suffered a fatal heart attack as they were loading her into the ambulance.

The witnesses were dead, the owners were still at large, and the security guard had vanished into thin air.

David stood with his team outside the gates of the brothel and stared at their blank, exhausted faces. He felt sick inside, filled with a toxic mix of anger and desperate anxiety. This disastrous, failed raid marked the end of Project Priscilla.

Worse still, all the daily markers—rush hour, home time, sunset, supper time, each one inspiring a new surge of hope, had been and gone. Now it was midnight. It was indisputably the end of the day, and Kevin was still missing.

Standing in the yellowish glow of a streetlight, David pressed his fists to his chest as he felt his world shatter around him.

53

"Xavier's not your friend?" Salimovic smiled at Jade again. "That's a pity. Such a shame. It would be so easy for me to open the front door and let you go."

"You aren't going to let me go," Jade said. "Even if I told you Xavier's life history and gave you his exact GPS coordinates, you still wouldn't let me out of this house."

She stood her ground, even though she was tempted to turn and run. The action would be pointless. If she did, she knew she'd have four bullets in her before she even reached the door.

She couldn't see a way out of this.

Suddenly, Jade wished she could speak to David, just one last time.

The stuffed animals on the wall looked down at her, their beady eyes seeming to convey silent sympathy.

"True," Salimovic said. He thought for a moment and then nodded once, as if he'd reached a workable solution to a problem that had been bothering him. "And you know what? I think I believe you. If you aren't with him, I have no further use for you."

He raised the gun.

And then Jade heard the whisper behind her, as soft as smoke.

"Toulouse."

Down.

Without giving herself time to think, Jade flung herself onto the floor, her chin hitting the flagstones just as a shot went off, so loudly she thought her eardrums might burst.

Salimovic staggered backwards, looking down in disbelief at the bloody hole in his stomach. He tried to raise her Glock, but Jade was too quick for him. On her feet in an instant, she managed to wrench it out of his hand. The effort made her wrists burn, and she was forced to hold the gun in a two-handed grip.

She backed away from Salimovic, swinging her weapon round to aim it at the black man who had now emerged from behind the curtain.

Xavier Soumare simply held out one rake-thin arm and limped towards the trafficker. Salimovic had dropped the knife and was clutching his stomach, his face twisted with pain and his hands slippery with blood.

Xavier shot him again in the gut, and Salimovic grunted. He took another step backwards, and then his knees buckled and he sat down hard, as if he had been pushed.

His fingers scrabbled for purchase on the flagstones as he tried to get up again.

Aiming carefully, taking his time, the black man fired two more shots, one into each of the trafficker's hands.

Salimovic let out a high-pitched wail.

He lifted his arms and gaped at his damaged hands. Sheets of blood flowed over his wrists and down onto the floor. He sagged sideways and, with an agonised groan, crumpled to the floor.

Lying in a pool of his own spreading blood, he started to scream and shout out words in a language Jade did not understand.

Then Xavier turned to face her, but even with her trusty Glock aimed squarely at his chest, Jade still shivered when she saw the coldness in his eyes.

"Out," he said.

Slowly, Jade moved towards the doorway.

Outside, Salimovic's tirade was still audible. The wind had dropped and a few stars were visible. No storm after all, not tonight. Just the threat of one.

After he had slammed the front door, Xavier began to cough; it was a rough, rattling, phlegmy sound. And once he'd started, he couldn't seem to stop. At one point he doubled over, spluttering and gasping for breath so desperately that Jade thought he was going to choke to death. She watched him intently, gripping her gun with hands that felt increasingly stiff and painful.

Toulouse.

By whispering that word, Xavier Soumare had saved her life.

Jade bit her lip. How could this man have known the secret language that she and her father had shared?

When he had stopped coughing, Xavier collapsed onto the grass like a puppet whose strings had been cut. Struggling into a sitting position, he turned his blank, unsettling gaze on Jade again.

He wiped his mouth with the back of his sleeve. It was difficult to see in the poor light, because both the sleeve and his skin were dark, but Jade thought that what he was wiping away was blood. "Jade de Jong," he said in a hoarse, unsteady voice.

Jade felt her mouth fall open.

"How do you know who I am?"

"I found out. Asked some questions. I even watched you at home with your police detective friend one evening. I took photos of you, too."

Xavier's teeth gleamed in the dim light.

Jade swallowed as she remembered the three distinctive marks of the tripod, aimed directly at her window. That had been Xavier? But why?

"Somebody asked about me at the hospital where I was born, as well. Was that you too?" she said.

A small headshake. "No. Mathilde did that. We thought she would cause less suspicion."

"Why did you want information on me?"

"Curiosity."

In response to Jade's incredulous glance, he continued.

"I knew your mother. Elise Delacourt. At one time, we were very close."

His words punched Jade's breath out of her lungs more effectively than a boxer's right hook.

"How . . . how did you know her?" she asked, when she could speak again.

"We worked together." Xavier regarded her closely as he spoke. "She was one of us, a long time ago. Just like Mathilde."

Then he bent over and coughed up what was undeniably a large clot of blood.

Jade's mind was churning.

Xavier was a criminal in the foulest sense of the word; a modern-day slaver whose preferred currency was the very lives of the victims he trafficked.

She remembered the photo of her gentle, smiling mother, looking down with utter love at the baby in her arms.

Elise Delacourt, a criminal?

Impossible.

"No." Her denial was automatic, but as she spoke, it dawned on Jade just how very wrong she had been.

Xavier Soumare and Mathilde Dupont were suspected traffickers only because of their association with Salimovic. The Scotland Yard detectives had assumed they were his accomplices. But it was now clear to her that the brothel owner had never even seen Mathilde, and had no close association with Xavier.

Was it possible that the pair had not been following Salimovic in order to do business, but rather hunting him down in order to kill him?

If that was true, then Xavier Soumare was not a trafficker at all, although he was undoubtedly a criminal. And, if he had worked with her mother in the past . . .

With a sudden rush of understanding, Jade realised that if she wanted to find out who her mother had really been, she could look to only one person for the truth.

Herself.

54

Edmonds stood at the top of the stairs leading down to the wine cellar. As the sun set, she had been listening to the sound of birds going to roost in the trees surrounding the villa.

After the birdsong had gradually died away, the only sounds left were the harsh shrieks of metal on metal coming from the cellar below, where the safe-crackers, who had arrived two hours ago, were hard at work.

Barak was leaning against a nearby wall. He stubbed out his cigarette and put the butt carefully in a plastic bag before lighting up a fresh one.

It was a tricky safe. They'd had to knock away half the wall to get it loose, and now they were having to cut their way into it.

"Well, I've got accommodation organised for us," Richards said, closing his mobile phone. "Two rooms at a little place in the village."

"Thanks."

"The detectives were telling me that there's a rather scenic waterfall a short way up the hill from here." Richards shifted from foot to foot and Edmonds thought she heard an unfamiliar tone in his voice. Was it nervousness?

"It's a bit late now, and we'll have a busy day tomorrow I'm sure, but I wondered if you'd like to take a walk up there with me? Before breakfast, perhaps? When I'm working in a foreign country I always try to walk somewhere. It gives you the feel of the place, you know."

Edmonds stared at Richards in surprise. She had the distinct impression that he was not just inviting her to do some exercise with him, but pretty much asking her a date. And while taking a walk in the early morning to visit a waterfall might not be the most romantic proposition she'd ever had . . . well, now that she thought about it, it was certainly not unromantic. In fact, it sounded pretty good.

Even so, Edmonds decided she should say no.

The reasoning behind her decision was just too long and complicated, and she was getting tired of explaining it to prospective suitors. She'd had a disaster of a relationship a few years back. The man had hurt her, physically and mentally, and his abuse had left scars—scars of both types—that still hadn't completely healed. Even three years down the line, romance and relationships had yet to re-enter her life plan.

Seeing that Richards was already looking disappointed, she realised that her body language must have given her decision away.

Which was why Edmonds was as surprised as anybody to hear herself say, "Thanks. I'd like that."

Richards blinked. Then an enormous smile spread across his face. Behind him, through a cloud of smoke, she could see the Cypriot detective nodding in solemn approval.

"Great. That's wonderful. You know, I didn't think . . . I mean . . ."

At that point, Richards was interrupted. A shout from downstairs signalled that the safe was finally open.

Edmonds hurried down the staircase and pulled on a pair of gloves in case any trace evidence could later be obtained from the items inside its thick steel shell. Then she knelt down on the cold concrete floor next to Barak. Down in the cellar the air was thick with the smell of scorched metal. The safe hadn't given up its contents without a fight.

Edmonds removed a few thick bundles of high-denomination notes. Money that she was no longer used to seeing because, since the introduction of the Euro, it had quickly disappeared from circulation. Swiss francs, lire, Deutschmarks. The bundles were old, with the peculiarly dirty smell that Edmonds always associated with money. Behind the money were five velvet pouches, each containing a sprinkling of gemstones. Edmonds guessed that the large, blue-white ones must be diamonds. The others, from their colour, were probably rubies and emeralds. In total, a small fortune. Conveniently portable assets. Edmonds was sure that selling just one bag would allow the criminals to live out their days in luxury.

The last item in the safe was a slim stack of documents held together by a rubber band. Old documents, their pages crisp and yellowed. Edmonds removed the band and unfolded them with great care, peering down at the printed words and wishing that she had a translator to help her, because some of them were in French. She carefully read each one through twice.

"Richards, look here."

"What?" He was by her side in an instant, peering over her shoulder.

"These documents . . . it looks like Xavier Soumare was adopted."

Edmonds' head was spinning with the implications of what that might mean. "Look here. He was adopted by Mr. Bernard Soumare, a doctor. Bernard is Amanita's grandfather, so I was right about the connection between them. Xavier and Amanita are related."

With a small surge of relief, Edmonds realised she wouldn't have to mention her earlier phone call at all now. "This document says he was a war orphan from Nigeria."

"Lost his parents in the Biafran conflict, I suppose," Richards said. "I guess he must have seen his share of horrors during that time."

He sounded thoughtful, and Edmonds wondered whether he was trying to understand what might have made Xavier Soumare the criminal he was today.

"According to this form, he took a new first name as well; a French name. Xavier is not his original forename. Trying to put his past behind him, do you think?"

Edmonds didn't know. She sat, breathing the scorched-smelling air, thinking about what Soumare might have suffered during the war, and how it had changed him.

Or perhaps it hadn't. Perhaps he had been evil all along.

The next document revealed another one of Xavier Soumare's secrets.

"Well, he didn't give up his previous identity altogether," Edmonds said. "This is a Nigerian passport, but it's in his old name. Obesanjo Achebe. And he's done a lot of travelling on it."

"Call Mackay," Richards advised. "Ask him to run the name through the system and see what it comes up with. If that old passport's been so well used, we might just find our man's committed crimes using his Nigerian identity, too."

Edmonds and Richards were on their way to the guesthouse when Mackay called back.

The name Obesanjo Achebe had hit paydirt. The Interpol computers were buzzing.

Achebe was a dangerous man, a wanted criminal in seven different countries. He was infamous for fabricating plausible stories to get close to his targets, a couple of whom had been high-profile businessmen and government officials. He'd been assisted by a number of attractive female accomplices who, in turn, had also proved to be untraceable.

And then he had disappeared.

After committing a series of crimes throughout the 1970s and 80s, Achebe had gone to ground. Fallen right off the radar.

Dead, the authorities had hoped.

The only problem, as Mackay explained, was that he had never been under any suspicion of trafficking.

All the crimes that Achebe was suspected of committing had been murders.

55

Xavier Soumare was no trafficker. He was an assassin.

Jade stood, staring at his hunched form while her mind struggled to accept the impossible truth.

The man in front of her, though elderly and sickly now, had worked as a hired killer.

And so had her own mother.

The code words that they used must have been crucial in tight situations. So critical that Elise Delacourt had held onto that part of her old life. She had taught them to her unwitting husband, who had later taught them to Jade.

Or had Commissioner de Jong known the truth about his wife? Jade didn't even want to think about that.

She remembered the way she had felt when she'd aimed her gun at her first victim, the man who had murdered her father.

It had been so easy to pull the trigger, to take him down. She hadn't hesitated, not even for a split-second. Her hands had been rock-steady, her aim true. And as she'd watched her target collapse onto the pavement, she'd felt, for an instant, an emotion she could only describe as joy.

Afterwards, she'd tried to convince herself that she'd been confused; that she could never have felt such hot, euphoric delight in taking the life of any human being, even one so evil.

Now, Jade swallowed hard as she realised that Elise Delacourt had passed on more than her physical appearance to her daughter. And, although Jade had only ever taken the lives of murderers, her mother had done far worse.

She had taken the life of whoever she'd been paid to kill.

"I can't believe this." Jade shook her head, tears stinging her eyes. "She couldn't have done that."

Xavier shrugged. Then he wiped his mouth with a trembling hand, leaving a bloody streak across his lips.

In the silence that followed, Jade realised that Salimovic had stopped screaming. All she could hear from the house was an occasional low groan.

"Did you kill Tamsin, too?" she asked.

A nod. "It was quick. Better than she deserved. She didn't suffer much."

"Who paid you to do it?"

"This was not a paid job." His voice was weak, breathy. He spoke in gasps. "Amanita is my brother's child. He died last year." Xavier pressed a finger to his chest. "Heart attack. He was a good man, a family man. My opposite, you could say. He and his father, Bernard, who adopted me when I was a boy, hated what I became. But when Amanita phoned to say she was a prisoner, Bernard begged me for two favours. To rescue the innocent girl, and to kill those who trafficked her."

Xavier made a coughing sound that Jade thought might have been an attempt at a laugh. "The police raid interrupted the rescue, but we knew she would be safe. Then we had to find her traffickers, and get close. Finding them was difficult. The killing . . . was the easy part."

With effort, Jade pulled her thoughts into focus. It was time for the question that was already causing her stomach to twist with anxiety. Xavier might not be a trafficker, but in order to get close to Salimovic, he and Mathilde had abducted an equally innocent boy.

Jade prayed that the black man would give her the answer she needed.

"Where is Kevin Patel?" she asked.

Xavier cleared his throat.

"The day is not over," he said.

Jade blinked. "What do you mean?"

"I mean you still have other business to finish here. I need you to do it for me, because I can't . . ." He gave a humourless smile, looked down at his bloody shirt. "I can't do it."

"I have other business?" Jade stared at the black man. "I don't understand."

Xavier propped himself onto his elbow.

"Jade de Jong," he said again. "You will understand. You're a good detective, it seems. One of the best. Good instincts. Otherwise you wouldn't be alive now." He paused to gather breath. "Elise was good, too. The very best. I still miss her."

Jade found herself blinking furiously once again because her eyes had unexpectedly flooded with tears. In the silence, a cricket chirped.

"I thought I did my last job many years ago," Xavier said. "But then I was asked to do this one. The first I have ever done for honour, not for money. A chance to settle a debt that can never be fully paid. Au revoir, Jade."

Then, as fluid as a cat, he sat upright and turned his wrist to point the muzzle of the Colt at himself.

"No!" Jade shouted, leaping forward in a desperate attempt to grab his arm. "Please, don't . . ."

But before she could reach him Xavier had tipped back his head and placed the barrel in his mouth.

The noise of the shot echoed off the faraway hills.

■

David's phone rang as he was climbing into the passenger seat of the unmarked. The first time he and Thembi had driven together, David had taken the wheel. After that eventful ride, Thembi had politely insisted that he do the driving. He'd come up with a variety of excuses so far, the most bizarre being that he was suffering from terrible car-sickness due to an ear-canal imbalance which could only be alleviated if he had an open window on his right side.

"If you don't mind, Sup, I'll drive," he said, sounding apologetic. "My left hip's killing me, and for some reason, sitting in that passenger seat only makes it worse."

At any other time, David would have responded with a caustic remark.

Right then he couldn't have cared less who did the driving, or why.

He nodded glumly, opened the passenger door, and heard the phone start to trill as he was about to get in.

He clapped a hand to his pocket as the ringing caused reality to catch up with him in an unwelcome rush.

Jade.

With everything that had happened during the raid, he hadn't had time to think about her at all. Now, anxiety came flooding back.

Where was she? Was she all right?

God, let nothing have happened to her. Surely, in one terrible night, he could not have lost both the people he loved the most?

"If you don't mind," he said to Thembi. He pulled the phone out and moved away from the car, squinting down at the display.

00.01 a.m. And the caller wasn't Jade. It wasn't a number he recognised at all.

"Patel," he snapped.

"Mr. David Patel?" The voice was middle-aged, female and worried. "It's Sister Baloyi here, from the Nelson Mandela Children's Hospital in Soweto. I'm so sorry to call at this hour, but your wife said you'd only be available after midnight."

His wife? What on earth?

David's first thought was that the stress of Kevin's disappearance had caused Naisha to have some kind of breakdown.

"What's happened? Is she all right?"

A pause. Then Sister Baloyi spoke again, sounding almost as confused as David.

"Your wife was here earlier today. At least, she said she was your wife. A white woman with brown hair. She told us she was on the way to the airport to catch an international flight, but she was very worried because your son passed out after he came home from school. That's why she brought him in."

"Kevin's there?" The words burst out of David's mouth. "Kevin's at your hospital?"

"Oh yes. He's awake now, and he seems fine. He's been asking for you. We've checked him out, scanned him and tested him. The doctors did notice slightly elevated levels of GHB in his bloodstream, so it's possible that he might have got hold of some tablets while he was at school. We'd like him to spend the night here for observation just in case, but you are welcome to come and fetch him tomorrow. He's in the high care ward, next door to the burns unit. Oh, and your wife said I must tell you she has already settled the bill in full. In fact, she made a generous donation to the hospital as well." Sister Baloyi sounded pleased at being able to convey this good news.

"Please, can I talk to him?" David said. "Is he well enough to talk? I need to speak to him now."

When he heard Kevin's voice, David felt as if the weight of the world had been lifted from his shoulders.

"Dad! Hey, Dad? It's me. Are you there?"

Kevin's voice. High-pitched, upset, but unbearably real.

David found he was so choked up that it took him a while before he could speak to his son with any coherence.

56

"Your work here is not done."

What had Xavier meant by that?

Jade wondered for an uneasy moment whether this was why the assassin had alerted her to his presence, allowing her to duck and avoid his bullet, instead of simply shooting her first, and then Salimovic.

Jade stared down at Xavier's body, and a number of random thoughts passed through her mind.

Pamela assuredly telling her that Terence had escaped his pursuers the first time round by going underground.

Naude, swivelling round on his motorbike, to fire the shot that left a double hole in Jade's black jacket.

Salimovic, grasping a smouldering coal in the fire tongs, sneering as he called her bluff. Why had he done that straight after she had told him that Pamela and Naude had been arrested?

Suddenly, Jade understood.

"Salimovic had three passports," she said aloud. "Three, not two. And an open-plan house with big windows and a rickety French door. And there are no beds in the spare bedrooms, no locks on any of the inside doors. There's no way the victims were broken in here."

The Colt .45 that Xavier had used had fallen onto the grass. Jade picked it up. She'd have to wipe her prints off it later, but for now, this was the gun she needed. She also needed a torch. She remembered seeing one in the hallway, and ran to get it.

The tracks leading away from the parking area were difficult to spot. In daylight she might not have noticed them at all, but under the low beam of the torch, the grass on either side of the short, flattened blades cast a sharp shadow.

Jade followed the narrow, winding route down the rocky slope. As soon as she heard human activity, she switched off her torch and waited for her eyes to adjust to the darkness. She carefully picked her way closer to the source.

Peering around a large granite boulder, Jade saw light pouring out of a square-ish opening in the hillside. The solid steel door that guarded it was standing wide open.

When Pamela had said Terence had gone underground, she'd meant it quite literally. He'd built the house on the top of the hill, and then, lower down, he'd built a bunker, a place to hide out in total safety.

Jade realised now that her intuition had been correct. She just hadn't followed the process through to its logical end.

The victims had been hired by Tamsin. They had been transported in the white-painted people carrier. And they had been brought to the secure bunker on Terence's country estate.

And, finally, they had been broken in. But by whom?

In the dim light, the bright red motorbike parked nearby was a dull maroon.

Jade caught a whiff of something familiar, and it took her only a moment to identify it.

Jeyes Fluid. Well known among criminals for its ability to eradicate trace evidence.

A shape emerged from the door and Jade shrank back.

She needn't have worried. Naude was too busy to notice her. He was dragging a mattress behind him, pulling it out of the bunker, and doing so with some difficulty because he could only use one arm effectively.

He squinted into the night as he emerged from the well-lit underground rooms.

Once out, he hefted the mattress awkwardly onto his head and carried it over to where three others and a heap of bedding were already piled up next to two petrol cans.

He flung the mattress onto the pile with a grunt, then turned around and walked back to the door.

Jade wished she had made the connection sooner. After all, Naude himself had told her that he'd been Pamela's lover, long ago, and run a business with her.

And David had said that, in partnership with a boyfriend, Pamela had gone into business organising sex parties for men.

It was so obvious now.

When the parties had become too wild, Pamela had got out of the business for good, but Naude must have come back to it later, and made his living that way again. At first, she guessed he'd hired willing girls—including those referred to him by Tamsin.

Then, when Tamsin met Salimovic, there had been groups of victims to break in. A simple move, surely, to change the programme from sex to rape. Invite a hard-core group for a weekend away, in the most private of locations, to share in the fun of training a new batch of victims.

Naude's behaviour now, as he piled the mattresses ready for burning, after scrubbing down the interior of the bunker, was more eloquent than any confession could have been.

Pamela had paid Naude good money to murder her husband.

Jade was certain that Salimovic had paid him to leave Terence alive. And, for good measure, sweetened the deal with a passport.

Another rectangular shape blocked off the light in the doorway.

Another mattress, contaminated with sweat and skin cells, semen and hair, being dragged out to be destroyed.

From inside the thick walls of the underground building, she thought the earlier gunshots must have been inaudible, because Naude didn't glance in her direction; didn't appear worried at all. He was going about his shameful business with what appeared to be a complete lack of remorse.

"I'm sorry, David," Jade whispered. "But some people are better off dead."

The Colt .45 felt heavy and unfamiliar in her hands, but at this distance, she couldn't miss.

There was only one question left.

Quick or slow?

Xavier had shot Salimovic in the gut, sentencing him to a prolonged and hideously painful death.

What would Elise Delacourt have done?

Raising the gun, Jade felt her mother's tainted blood coursing through her veins. Her mother the killer.

You could give up your job, but you could never turn your back on who you were.

Head or gut?

Suddenly Jade knew for certain which it should be.

The tall, moustached man dumped the fifth mattress on top of the pile, and, breathing heavily, turned to go back to the bunker.

"Naude!" Jade shouted.

As he spun round, she pulled the trigger.

Acknowledgements

Firstly, thank you to my beloved parents Ann and Mac Mackenzie, for teaching me to read when I was very young and helping me develop a lasting love of books.

Thank you to Detective Sergeant Roddy Llewellyn and Detective Constable Leia Shearing from the Maxim Human Trafficking team at Scotland Yard, as well as Detective Sergeant Brian Faulkner from the Proceeds of Crime Implementation Unit, for all the help they gave me on police procedure in human trafficking cases. (Any discrepancies and inaccuracies in my writing have been deliberately included in order to safeguard their top-secret methods.) And Roddy, the beef stroganoff at the canteen was excellent!

A big thank you to my sister Sophie Mackenzie for letting me stay in her lovely London flat while I was doing my research, and to Dr. Ruth-Anna Macqueen for the information on medical problems commonly experienced by sex workers.

Thanks also to the Internet Writing Workshop, whose members gave me hundreds of constructive comments when they critted the first few chapters of this book, and to Mark Stanton for reading and commenting on the entire manuscript.

A huge thanks to my editor Frances Marks, who has saved me from myself more times than I care to remember, to Frederik de Jager, Fourie Botha and Fahiema Hallam at Umuzi for all their support and enthusiasm, and to Michiel Botha for the book's stunning cover design.

Thank you to Camilla Ferrier, Geraldine Cooke and Hannah Ferguson from the Marsh Agency in London as well as Debbie Gill from Maia Publishing Services for the amazing work they have done on my behalf.

I am thankful to the late, great Laura Hruska of Soho Press, as well as to Soho's Bronwen Hruska, Justin Hargett, Katie Herman, Ailen Lujo and Mark Doten – a fantastic team of people that I look forward to meeting soon.

My thanks, and all my love, goes to my wonderful partner Dion, who is the first person to read every word I write. Dion, you are my support and my inspiration and I feel happy every time I think of you.

While doing research on bodyguarding, I found one book particularly informative and interesting. This was *The Bodyguard's Bible* by James Brown.

Turn the page for a preview from the next
Jade de Jong investigation

THE
FALLEN

I

Themba Msamaya didn't suspect a thing on the morning he opened his door to death.

He was halfway through his first cup of tea when the knock came. Over the past few months, he'd developed something of a ritual. He'd get up early, boil the kettle and dunk a bag of cheap, Shoprite own-brand tea into a chipped South African Airways mug. He'd learned to do without milk, but a teaspoon of sugar was an essential he couldn't forego. Black tea didn't have to be so strong—it tasted better weak, in fact—and he had discovered one teabag could easily stretch to two mugs.

He would drink the steaming, reddish brew while sitting at the desk in his tiny Yeoville bedsit, yesterday's papers open at the Classifieds, his elderly laptop ready to browse the Jobsearch websites.

Over the last few days, his searching had become more stressful, because his useless Internet connection, slow at best and unreliable at worst, was close to reaching its cap. He'd nearly got through the five hundred megabytes that his low-spec package allowed him, God knew how, seeing it was only the twenty-second of the month, and all he'd been using it for was trying to find work. But once the threshold was reached, he would be cut off. Rudely, instantly and without any warning. It had happened a couple of times recently, once while he was right in the middle of sending off his cv.

Today, JobSA was slow to load and Workopolis had no new listings, but his favourite site, NATs Careers, was advertising a position that looked promising.

Email us your application and cv, the advert read. All companies required candidates to do that these days. Phone calls appeared to have become redundant.

A quick read through the well-worded cv that he'd paid a

specialist company to put together for him five months ago. Now he wished he hadn't wasted the money on it.

Did he need to change anything in the accompanying letter?

He scanned the document once more, slowly, even though he knew the damn thing off by heart. He thought it sounded fine. As fine as was possible, at any rate. He attached it and pressed "Send," willing the email to go through the first time, praying that the connection would not drop, as it often did, forcing him to repeat the task and gobbling up even more of his precious bandwidth allocation.

A series of clanging sounds and shouts from outside disturbed his concentration, and he looked up, frowning. Was this his neighbour causing trouble again? Themba didn't know him by name, but he was convinced the guy was a drug dealer. People were in and out of that room at all hours, talking, partying, banging on his door late into the night, and occasionally on Themba's door by mistake; and just last week he had overheard an argument that had ended in a gunshot.

No, it couldn't have been his drug-dealing neighbour. The morning after the gunshot, he'd been on his way to the shops when he'd seen the man hurrying down to the garage, carrying what looked like a hastily packed gym bag, half zipped up, in one hand, and his firearm in the other. A few minutes later, Themba had heard the unmistakable roar of his black, souped-up, spoiler-decorated BMW. The man had left and, as far as he knew, he hadn't been back since.

Then Themba realised what the sound was. It was the dustbins being emptied. There had been a municipal strike for weeks, and the bins lined up on the uneven paving outside the building had quickly gone from full to overflowing. Black bags had split open and vomited their contents onto the pavement and into the road. Those that hadn't split had been torn apart—by stray dogs or vagrants or both, he guessed. Crumpled plastic now littered the sidewalks, mushy piles of leftover food had swiftly started stinking in the heat, and dirty nappies disgorged their foul contents, which were soon blanketed by flies.

Now he could hear the loud drone of the garbage truck and the clanking of its crushing mechanism. Above this, the shouts of the workers, more clanging as empty metal dustbins were flung on their sides, and the clatter of the plastic wheelie bins being upended.

And then a second, closer sound, only just audible above the racket. A quick, polite-sounding rat-tat-tat on his door.

Themba glanced at the email. It looked like it was going through. Then he got up from his wooden chair and squeezed past his bed. As he wasn't expecting anyone, he was sure that whoever was outside the door was yet another customer looking for his drug-dealer neighbour.

He twisted the Yale latch open with his right hand, pulled the door handle down with his left, and opened the door a crack, snapping out a rather irritated "Yes?' before squinting out into the shady corridor.

That one word was all he had time for. The door exploded open, its handle wrenched out of his hand, its edge smashing against his temple as he staggered backwards and a sharp, stabbing pain lanced through his gut.

Themba slammed against the rickety desk and sprawled down onto the floor, blinking as hot rivulets of spilled tea splashed down onto his face.

And then a black-clad figure wearing a dark mask was inside, standing over him. The pain in his stomach was dreadful; he could taste blood in his mouth, but in his shock he hadn't begun to associate any of this with the slim black handle that now jutted from his midriff.

Until his assailant leaned forward, grasped the handle with a gloved hand, and pulled.

The pain was sickening. Themba screamed, a shrill, breathy sound, and clamped his hands over the deep gash, now pouring blood. He glanced up, only to see the knife coming at him again.

"Don't . . ." he begged, but his voice had reduced to a whisper. He mouthed the words, "Please don't."

He wanted to plead for his life, to explain that this wasn't fair, that this was the wrong room, that he was not the right man. That he didn't deal in drugs and never had. That this was all a terrible mistake.

But there was no time.

He tried to stop the blade, tried to grab it with his right hand, but it sliced cleanly through his palm and buried itself in his chest.

And then his attacker was gone.

Themba found he couldn't move. He wanted to cough, but he couldn't do that either. All he could do was lie in his own blood, watching as a dark mist rushed to cover the smeary ceiling.

Outside, the clanging of the garbage truck faded into silence.

2

Jade de Jong was fighting to convince herself she wasn't going to drown.

She was six and a half metres under the surface of the sea and sinking, with tons upon tons of water forcing her downwards. She was burying herself in a pale-blue grave, every movement of her fins taking her closer to the ocean's sandy floor and further from the sky and sun above.

She reached out in front of her, striking forward, pushing just a tiny fraction of all that water aside, noticing that her cupped hand looked sickly white in the dim light. Like a sea spectre. Or perhaps more like a corpse.

The thought paralysed her with fear—she was unable to keep going down, unable now even to breathe. Just as she had been on the dive before. And the dive before that.

God, get me out of here, she thought frantically. She knew how easy it would be to escape. A few kicks with her flippers and she could be hurtling up out of the depths, shooting to the surface, ripping the mask off her face. The next big breath she took could be real air. Proper air, not the dry-tasting canned stuff in the tanks on her back.

With her heart banging so hard she was sure it must be sending a subsonic message of panic to all sea life within a two-kilometre radius, Jade forced herself to stay put. She did what Amanda Bolton, her personal scuba-diving trainer, had told her to do. Gently exhale and send a rush of bubbles upwards. Then breathe in again. Slowly and easily. She had to force herself to relax, a command that Jade had realised on her first dive was physically impossible. This time, though, she managed to keep her fear at bay. She took a long, relieved gulp of air and then signalled to the wet-suited figure who was a few metres in front of her and looking at her enquiringly, waiting for her to communicate what she wanted to do next.

Closing her fist with her thumb towards the surface, Jade gestured upwards.

Get me out of here.

Amanda signalled back "okay." Escaping locks of her dark hair swirled, mermaid-like, around her face. Then she made another sign that Jade knew meant: slow. Take it slow going up. No panicking.

As Jade kicked towards the surface, she saw a shoal of fish swimming past. Small silvery-looking fish that seemed almost impossibly bright in the clear water—a scattering of marquise-cut diamonds on an aquamarine backdrop. They swam fast and purposefully, as if they were late for an important appointment.

Pretty, yes. But worth the dive? Jade didn't think so. And as for the rest of the sea life she'd heard so much about but hadn't seen yet, like the huge leatherback and loggerhead turtles that the St. Lucia estuary was famous for—well, she was sure there'd be some in a glass tank, ready for viewing, at uShaka Marine World in Durban.

Jade had thought learning to scuba dive would be easy, but it was proving to be the opposite. She'd managed her training dives—eventually—but open water terrified her, and she had never thought it would.

She'd expected that she'd take after her mother in this regard, as she did in so many other ways. Her late father had been a reluctant swimmer, a man much more comfortable out of the sea than in it. Although he'd never spoken much about her mother, Jade was certain that she remembered him saying once how much she had loved scuba diving.

Now she realised she must have inherited her father's dislike of the ocean.

At last she broke the surface and pulled off her claustrophobic mask. Treading water, she looked up gratefully at the cloudless sky and felt the coolness of the air against her face. It wouldn't have this effect for long—not in this heat, with the humidity smothering the estuary like a pillow, but the first few minutes out of the water always felt refreshing.

Miles of sea all around her in every direction, stretching all the way to the horizon on the seaward side, and the faraway rolling outline of the forested dunes on the shoreward side. The vastness of that distance didn't worry Jade too much. It was the depths below her that gave her the shivers.

Then Amanda surfaced beside her.

"Short break?' she suggested.

Jade nodded and they swam over to the dive boat waiting nearby and clambered on board.

"Well, that seemed to go better," Amanda said in an accent that Jade had originally thought was from southern England, but which she had laughingly confessed was pure East End. "Fifteen minutes under, this time. That's two minutes longer than on the last dive, and you went further, too. Quite an improvement, I think. How do you feel?"

Jade frowned.

"It still doesn't feel like my environment. I'm just not comfortable going so deep, although I know by scuba standards six metres is barely under water.' Bending over, she eased her fins off, then unzipped the wetsuit, which was already feeling too warm, and pulled it down off her shoulders.

"You'll get there, don't you worry. Most people take to it like a fish to water, 'scuse the pun, but some never get the hang of it. Others learn how to do it, but just don't like it."

"Does that ever change?' Jade asked, glancing longingly at her T-shirt and shorts that were folded up on the bench.

"Oh, it often does."

Amanda sounded so chirpy that Jade had no idea whether she was humouring her or not.

"Just you wait. In a couple more days, we'll have you out on the big boat, diving in a group with your boyfriend. That's where you really want to be, isn't it?"

Jade didn't miss the sympathy in her voice. But she couldn't argue with her, because the scuba instructor was spot on. One hundred per cent correct. She didn't want to be here, taking private lessons that were being offered at no extra charge, thanks to Amanda's kind-heartedness. She did want to be out on the big boat with police Superintendent David Patel, who might or might not be her boyfriend, but who was most definitely going to be her partner on this trip.

David already knew how to scuba dive, so Jade's plan had been for her to complete the diving course with a couple of other beginners at the resort, which rejoiced in the name of Scuba Sands, and then to join David in exploring the rich coral reefs that lined the estuary in the iSimangaliso Wetland Park—reefs that Jade had been interested to learn were the southernmost in the world.

But nothing had gone as planned.

Jade's own fear of open water had held her back. The other beginners had completed the course without trouble and had left that morning for a full-day's diving out on the reef with Monique du Preez, the other instructor.

And David wasn't even at the resort yet. He'd been supposed to drive down with Jade at the start of the week, but he had been delayed in Jo'burg after a drug-smuggling case he was working on had, in his own words, "hit the bloody fan harder than a shit-bomb."

He'd messaged her last night to say that he was getting an afternoon flight from Jo'burg today and would be landing at King Shaka International Airport in Durban at four-thirty. As soon as she and Amanda got back to shore, Jade would set off to fetch him. But before that, she had one more dive still to get through.

She stepped over to the prow of the boat and grasped the metal railing. Just a few minutes out of the water and she was already starting to feel sweaty in the oppressive humidity. The sea was as flat and still as a pond, and the sun burned down from a metallic sky.

"I'm not used to failing," she admitted. It was easier to say the words when she wasn't looking at the other woman. "Up till now, I've always managed to do everything I've wanted to do. Some things have been easy, like . . ."

She stopped herself. She'd been going to say: like shooting. That had come naturally to Jade. The first gun she had fired at the age of twelve had been a rifle almost as tall as she was, and she'd hit her target—a Coke can—at a distance of more than a hundred metres.

Admittedly, that gun had had telescopic sights. But

the handguns she'd fired since then had not. Guns felt like an extension of her own body; shooting was almost as instinctive as breathing.

She had made a promise, though, that she wasn't going to talk about her work activities on this holiday. Not with David there. Her ability to shoot, and what she had used it for, had caused problems between them that, at one stage, Jade had feared were permanent and would never be resolved.

Amanda laughed, obviously misinterpreting Jade's sudden silence. "Yeah, I know. You can never remember all the things you can do easily when you're thinking about the one thing you can't."

"Cycling," Jade said, picking a safer subject. "I love to cycle. I bought a mountain bike a while ago and I try to get out on it at least three times a week. I'm good with uphills. They don't bother me at all. Not when I'm cycling or when I'm running. I do that as well, and I've been training myself to run barefoot."

"Well, that's incredible. Hills just about kill me, whether I'm on a bike or my own two feet. But I can see you keep yourself fit."

"I'd like to do the long cycle races one day. The 94.7 kilometre one up in Jo'burg and the Cape Argus."

"Ah," Amanda said. "And have you done the L'Eroica Chianti cycling race in Italy? I was wondering when I saw your shirt."

Jade glanced across at her faded T-shirt that had, indeed, been a free gift to all entrants from the race organisers a few years back. She hadn't completed the ride, though. She'd been assigned as security detail to a wealthy British businessman's wife who'd gone there hoping to cycle the medium-distance route. But the woman hadn't put in nearly enough training for the tough, 135-kilometre course over rough, hilly terrain, and she'd been forced to retire before she'd even reached the halfway point. That meant that, as her bodyguard, Jade had had to swallow her disappointment and put her own bicycle in the back of the pick-up van together with her client's when it came round to collect the stragglers.

"I didn't finish it," she said. "I was there with a client who pulled out before the halfway mark. I was disappointed, but there was nothing I could do. It felt like a failure, too, even though it wasn't my fault."

Amanda gave a small nod and a shadow crossed her face.

"Failure's never easy to cope with," she said in a soft voice. "Especially when it's not your fault."

Her hand strayed to the small gold airplane pendant that she wore on a chain around her neck, and she slid it from side to side; an instinctive gesture that Jade had seen her make before, but thought Amanda herself was unaware of.

Taking comfort from the familiar action, perhaps.

Jade wondered what failure Amanda had experienced. Whatever it was, she clearly didn't want to talk about it, and Jade wasn't going to ask.

Changing the topic, she said, "That's a pretty piece of jewellery."

The dark-haired woman smiled.

"My mother gave it to me when I started work at Heathrow."

"Flight attendant?"

Now Amanda's smile widened. "No. Actually, I'm an air-traffic controller. I started out in England and then travelled around the world. That's what I'm qualified to do; what I've always done. The scuba diving is just a hobby, really."

Jade nodded, hoping her surprise didn't show on her face. She'd never have imagined that the woman who had been so patiently teaching her to dive had held down one of the toughest and most responsible jobs in the world—co-ordinating the approach and departure of airplanes at what must be one of the world's busiest commercial airports.

"I see," she said. "Sorry."

"For what?"

"Underestimating your abilities."

"You wouldn't be the first one to do that. People see a dive instructor in her thirties, working in a little resort like this, and they assume she's a drifter who never had any ambitions in life. At least you asked."

Jade smiled.

"That was my old life," Amanda continued. "Up until last year. I've been here almost six months now."

"Are you enjoying the change? It must be far less stressful."

Jade had thought Amanda would agree, but instead she looked away.

"Not really," she said.

Her words struck a chord with Jade. Made her reflect on her own situation. She was qualified as a bodyguard and had years of experience as a private investigator, working on her own and with big firms. But that might well have to change now.

She knew David didn't approve of the work she did, because of the danger to which it exposed her. Not to mention the fact that in solving her cases she often chose to go beyond the law, or that some of the cases she handled were not legal at all.

Could she do what Amanda had done? Turn her back on her previous life and start afresh doing something else? And if so, what on earth would that new career involve? Would it be too late to finish the law degree she'd started long ago, before she had decided that her heart and her talent lay elsewhere?

One thing was for sure—becoming a scuba-diving instructor was definitely out of the question.

"Shall we go under again? Aim for sixteen minutes this time?" Amanda asked.

Jade dug her fingernails into the palms of her hands. One more dive. Another visit to the depths. The time stretched ahead of her, endless as a prison sentence, but she had to do it. The only thing she feared more than being under the water was giving up on trying.

"Okay. Let's give it a go," she said.

OTHER TITLES IN THE SOHO CRIME SERIES

David Downing cont.
(World War I)
Jack of Spies
One Man's Flag
Lenin's Roller Coaster

Agnete Friis
(Denmark)
What My Body Remembers

Leighton Gage
(Brazil)
Blood of the Wicked
Buried Strangers
Dying Gasp
Every Bitter Thing
A Vine in the Blood
Perfect Hatred
The Ways of Evil Men

Michael Genelin
(Slovakia)
Siren of the Waters
Dark Dreams
The Magician's Accomplice
Requiem for a Gypsy

Timothy Hallinan
(Thailand)
The Fear Artist
For the Dead
The Hot Countries
Fools' River

(Los Angeles)
Crashed
Little Elvises
The Fame Thief
Herbie's Game
King Maybe
Fields Where They Lay

Karo Hämäläinen
(Finland)
Cruel Is the Night

Mette Ivie Harrison
(Mormon Utah)
The Bishop's Wife
His Right Hand
For Time and All Eternities

Mick Herron
(England)
Down Cemetery Road
The Last Voice You Hear
Reconstruction
Smoke and Whispers
Why We Die
Slow Horses
Dead Lions
Nobody Walks
Real Tigers
Spook Street
This Is What Happened

Lene Kaaberbøl &
Agnete Friis
(Denmark)
The Boy in the Suitcase
Invisible Murder
Death of a Nightingale
The Considerate Killer

Heda Margolius Kovály
(1950s Prague)
Innocence

Martin Limón
(South Korea)
Jade Lady Burning
Slicky Boys
Buddha's Money
The Door to Bitterness
The Wandering Ghost
G.I. Bones
Mr. Kill
The Joy Brigade
Nightmare Range
The Iron Sickle
The Ville Rat
Ping-Pong Heart
The Nine-Tailed Fox

Ed Lin
(Taiwan)
Ghost Month
Incensed

Peter Lovesey
(England)
The Circle
The Headhunters

Peter Lovesey cont.
False Inspector Dew
Rough Cider
On the Edge
The Reaper

(Bath, England)
The Last Detective
Diamond Solitaire
The Summons
Bloodhounds
Upon a Dark Night
The Vault
Diamond Dust
The House Sitter
The Secret Hangman
Skeleton Hill
Stagestruck
Cop to Corpse
The Tooth Tattoo
The Stone Wife
Down Among the Dead Men
Another One Goes Tonight

(London, England)
Wobble to Death
The Detective Wore
Silk Drawers
Abracadaver
Mad Hatter's Holiday
The Tick of Death
A Case of Spirits
Swing, Swing Together
Waxwork

Jassy Mackenzie
(South Africa)
Random Violence
Stolen Lives
The Fallen
Pale Horses
Bad Seeds

Francine Mathews
(Nantucket)
Death in the Off-Season
Death in Rough Water
Death in a Mood Indigo
Death in a Cold Hard Light
Death on Nantucket

Seichō Matsumoto
(Japan)
*Inspector Imanishi
Investigates*

Magdalen Nabb
(Italy)
Deat
Dec
De... ...Spr... ...ne
Death in Autumn
*The Marshal and
the Murderer*
*The Marshal and
the Madwoman*
The Marshal's Own Case
*The Marshal Makes
His Report*
*The Marshal
at the Villa Torrini*
Property of Blood
Some Bitter Taste
The Innocent
Vita Nuova
The Monster of Florence

Fuminori Nakamura
(Japan)
The Thief
Evil and the Mask
Last Winter, We Parted
The Kingdom
The Boy in the Earth

Stuart Neville
(Northern Ireland)
The Ghosts of Belfast
Collusion
Stolen Souls
The Final Silence
Those We Left Behind
So Say the Fallen

(Dublin)
Ratlines

Rebecca Pawel
(1930s Spain)
Death of a Nationalist
Law of Return
The Watcher in the Pine
The Summer Snow

(Ghana)
...der at Cape
Three Points
Gold of Our Fathers
Death by His Grace

Qiu Xiaolong
(China)
Death of a Red Heroine
A Loyal Character Dancer
When Red Is Black

John Straley
(Alaska)
*The Woman Who
Married a Bear*
The Curious Eat Themselves
The Big Both Ways
Cold Storage, Alaska

Akimitsu Takagi
(Japan)
The Tattoo Murder Case
Honeymoon to Nowhere
The Informer

Helene Tursten
(Sweden)
Detective Inspector Huss
The Torso
The Glass Devil
Night Rounds
The Golden Calf
The Fire Dance
The Beige Man
The Treacherous Net
Who Watcheth
Protected by the Shadows

Janwillem van de
Wetering
(Holland)
Outsider in Amsterdam
Tumbleweed
The Corpse on the Dike
...a Hawker
...ese Corpse
...d Baboon
The Maine Massacre
The Mind-Murders
The Streetbird
The Rattle-Rat
Hard Rain
Just a Corpse at Twilight
Hollow-Eyed Angel
The Perfidious Parrot
*The Sergeant's Cat:
Collected Stories*

Timothy Williams
(Guadeloupe)
Another Sun
*The Honest Folk
of Guadeloupe*

(Italy)
Converging Parallels
The Puppeteer
Persona Non Grata
Black August
Big Italy
*The Second Day
of the Renaissance*

Jacqueline Winspear
(1920s England)
Maisie Dobbs
Birds of a Feather